Writers and Rebels

EURASIA PAST AND PRESENT
General Editors

Catriona Kelly
University of Oxford

Douglas Rogers
Yale University

Mark D. Steinberg
University of Illinois

Writers and Rebels

The Literature of Insurgency in the Caucasus

REBECCA GOULD

Yale UNIVERSITY PRESS / NEW HAVEN AND LONDON

This work was generously supported by Yale-NUS College and the University of Bristol.

Set in Minion type by Newgen.
Printed in the United States of America.

Library of Congress Control Number: 2016936484
ISBN: 978-0-300-20064-5 (hardcover : alk. paper)

A catalogue record for this book is available from the British Library.

This paper meets the requirements of ANSI/NISO Z39.48-1992 (Permanence of Paper).

10 9 8 7 6 5 4 3 2 1

For Kate Gould

The law's concern with justice is only apparent . . .
[I]n truth the law is concerned with self-preservation.
In particular, with defending its existence against its own guilt.

—Walter Benjamin, "Das Recht zur Gewaltanwendung" (1920)

Colonialism orients itself to the past of an oppressed people and aims for its distortion, disfiguration, and annihilation. The devaluation of precolonial history acquires a dialectical significance today.

—Frantz Fanon, *Les damnés de la Terre* (1961)

Contents

Note on Transliteration and Method

The conversations on which the ethnographic material in this book is based were conducted in Russian, Georgian, and Chechen from 2005 to 2013, with funding provided by the American Councils for International Education and the International Research & Exchanges Board. In keeping with standard ethnographic practice for describing life in war-torn societies, the names of all my informants have been changed.

For the purposes of this book, the Caucasus encompasses the northern regions of Daghestan and Chechnya, as well as southern regions such as Georgia and Azerbaijan. Armenia is not discussed because the dominant form of anticolonial resistance was quite different from the types of violence studied here, and the Armenian literary tradition reflects this distinction. To avoid conflation with the pseudoscientific associations of the term *Caucasian*, I have used *Caucasus* here both as a noun and as an adjective to reference the mountain range as well as the people who inhabit it. I have also avoided using the term *North Caucasus* to reference the region to the north of the mountains where resistance to Russian rule was most violent because it implies the existence of an impermeable border between north and south that did not exist prior to the contemporary moment.

For Islamic names and terms, I adopt a modified transliteration system based on that used by the *International Journal of Middle East*

Studies, except when an orthographically and phonetically correct transcription would conflict with the source I am citing from. Thus, I give Qalʿa Quraysh generally but transliterate Kalakoreish when citing a Russian book on the subject in the bibliography, Najm al-Dīn al-Ḥutsī but Nadzhmuddin Gotsinskii when citing the Russian biography, and al-Alqadārī but Alkadari when citing modern Russian sources and editions. The names of this narrative's major protagonists, such as Imam Shamil (Imām Shāmil), Titsian Tabidze (T'itsian T'abidze), and Leo Tolstoy (Lev Tolstoi), are given in their most accessible forms, without diacritics. Terms in common English usage, such as *imam*, *jihad*, *hadith*, and *Quran*, are given without diacritics and are not italicized.

For words in Arabic and Slavic scripts, a simplified version of the Library of Congress transliteration system is used. I have simplified the ский ending to *–sky* in the main text, while keeping *–skii* in the notes and critical apparatus. For Caucasus vernaculars such as Chechen, glottal stops are represented by the sign (ʿ) used for the Arabic ʿ*ayn*. Because there is no single widely accepted transliteration system for Georgian and Chechen, and the number of potential readers with expertise in these languages is smaller than that of the other literatures I engage here, I have avoided diacritics wherever possible and have chosen spellings that indicate the best English pronunciation. The Georgian წ and ც are both transliterated by *ts*. Because Georgian has no capital letters, capitals have been used as sparingly as possible when transliterating Georgian titles.

Where authors' names are frequently encountered in multiple transliterations, I have aimed to provide alternate spellings. For well-known places, the most common spelling has been preferred, including in bibliographic citations, on the understanding that experts will know the location referenced regardless of how it is spelled. Hence *Grozny* and *Tbilisi* are used in lieu of *Groznyi* and *T'bilisi.*

All translations from Russian, Georgian, Arabic, German, French, and Chechen are mine except where otherwise noted or when I cite from a published translation. For reasons of economy, translators' names are given in full in the bibliography but not in the notes, except in cases of important editions or when their identities are part of the literary history I am excavating.

Arabic, Russian, and Georgian terms not in current English usage are defined in the glossary. Archival materials located in Russia are organized by *fond* (f.), *opis'* (op.), and *nomer* (no.). Archival materials located in Georgia are organized by *fond* (f.), *aghtsera* (a.), and *okmi* (o.).

Hijra dates are given only occasionally and are accompanied by the year according to the Christian calendar. Given that most of the Muslim authors whose works are discussed here engaged extensively with European, and particularly Russian, sources, the omission seems justified.

Endnotes refer to works in abbreviated form, with full references in the bibliography.

Map of the Caucasus Region, 1871–1888. Map copyright © 2015 by XNR Productions Inc

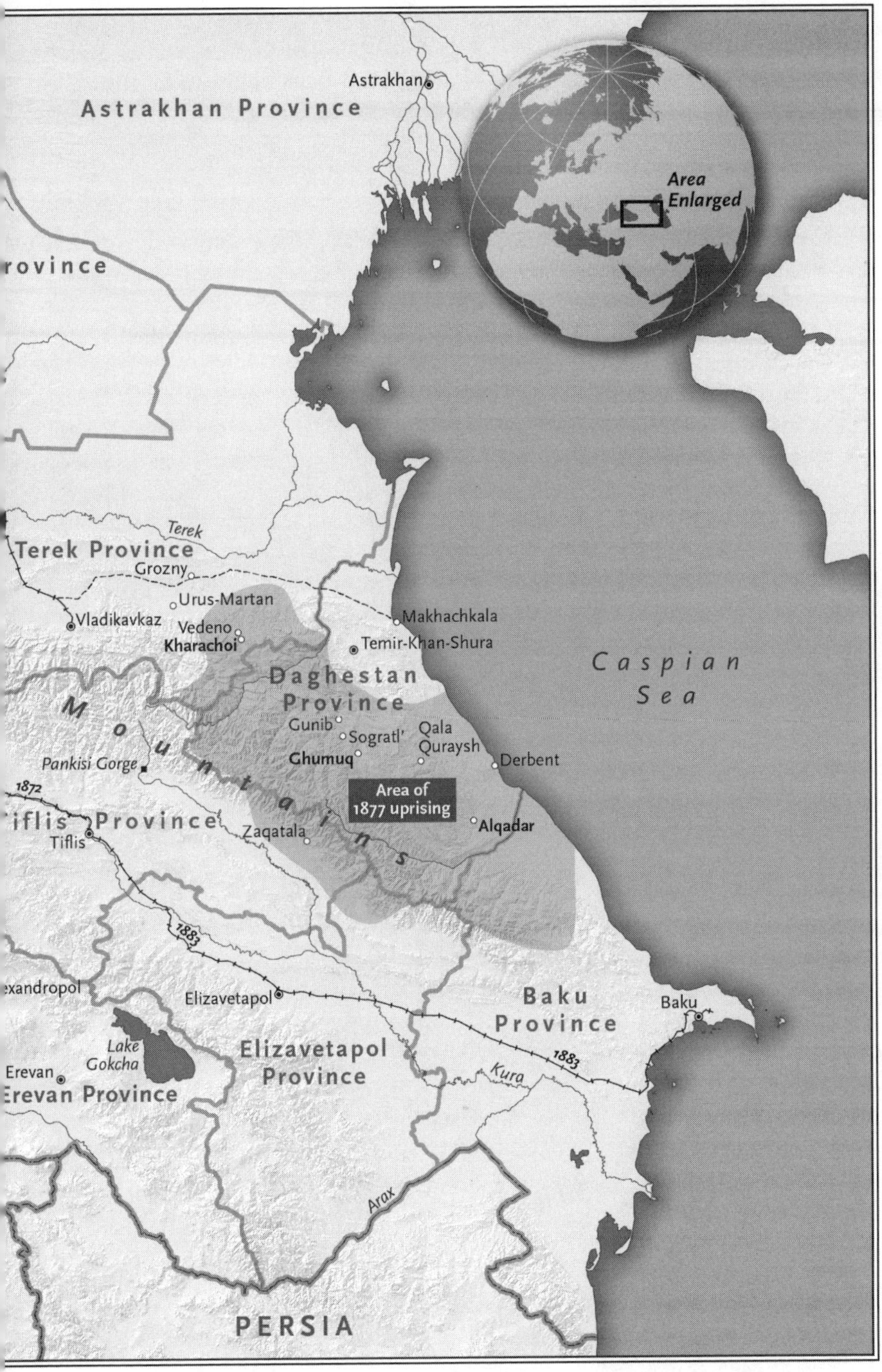
Astrakhan
Astrakhan Province
Area Enlarged
rovince
Terek
Terek Province
Grozny
Urus-Martan
Vladikavkaz
Vedeno
Kharachoi
Makhachkala
Temir-Khan-Shura
Caspian Sea
Daghestan Province
Mountains
Gunib
Sogratl'
Qala Quraysh
Ghumuq
Derbent
Pankisi Gorge
1872
Area of 1877 uprising
Alqadar
Tiflis Province
Tiflis
Zaqatala
1883
exandropol
Elizavetapol
Baku
Baku Province
1883
Lake Gokcha
Elizavetapol Province
Kura
Erevan
Erevan Province
Arax
PERSIA

Introduction

The Caucasus as Region, Literature as Method

Although he surrendered after a quarter century of leading the peoples of Chechnya and Daghestan in their resistance to imperial rule, Imam Shamil has never lost his preeminent position in the Caucasus literatures of anticolonial insurgency. Among his many accomplishments, Shamil's small Islamic state successfully withstood incorporation into a colonial empire from 1834 to 1859, longer than any of its counterparts across the Islamic world. A brief reflection on the biography of this individual and the methods through which he asserted his power will set the stage for the vacuum in political authority that ensued following the destruction of his imamate. This destruction laid the groundwork for the literatures of anticolonial insurgency with which this book is concerned.

Born in 1797 in the village of Gimri in mountainous Daghestan, Shamil's original name was ʿAlī. During a childhood illness, ʿAlī was renamed Shāmwīl. Shāmwīl was later simplified to Shamil, the name by which he is known to history. A weak child from birth, after his name change Shamil grew to be strong, courageous, and widely esteemed for his eloquence and learning. By the age of twenty, Shamil had mastered all the traditional subjects taught in local madrasas: Arabic grammar and rhetoric, jurisprudence (*fiqh*), and dialectical theology (*kalām*).

Shamil received his initial training from Ghāzī Muḥammad, the first imam of Chechnya and Daghestan. In 1832, soon after obtaining permission to wage jihad against the Russians, Ghāzī Muḥammad was killed by the Russians. He was succeeded by Ḥamza Bek, who himself was killed two years later by his own followers. This opened the path to Shamil, who in 1834 was chosen by the scholars of Daghestan to lead a united Daghestan and Chechnya against the tsarist army and simultaneously to serve as head of a northeastern Caucasus imamate. Through such rapid transfers of power, Shamil became the third imam of the Caucasus. Shamil's historian Muḥammad Ṭāhir al-Qarākhī describes his rise to power in eulogistic terms. Al-Qarākhī writes of how the "able scholar Shamil" was so "famed in the east and the west for his jihad that the people of Mecca and Medina, the scholars of Balkh and Bukhara, and pious people from all over the world . . . prayed for his victory, success, and prosperity."[1] Scholars in Shamil's service drew on Islamic law to mount a critique of both the colonial infidels (*kuffār*) and the ignorant (*jāhilī*), not-fully-Islamicized mountaineers of Daghestan and, especially, Chechnya.[2] Partly for this reason, Shamil's imamate marked a turning point in the political foundations of governance in the Islamic Caucasus.

More than a military leader, Shamil was the architect of a new state. In addition to adapting *sharīʿa* to his local environment, the third imam formulated ordinances for situations *sharīʿa* had yet to address. His second set of regulations resulted in a body of law he called *niẓām*, which was modeled on *qānūn*, the legal system prevalent in the Ottoman empire.[3] In formulating his legal system, Shamil introduced innovations that went beyond both indigenous law (*ʿādāt*) and *sharīʿa* as traditionally understood. For example, whereas *ʿādāt* prescribed fines for thieves and *sharīʿa* prescribed amputation, Shamil prescribed imprisonment and, if the offense was repeated, execution.[4]

Alongside his role as a lawmaker, Shamil was the leading diplomat in his self-built state. In his official correspondence, he applied to himself the term *amīr al-muʾminīn* (commander of the faithful), generally reserved for the caliph, alongside more pedestrian titles such as *qāḍī* (judge).[5] Aside from Ottoman sultans, few Islamic leaders called themselves *amīr al-muʾminīn* in the colonial period. Most significant among the titles Shamil claimed for himself, and the title by which he continues to be remembered, is *imam*, a term that has referred to the supreme leader of the Muslim community since the founding of Islam in the seventh century. In Sunni Islam (most relevant to the literatures studied here), the imam's original function was to defend "the unity and internal peace of the Muslim community . . . against the threat posed by the claims of the opposition movements."[6] Although the original opposition movements threatened the internal stability of the caliphate, by the beginnings of the colonial period, the threat to the Muslim community lay elsewhere, outside the Muslim sphere. In light of the altered political landscape, the meaning and function of the imam shifted. No longer a political leader who presided over a prosperous community in its political ascendency, the imam became a protector of the beleaguered Muslims under his domain from annihilation.

In the aftermath of Shamil's imamate and from within the vacuum of authority that followed its disappearance, the guiding concept of this book, transgressive sanctity, was born. Stated briefly, transgressive sanctity is the process through which sanctity is made transgressive and transgression is made sacred through violence against the state. Through this process, violence is aestheticized and aesthetics is endowed with the capacity to generate violence. Beyond signifying transgression against an externally imposed legal order, the violence entailed in transgressive sanctity intervenes in local laws. While the laws transgressed within this paradigm are necessarily alien to the community that transgresses them—otherwise no ethical value would attach to their transgression—the transgressive act has the consequence of altering local legal, aesthetic, and ethical norms. Generated by legal norms that, because they have been illegitimately imposed, can be legitimately violated, transgressive sanctity indicates how rebellion is sacralized in and through transgression. The contentious yet generative relation between a normative legal order and a nonnormative ethical position that is crystallized by transgressive sanctity is, I argue, a constitutive feature of colonial modernity, which is brought into relief on Caucasus borderlands.

Because the violation entailed in transgressive sanctity is never singular, transgressive sanctity refers to a process rather than a result.

First, a colonial norm is violated. Second, an indigenous legal system is transformed. The violation of colonial law, together with the transformation of indigenous law, brings us to the third moment in transgressive sanctity: its reconstitution in and through literary form. Transgressive sanctity's fluidity sets it apart from the monolithic accounts of resistance that shaped prior anticolonial critiques. These earlier accounts tended to ignore the aesthetic dimensions of local anticolonial sentiment in favor of a focus on the metropolitan currents of power. Entailing the transvaluation of religious categories, transgressive sanctity arises at the intersection of politics and aesthetics. It is crystallized in the literary imagination. In disciplinary terms, transgressive sanctity traverses literature, law, and anthropology while reconfiguring each of these disciplines as self-sufficient knowledge forms.

Transgressive sanctity derives its meaning and authority from the encounter between nonhegemonic legal orders, especially colonial structures of governance, and hegemonic but noncoercive indigenous law. While indigenous law (*ʿādāt*) wielded hegemony before colonialism through authority that was (to adapt Gramsci) secured and internalized through "the diffusion and popularization of the world view of the ruling class," this authority was reconfigured by colonial rule.[7] Even after the material force of indigenous law was vanquished, its cultural prestige persisted in colonial contexts. At this juncture, amid the near-total victory of colonial regimes across the Muslim world from the final decades of the nineteenth century to the early decades of the twentieth, transgressive sanctity entered literature, history, and culture.

Transgressive sanctity is generated when indigenous law is emptied of its old meaning and filled with new content. This new content asserts its power by staging acts of violence against the new legal order. Transgressive sanctity differs from other kinds of violence, as well as from other kinds of sanctities, in that it thrives on performance and display. Aesthetic and literary, transgressive sanctity is a product of the imagination and an expression of the will. Its relationship to history is among the most contentious aspects of my argument. Although transgressive sanctity entered the world historically, by inverting legal norms, its deepest life is lived in literature. By examining literary and historical accounts of anticolonial rebellion across multiple Caucasus literatures, this book demonstrates how and why transgressive sanctity gave anticolonial violence literary form.

The last imam prior to the incorporation of the northern Caucasus into the Russian empire (a process that extended from 1859 to 1864), Shamil was followed by Najm al-Dīn al-Ḥutsī (d. 1925). Although he tried to prevent the incorporation of Daghestan and Chechnya into the Soviet Union, Najm al-Dīn was himself heavily influenced by Bolshevik idioms of governance. In between the political ascendency of these imams, whose power was underwritten by actual Islamic states, unofficial insurgents were memorialized, honored, and, in some cases, sacralized by their communities. This group of unofficial insurgents included the Chechens Vara and Zelimkhan, discussed in chapter 1, and ʿAlībek Ḥājjī and Muḥammad Ḥājjī, discussed in chapter 2. Because they lacked the power of their official counterparts, these unofficial imams promulgated transgressive sanctity as the source of their legitimacy. In late tsarist and early Soviet times, the populist sanctity that circulated around these unofficial imams contributed to an anticolonial literary culture. Unable to rule through force, these figures were compelled to rule through sanctity. The means through which these insurgents acquired their prestige is an object lesson in the process through which anticolonial resistance is sedimented into ideology, and how anticolonial ideology generates anticolonial literary form.

This book examines the aestheticization of violence in the vernacular literatures of the Caucasus from the nineteenth century to the Soviet period through the framework of transgressive sanctity. Across Chechen, Daghestani, Georgian, and Russophone literary modernisms, I attend to worlds that were locally imagined even when they were managed by Russian and Soviet ideologies. It is primarily with respect to Chechen culture that I have, over the course of writing this book, developed the concept of transgressive sanctity, which I conceive as an aesthetic consciousness that arises in vacuums of legal authority when states coercively impose their laws on unwilling populations.[8] Codifying the immanent logic of anticolonial violence, transgressive sanctity is continuous with the aestheticization of violence in postcolonial and post-Soviet modernity. In the context of the literatures studied here, transgressive sanctity is most fully realized in the outcast-bandit figure known as the abrek (Chechen, *obarg*), who was variously configured, contested, appropriated, and rejected by the major figures in Caucasus literary modernity.[9]

Although transgressive sanctity requires the full breadth of this book for its unfolding, it can be noted by way of introduction that, in his modern iteration as an anticolonial bandit, the abrek epitomizes the paradoxes of transgressive sanctity as a political principle. Animated by a panache for display, transgressive sanctity gives literary life to tensions between anticolonial actors (including authors and their readers) and the agents of colonial rule. By engaging with transgressive sanctity's unfolding across the Caucasus from the late nineteenth to the mid-twentieth century, this book advances our understanding of the aestheticization of violence by the anticolonial imagination. I engage with Walter Benjamin, most explicitly in concluding, as I propose a critique of violence that is not merely negative. This critique takes seriously the power that is intrinsic to, and legitimated by, anticolonialism's aesthetics of transgression.

Given its focus on transgressions by individuals rather than collectives, my concept of transgressive sanctity diverges from many key contributions to political anthropology, including James C. Scott's "hidden transcripts" of subaltern groups and Pierre Clastres's account of how "primitive societies" resist governmentality.[10] Also, unlike much political anthropology, beyond being concerned with the dynamics of violence, transgressive sanctity is concerned with violence's cultural and aesthetic effects. It is engaged less by the *origins* of antistate violence than by the *repetition* and *performance* of that violence in cultural production. This study of the aesthetic reproduction of violence elucidates the persistent power of a political form that, because it generates and propagates suffering, needs to have its attractiveness explained. With anthropologist Steve Caton, I examine the appeal of certain forms of political life in the understanding that "force is only one aspect of the total picture in which power must be viewed."[11] Alongside the fear it inspires, force is also attractive from certain points of view. What Gramsci called hegemony

Caton calls persuasion in his effort to better understand the power of aesthetic representations in traditional Middle Eastern societies.

Transgressive sanctity is concerned less with the traditional questions of political science—such as why antistate actors rebel—than with the literary and aesthetic question of why and how anticolonial violence mesmerizes and mobilizes religious sensibilities.[12] Such foci work in tandem, enriching and implicating each other. When we better understand violence's aesthetic, then we will also have a firmer grasp of how violence can become a viable—and often the *only*—modality of social existence, and of resistance, in societies ravaged by colonial and neocolonial rule. Examining the permeation of modern Caucasus literatures by violence is one way of answering Charles King's question: "why do some social conflicts appear to endure across the centuries" while other forms of violence are neutralized by popular memory?[13] Amid such concerns, and particularly with respect to their engagements with the perspectives of nonstate actors, Clastres's and Scott's anthropologies of resistance shed the clearest light on the sanctification of transgression when they are in dialogue with the anthropological reflexivity of Talal Asad on the one hand and the political aesthetics of Walter Benjamin on the other.[14]

In Chechen literary and cultural memory, the abrek violates coercively imposed legal norms in the process of fulfilling the mandate of a higher ethical order. In crafting an alternative ethical system by violating an external legal order, he also reconfigures indigenous norms. Paradoxically, these violations, when performed against laws that have been coercively imposed, validate transgressions that would otherwise be seen as unethical. Transfixed by an ethically ambiguous aestheticization of violence, transgressive sanctity makes the profane sacred and the sacred profane. Through the workings of transgressive sanctity, figures who violated indigenous laws came to be locally regarded as sacred as a result of the colonial dispensation's naturalization of violence.

From an eclectic array of legal systems, including colonial, Islamic, and pre-Islamic social codes, the abrek forges an ethics and an aesthetics to sustain his community in times of war. Chechen transgressive sanctity was conditioned by the distance of Chechen vernacular literature from Daghestani Islamic cultural hierarchies as well as from imperial ideologies of governance. While Daghestani insurgency was shaped by a legal discourse cultivated by a learned elite, the Chechen ethos of rebellion was epitomized in popular and folkloric traditions, and, later, in Soviet literary culture.

Alongside its contribution to the aesthetics of violence and the violence of aesthetics in literary modernity, this is the first study to compare the anticolonial literatures of Chechnya, Daghestan, and Georgia. By way of laying the groundwork for the tours through literature, culture, and history that follow, I briefly survey here the precolonial vernacular and cosmopolitan literatures that informed anticolonial poetics during the tsarist and Soviet periods. Given its pivotal role in shaping Chechen literature, I begin with Daghestan. I consider how this region has functioned as a nodal point within the precolonial Caucasus, not least through its early and extensive contacts with the wider Islamic world. After viewing Daghestan as a crossroads of multiple civilizations, I consider how Chechen and Georgian literatures enrich the framework within which Daghestani literature circulated. I conclude by examining how the literary anthropology of transgressive sanctity enriches the study of both literature and anthropology through its politics of literary form.

Daghestani Crossroads

Home to one of the oldest Islamic cultures in the world, Daghestan is today located within the boundaries of the Russian Federation. For most of its history Daghestan has variously marked the northernmost extent of the Sassanian, Umayyad, Abbasid, and Safavid empires. Whereas most former Soviet autonomous republics were retrofitted to ethnolinguistically defined territories, Daghestan successfully resisted such demographic engineering thanks to the diversity of its cultures, languages, and religions. While in the Soviet period the republics of Checheno-Ingushetia, Kabardino-Balkaria, Karachay-Cherkessia, Georgia, and Abkhazia conflated the dominant ethnicities residing in the region with a single or at best dual political identity, Daghestan was always *Daghestan*, Turkic for the "land of mountains," a taxonomy onto which no ethnic label could be imposed.

Brought under Russian rule in the nineteenth century, Daghestan was linguistically, ethnically, and culturally the most diverse region of the Russian empire, and "one of the most varied in the world."[15] Arabic, Turkic Qumuq, and Russian have all been linguae francae, often contemporaneously. Until anti-Islamic campaigns under Stalin mandated the use of Russian, Arabic was the standard language for written communication, while Islamic teachings and pagan beliefs generated unique folkloric and literary traditions. Among its many distinctions, Daghestan's traditions of Arabic learning have given this small corner of the world "a leading position in the whole of the Muslim world in terms of the 'thickness' of the spread of manuscript collections."[16] New manuscript collections continue to be discovered regularly, revealing the vibrant life of Islamic knowledge systems in the contemporary Caucasus.[17]

Most Daghestanis identify as Muslims, although Daghestani Islam, like all religious belief in the Caucasus, is internally diverse. Until the emigration of the Jews from formerly Soviet territories to modern Israel, ancient communities of Mountain Jews, who spoke an Iranian dialect known as Tat, also made their home in Daghestan.[18] In southern Daghestan, this Judaic culture, which dates back to the Khazar period (618–1048 CE), was shaped by Christianity and Zoroastrianism. Minimally, this diversity of languages, peoples, and religions suggests the impossibility of mapping a single language and ethnicity onto a given territory. Maximally, it shows that the long history of interaction between cosmopolitan and vernacular languages in the Caucasus challenges area studies models calibrated to the nation-state. Even when national consciousness came to influence cultural life in the Caucasus, these alien structures were heavily inflected by nonnational understandings of language and community. Until the twentieth century, cosmopolitan languages (Arabic, Persian, Turkish) prevailed over the vernaculars (Qumuq, Avar, Darghi, Lezgi) for the purposes of literary expression.[19] While much of the world witnessed an increased emphasis on national formations, Soviet modernity ushered in a turn to vernacular literary expression, above all in indigenous languages such as Qumuq, Avar, and Darghi.

The cultural palimpsests of premodern Daghestan persisted deep into the modern period. Shortly before the Bolshevik Revolution, the

Daghestani publisher and intellectual Magomed Mirza Mavraev traveled to the mountainous regions of his homeland in the company of a government official.[20] Their trip was ordinary in nearly all respects. All that distinguished it from many similar trips made that day throughout Russia's borderlands was the technology that made it possible. Mavraev and his companion were traveling in a car. As they drove, the travelers were approached by a convoy of five mountaineers in a cart. The mountaineers wanted to know how it was possible that a cart made of steel could travel at a high speed without the help of either a horse or an ox. "How talented the people who created this cart must have been!" they exclaimed. "Glory be to Allah," one of the mountaineers added in Arabic to the chorus of praise that had been delivered in Qumuq, Daghestan's most widely spoken Turkic language.

At a time when, across the former Russian empire, Muslims were complaining that their coreligionists lacked access to worldly knowledge, Mavraev's remark caused the villager to despair. Infected by an anxiety reverberating from Cairo to Bukhara that Islamic traditions were not up to the task of forging a modernity on local terms, the villager pointed to a gap dividing his homeland from technological advances outside the Islamic world. "Why can't we create such ingenious devices?" he asked Mavraev. Receiving no answer, the villager continued, "Muslims will never be able to fashion the objects that the infidels have fabricated with their devilish tricks." Mountaineers, he lamented, were doomed to follow in the footsteps of the infidels, imitating without creating, copying without inventing.

The complaint of the Qumuq mountaineer touched on Mavraev's favorite theme. In his weekly columns for *Musavat* (*Equality*), the newspaper he had founded that same year, Mavraev had repeatedly raised the problem of how to understand what he saw as the modern Islamic world's backwardness. Why, he had asked a month prior to his visit to the mountains, were the Muslims of the Caucasus so behind the times? In responding to this question, Mavraev fleshed out a critique of Daghestani society, which in his view, had failed to modernize. "God bestowed on the infidels the ability to create such miraculous objects while denying this talent to us pious Muslims," Mavraev proposed, "because we do not study. If we studied, then we would be able to create objects as miraculous as those the infidels create." Mavraev's lament overlooked the intellectual ferment that was spreading across the Islamic world at that time and in journals he read on a regular basis. At the same time, his critique was typical of the *jadidis* (reformists) who, from Daghestani to Central Asia and Tatarstan, believed that Russia's Muslim subjects lagged "far behind other peoples."[21]

Mavraev recounted his encounter with the Qumuq mountaineer in a regular column for *Musavat.* Although his willingness to forgo Russian-language education is at odds with his insistence in other columns on the importance of Russian, Mavraev is consistent in his anticipation of the collapse of a colonial education system that privileges Russian to the exclusion of all other languages. While Mavraev presents himself as an advocate for modernization, his articles systematically expose the dangers of suppressing vernacular knowledge and reflect on how, during the tsarist era, government officials "crushed and oppressed" Daghestani learning by prohibiting education in Arabic, Ottoman Turkish, and Daghestani languages.[22] Among his many ambitions, Mavraev wished with his writing and publishing activities to preserve Daghestan's Islamic heritage from this kind of destruction.

Far from being uniformly hostile to Islamic learning, the Soviet state allowed Arabic to flourish in Daghestan during the early decades of Soviet rule. Many major centers for the study of Oriental languages were founded throughout Central Asia and the Caucasus during the Soviet period.[23] As late as 1927, ten years after the Bolshevik Revolution, Arabic-script publishing flourished in Daghestan under the auspices of Mavraev's publishing house, based in the ancient city of Temir-Khan-Shura (today called Buinaksk).[24] The multilingual *Daghestan Anthology* (*Dāghistān mejmūʿasï / Dagestanskii sbornik*), edited by Bolshevik activist, ethnographer, and Orientalist Alibek Takho-Godi (1882–1937) and discussed in chapter 2, had Arabic script emblazoned on its masthead well into the Soviet era.

Islamic learning was cultivated throughout the territories of the former Soviet empire, but Daghestan is unparalleled for its cultivation of Arabic and classical Islamic learning, as well as for the interface of its vernaculars with cosmopolitan tongues. Areas of outstanding achievement include jurisprudence, lexicography, Sufi hagiography, and historiography.[25] Arabs settled in the region following the Umayyad conquest of the eighth century. As medieval travelers to Daghestan attest, many Arabs who arrived as conquerors settled there permanently. Residents of the village where many Arabs settled in the Tabasaran region of southern Daghestan spoke Arabic as a native language well into the Soviet period.[26] But the real renaissance in Arabic learning was stimulated in the nineteenth century by local scholars, for whom Arabic was a nonnative language that was nonetheless intimately intertwined with their culture and identity. In the world of this book, Lak, Darghi, Qumuq, and Avar circulated like close acquaintances alongside Arabic, Turkic, Persian, and Russian, with separately assigned places within a single cultural sphere. Studying Caucasus literatures through their cosmopolitan and vernacular lenses means replacing the nativisms fostered by Soviet ethnic engineering and the current area studies frameworks derived from this precedent with nonethnic understandings of the circulation of languages, literatures, and cultures.

As early as the twelfth century, Arabophone travelers such as the Andalusian al-Gharnāṭī (d. 1170) attended lessons in Islamic law delivered by the amir of Darband (modern Derbent) in multiple Caucasus languages. According to al-Gharnāṭī, the amir translated his own speech into Lakzani, Tabalani, Filani, Zakalani, Haidak, Qumuq, Sarir, Alanian, Assi, Zarihgarani, Turkic, Arabic, and Persian.[27] Although al-Gharnāṭī's list may be exaggerated, the perception of Daghestan as a "mountain of tongues [*jibal al-alsun*]," as it is referred to in medieval Arabic historiography, says much about diversity in the Caucasus before modernity.[28] That this plurality was not solely linguistic is indicated by the evidence for polylingual translation adduced by al-Gharnāṭī. Beyond facilitating the oral translation from global languages such as Arabic, these vernaculars were committed to writing in the form of "short notes, often in the margins of Arabic books."[29] As in much of premodern Eurasia, the vernaculars had to wait for early modernity for their literary fruition.

Concurrently with Arabic, Persian was cultivated in Daghestan from the medieval period onward, especially in Darband and elsewhere in southern Daghestan and northern Azerbaijan, where Persian superseded Arabic as the primary language of literary culture. Persian took root as the primary literary language of Azerbaijan in the eleventh and twelfth centuries, from where it influenced the development of Georgian literature. From the fourteenth century onward, Persian inscriptions on Darband's tombstones quote verses from the Persian poets Saʿdī and ʿOmar Khayyām.[30] Occasionally, Persian was the intermediary language through which Arabic texts were rendered into the vernaculars Qumuq and Lak, as with Muḥammad Deylamī's medical treatise *Tuḥfat al-muʾminīn* (Gift of the Believers).[31]

Concurrently with Persian in southern Daghestan and Arabic in the mountainous north, in addition to functioning as a native language for people like Mavraev and as a spoken lingua franca across the northern Caucasus, Qumuq was in common use as a literary language in the lowlands, among Chechens, Avars, Darghins, and Nogais. Following the 1917 revolution, rather than turning to Avar, which had the largest constituency, Daghestani intellectuals recommended Qumuq, which was the language used by largest range of "linguistically diverse people," as the official language of Soviet Daghestan.[32]

Daghestani literary culture was enriched as well by the non-Arab (*ʿajam*) culture that circulated throughout Muslim-majority peripheries.[33] Among the innovations of Daghestani scholars was the introduction of a system of syntactical aids to facilitate adaptation of the Arabic script to Daghestani vernaculars. In distinguishing between verbs and nominal subjects, local scholars overcame the phonic imprecisions endemic to unvocalized Arabic texts.[34] The best-documented modification of the Arabic script to accommodate a north Caucasus vernacular is Dibīrqāḍī al-Khunzakhī's (d. 1817) Avar alphabet, which comprises thirty-eight letters.[35] This same Dibīrqāḍī composed a Persian-Arabic-Turkish dictionary entitled *Jāmiʿ al-lughatayn* (*Gathering of Languages*) on the order of Avar ruler Umma Khan (1774–1801), as well as a Persian conversation manual and a Persian-language textbook.[36]

Among the more significant monuments in the history of Daghestan's vernacular literary history is the legal Codex of Rustam Khan in the Darghi language. This work synthesizes local understandings of sovereignty, which were distinct both from Islamic law and colonial legal norms. Extant only in an Arabic translation copied in the eighteenth century, this compendium of local customs that both preceded and coexisted with the Islamic legal order likely dates back to an earlier period. Among the other grounds of its significance, Codex of Rustam Khan serves as a valuable repository of precolonial legal norms.[37]

Another major Daghestani monument that bears the palimpsests of the region's multifaceted history is Qalʿa Quraysh. Named after the Meccan tribe of the Prophet that guarded the Kaʿba in pre-Islamic days, this fortress was the capital of Qītāgh, a settlement built by Arab migrants who arrived in Daghestan during the Umayyad period to propagate Islam. The fortress, now in ruins, still stands in the mountains, an "image of ruins [*ʿibrat al-aṭlāl*]," testifying to its "former power and glory," in the eulogy of a contemporary commentator.[38] Qalʿa Quraysh was referenced frequently in Arabic and European travel literature from the early medieval period onward. A century before al-Gharnāṭī set foot on Daghestani territory, the Persian geographer Ibn Rusta visited Daghestan. At that time, the region was known as al-Sarīr (homonymous with the Arabic word for "throne"). Ibn Rusta recorded his visit to this fortress in his travelogue, wherein he delineates the peculiar policy of Qalʿa Quraysh's local ruler (*malik*) toward religion. According to the medieval traveler, the ruler acknowledged the equality of all faiths. "The ruler adheres to three religions," noted Ibn Rusta:

> On Fridays he prays with the Muslims, on Saturdays [*yawm al-sabat*] with the Jews [*al-yahūd*], and on Sundays, with the Christians [*al-naṣranī*]. He explains to everyone who visits him that people from each of these faiths tell him that the truth is only found in their creeds and that all other religions are false. His solution is to follow the creeds of all three faiths, in order to attain to the highest truth of all religions [*ḥaqq al-ādīān*].[39]

While modern scholars may doubt the historical authenticity of Ibn Rusta's statements, they tell us much about Daghestan's religious and linguistic pluralism. Ibn Rusta's account of this multiconfessional Arab settlement high in the Caucasus mountains suggests that the region's religious diversity informed the plurality of its literary cultures. Alongside such external travel narratives, Arabic poetry indigenous to

Daghestan has been dated to as early as the seventh century.[40] Arabic and Persian epigraphy further attests to the confessional and linguistic diversity of the Islamic Caucasus.[41]

Local historiographies reveal the extent of the interaction among Arabic, Turkic, and Persian literatures in the constitution of Daghestani historiography, which was inaugurated by Mammus al-Lakzī's twelfth-century chronicle, *History of Darband* (*Tārīkh al-Bāb*). *History of Darband* begins its narrative in the eighth century and ends in 1075.[42] Two fourteenth-century Arabic works, both called *History of Daghestan* (*Tārīkh Dāghistān*), by Muḥammad Rafīʿ and Maḥmud Khinaluqī, respectively, pick up the narrative thread abandoned by the earlier chronicle.[43] In addition to the works of al-Lakzī, Muḥammad Rafīʿ, and Maḥmud Khinaluqī, there are two major sources for precolonial Daghestan's Islamic history. The first is Muḥammad al-Awābī al-Aqtāshī's sixteenth-century *Story of Darband* (*Darbandnāma*). Although the extant *Darbandnāma* is in a Turkic language, this text is believed to have originally been composed in Persian many centuries prior.[44] The second is an abridged Turkic version of al-Lakzī's *History of Darband*, preserved in *Gathering of States* (*Jāmiʿ al-duwal*), an Arabic-language "encyclopedic account of numerous dynasties, both Muslim and non-Muslim" by the Ottoman historian Aḥmad ibn Luṭf Allāh Munajjim Bāshī (d. 1702).[45]

Whereas the sixteenth-century Turkic *Darbandnāma* was originally composed in Persian, the *History of Derbent* (*Tārīkh al-Bāb*), from roughly the same period, was originally composed in Arabic by al-Lakzī. The Turkic *History of Derbent* in Munajjim Bāshī's *Gathering of States* reproduces and updates its Arabic predecessors. Although it does not correspond to the original Persian, al-Awābī's Turkic *Darbandnāma* is by far the best known and most complete.[46] The Turkic *Darbandnāma* was in turn later translated into Persian in 1825–1826 by ʿAlī-Yār bin Qāsem.[47] Arabic fragments bearing the title *Darbandnāma* were incorporated into later Turkic versions.[48]

The final synthesizing contribution to Daghestani historiography before modernity is Muḥammad-Ḥaydar bin Ḥājjī Mīrzā Āqāsī's *New Book of Darband* (*Darbandnāma-ye jadīd*).[49] Composed in Persian in the middle of the nineteenth century, this work uses Arabic, Turkic, and

Persian sources to construct a history of Derbent in a newly systematic manner. Responding to shifts in local distributions of sovereignty and to the new importance ascribed to the vernacular languages that partially displaced Arabic, Daghestani historiography united two literary traditions, Persian and Arabic, into a multilingual ecumene. Congruent with Sheldon Pollock's formulation of the premodern cosmopolis as a space where culture and power were mutually imbricated rather than overdetermining, and where literary languages created identities that spanned vastly disparate geographies, the Caucasus before colonialism replicated on a smaller scale the "imperial culture-power formation" brought into being by the circulation of Islamic knowledge.[50]

The major distinction between Pollock's cosmopolis, based on an expansive South Asian geography, and the literary cultures that circulated throughout the Caucasus, is that always more than one cosmopolitan language held sway in regions that were to come to constitute the Russian empire. Arabic, Persian, Turkic, and subsequently Russian contributed a literary culture that was more heteroglossic—more plural in its range of languages—than were other cosmopolitan formations, which tended to coalesce around a single cosmopolitan language, such as Sanskrit, Persian, or Arabic. This heteroglossia of Caucasus literatures gives it a special place in the ecology of world literatures.

Chechen and Georgian Intersections

While Daghestan's precolonial literary cultures were situated at multiple civilizational crossroads, until the beginning of eighteenth century, Chechnya was by comparison less intensively affected by Islamic globalization. Because written Chechen literature was first introduced in the early years of the Soviet experiment, Chechen literary representations of violence differ from that of the neighboring literatures of Daghestan and Georgia. Daghestan and Georgia nourished flourishing literary cultures long before colonialism came to influence the local literary economy. Chechen textuality was by contrast born from a violent confrontation with governmentality, the distinctively modern form of power that, per Foucault, "is not purely one either of freedom or of domination," and that oscillates between accommodation and resistance.[51] Beyond simply reflecting colonial violence, many of the Chechen texts discussed in this book refract new forms of violence, newly inflected by colonial governmentality.[52]

The intense politicization of Chechen culture has given more visceral markings to Chechen literature than neighboring Daghestani and Georgian literary traditions. Equally, the three legal systems that grounded social life in the Islamic Caucasus, each of which makes conflicting claims on the colonial subject—*sharīʿa* (Islamic law), *ʿādāt* (indigenous law), and *zakon* (imperial law)—have similarly generated polarities less visible in neighboring cultures. Chechen literature does double duty as ethnography, refracting violence across a wide dispersal of classes and clans. One sign of the role of colonialism in early Chechen literary history is that the first published work in Chechen was authored by an officer in the tsar's army named Umalat Laudaev (1818–1883).[53] By contrast, none of the major Daghestani authors discussed in this book wrote primarily in Russian.

Among the variables that formally constitute legal and political existence in Caucasus societies—*sharīʿa*, *ʿādāt*, and *zakon*—the second and third are the most salient for the study of Chechen literary culture. Whereas the right to rebel was articulated among the Daghestani literati through a millennium-old engagement with *sharīʿa*, attitudes to rebellion were more heavily mediated in Chechen literature and folklore by indigenous, and often pre-Islamic, conceptions of the sacred. Chechen perspectives could also be more easily adapted to vernacular traditions, and in particular to practices within the Sufi Qādiriyya order to which Chechens were more closely aligned than to the Naqshbandiyya order that dominated Daghestani religiosity.

The confessional plurality of the premodern Caucasus is illustrated well by the actions of King Dmitri (r. 1125–1156), the Georgian king of Christian Georgia. Conscious of his status as a Saljuq vassal, and wishing to incorporate his domains into a larger Islamic ecumene, the Georgian king prayed at a Tbilisi mosque every week.[54] Also because of King Dmitri's initiative, Georgian coins with Arabic inscriptions circulated throughout the Caucasus.[55] The Shirwānshāhs who ruled parts of Daghestan and Shirwān (Azerbaijan) claimed descent from pre-Islamic

Iranian kings, even when they could not reconcile their Iranian lineages with their claims to Arab descent.[56]

The literature of Georgia, the only non-Islamic culture studied extensively in this work, combines Daghestan's textualized traditions of Islamic learning (albeit with a more Persianate genealogy) with the vernacular idioms of Chechen folklore.[57] Christianized in the fourth century, Georgia's literary traditions predate those of Daghestan, not to mention Russia. The antiquity of the Georgian literary language has both inspired and blinded its most visionary authors, offering depths of tradition to engage while cutting Georgian poets off from neighboring Islamic cultures. Surrounded by Muslim neighbors to the east, north, and south, Georgian authors were compelled to address cultural and religious difference every time they engaged with their neighbors.

Figuring themselves alternately as Eastern Orthodox Christians aligned to Russia and as mountaineers whose geography and cultural ethos converge with that of Daghestani and Chechen peoples, Georgian poets have been historically situated on both sides of the colonial divide. Like their Ossetian counterparts, who were Christianized at a later moment in their history, Georgian authors adapted pan-Caucasus idioms of insurgency to Soviet modernity. *Writers and Rebels* maps Georgia's diverse and internally conflicting engagements with anticolonial violence at the intersections of Chechen, Daghestani, Russian, and Ossetian literatures.

One of the most powerful contributions to the literature of insurgency in the Caucasus is a proclamation by the Georgian modernist poet Titsian Tabidze (1895–1937), which draws on the Islamic concept of the *murīd*, a Sufi adept now refashioned as an agent of anticolonial resistance, to draw new connections between the Daghestani discourse of jihad and Georgian avant-garde poetics. "I—an infidel [*giaouri*]," writes Titsian, "now a *murīd* / write poetry / to redeem your treachery."[58] That the poet, writing from a Christian background and addressing a culturally Christian audience, renounces his literature's colonial entanglements by drawing on an Islamic idiom of anticolonial militancy (albeit one mediated through Soviet paradigms) attests to the wide reach of the poetics of insurgency across Caucasus literatures.

Recent studies of Imam Shamil's anticolonial jihad have considerably nuanced Soviet representations of anticolonial militancy in Daghestan and Chechnya.[59] Many Soviet and post-Soviet accounts of this movement propagated the image of a monolithic "*murid* movement," named after the Sufi adepts whose religion supposedly drove them to make war on the Russian empire.[60] The chapters that follow support this critical turn within Caucasus studies against the romanticization of times past. I show how greater access to Daghestani Arabic texts delineates a Caucasus literature of anticolonial insurgency that is more nuanced, more textualized, and less indebted to still-regnant tsarist and Soviet paradigms.

Recent historiography of jihad in the nineteenth-century Caucasus takes us well beyond Soviet paradigms.[61] Meanwhile, notwithstanding the extensive multilingual literary archives that are becoming increasingly accessible after the fall of the Soviet Union, there have been few attempts to situate these literatures as world literatures, or indeed to engage with them at all.[62] In the aftermath of the Boston Marathon bombings, orchestrated by two Chechen brothers, the *New Yorker* falsely claimed that "of all the literature about the Caucasus almost none is written by Caucasians themselves."[63] Although the author later edited his online remarks to clarify that "almost none" referred to "what is widely read and celebrated," rather than to the literature as such, this elision reveals a broader ignorance. The media is broadly implicated in the occlusion of local angles of vision from our understanding of the Caucasus, but contemporary scholarship also bears much of the blame for not having made the relevant works available in translation or accessible editions.

This book is concerned as much with the nonevent—with how worlds are imagined into being even when they do not attain historical actuality—as it is with the event. Rather than trying to determine the role of Sufism in stimulating jihad, as scholars such as Kemper have done, this study aims to better understand violence's aesthetic appeal, which lies at the basis of its material power. As I understand and seek to practice it, literary anthropology counters the customary privileging of event-based history with stories from archives that have been forgotten and suppressed. Although literary scholars have addressed anticolonial violence in the Caucasus, they have not generally looked beyond Russian material.[64] Meanwhile, the literatures local to the Caucasus, including the poetry and prose in Arabic, Chechen, and Georgian that form the basis of this study, remain ignored.[65] So too have many groundbreaking Russian texts composed by non-Russian authors from the Caucasus been overlooked, as a result of the entrenched tendency in literary studies to privilege the canonical and the many times read over the marginal and unknown.

Because this work is in close dialogue with historical materials, particularly in its early chapters, it is necessary to clarify my relationship, as a scholar of literature, to history as a method.[66] For the purposes of the work, history possesses significant narrative value. To appreciate the abrek's literary metamorphosis, it is necessary to cognize his role in historical memory. Furthermore, any engagement with transgressive sanctity must address its historicity in the process of attending to how literary texts act in the world. For each of the literatures studied in this book, there is, however, an important moment, which is most in evidence in the treatment in chapter 3 of Georgian modernism but pertains to my Chechen, Daghestani, and Russian material as well, when transgressive sanctity inverts the historical record. These moments situate the historical event within the imaginative landscape that is constitutive of literature. At these crucial junctures, the turn against history necessitates literary form. The purpose, then, of my engagements with history, is not only to elaborate on the narratives it generates but also to invert and contest what it presents as normative.

History possesses aesthetic rather than explanatory power within this narrative. At the same time, I want to show that aesthetic power *is* power, however innocent of the laws of cause and effect. Rather than directing us to the causes of violence, for the purposes of this literary account, history is a text that generates multiple, and mutually contradictory, readings. While the historical record offers an important narrative background against which the literatures of anticolonial insurgency are written, it does not and cannot offer a definitive explanation of violence, nor can it adequately account for the power conferred on the imagination by violence. By way of elucidating literature's counterhistorical dimensions, I turn to other disciplines, in particular anthropology and political theory, that are better able to navigate between the world and the text and which do not require causal explanations for aesthetic processes.

Instead of seeking to establish transgressive sanctity as an historical event, I propose literature as a means of understanding violence. Stated otherwise, my evidence for transgressive sanctity is the literary texts through which I reconstruct the anticolonial imaginations of Caucasus literatures. Far from reducing the significance of this inquiry, this approach illuminates the aesthetic foundations of violence, and suggests how transgressive sanctity can help us critically cognize our attraction to violence. I prioritize the aesthetics of the encounter over the historicity of the event in order to view violence as a performance that draws its power from its effect on observers. If engaged critically, such cognition will help us control violence's effects, at least at the level of individual agency.

Although Titsian's deployment of militant Islamic lexicons privileges literary over historical veracity, his imagery aspires toward a pan-Caucasus poetics of insurgency. Titsian's literary discourse on the enemy within himself (a self-styled *giaour*) and on himself within his enemy (the Sufi *murīd*) shows that anticolonial poetics confounds the dichotomous politics of armed militancy and coercive colonialism. For this Georgian modernist, anticolonial poetics makes the world new. Insurgency for Titsian is a faculty of the literary imagination rather than a function of material force.

Provocatively merging poetry and politics and reading resistance against the grain of both the Muslim and the Christian tradition, Titsian's laconic indictment of Georgian literature's historical entanglement in the imperial project resonates far beyond the region that birthed his verse. Titsian's poetic critique also substantiates the argument of this book, which is the argument of transgressive sanctity: the literary imagination rearranges the political relations naturalized by colonial rule. If violence is a performance, as this book presumes, then it follows that aesthetics shape political reality. As detailed in the chapters that follow, Daghestani scholars broke with Chechen idioms of anticolonial insurgency when violence was aestheticized within Daghestani culture. Similarly demonstrative of the primacy of the aesthetic in constituting history is the fact that Georgian modernism's break with the colonial past was enabled by its elaboration of a poetics of insurgency that drew inspiration from Daghestani and Chechen examples.

Having contrasted the multilingual literatures of Daghestan, Chechnya, and Georgia to the monolingual narratives that dominate the study of this region, I close by explicating the disciplinary orientation that, in my estimation, is best suited for the study of the Caucasus, a region, that, given its small scale, is almost unparalleled in its literary, linguistic, cultural, temporal, religious, and ethnic diversity.

Literary Anthropology as Method

A method that combines literature and anthropology to emphasize literature's infrastructural impact on the social realm is ideally poised to explicate the aesthetics of insurgency. While the anthropology of literature undertaken in the pages that follow benefits from prior interventions within literary studies, including New Historicism and reader-response criticism, the intensified forms of both aesthetics and politics in the literatures of the Caucasus calls for a new understanding of the relation between anthropology and literature. Responding to this exigency, the literary anthropology cultivated in these pages reads literature as a performance rooted in power, and conceives of anticolonial aesthetics as the mediation between the power of the text and the power of the state.

For too long, the Caucasus has been dominated by disciplines that conceive of literary form as epiphenomenal to political history. In part as a result of this denial of local literatures, Russian representations of the region have largely remained normative in the study of the Caucasus. Even critiques of Russian Orientalism rarely engage with non-Russian sources.[67] While this bias is increasingly problematized as a matter of culture and geography, its disciplinary implications have not been adequately explored. The devaluation of the literary within Soviet and post-Soviet studies results in part from the severance of literary studies from anthropological methods, as well as from the tendency, especially strong within the social sciences, of isolating aesthetics from politics. Even when the Caucasus is studied within a transdisciplinary context, multiple disciplines are yoked together without actually being brought into conversation. Symptomatically, scholars of the Caucasus possess no interdisciplinary regional manifesto comparable to the calls to action that have shaped the study of the Caribbean, East Asia, and the Levant.[68] Even regional subfields of recent coinage, such as Southeast Asia, have attained greater institutional recognition than the Caucasus, which hovers uncomfortably between Asia and Europe, or Russian studies and the Middle East, straddling the margins of each of these imperfect configurations.[69]

By studying the figure of the abrek through the framework of transgressive sanctity, this literary anthropology of anticolonial insurgency establishes the aesthetic as a political category. My approach follows the emphasis of New Historicism on the "interpretive constructions the members of a society apply to their experiences" while supplementing the New Historicist agenda with an ethnographic method.[70] Integrating "several kinds of ethnography and ethnology,"[71] literary anthropology elucidates the aesthetics of insurgency while attending to affective forms of life generated by this violence. Focusing on the juncture of texts and their reception, literary anthropology brings the anthropological question "how can . . . archives . . . be converted into texts that represent and even participate in a way of life?" into dialogue with the immanent aesthetics of literary form.[72]

Through its examination of the social mediation of textual representations, literary anthropology confounds the disciplinary strictures that sever the social sciences from the humanities. It also enables us to read violence as a performance rather than as the mere application of force. While the traditional field of literary studies has long been preoccupied with how history and experience shape literature, literary anthropology documents the processes through which literature shapes history and experience. In terms of the literatures that are the subject of this book, literary anthropology examines how Daghestani, Georgian, and Chechen texts influenced the Soviet experience, giving birth to new ways of conceiving political life. It also considers how tsarist and Soviet violence was refracted into post-Soviet war, generating new idioms of resistance and new and ever more complex languages of accommodation.

for someone who wants to think beyond causal relationships cf. pg. 21

The dialogue between literature and anthropology unfolds in this book through a nonlinear chronology that is calibrated to the genres that are most significant within their respective literatures. The Soviet-era Chechen historical novel predominates in chapter 1, nineteenth-century Daghestani Arabic historiography and poetry predominates in chapter 2, and the poetry of Georgian modernism predominates in chapter 3. Unlike most temporally attuned scholarship on the Caucasus, which begins with the historical record, I begin with literature. From literature, I turn to history and finally to contemporary experience. Opening with Soviet texts that reconstruct tsarist-era anticolonial violence, I work backward in time, to colonial-era Daghestani reflections on insurgency. While this method runs against the grain of certain historicist methods, my chosen temporal sequence prioritizes literary over historical categories and reveals violence as a performance more thoroughly than a chronological organization could sustain.

When anthropologist Paul Friedrich takes Susan Layton's landmark study of Russian literary representations of the Caucasus to task for its failure to distinguish among "Chechens, Circassians, and other peoples of the Caucasus," he pinpoints one contribution that literary anthropology can make to the study of Caucasus literatures.[73] The error of such homogenization is obvious to any historian or anthropologist, indeed to anyone whose discipline prioritizes empirical research over its imaginative refraction. While at an empirical level we can document what is lost when Caucasus literatures are homogenized, we also need to understand this loss in literary terms, as an impoverishment of world literature and not only a simplification of the historical and ethnographic record. This work reveals the aesthetic costs of the linguistically reduced Caucasus that remains normative within Russian and Eurasian studies. Friedrich's call for greater ethnographic specificity suggests how scholars of Caucasus vernacular literatures can complicate influential paradigms of subaltern resistance, including those advanced by James C. Scott and Ranajit Guha. An anthropological aesthetic lays at the foundations of transgressive sanctity.

While literary engagements with the Caucasus privilege Russian literary representations, the anthropology of this same geography, most notably those of Valery Tishkov, tends to privilege the neocolonial

Russian state as the locus of political agency.[74] Literary anthropology, by contrast, offers a more fluid account of power and agency. I trace the birth of Chechen, Daghestani, and Russophone Ossetian literatures from within colonial violence to their Soviet-era refinement in the elite universities of Moscow and Leningrad, and to the second life they acquired in the Caucasus, where they helped to generate the vernacular nationalisms of the post-Soviet periods.[75]

Literary studies traditionally privileges the canon and political theory traditionally privileges the state. By contrast, the anthropology of literature displaces the hegemonic state formations that canonical textual traditions have helped consolidate by introducing literatures outside the received canon. Counterhegemonic and countercanonical, literary anthropology is a useful tool for recovering the aesthetics of vernacular literary forms, including but not exclusively oral genres. In keeping with recent trends in postcolonial studies, vernacular is used throughout this book to reference "the arguments and assumptions" that inflect the "social meanings" of literature outside the metropole.[76] In contradistinction to a purely linguistic understanding of vernacularity, literary anthropology showcases the aesthetic and political specificity of vernacularity in modern culture.

Political theorists have long been familiar with the entailment of language within sovereignty. The early modern political theorist Jean Bodin articulated this relation well while also outlining a useful conceptual framework for the elaboration of insurgency. In 1576, amidst the Wars of Religion that devastated Huguenot Europe, Bodin declared that the ability to compel "subjects to change their language is a mark of sovereignty."[77] Following on Bodin's insight, this book traces the genesis of Caucasus literatures with reference to the political entanglements of language and governmentality that Bodin associated with the inception of sovereignty. Hence, literary anthropology functions here, in part, as a political theory that mediates between the anthropology of violence and the aesthetics of transgressive sanctity.

The insights of Clifford Geertz and James Clifford concerning the primacy of vernacular knowledge to the task of writing culture have long been internalized in anthropological inquiry.[78] Yet literary studies lags behind the social sciences in terms of its ability to engage with vernacular literary forms. Reader-response theorist Wolfgang Iser perceives literary anthropology as a "divining rod" that identifies in literary texts the "dispositions, desires, [and] inclinations" of readers past and present.[79] But while Iser formulates literary anthropology as an "offshoot of reader-response criticism," I conceive of literary anthropology as a method for grasping the process through which violence is aestheticized. Whereas the anthropological project of writing culture, or Iser's more diluted concept of literature as a divining rod, is ultimately subservient to specific canons, literary anthropology in the sense deployed here uses aesthetics as a method for reading political violence.

In my endeavor to use literary form to elucidate political violence, I draw inspiration from the oeuvre of Walter Benjamin, and specifically his "Zur Kritik der Gewalt" (On the Critique of Violence, 1921). In this essay, written in the early years of the Weimar Republic and in uncanny anticipation of the fascism that was to drive him to suicide, Benjamin developed a critical account of the evolution of political power in modernity through its relationship to violence. The title Benjamin gave to his account, *Kritik*, referenced a style of philosophical analysis that in the Kantian tradition entails a provisional acceptance of the terms through which the object of analysis is constituted, without foreclosing its eventual rejection.[80] Similarly, in this book, I resist the temptation to criticize the aestheticization of violence that suffuses many of my literary sources, just as it suffused the politically saturated atmosphere of the Chechen homes where I resided during the closing years of the Second Chechen War (1999–2009). Following Benjamin, I cultivate a dialectical relationship to my subjects, which includes peoples, traditions, texts, and cultures associated with the perpetration of violence. This relation requires me to live with and within the aesthetics of violence and the images this aesthetics generates rather than to regard sympathetic representations of violence in anticolonial texts as mere symptoms of false consciousness.

To judge violence and then summarily castigate those who are enmeshed within its machinations is easy, particularly when one is observing from afar. Unsurprisingly, such summary judgments, of Chechens and of the propensity to violence that is presumed to be endemic to the Caucasus, permeate the global mass media as well as the scholarly literature. One purpose of this book is to write against this tradition, and to replace it with a more dialectical understanding of violence as a generator of value, including sacred values that have substantive political and historical implications. By contrast with the commonplace refusal to come to terms with violence's productivity, a *Kritik* of violence engages this concept from within the understandings of its perpetrators. *Kritik* performs this identification in the interests, ultimately, of overcoming violence, but it does not evade the ethical challenge that is entailed in the recognition that one person's violence is another person's peace, a challenge that the modern historical method evades through its cultivation of hermeneutic distance.[81] In this Benjaminian iteration, the *Kritik* of violence entails a disciplinary repertoire, and an ethical position, unlike those that inform most scholarly accounts of political violence, in the Caucasus and throughout the world.

When Benjamin states cryptically that the "*Kritik* of violence is the philosophy of its history," he means that, to overcome any influential concept, destructive or otherwise, a critical understanding of its historical constitution is necessary.[82] A philosophy of a concept's history is not equivalent, however, to a history of the concept itself.[83] This book opts for genealogy over chronology: I seek to generate a conceptual account of violence's historical constitution in modernity rather than an historical account that severs the observing subject from the object analyzed. The structure of this book conforms to a *Kritik* in that it begins by seeking to understand violence from within, particularly in the first chapter, while moving toward a more ambivalent account of militant resistance in the chapters that follow. By attending to the mediation of violence by aesthetic form, I argue that, just as aesthetics sacralizes violence, so too is it able to bring about violence's desacralization.

In terms of Gadamerian hermeneutics, this book has as its primary goal *Verstehen* (understanding) rather than *Wissen* (knowledge).[84] As I seek to understand violence from within, I make use of anthropology's deep history of empathetic engagement to read texts (in chapters 1–3), and I draw on literary analysis to carry out ethnography (in chapter 4 and the epilogue). That many of the chapters that follow juxtapose incommensurable contexts necessarily obscures certain historical nuances; however, this loss is partly ameliorated by a growing historical literature concerned with anticolonial violence in the Caucasus, most notably in the pioneering historical ethnographies of Vladimir Bobrovnikov.[85] Conjoining imaginative and documentary representations, the method adopted in the pages that follow aims to reproduce the experience of reading in a local context. In contradistinction to a historicist method, which assumes a view from nowhere, literary anthropology situates historical meaning within the literary text.

Finally, a more precise description of the concept of modernity that frames my inquiry into the relationship between aesthetics and violence is in order. Although this work is concerned almost exclusively with the production of literature during the colonial, Soviet, and post-Soviet periods, I do not intend for this framework to be comprehensive of Caucasus modernities. Modernity is not reducible to colonialism anywhere in the world, and least of all in the Caucasus. The frequent recurrence of these terms together, in phrases such as "colonial modernity" and "Soviet modernity," is intended to underscore the specificity as well as the plurality of modernity's many forms, for if modernity were always colonial, then it would not require such qualification. Like transgressive sanctity, modernity, which can be provisionally described as any systematic and self-conscious deployment of cultural, literary, and linguistic forms of newness, is a heuristic that is best left untethered to any single time or place.[86] As a concept, modernity is useful, less for its internal content than for its mediatory effects, and for demonstrating the contemporaneity of past forms of reasoning with our political present.

This book understands modernity in terms of its placement within the social sciences, wherein it functions as a provocation by shifting the terms through which specific canons and archives are commonly conceived. Modernity is not a final or authoritative account or any given historical juncture; rather it is malleable and forever subject to change. Modernity in this usage should also be distinguished from modernism, for the latter entails a conscious "contestation of political projects," whereas the former may lack a unified agenda.[87] Just as it refuses existing historicist paradigms, this book rejects existing definitions of modernity. Rather than define a term that has primarily heuristic value, I aim to deploy it productively, and in terms that elucidate our political present. Far from erasing past forms of life, modernity in this usage seeks ways of being that counter contemporary paradigms.

While I recognize that any usage of the term *modernity* will be overdetermined, at this preliminary juncture in its usage, by its European genealogy, I join with a growing contingent of scholars who seek to appropriate the term in ways that enable it to signify in post-Eurocentric (as well as pre-Eurocentric) ways.[88] The rubric of early modernity, which frames other aspects of my work, draws attention to the precolonial variants on the forms of modernity that are best known to us in their colonial iterations.[89] Rather than positing a singular modernity, I offer a plurality of ways of coming to terms with newness across time and space. Elsewhere, I have used the early modern concept to explore the alternative modernities that were generated from within the Islamic world prior to the colonial encounter, modernities with which Mavraev and other jadidists were in dialogue when they refashioned them for a later temporal horizon.

Such is the temporal framework, at the intersection of these multiple modernities, within which the present engagement with Caucasus literatures transpires. Many of the authors considered in this book, particularly those from Daghestan, were in dialogue with precolonial textual traditions. Although interfaces between past and present are not my focus here, their textual encounters, some of which have been alluded to in the preceding pages, attest to the many temporal palimpsests that characterize literary form in the Caucasus. Collectively, these pluralities of time, space, language, and conviction constitute an important background against which and through which anticolonial insurgency is given literary form.

The Road Ahead

I conclude with a road map for the road ahead. Chapter 1 traces the emergence of the anticolonial bandit (abrek) in Chechen Soviet literature. Beyond mapping this institution onto its broader social context, I study how the sanctification of social banditry in Soviet literature recalibrates the dialectic between colonial and indigenous law in the nineteenth-century Caucasus. This dialectic is further complicated by the plurality of local legal norms, which oscillated between indigenous law (*ʿādāt*) and Islamic jurisprudence (*sharīʿa*). Rooted in precolonial traditions, the abrek functioned as the dominant idiom of indigenous insurgency during the second half of the nineteenth and early twentieth century as the Muslim peoples of the Caucasus confronted the overwhelming force of Russia's imperial army. During the Soviet period, representing the abrek was one of the most powerful ways for the indigenous literary elite to contest imperial law. Drawing on Chechen, Russian, and Georgian literatures of anticolonial insurgency, chapter 1 reverses the causal relations between base and superstructure that obtain in Ranajit Guha's "elementary aspects of peasant insurgency" to document how the literary imagination mediates the memory of popular insurgency.

Chapter 2 explores literary and historiographic renderings of Daghestani rebellions from 1877 and 1921 across Arabic and Russian sources. I focus in particular on the Arabic historiography that coalesced around the 1877 rebellion that swept through Daghestan and Chechnya following Shamil's surrender. These historiographic texts are read alongside the Arabic poetry of major Daghestani writers, especially Ḥasan al-Alqadārī and Najm al-Dīn al-Ḥutsī. This chapter is linked to the chapter that follows through its exploration of the representation of Ḥājjī Murād in vernacular Daghestani literatures.

Chapter 3 completes the arc of my comparative investigations into the literatures of anticolonial insurgency. In this chapter, I compare Leo Tolstoy's writings on the Caucasus, beginning in his early short stories and culminating in his posthumously published masterpiece *Hadji Murad* (1912), with Georgian poet Titsian Tabidze's poems on Imam Shamil, the most striking among which is "Gunib" (1928), a text written to eulogize Daghestan's political defeat. Reading Georgian poems against and through Russian intertexts, I show how Georgian poets aestheticized transgressive sanctity in ways that paralleled the Chechen novels introduced in chapter 1. Critically interrogating their own literary traditions, and seeking in neighboring literatures alternative languages for dissent, Georgian writers such as Titsian Tabidze pioneered a literary form that was at once anticolonial, self-consciously modernist, and pan-Caucasian.

Congruent with the reading of Dzakho Gatuev's *Zelimkhan* (1926) that preoccupies chapter 1, chapter 3 dwells on writers who forged vernacular poetics from courageous critiques of colonial rule and creative contestations of violence. While the terms through which colonialism was negotiated differed radically from Gatuev to Tabidze, both writers paid for their political dissidence with their lives. Beyond this biographical happenstance, both writers crafted literary grammars of insurgency that contributed in the longer term to a pan-Caucasian anticolonial poetics. For each of the texts discussed in these chapters, the penultimate source of inspiration is the Chechen abrek, who is this book's dominant motif and guiding light. As the condensation of transgressive sanctity's paradox, the anticolonial abrek marks the moment when the unholy violation of local law is sacralized in order to dismantle a coercively imposed legal system. Poetics becomes political critique and political critique becomes a poetic act.

Turning from literature to ethnography, and text to image, chapter 4 examines transgressive sanctity's most recent iteration in wartime Chechnya. My examination revolves around local memories of Chechnya's first female suicide bombing in 2001. As I excavate the spaces of political life that remain unclarified by analyses grounded in the state, I draw on anthropological reflections on suicide bombing as a practice that aims at earthly immortality by Talal Asad and other theorists of secular modernity. I also explore how suicide bombing converges with and diverges from Hannah Arendt's reading of political life in antiquity as a striving for freedom from coercion. Even as I document the post-Soviet recourse to violence in order to achieve recognition, I also seek to reframe the anthropological concept of resistance. While much has been published concerning Chechen defiance of Russian rule, little has been written about the creative strategizing within coercive political systems that in Arabic is called *ṣumūd* (steadfastness) and yet permeates everyday life in the Caucasus.[90] Ultimately, I argue that the shift in the discourse of transgressive sanctity from text to image, and literature to mass media, to which the suicide bomber attests, harbingers this ideology's degeneration. In late post-Soviet modernity, violence has become aestheticized to the point of relinquishing its former power. At such a juncture, the state gains in power, because it is able to deploy force without being dependent on violence's aesthetic power.

In arguing for the relevance of area studies to diasporic inquiry, postcolonial theorists have promoted subaltern studies as a framework within which to document the destabilization of imperial reason by vernacular literary forms.[91] The time has come to reconceive the Caucasus in similarly global terms. Within such a framework, the Caucasus would not simply be postcolonial theory's afterthought, or a battleground upon which to provide or disprove the theories of Edward Said.[92] Rather, it would offer a space for generating new meanings, new ways of seeing, and new ways of being to readers around the world. While Guha and other historians of peasant insurgency have taught us to read indigenous violence as a grammar unto itself, we are much less informed about the poetics that gave this grammar meaning.[93] By engaging with literary texts that circulated across Caucasus from the beginning of the colonial period into late Soviet modernity, this book seeks to make the aesthetic redemptions of treachery elaborated across multiple Caucasus literatures legible as critiques of empire and as endeavors to articulate a cogent vision of a world region that has over the course of its long history confounded our most deeply engrained prejudices. Through its plurality of cultures, confessions, literatures, and languages, the Caucasus has hosted a remarkable diversity of approaches to the problem of violence. This book seeks to bring some of those approaches to light, in the interests of confounding our own stereotypes.

O·N·E

The Abrek in Soviet Chechen Literature

The anticolonial literatures of Chechnya, Daghestan, and Georgia were differently shaped by colonial violence. This chapter engages with some key moments in the history of Chechen anticolonial insurgency while examining how they contributed to the birth of Chechen literature in the Soviet period. During the final decades of this conquest, the famed Daghestani warrior Imam Shamil presided over the longest-lasting *sharīʿa*-ruled government in a world region controlled by colonial powers. And yet, notwithstanding Daghestan's centrality to anticolonial insurgency both globally and locally, the Chechen idiom of insurgency reverberated even more widely across the region. This is one reason for beginning this book with Chechnya, the culture that served as a fulcrum for so much violence in the Caucasus. It was also in Chechnya that the abrek contributed most formidably to development of transgressive sanctity in the aftermath of political defeat. Known in Chechen as *obargalla*, and in Russian by the term *abrechestvo*, social banditry was first aestheticized in the waning years of the Russo-Caucasus War.

While the precolonial abrek (Chechen *obarg*) participated in raids on other villages, the anticolonial abrek contributed to the formation of an indigenous colonial modernity. Whereas before colonialism, the abrek was a social outcast, the anticolonial abrek was regarded as sacred by his community in proportion to his transgressive activities.[1] When Chechnya was formally incorporated, along with the rest of the northern Caucasus, into the Russian empire, acts that in premodern contexts were understood as crimes came to be locally viewed as insignia of courage. Drawing on while also diverging from his precolonial predecessors, the anticolonial abrek dedicated his life to destroying the colonial administration that "recognized the state's sovereignty and gave it life."[2]

The year 1859 marks the beginning of the process that structures this book, repeatedly through a kind of repetition compulsion, across Chechen, Daghestani, Georgian, and other Caucasus literatures. In that year, Shamil surrendered to the Russian field marshal Bariatinskii.[3] This surrender is the event with which the most important primary source on Shamil's jihad, Muḥammad Ṭāhir al-Qarākhī's *Bāriqat*, was intended to conclude before a sequence of poems (discussed in the following chapter) was later grafted onto it.[4] Shamil was then exiled to Russia's interior, where he peacefully resided until he was given permission to leave Russia for Mecca in 1869. Unsurprisingly, his lionization in Russian popular culture also begins with his 1859 surrender (figure 1).[5] Notably, this event is referred to among Daghestanis today as Shamil's captivity (*plenenie shamiliia*), even though Shamil surrendered of his own free will.

In Daghestan, Shamil is remembered as "a national hero, a strong ruler, a gifted general and an accomplished statesman," as well as the forger of "a united Daghestan."[6] Meanwhile, in Chechnya, although he is revered as a local hero, Shamil is also regarded by many as a traitor whose surrender did not and could not normalize the new colonial dispensation. Chechens were acutely conscious of the negative effects of Shamil's surrender, and their attitude influenced some Daghestanis as well to adopt a more negative account of Shamil's legacy in general and of his surrender in particular. In this spirit, a contemporary Daghestani historian writes that, after Shamil's surrender, Tsar Aleksandr II began to "suppress Islam, Muslim scholars, and *sharīʿa*, and to increase [the mountaineers'] economic and social burdens."[7] The most searching investigations into the aftermath of Shamil's surrender are, however, predominantly the domain of Chechen narrative prose, including the texts studied in this chapter.

Figure 1. Photograph of Imam Shamil, taken in 1859. Courtesy of Khadzhi Murad Donogo.

In a post-1859 world, few Chechens would have regarded their struggle against the tsar as likely to result in victory. Under the new dispensation, political autonomy came to seem like an empty fantasy. After 1859, Chechens, together with other peoples of the northern Caucasus, were constrained to turn to the abrek, a figure who offered less political leverage but perhaps for that very reason more cultural capital than the more familiar forms of resistance that had animated Shamil's jihad. This historical shift from institutionalized resistance to anticolonial banditry laid the groundwork for Chechen literature's grammar of indigenous insurgency.

Shamil's surrender radically altered the balance of power in the Caucasus. Whereas the mountaineers had been fighting the Russians under Shamil's leadership for the preceding quarter century, in the aftermath of their leader's defeat, they were left to fend for themselves. Shamil's surrender ushered in a new kind of violence. Lacking a centralized state to organize resistance, the mountaineers of the Caucasus organized from within the vacuum of authority created by their leader's abdication. Originating in defeat, anticolonial resistance in post-Shamilian Chechnya is marked by the fragility of indigenous political institutions, on the one hand, and by the rise of new social institutions, less governed by centralized authority, on the other hand.

Beginning with the pivotal year of 1859, the atmosphere of defeat that pervaded post-Shamilian Chechnya led bandits, rebels, and saints to sacrifice themselves for the benefit of their community. This chapter examines how Soviet-era Chechen, Ossetian, and Georgian intellectuals were inspired to eulogize in literary form bandits, rebels, and saints as they reflected on Chechnya's political defeat. In tracing how the mountaineer insurgent was rendered in multiple Soviet literatures, I show how violence became constitutive of literary modernity in these colonial borderlands.

Given the Islamic traditions that have spread unevenly throughout the Caucasus for many centuries, it is not surprising that the most effective mobilizations of local political sentiment merged the struggle against the tsar with Muslim piety. An influential folk song dedicated to Baisangur (c. 1794–1861), a Chechen *nāʾib* (lieutenant) of Shamil who stayed behind to fight after his leader surrendered, epitomizes the sense of betrayal experienced by those who did not wish to make peace with the Russians. According to this folkloric narrative, which circulated widely in post-Soviet Chechnya, Baisangur, from the village of Beno in mountainous Chechnya, resorted to a veiled threat to dissuade his leader from surrendering. "Chechens don't shoot in the back, Shamil,"

Baisangur said, "but you should beware. I have a pistol on me now."[8] Shamil asked his *nā'ib*'s forgiveness but refused to follow his advice. He explained that he was tired of fighting and that there was no point in resistance. Defeat was inevitable.

Unimpressed by Shamil's diplomacy, Baisangur summoned his men to Chechnya, to the epicenter of the battle, where, so the song prophesies, only thirty of every hundred fighters will survive. Baisangur knew the meaning of sacrifice: he fought to his death with his sole remaining arm and mutilated eyes. From the middle of 1860 to the beginning of 1861, Baisangur led a rebellion in the Chechen highlands against the army of the tsar. By the time the rebellion was quelled, fifteen villages had burned to the ground, including Beno, Baisangur's native village.[9] In the spring of 1861, Baisangur was hung, like so many of the insurgents who populate these chapters and who were eulogized in the anticolonial literatures of the Caucasus, in Khasav-Yurt, a Chechen village on the Daghestan border.[10]

After the incorporation of the north Caucasus into the Russian empire, many stories circulated concerning Shamil's former *nā'ibs* who resented their master's surrender, including, in addition to Baisangur, Ḥājjī Murād, whose life story was famously dramatized by Tolstoy, as well as by multiple Avar and Georgian authors discussed in chapters 2 and 3. Such stories laid the groundwork for transgressive sanctity, the guiding concept of this book. Understood politically, transgressive sanctity is the process through which state-sanctioned coercion generates a new ethical and aesthetic relation to violence. Although it attained its fullest form in the early Soviet period, transgressive sanctity was inaugurated in the tsarist period through the encounter with colonial law generally and the violent application (and violation) of these laws specifically.

For a political concept, transgressive sanctity is unique in that it is forged from literary archives and cultural memories. Because my primary evidence for transgressive sanctity is literary, this argument is also a theory derived from a literary canon's representation of violence. To ask any theory to do double work, as a description of a textual archive and an historical process, is to court accusations of partiality. Although it cannot wholly account for either the aestheticization of violence in history or the refraction of this process in literature, transgressive sanctity does enable us to see these two distinct topics as intimately related. Transgressive sanctity also fruitfully suggests how literature can sometimes deduce from the historical record dynamics that mainstream political history is not equipped to see.

Although transgressive sanctity can be discerned in many anticolonial literatures, it has a particularly prominent place within the Caucasus literatures of insurgency. Composed by the descendants of insurgents and their literary admirers, these texts rework the relation between anthropology and literature. As the prospect of full political autonomy faded from the realm of the possible, the sacred bandit came to epitomize the last hope of a conquered people. While some bandits lived genuinely spiritual lives and performed miracles, others used spirituality as a cover for militancy. Their collective memorialization was one of early Chechen literature's basic accomplishments.

As an institution for regulating—and punishing—transgression, the abrek is ancient to the Caucasus. Like blood revenge (*kanly*) and the attendant custom of safe passage (*amān*), whereby a member of one clan found guilty of a crime sought refuge with another clan and changed his identity in the process, the abrek has functioned over the centuries as a tool for managing violence among neighboring communities.[11] In addition to changing identities, the abrek economically supported his adopted clan by raiding neighboring villages. Although often violent, the raids initiated by abreks were distinct from other forms of aggression between villages and clans. Governed by rules of reciprocity, the abrek's raids aimed to capture livestock and other food, and it was expected that the raided villagers would respond in kind. A kind of circular justice was thereby already attendant on the abrek before colonialism. The abrek's circular justice morphed into an ambivalent relationship to violence, first with the colonial dispensation and secondly with the Soviet experiment. As the threat posed by the colonial regime to local ethics became increasingly clear, the abreks' raids came to be directed against Russian settlements rather than against other Chechens. This colonial-era reconfiguration of the enemy laid the groundwork for transgressive sanctity.

While the precolonial abrek moved between villages, he only came to underwrite an ethics of transgressive sanctity in late tsarist and early

Soviet periods. After 1859, as contacts with the colonial administration increased in both intensity and frequency, the abrek became the primary means through which insurgency was waged. After 1917, through the Soviet refashioning of cultural memory, the abrek was further aestheticized. Ultimately, this "infrapolitics of the powerless" created a situation whereby violence appeared ethically legitimate.[12] As the mountaineers' prospects of political autonomy declined, the empire that ruled over their lands grew in power, creating the need for a new aesthetic register to navigate the loss of local sovereignty. In response to this exigency, the anticolonial abrek acquired literary form.

In the introduction, I suggested that the abrek's genesis breaks the chain of cause and effect, whereby history is seen to generate literature, and literature either reflects or distorts the historical record. While there are many cracks in the Soviet narrative, and many instances of anachronistic refashioning, more important to my purposes than tabulating the tension between literary accounts and the historical record is coming to terms with the effect of the abrek's engagement with violence on literature. Literature and history intermingle in this work like siblings separated at birth. One contribution of the study of the literature of anticolonial insurgency is to bring about their provisional and inevitably contentious reunion.

While the anticolonial abrek was forged by the nineteenth-century encounter between indigenous and colonial norms, this social institution was given literary form only in the Soviet period, as the colonial inversion of local legal codes entered into the infrastructure of everyday life. The coming-into-being of banditry at the nexus of aesthetics and politics was facilitated by a colonial discourse that, in conflating "all bandits with abreks and, vice versa, all abreks with bandits," made crime controvertible with sanctity.[13] In ways subsequently mirrored in the literatures of Georgia and Daghestan, Chechens' encounter with the colonial legal order was memorialized as transgressive sanctity.

The pages that follow trace the embrace of indigenous violence through the abrek's transgressive sanctity. Colonial stereotypes are interpolated with the counternarratives they evoked among anticolonial Chechen, Ossetian, and Georgian writers. The abrek who is the subject of this analysis was forged in the interstices of domination and resistance, politics and culture, anthropology and literature. His quixotic militancy proliferated in periodicals, novels, folklore, and film in the latter half of the nineteenth and the early twentieth centuries concurrently to literary rewritings of the colonial dispensation. As an invented tradition, the transgressively sanctified abrek refashioned the cultural memory of anticolonial resistance.[14]

I consider the constitution of abreks in and through the vernacular literatures of the Caucasus, including texts produced by Muslim Chechens, Avars, Qumuqs, Adyghes, Kabardians, Ossetians who straddle the Christian-Muslim divide, and Christian Georgians. A literary history of the Chechen abrek must cultivate different angles of vision. Beyond inquiring into why Chechens were demonized in colonial discourse, we must ask what Chechen authors have invested historically in their culture's self-representations and what the worlds they imagined into existence tell us about the relationship between a subaltern culture and the empire that both fostered and suppressed it.

Following the colonial dispensation, the transgressively sanctified abrek relinquished his function as a leverager of violence within the community and began instead to leverage violence between the colonial regime and its subjects. The rapid spread of literacy throughout the northern Caucasus under Soviet rule stimulated the abrek's life in literature. The literary abrek was grounded in the historical figure who roamed the mountains dividing Georgia's Pankisi Gorge from Chechnya as late as the 1970s. Yet he was also a figure apart, a product of the anticolonial imagination that has profoundly influenced the development of Chechen literature.

Our knowledge of the historical abrek is based on five types of sources. Most important are *ʿādāt* compendiums, many still unpublished, mostly in Arabic but also in vernacular languages.[15] Extending from the early medieval to the early modern period, these texts typically describe the abrek as someone who is "deprived of an inheritance and banished from his family and clan."[16] A second source, used here, but only by way of supplementing literary accounts, is oral poetry in Chechen, Georgian, Daghestani, and Circassian languages.[17] A third source is the works of local and Russian ethnographers that were published in the Russian periodical press during the late nineteenth and

early twentieth century.[18] A fourth source, now at a significant remove *vice*
from local contexts, are discussions of mountaineer societies by colonial (4)
officers and military historians, which are frequently interwoven into
accounts of tsarist military campaigns.[19] Finally, the fifth source—
Soviet-era historical novels—traverses the divide between history (5)
and literature. These novels are the key building block in the edifice of
transgressive sanctity. They are consecrated by and large to one abrek,
Zelimkhan, whom three mountaineer intellectuals studied intensively:
Aslanbek Sheripov, Dzakho Gatuev, and Magomed Mamakaev.

While many of the Chechen and Ossetian writers who created
the literary abrek were Moscow educated, their elite education did not
stop them promoting indigenous literatures. As they contributed to the *But this*
Soviet discourse concerning the brotherhood of peoples, through their *was*
reinvention of local literatures, these writers tried to steer this conversa- *Soviet*
tion in a direction it did not otherwise travel, toward the critique of *policy — see*
colonialism. Like the other four sources for our knowledge of the abrek, *Sam,*
Chechen and Ossetian literary texts had distinct agendas. Crafting *Rossen*
a literary anticolonialism from indigenous traditions, these authors
experimented with Soviet realities in local terms. Even when their mod-
ernist orientations relegated jihad to a holdover from a bygone era, they
successfully brought together anticolonialism and the Soviet dream. *– but still,*
these seem like
neglected case
studies

The First Abrek

As with many colonial conflicts, the death toll for the Battle of the
Daggers (1864)—the first large-scale conflict in Chechnya following
Shamil's surrender—depends on which side is counting. Half a cen-
tury after the event, the secretary for the Terek Statistical Committee
estimated one hundred casualties on the Chechen side.[20] By contrast,
an early Soviet Chechen historian estimated four hundred Chechen
deaths.[21] With similar sources at their disposal, the authors reached
sharply different assessments of the fallout of this battle, which has been
alternately described as a massacre and a declaration of war.[22] All that
is known is that at a Russian fort bordering the village of Shali, three
thousand pious Muslim men and women gathered to protest the recent
imprisonment of their Sufi leader, Kunta Ḥājjī. The violent suppression

of their peaceful protest radicalized piety, which until then had been noted for pacifism.

Kunta Ḥājjī, the protestors' imprisoned leader, was a Qumuq shepherd born around 1830 in the village of Mel'cha-Khi.[23] Drawn to religious studies from an early age, Kunta Ḥājjī memorized the Quran at the age of twelve. He then went on to study with the leading Chechen Sufi sheykh of his day, Ḥājjī Tashaw al-Indīrī, a *nā'ib* (lieutenant) of Imam Shamil. In 1849, the young shepherd and his father were granted permission to complete the hajj a privilege rarely granted in the tightly controlled imamate. While traversing the Arab world, Kunta Ḥājjī—now bearing the honorific affirming that he had completed the hajj—received an *ijāza* (authorization to preach), which officially inducted him into the Qādiriyya order. One of the four oldest Sufi orders, the Qādirīs followed traditions that were distinct and at times openly in conflict with the politically dominant Naqshbandīs.[24] Following his initiation into Qādiriyya Sufism, Kunta Ḥājjī returned to his homeland. A decade later, in 1858, as Shamil was on the verge of surrendering, Kunta Ḥājjī left his home in the Caucasus for a second pilgrimage.

Kunta Ḥājjī's forced exile was as much a blessing as it was a curse, for it afforded the opportunity to obtain deeper knowledge of the thinker from whom Qādirī Sufism derived its name, ʿAbd al-Qādir al-Jīlānī (1077–1166). Born near the Caspian Sea and buried in Baghdad, al-Jīlānī's grave became a major pilgrimage site for Qādirī Sufis.[25] Unwanted in his native country, the Qumuq shepherd traveled to Baghdad, where he immersed himself in the teachings and legacies of his Sufi master. Kunta Ḥājjī returned in 1861 to a post-imamate Chechnya, this time with the permission of Russian authorities who sought, at that early stage in their relations with this unknown branch of Sufism, to increase the pacifist leader's leverage over his Naqshbandī rivals in the hopes of eliminating "all remnants of resistance" from an already-defeated Chechnya.[26]

The alliance between the tsarist state and Qādirī Sufism was short lived. Although the initial tensions were between the Naqshbandīs who supported militant resistance and Kunta Ḥājjī's more ambiguous pacifism, soon after his return to Chechnya, Russian authorities came to fear Kunta Ḥājjī's teaching even more than that of his jihadist rivals. The colonial administration's policies were ironic in that while many

Naqshbandīs supported jihad against the Russians, Qādirīs initially campaigned for the cessation of violence.[27]

In addition to its pacifist dimensions, the primary hallmark of Kunta Ḥājjī's teaching was the loud recitation of the name of God (*dhikr jahrī*) that accompanied Sufi religious ceremonies and that distinguished his order from the Naqshbandiyya, who performed the quiet recitation of the name of God (*dhikr qalbī*). "The *zikrist* teaching," wrote the governor of the Terek district (which included Chechnya) Loris-Melikov with reference to Kunta Ḥājjī's style of chanting, "is consistent with *gazavat* [holy war], is a powerful tool for [creating] national unity, and waits for a propitious moment for its fanatical power to be reawakened."[28] Even when the tsarist administration recognized that, as one official put it, Kunta Ḥājjī's mystical teachings had acquired a militant character, the shift from pacifism to violence in the indigenous response to colonial law did not alter the state's practices of governance.[29]

Along with his brother and several of his followers, Kunta Ḥājjī was arrested in the Chechen village of Serzhen-Yurt. He was then transferred to a military prison in Novocherkassk in western Russia.[30] After serving hard labor in Novocherkassk for half a year, Kunta Ḥājjī was exiled to central Russia. His subsequent fate is unknown. According to popular belief, Kunta Ḥājjī is still alive and bestows his blessings on the faithful.[31] Long after his death, the violent persecution of Kunta Ḥājjī and his followers stimulated the spread of Sufi orders across Chechnya and Ingushetia.[32] More immediately relevant to our purposes, the memory of Kunta Ḥājjī influenced the development of transgressive sanctity within Soviet Chechen literature.

When their demand for Kunta Ḥājjī's release was refused, the Chechens assembled at the Shali fort in 1864 and began loudly performing the chanting ritual (*dhikr*) their leader had learned in Baghdad. Traditionally addressed to God, the *dhikr* as practiced by Chechens had more recently come to be associated with anticolonial protest. The protestors' peaceful chanting frightened the soldiers, who began shooting in the air. The Chechens then picked up their daggers and stormed the troops. Daggers were no match for bullets, and the pious but weakly armed insurgents were drastically unprepared for the confrontation that awaited them. According to the commander of the tsarist army, along with 150 Chechens, 8 Russian soldiers were killed.[33] The full death toll remains unknown.

According to the Soviet literary reconstruction, Shamil's surrender weakened the institutional foundations of anticolonial insurgency. Similarly, the Battle of the Daggers marked the moment when hitherto-pacifist mountaineers found their conceptions of the sacred politicized and their relationship to violence aestheticized. Kunta Ḥājjī's followers had thrown away their guns before they approached the fort where they believed their spiritual leader was imprisoned. Assuming that God would protect them, they confronted their enemies bolstered by faith alone. The peaceful protest that was motivated by the arrest of Kunta Ḥājjī launched the career of the first transgressively sanctified abrek, Vara, from Baisangur's village of Beno. A follower of Kunta Ḥājjī, Vara had joined the other protestors at Shali to launch the Battle of the Daggers.

Because he sought to emulate Kunta Ḥājjī's pacifism, Vara joined the protest at Shali unarmed.[34] As Chechen writer Abuzar Aidamirov wrote in 1972, in his literary reconstruction of this historical event, Vara rushed into the fight believing that "Allah, the Prophet, and his teacher [Kunta Ḥājjī] would immediately come to his aid" (286). When, in spite of his faith, his companions died through violence, Vara left his "home, family, and native village" to become an abrek (285). Here as elsewhere, in addition to perpetuating violence, anticolonial insurgency is born in response to another kind of violence. According to Aidamirov, Vara was the first modern abrek to avenge his people's suffering (*bekxamxoin xalq'an*). He became "the first rising star" of the movement that later "was made famous as Chechen banditry [*noxchiin obargiin*]" (285). Although Vara initially heeded his teacher's injunction to peace, after the Battle of the Daggers, he turned to violence. Following the arrest of his teacher and the murder of his fellow protesters, Vara passed the remainder of his life wandering from village to village, waging war against the tsar.

While Vara was one of the first abreks whose life trajectory was directly affected by the defeat of Shamil's imamate, he was by no means the last to feature in Soviet literature. As an erstwhile disciple of Kunta Ḥājjī, Vara is remembered to have ceremoniously recited from the Quran shortly before his death.[35] In his spirituality as in his politics, the first anticolonial abrek set a precedent for the many abreks whose lives and, no less importantly, deaths were refashioned by Soviet literature. A religious teaching that was, in essence, "alien to any kind of worldly movement" was thereby seen to underwrite an anticolonial political agenda.[36] Having reviewed Soviet reconstructions of nineteenth-century Chechen violent resistance, I now turn to Soviet renderings of the next juncture in the literary history of anticolonial insurgency. Each of these narratives epitomizes the complex modulations between resistance and accommodation so characteristic of Soviet modernity, and each, in its own specific way, aestheticizes violence.

Terrorizing Power

The Chechen Bolshevik leader Aslanbek Sheripov, a founder of Soviet Chechen literature, was among the first to draw attention to the abrek's importance for Soviet modernity. In the 1918 introduction to his Russian translations of Chechen folk songs, the Bolshevik intellectual outlined a genealogy for the modern abrek on the basis of Chechen folklore that shaped subsequent renderings of this figure across the literatures of the Caucasus. Merging Romantic poetry with revolutionary ideology, Sheripov argued that prior to the colonial period, "abreks were 'Byronic' types" who, because they could not adjust to their social milieus, "cut their ties" with their communities and pursued lives of solitude and exile. As "internationalists," abreks identified "neither with their own circle, nor with foreigners. . . . The people [*narod*] feared and therefore hated them."[37]

As an early Chechen attempt to reinvent the abrek for a Bolshevik readership, Sheripov's work merits close consideration. The abrek in his original incarnation was, according to Sheripov, simply someone excluded from the community. This precolonial abrek was typically a target of a blood feud. Guilty of a crime for which neither he nor his relatives could compensate the victim with cattle or other commodities, he was compelled to hide from his own community, which in those days administered punishment according to *ʿādāt*. Either he took up residence in a new community under a new name and concealed his prior identity from his new neighbors, or he roamed the mountains and forests until he met a tragic death from starvation. Even at this early moment in the Caucasus literatures of insurgency, Sheripov incorporates Russian literary sources, such as Lermontov's *Demon* (1841), into his conception of the abrek as a Byronic hero. The incorporation of canonical Russian poems into a proto-national defense of Chechen insurgency attests to the conflicting political agendas that were internal to this literary tradition.

From the perspective of Sheripov's anticolonial genealogy, the subsequent two stages in the abrek's evolution are of greatest salience. Sheripov dwells on these stages when he considers the aestheticization of the abrek's violence in relation to his newly acquired sanctity. "When Russian conquerors appeared in the Caucasus," Sheripov writes, "the people transferred their terror of the abreks onto the uninvited guests; during the war, abreks came to lead the Chechen resistance. Banditry [*abrechestvo*] acquired its most specific form only with the establishment of Russian rule in the Caucasus."[38] The last two stages in Sheripov's tripartite genealogy are intimately linked to the growth of the Russian empire. On this account, only after defeat did the abrek's violence become sacred. Defeat made the abrek a repository of a community's most sacred aspirations. When they were not overwhelmed by an enemy that wielded infinitely greater military resources, the common people, according to Sheripov, despised abreks and even killed them. Only after Shamil's captivity formalized Russian sovereignty in the Caucasus did abreks come to be venerated as bearers of sanctity. Onto their images were projected the trauma of war, the fear of annihilation, and the hopes of the vanquished. From his origins in precolonial society to his anticolonial iteration, the abrek has always been on intimate terms with violence. But only when his violence became anticolonial did it become fit for literature.

The decades following Shamil's captivity were also marked by an unprecedented proliferation of texts pertaining to anticolonial banditry in Caucasus folklore Caucasus, especially Chechen. Sheripov played a major role in incorporating this folklore into the Soviet literary canon by transcribing and translating into Russian an *illi* (Chechen folk ballad) pertaining to Gekha, a colonial-era abrek whose biography converges closely with that of Vara.[39] Beyond Gekha's *illi*, anthologies of Chechen folklore include *illi* for Vara and Zelimkhan that date to this period.[40] Further aligning transgression and sacralized insurgency in modernity, Soviet literature distinguished between folkloric abreks who were reviled by society and abreks who entered their vocation following Shamil's surrender. As the aesthetics of transgression proliferated, the post-Shamilian abrek ultimately became the norm. Whereas abreks featured broadly in the early colonial period across the Caucasus, including in Christian Georgia, the most famous example being that of the Georgian abrek Arsena Odzelashvili (c. 1797–1842), after Shamil's surrender, the abrek's geography was restricted to Muslim-majority regions of the Caucasus. Table 1 outlines the historical typology I have delineated for the abrek in terms that clarify the links between this social institution and the history of colonial rule in the Caucasus.

In his brief introduction, Sheripov rehearses the abrek's subsequent sanctification, tracing his transformation from bandit to saint. At the same time, this Chechen dissident establishes what would later become an orthodox Bolshevik teleology. Breaking with past tendencies to neutralize the damage inflicted by Russian rule, Sheripov took advantage of the new Soviet moment to argue out an anticolonial aesthetics. In forecasting the abrek's future, Sheripov evinced sensitivity to what was at the time a genuinely revolutionary idea. The trajectory he delineated would be adopted by many Caucasus writers who tackled the abrek theme in future decades, despite the frequent fluctuations in official attitudes to the subversive yet ideologically malleable figure.

Like nearly all accounts that followed, Sheripov's genealogy of social banditry originates in the tension between indigenous law (*ʿādāt*) and the law of the colonial state (*zakon*). This tension overwhelmingly structures Chechen literature and lays the groundwork for the forms of its insurgency. According to Sheripov, the discrepancy (*nesootvetstvie*) between "Russian justice" and the mountaineers' "local law" together with "the criminal administration of the Caucasus and the general politics of colonialism" forced many respected Chechen leaders to embrace illegal modes of life while the colonial state

> exiled these people from civil society. . . . People were made to suffer who had the bad fortune to be related to or simply to be from the same village as these "criminals." . . . Then

Table 1: The abrek's historical trajectory

Era	Transgressing against	Sanctified by	Primary sources	Secondary sources
Precolonial	clan (*taip*); ʿ*ādāt*	no one; an object of pity and contempt	ʿ*ādāt* codices; historical and sociolinguistics	Anchabadze; Botiakov; Akhlakov
Russo-Caucasus Wars (1824–1858)	Shamil's imamate; no collective agenda	impoverished mountaineers (in the case of Arsena); in general not supported	Arabic chronicles and poetry; European travel accounts	Bobrovnikov; Khojaev; Javaxishvili (fiction)
After Shamil's surrender (1859–1916)	*zakon* (colonial law); tsarist regime	parts of the mountaineer community; Chechen vernacular Islam	colonial-era *illi* (Gekha, Zelimkhan, Vara); Zelimkhan's letters	Vagapov; Gatuev and Mamkaev (fiction)
Soviet (1917–1990)	unequal distributions of wealth; Soviet violence (including deportation)	official Soviet policy; indigenous intelligentsia	novels; film; state-sponsored historiography	Gudaev; Khoruev
Post-Soviet (1991–)	post-Soviet Russian law	national liberation movements	popular culture (especially music); nationalist historiography	mass media

interesting that both sides claim this figure

> they began to take revenge on the authorities: abreks killed officials, robbed the post and Cossacks, as well as other official institutions . . . but those in power continued to punish [innocent] civilians with fines, executions, exile to Siberia, and hanging.[41]

Because the criteria used to determine punishment were as random as being born into the same village as an abrek, the legal apparatus that criminalized the abrek came increasingly to be associated with the arbitrary exercise of power. As in subsequent articulations of insurgency, the tension between the arbitrary bureaucracy normalized by imperial rule and native legal systems (such as ʿ*ādāt* and *sharīʿa*) to which colonial law could not adapt politicized banditry and stimulated a merger between anticolonial violence and religion. This new relation was expressed in transgressive sanctity. Colonial governmentality legitimated violence not only through its direct practices of governance but also by stimulating the sanctification of violent resistance. While the abrek as a social institution long predates the first clash between imperial power and local norms, the anticolonial abrek had to wait for the Soviet period to attain his fullest literary articulation.

Having seen how Sheripov accounted for the role of colonial law in the abrek's historical genesis, let us consider how he conceptualized the contribution made by the people (*narod*). How did the masses raise the abrek from his formerly despised status and crown him with a martyr's halo? Here is Sheripov's answer:

> Power terrorized the peaceful population, and abreks terrorized those in power. Of course, too, the people regarded abreks as fighters against the barbarism of the colonial authorities. . . . "Abrek" became a term of respect, and the people did not honor just anyone with this title. The most respected and successful abreks so captivated the Chechen people that they were considered to be carrying on the battle initiated by Shamil and his *murīds*. At one time, rumors even circulated that Zelimkhan had declared himself to be an imam and an annihilator of tsarist power.[42]

Sheripov does not dwell on the point that one crucial factor in the abrek's rise to the position of hero, and even, in the case of a specific abrek named Zelimkhan, of his association with the Islamic office of imam, was the popular reaction against the institutionalized militancy that dominated the most auspicious years of Shamil's imamate. This point is, however, taken up by Sheripov's brother Zaurbek in a series of sketches he published in a remarkable anthology that appeared in Grozny a decade after Aslanbek's abrek speech. Entitled *Concerning those who were called abreks* (*O tekh kogo nazyvali abrekami*, 1927), this work gathered together folk stories concerning abreks, scholarly articles on Chechnya's "musical culture" and "socioeconomic condition," with vignettes of major figures in Chechen anticolonial insurgency, including Beibulat Taimiev and Sheykh Mansur. Five of the sketches are attributed to Zaurbek—more than that of any other author included in the collection.[43] The cover of this book, displaying Chechens engaged in various forms of manual labor against a backdrop of mountains and auls (figure 2), reinforced Aslanbek Sheripov's revisionary account of Chechnya's past in light of the new possibilities opened up by the Soviet dispensation.

The Soviet break with the past that was heralded in Sheripov's speech is conveyed with particular clarity in a footnote that prefaces a sketch of the Chechens by the German travel writer Moritz Wagner (1813–1887).[44] While noting that Wagner's essay was of interest to the Soviet reader for its foreign perspective on the Caucasus wars, the footnote adds that the text contains "several false suppositions and mistaken conclusions" that are immediately discernable to the Soviet reader.[45] The conspicuous break with the colonial past brought about by the Soviet dispensation is evinced in this anonymous criticism in the pages of a publication closely linked to Sheripov. The oppositional relation to prior representations of Chechen culture on display here is one crucial element in the abrek's anticolonialism.

Fighting as he does a battle he is predestined to lose, the abrek is the pivot around which the Chechen literature of anticolonial insurgency turns. The abrek is the standard-bearer for the cause abandoned by Shamil in 1859, but with the crucial difference that, whereas Daghestani insurgents endeavored to bring about the imamate's victory,

Figure 2. Cover of *O tekh, kogo nazyvali abrekami* (Grozny, 1927).

the Chechen abrek's defeat was a foregone conclusion.[46] Whereas the Daghestani Arabic literature of insurgency begins with the jihad against the tsar, the Chechen literature of insurgency begins with defeat. This specificity of Chechen literary history has implications for the advent of transgressive sanctity, which in the Chechen context is grafted onto figures who, notwithstanding their courage, are destined for defeat. Because the Chechen abrek was weak in the material sense, his violence could be sacralized. In contrast to Daghestani insurgency, which regulated violence through Islamic law, the vacuum of authority in Chechen domains created a defeatist foundation for an aesthetics, ethics, and politics of sanctified transgression.

Colonial officials demonized the abrek when they perceived the threat he posed to a political order that supported the colonial state's monopoly on violence. Through such demonization, the abrek became a competitor for power, not in the realm of governance but in the realm of aesthetics. This demonization in turn filtered into local perceptions, where it acquired politically subversive nuances. The most important abrek in this regard is Zelimkhan Gushmazukaev (1872–1913), the next major abrek after Vara. Zelimkhan imparted to banditry its most politically loaded and spiritually most intense formulations. Zelimkhan's posthumous canonization shows that even as banditry was "liquidated" during the Soviet period, it was mythologized by Chechen and Ossetian authors for whom the abrek's transgressive sanctity was the penultimate resistance colonial rule.

Like the Russian Romantics, although with more emphasis on colonial inequities of power, Chechen, Ossetian, and Daghestani authors used the trope of banditry to critique a regime that made crime controvertible with sanctity and thereby compromised its ethical integrity. The indigenous intellectuals who canonized the abrek invested their dreams and yearnings in these elusive heroes—who were criminals according to external legal norms—and who sacrificed their lives and comfort for a higher cause. The texts that coalesced around the Chechen abrek during the Soviet period generated an new subject, and thus a new relation between violence and the state.

The Caucasus literatures of insurgency are multilingual, both externally across different literary traditions, and internally within every given text. The influence exerted by Russian literary conventions on this tradition complicates monolithic understandings of anticolonial resistance. Dialogic as well as generative, the Soviet Chechen literature of insurgency produced an aesthetic of violence newly marked by modern technologies of governance. This literature calls for an account of resistance more nuanced than those currently on offer for the Caucasus. Such an approach will speak to anthropologist Sherry Ortner's account of how colonial subjects "resist, or anyway evade, textual domination." Ortner adds that "the politics of external domination and the politics within a subordinated group may link up with, as well as repel, one another; the cultures of dominant groups and of subalterns may speak to, even while speaking against, one another."[47]

Although Ortner does not dwell on the colonial dimensions of the confrontation between subalterns and their rulers, the abrek's paradoxical authority supports her conception of resistance as an event engages many different nodes of power. Not long after the Soviet dispensation introduced a new kind of political life into the Caucasus, anticolonial resistance was given literary form. This encounter between poetics and violence inverted normative social codes. When Chechen literature was formalized amid a clash between indigenous norms and colonial governance, the abrek became a text, and this text became a new world.

The Abrek as Anticolonial Rebel

In 1926, a little-known Ossetian writer named Dzakho Gatuev (1892–1938) published the first literary account of the anticolonial abrek. His subject was Zelimkhan, from the mountainous village of Kharachoi. As Chechnya's most articulate abrek, and more keenly attuned to the emergent public sphere his predecessors, Zelimkhan's legacy centrally shaped Soviet literature.[48] Gatuev chose for his documentary novel a title that reverberated with historiographic ambition: *Zelimkhan: From the history of the national liberation movement in the north Caucasus* (figure 3). That the book was written in Russian was typical of much Ossetian literature of the period, in contrast to the literatures of other northern Caucasus peoples, which continued to be composed in indigenous languages. Zelimkhan had been executed by tsarist troops thirteen years prior to the publication of Gatuev's text. Although Zelimkhan's exploits had been making newspaper headlines for years, Gatuev's work was the first book-length account of the abrek's life. The official attitude during the early days of the Soviet Union toward anti-tsarist insurgency is indicated by the book's unabashed call for political liberation. In battling the Russians, the author tells us, Zelimkhan fought to free the entire northern Caucasus.

In his novel, Gatuev directly assaults Russian ethnographic representations of the mountaineers and replaces those stereotypes with

Figure 3. Cover of Gatuev's *Zelimkhan* (Rostov and Krasnodar, 1926).

other, equally romantic representations. "In the ethnography of the Caucasus," Gatuev announces, some Russian scholars aim "to prove that the mountaineers have neither culture nor civilization and can be called human only by a stretch of the imagination."[49] As we have already seen in the anonymous Chechen critique of Moritz Wagner that was published one year after Gatuev's *Zelimkhan*, in the early years of the Soviet experiment, Gatuev's critique of Orientalist ethnography, exemplified by authors such as P. I. Kovalevsky, was tolerated and at times even welcomed.[50] Gatuev's account is marked by passionate sympathy for his hero Zelimkhan, whom he portrays as a leader of the Chechen people.

As one of the founding documents in the literature of anticolonial insurgency, Gatuev's novel had a tremendous impact over the *longue durée*. Four decades after its publication, Gatuev's book gave birth to another text in another language. Called simply *Zelamkha*, after the Chechen form of the abrek's name, and authored by the Chechen poet and scholar Magomed Mamakaev (1910–1973), this novel did even more to aestheticize the violence of anticolonial insurgency.[51] As Mamakaev's first major novel, *Zelamkha* moves significantly beyond Mamakaev's earlier fictionalized account of the exploits of Aslanbek Sheripov (*Murid of the Revolution*, 1963). While oral accounts of Zelimkhan's exploits circulated widely across Chechnya during the abrek's life, Mamakaev's *Zelamkha* was one of the first historical novels in the Chechen language.

Zelamkha was published in Chechen in 1968 (figure 4). Mamakaev points out in his afterword (never translated into Russian) that as early as 1926, not coincidentally the same year that Gatuev's *Zelimkhan* was published, he aspired to "create a memorable image of the famous abrek [*Zelamkhanan surt*]" (293C) that could compare with the most elevated poetry. The Chechen author's youthful ambition to generate an indigenous representation (*surt*, after the Arabic *ṣūrat*) of the abrek was destined to remain unrealized for the forty years that intervened between the publication of Gatuev's novel and his own. Concluding with the statement that "Zelamkha was a great abrek [*obarg*], and the violence he endured from the clerks of the state was the same as that experienced by the simple Chechen peasants" (294C), the author associates the abrek with a pan-Caucasus anticolonial discourse. In this way,

Figure 4. Cover of Mamakaev's *Zelamkha* (Grozny, 1968).

the Chechen Soviet literature of insurgency removed the stigma attending the evocation of banditry from the abrek's legacy and aestheticized his violence for future readers.

Mamakaev's preface to the Russian edition of *Zelamkha* addresses Gatuev's contribution to shaping Zelimkhan's legacy, which was in turn to shape Mamakaev's own masterpiece. In Mamakaev's view, Gatuev's *Zelimkhan*, along with another book of Gatuev's, titled *Ingush*, were "the only literary works of their time that acquainted the reader with Chechen and Ingush life-worlds." Mamakaev also sees Gatuev's engagement with Zelimkhan as a way of writing against colonial stereotypes: "In place of the 'bandit' [*razboinik*] Zelimkhan," Gatuev, in Mamakaev's account, resurrected "an authentic [*podlinnyi*] Zelimkhan, to whom nothing human was foreign, a brave and fearless warrior, who fought for the interests of his people . . . [and] to change the existing order."[52] Even as it honors a departed teacher, this homage anticipates Mamakaev's own representation of Chechen insurgency at the apex of his literary career.

The abstract of Mamakaev's *Zelamkha* that appears on the title page of the 1981 Russian edition reflects a shift from the 1968 Chechen version with respect to the official attitude toward the abrek. No longer is the abrek the national hero of official Chechen Soviet discourse. In addition to being an "extraordinary person," the abrek is a "religious fanatic":

> There is no doubt that Zelimkhan is an extraordinary person, a legend. However, the author poeticizes him and his "feats" [*podvigi*], which at times were driven by religious fanaticism and the cult of blood revenge. . . . "In spite of all the heroism of the abreks," according to *Notes on the History of the Chechen-Ingush Republic* [1:218], their rebellions often bore the character of banditry [*razboi*], terror. . . . Social banditry [*abrechestvo*] was not connected with the broad revolutionary movement of the masses. It was without perspective.[53]

The final two sentences rehearse the typical Soviet formula for exposing the ideological inadequacies of a text that did not wholly conform to Marxism-Leninism. In Mamakaev's rendition, as in Gatuev's, Zelamkha is a liberator of his people. The shepherds of Chechnya regard Zelamkha as a political leader around whom to rally and through whom they will be saved. As the narrator reports:

> Thus the man from Kharachoi stood before them. Their only thought was for the abrek who stood before them. His amazing life only now struck them in all its power. No man was more beloved by the villagers than Zelamkha, but today he seemed as though on the verge of falling into an abyss. They observed Zelamkha, trembling beneath the generous light, full of the knowledge that, no matter how hard he tried, he was destined to die. (126C)

Mamakaev emphasizes that Zelamkha was *forced* into banditry, and indeed he uses as an epigraph to his Russian edition a letter Zelimkhan addressed to the State Assembly (Duma). In this letter, the abrek declared, "I was not born an abrek, nor was my father, brother or other comrades." Mamakaev's abrek is historically constituted by violence rather than prehistorically ordained. Once he begins to engage in violence, there is no turning back. The very fatality under which the abrek labors constitutes him as a hero. We will see violence's circular logic repeated under the drastically different, but equally politicized, conditions of post-Soviet post-war Chechnya in chapter 4.

Unlike Gatuev's Zelimkhan, Mamakaev's Zelamkha hesitates over his chosen vocation. He longs to return to the innocent life that preceded his entry into banditry. Tsarist imperialism is not, however, the only factor in Zelamkha's turn to banditry. In Mamakaev's narration, the indigenous ethics of transgressive sanctity makes the abrek's sacrifice both necessary and inevitable. One feature that runs through the polyglot literature of anticolonial insurgency, from the Muslim northern Caucasus to Christian Georgia, is that the abrek fights for the sake of an ethical code that aestheticizes violence. In Mamakaev's novel, Zelamkha is a chosen figure. His mission is much deeper than defending his own interest. In the epic world of holy banditry, heroes only indirectly participate in the process of their selection.

Another respect in which Mamakaev's Zelamkha differs from Gatuev's Zelimkhan is in his obsession with the ethical status of violence. At several crucial points in the novel, Zelamkha dreams of turning himself in to the authorities and of returning to civilian life, but he soon sees that this escape route is closed. Zelamkha realizes to his dismay that there is no turning back. After his native village of Kharachoi is invaded by the tsar's army, Zelamkha considers surrendering. He proposes implicitly to follow in Shamil's path by bringing a useless war to a defeatist conclusion. In the midst of such reflections, Mamakaev tells us, Zelamkha was prepared to "hand himself over to the authorities, if it would have brought the unjust abuse of the innocent to an end." At this juncture—the closest the abrek ever comes to swerving from his chosen path—Zelamkha "remembered the experience of his ancestors, and understood that there was nothing he could do" to avoid his fate (119C).

The mere fact that Zelamkha is powerless to resist the lure of transgressive sanctity does not, however, free his conscience from remorse over his chosen vocation. One indication of the abrek's ambivalence toward his calling is the conversation he has with his father Gushmazuko when the burden of being an abrek has become too heavy for him to endure. Zelamkha informs him of his dreams of resettling in Turkey with his family and beginning a peaceful life:

> "I am ready to go to the end of the earth, if only it means that innocent people will cease to suffer on my account. And if I didn't fear God. . . ." Zelimkhan didn't finish his words.
>
> "What would you do then?" his father asked him.
>
> "I would kill myself."
>
> "You should be ashamed! . . . Didn't Bakho [Zelimkhan's grandfather] teach us never to surrender to evil people? A true man kills anyone who keeps him from living a free existence."
>
> "I've had enough killing, Gusha! Enough!"
>
> Zelimkhan shouted. A note of repulsion trembled in his voice. (120C)

Elsewhere in the novel, Zelamkha's father doubts the morality of killing, but here it is his son who appears as an opponent to violence. In contrast to Gatuev's early Soviet transgressive sanctity, Mamakaev's late Soviet ethics emphasizes the ethical ambiguity of violence, as Zelamkha casts judgment on his murderous past.

In another scene, Zelamkha confides in his wife, Bitsi, his wish to immigrate to Turkey, and the abrek wavers in his commitment to the vocation of social banditry. As in Zelamkha's debate with his father concerning the ethics of murder and suicide, his wife keeps him fixed on the path of transgressive sanctity and sacralizes his violence. The author intervenes at this juncture to document the tension between the abrek's love for his family and commitment to his fellow Chechens:

> When Zelimkhan saw the half-burned homes of his fellow villagers, and their empty, desecrated courtyards, he decided to abandon Chechnya. Not for his own sake, not even for his family's safety, but to free his villagers from this nightmare. He still dreamed from time to time of ceasing to be an abrek. In Turkey, he would take up the most arduous, but at least peaceful, kinds of work. Then, with the passage of time, he would be forgotten by the authorities, and, if Allah willed, he would return to his native land. (137C)

When Zelamkha shares his dreams with his wife, she helps him overcome his self-doubt. In response to his plan to resettle with his family in Turkey, Bitsi, in what may be the only documented case of a female embracing this vocation, offers to become an abrek herself. "The main thing for me is to be with you," Bitsi tells Zelamkha. "But I don't believe that a man should abandon his homeland. It's better for me to be an abrek alongside you, if you'll take me" (138C). Even more than criminal banditry, sacred banditry is a communal activity. The abrek requires support from the community for whose sake he has gone into hiding. Even more than in Gatuev's polemical text, Mamakaev suggests that the violence entailed in the abrek's banditry is legitimized by its communal orientation. Hence we arrive at a major difference between the precolonial and the colonial-era abrek: whereas the first acts in isolation and against the interests of the community, the second acts as part of a collective wish, and in defense of a community that has been unified as a result of war. When wartime ethics becomes the norm, transgressive sanctity comes to feature permanently in a society's social ethics.

This exchange between the abrek and his wife illustrates the process whereby transgressive sanctity is generated. By sanctioning the violation of colonial law, the community which sustains the abrek creates a framework for the transgressive sanctity. It should be noted that violence is infused with ethical content only after it has been introduced by the colonial order. Prior to that introduction, violence lacked the sacred properties it acquired within the colonial dispensation. As an aesthetic principle, transgressive sanctity is socially constituted, politically fluid, and legally polysemous. This legal polysemy is visualized in table 2.

As table 2 indicates, transgressive sanctity is attained when colonial law (*zakon*) is violated. At the moment of that violation, violence is perpetuated, and indigenous law (*ʿādāt*) is transformed. This violation,

Table 2: Transgressive sanctity (TS) as a legal principle

Type of law	Status within community	Impact of TS
Colonial law (*zakon*)	external, coercive, nonhegemonic	violation; TS brings into closer relation to indigenous law
Islamic law (*sharīʿa*)	internal, degree of hegemonies varies according to time and place	neutral; minimal impact in the Chechen case (more in Daghestan)
Indigenous law (*ʿādāt*)	internal and hegemonic (the oldest legal norms; however, known to us only through Islam-era sources)	transformation; TS brings into closer relation to colonial law

and this violence, generates a new norm that wields greater, if still tenuous, authority than colonial law, and which has more hegemony than any other legal norm. Key to this process is the way in which transgressive sanctity impinges on two distinct legal regimes, of colonial and indigenous law. In the case of the abrek, transgressive sanctity adapts a mode of existence that was controversial and largely negative within its own indigenous world to a legal order infused by new pluralities. While transgressive sanctity is directly opposed to colonial law, it is also deracinated from indigenous legal norms.

In typically modern fashion, transgressive sanctity reifies indigenous law in light of colonial law. What distinguishes transgressive sanctity's modernity from its European counterparts is its method of intervening in the colonial legal order by drawing on an indigenous legal code. That many of the sources adduced in this chapter are Soviet is proof that transgressive sanctity entails a rupture with *ʿādāt*. But while the colonial and Soviet abrek breaks with the indigenous past, it is important, in our efforts to understand transgressive sanctity as an aesthetic and political category, to be mindful of its premodern and non-European foundations. Origins do not determine destiny, but they are an important element in it. In this process of legal and aesthetic refashioning, *sharīʿa* is relatively marginal to Chechen culture, although it more centrally inflects Daghestani conceptions of anticolonial violence (as discussed in chapter 2).

Whereas Gatuev celebrates his hero's bold feats, Mamakaev emphasizes the abrek's mission to fulfill the Chechens' collective yearning for freedom, peace, and justice. By underscoring Zelamkha's dependence on his community, the Chechen text socializes the heroism that Gatuev renders as the work of a solitary individual. Zelamkha's heroism derives from his consciousness of himself as a member of a community that has been targeted by the colonial regime for annihilation. This regime's genocidal intent makes its legal system untenable from a Chechen point of view. Notwithstanding his antagonism to its legal norms, the abrek appropriates certain aspects of colonial law, specifically its fixation on resolving conflict through violence.

And yet there are differences, for, when compared to his colonial counterparts, the abrek is figured in this literature as a more complete human being, both more cunning and more compassionate than his Russian foes. Whereas Mamakaev emphasizes the interdependency of Zelamkha's family and makes explicit his relations' willingness to support and die for one another, the Russian soldiers tasked with annihilating Chechen abreks like Zelamkha are alienated from their environments. Lacking any sense of community, the soldiers are as oblivious to ethics as they are insensible to the humanity of the Chechens they have been assigned to punish. They arrive in Kharachoi with the task of arresting innocent Chechens in retribution for Zelamkha's raids. Mamakaev masterfully contrasts the soldiers' indifference to human life with the Chechens' suffering:

> Long ago torn from their native land [*shain Daimaxkara*], their family and friends, they apathetically carried out the orders that they had been assigned, forgetting that somewhere far away in the depths of Russia, their family was enduring the same injustice from tsarist officials. Long accustomed to the subjugation of everyone around them, they did not understand that those Chechens whom they were exiling from their native land and deporting [to Siberia] were their brothers. (133C)

Here we witness a major distinction drawn in the literature of Chechen insurgency between local law, which is communal in its orientation even when it propagates violence, and colonial law, which is implemented by deracinated individuals who do not benefit from the social structures they serve. From this vantage point, transgressive sanctity can be seen as a critique of colonialism, not only from the vantage point of those who are the objects of conquest but also as a constraint on those charged with upholding colonial law. Mamakaev's account of the soldiers' estrangement from their homeland and the new circumstances in which they find themselves resonates with an earlier Georgian account of a similar deportation. In his classic short story "Eliso" (1882), Aleksandre Qazbegi, who became the leading nineteenth-century Georgian novelist on the basis of his literary representations of Chechens, memorably rendered the psychic deracination of the tsar's soldiers engaged in deporting a village of Chechens to the Ottoman empire following Shamil's surrender. "Who could fail to be touched by the Chechens' grief," asked Qazbegi, "aside from those soldiers whom someone had placed in charge of the deportation and whose job it was to ensure that the rules were obeyed, peace was maintained, and that operations were carried out successfully?" Qazbegi continues:

> Only they stood cheerful amid the general sorrow; only they laughed and mocked the Chechens' wordless grief. The soldiers were accustomed to life far from their homeland, their people and their hearth. They felt nothing in the presence of other's grief. Used to a life of aimless wandering, they couldn't understand what these people were complaining about. All their life, they had moved from one place to another at the behest of those who did not even know their names. Enslaved to what they didn't understand, the soldiers had no wishes or dreams of their own; they lived according to the others' orders and thought that the entire world should live as they did.[54]

Qazbegi here perceptively connects the ethical limitations exhibited by these servants of the colonial regime with their deracination. "Accustomed to life far from their homeland, their people, and their hearth," these soldiers are to be pitied for their lack of compassion.

"Eliso" was available in Russian and Chechen at the time of Mamakaev's writing. Qazbegi's stories were translated into Chechen in 1961, nearly a century after the Georgian publication of "Eliso." Wider dissemination of this translation in a textbook of Chechen literature made it available to all Chechen students a decade later.[55] Since the 1961 translation, Qazbegi has been a household name in Chechen-Georgian borderlands, where the Kist (Chechen-Georgian) translator Margoshvili, who decided to undertake the translation of Qazbegi's three Georgian masterpieces into Chechen while residing in Grozny, is often remembered.[56]

Given Qazbegi's popularity with Chechen writers, it is certain that Mamakaev was familiar with "Eliso." Together with Qazbegi's short story "Elberd," "Eliso" is the most influential literary account of the Chechen encounter with colonial rule in a language other than Russian. Both Mamakaev's and Qazbegi's descriptions of the colonial soldiers' deracination reveal writers struggling to articulate for a native audience the experience of being a Russian soldier and helping their readers understand how the soldiers' alienation and displacement intensified their indifference to Chechen suffering. Significantly, both writers go to great lengths to indicate that, in addition to not comprehending Chechen suffering, the soldiers are alienated from their homeland. They are, as Qazbegi puts it, "enslaved to what they didn't understand" with "no wishes or dreams of their own." On Mamakaev's and Qazbegi's accounts, the colonial encounter entails losses on all sides.

Unlike the Chechens, the Russian soldiers have no place they can call home. Their indifference to the Chechens' plight must be understood in light of this lack. One consequence of the soldiers' incapacity for empathy is that, in addition to being deaf to Chechen suffering, they lack compassion for themselves. Their lack of self-knowledge complicates the conflicts and affinities among Russian soldiers, officers, and the transgressively sanctified bandit. Their alienation from the violence within which they are implicated renders these soldiers serving in Chechnya vulnerable to the abrek's spiritual power. In Qazbegi's and Mamakaev's renditions, the encounter between the anticolonial insurgent and the soldiers of the tsar occurs at the intersection of conflicting legal norms. An ethics based on communal accountability violates the foundations of a bureaucratic state. But whereas violence degenerates the soldiers' ethics, its effect on the abrek is precisely the opposite. For the abrek, violence is first aestheticized and subsequently sanctified.

The villagers of Kharachoi stand by passively as their fellow Chechens are deported. As Mamakaev writes: "Within them a revolution was taking place. Every last one of them was ready to fight and to die, to crash against the rocks and break into pieces. Everyone was restrained by the fear of endangering the others." In sharp contrast to the soldiers, who think first of themselves, the villagers of Kharachoi elevate the welfare of their fellow Chechens above the satisfaction of their personal vendettas. Justified through solidarity rather than strength, their ethics contrasts with Russian military might. Mamakaev concludes by emphasizing the colonial regime's inability to come to terms with mountaineer insurgency. "The soldiers," he writes, "standing beside their guns, knew nothing of the despair palpitating inside the heart of every mountaineer" (133C). The colonial regime's inability to engage the mountaineers' hearts and minds is framed as a flaw even more egregious than its violence. Together with the tension it generates between colonial and indigenous law, this limitation accounts for colonialism's failure to acquire hegemony in the Gramscian sense as well as, by extension, its collapse. The gap between colonial hegemony and indigenous ethics is filled by transgressive sanctity.

Through the ethics of transgressive sanctity, which inverts the power differential between the colonial state and its subjects, Chechens prevail over their conquerors in spiritual, though not material, terms. Such political dynamics are foundational to the literature of anticolonial insurgency. Although they mirror the abrek in endorsing violence, the soldiers' violence is not modulated by the abrek's sanctity. Lacking the spiritual authority conferred by transgressive sanctity, they are carbon copies of each other.

A Quranic Death

In Gatuev's and, particularly, Mamakaev's account, Zelimkhan's spiritual gifts confer artistic proclivities. Often seen with a *chinar* (guitar) by his side, at pivotal moments in the narrative of his life, the abrek is found singing and improvising poetry to music. Gatuev's and Mamakaev's renditions of Zelimkhan converge in their representation of the abrek's aesthetic inclinations. Similarly, both accounts agree with respect to the last moments of Zelimkhan's life, when the abrek's spiritual and artistic propensities converge. According to contemporary accounts, Zelimkhan died singing Yā Sīn, the thirty-sixth sura (chapter) in the Quran, recited by pious Muslims before death.[57] This sura, recited by both Vara and Zelimkhan before their deaths, made its way into Gatuev's grammar of Chechen insurgency.

In his influential commentary on the Quran, the Egyptian Islamist Sayyid Quṭb (d. 1966), helps explain the power of this Quranic text. Quṭb points to the sura's aesthetic impact in his summary:

> The dead land as life begins to emerge in it; the night stripped out of the day to spread total darkness; the sun running its course up to its point of destination; the moon moving from one phase to another until it becomes like an old date stalk; the boats laden with the offspring of old human generations; the cattle made subservient to man. . . . It is by using all these scenes and images that the sūra emphasizes its message.[58]

Pertinently for a text that is more an exercise in prose poetics than a documentary narrative, Yā Sīn also stands out from among other sura*s* in the Quran for its abundance of end rhymes, with each of its eighty-three verses maintaining a full monorhyme.[59]

Gatuev's description of Zelimkhan's final moments, cited here, derives its power from parataxis, a literary technique wherein the "logical relationships among [grammatical] elements are not specified but are left to be inferred by the reader."[60] Gatuev's parataxis is intensified by the presence of multiple languages in the text, including Arabic and Chechen. The parataxis of the passage describing Zelimkhan's death replaces the hypotaxis that characterizes the surrounding text, wherein the logical relationships among the elements are made explicit through "a hierarchy of levels of grammatical subordination."[61] The sheer incomprehensibility of Zelimkhan's lexicon reinforces the reader's awareness of the abrek's sanctity. Typically for a paratactic exposition, the narrator's deceptively simple voice relies on defamiliarization to unsettle his readers' consciousness. The text's appearance on the center of the page underscores it status as poetry. Gatuev's narrative is punctured five times by a heavily distorted Cyrillic transliteration of the Arabic sura, reproduced here. I have noted in brackets the Quranic passages to which Gatuev's transliterations correspond:

> Zelimkhan sang and aimed at the Russians. He shot.
> —*Li tun zira qaumen ma in zira sa baa igim.* [39, 6]
> Zelimkhan sang. He sang a long time.
> As many hours as the battle dragged on, that many hours he sang.
> The battle began at nine in the evening.
> —*Fegim gi fil lush.* [39, 6]

The sky blanched white. Rain ceased to fall.
Only the trees trembled with their tears. The last drops.
—*La qad khakal kai lei. A la ek ser egim fegim. La ei minui.* [39, 7]
The sky blanched white. The grass turned grey from the drops of rain.
—*In na dzhaal ha fi agna kigim. A glalal fegnia il'ial azi ko'oni.* [36, 8]
Zelimkhan saw his enemies' hats making their way
toward him in the grass. Then he stood up. He could not raise
his gun anymore. He raised his Browning [pistol].
For the last time, he killed two more.
—*Fegyim. Moq mexui* [36, 8]. *Va dzhaal pa.*[62]

Although Gatuev's transliterations introduce changes at the level of word breaks and pronunciation, and represent the original Arabic with imprecision, these Quranic citations play a central role in the novel's sacralization of violence.[63] We have no evidence that Gatuev—or indeed any early twentieth-century Ossetian writer—formally studied Arabic, although he may have had access to Sablukov's bilingual Russian-Arabic edition of the Quran, published in Kazan in 1877.[64] Gatuev draws even more extensively on the Quran in his unpublished essay, "Sheikhizm v Chechne," discussed in chapter 2.

No less powerful than the interpolation of Quranic Arabic into his narrative of the abrek's death are Gatuev's decisions concerning the placement and handling of his Quranic citations. Notably, the Ossetian author does *not* translate the impenetrable text. He does not render his meaning transparent to the undiscerning reader. In addition to leaving the Arabic untranslated, at certain places he contorts the Arabic text beyond recognition and thereby obfuscates his source. Sablukov's Russian rendering of the three Quranic suras (36:6–8) that Gatuev weaves into his narrative reads:

6. In order that you may teach a people what
their fathers never knew, having been heedless:

7. Know the word [*al-qawlu*] has already been fulfilled
against most of them, and yet they do not believe.

8. We have put shackles on their necks
reaching to chins, crushing their movements.[65]

Most haunting among these lines, and most salient for a holistic read of Gatuev's text, is 36:6: "In order that you may teach a people what their fathers never knew, having been heedless."[66]

The Quranic text offers itself up here as what is in the Islamic tradition called *ʿibrat* (moral lesson, admonition). This particular *ʿibrat* is offered to the children of a heedless people. In the context of Gatuev's anticolonial poetics, this can mean only that the author's own text is intended as a pedagogical lesson to the proxies of a colonial dispensation, and specifically to the officers tasked to kill the abrek. The *ʿibrat* is intensified in the verses that follow, which state that the word (*al-qawl*) has been fulfilled, implicitly in Gatuev's own text, by virtue of Zelimkhan's transgressive sanctity, while the soldiers persist in unbelief. Hence the punishment the soldiers receive is just. The unbelievers deserve such punishment, on this reading, for making the innocent suffer. In a remarkable reversal of a colonial jurisprudence that regards *sharīʿa* as an inferior ethical system with purely local salience, Gatuev, a non-Muslim of Christian background, draws on Islamic traditions to contest colonial norms. This usage conditions the abrek's transgressive sanctity and adds a new dimension to his violence.

As we have seen, Gatuev assimilates the Quran into his Russian novel by weaving its Arabic cadences into the staccato rhythm of Zelimkhan's movement toward death. Immediately following the suspenseful Russian parataxis, we read that the abrek "raised his Browning. For the last time, he killed two more." Then comes a garbled and defamiliarizing sequence of Arabic sounds: "Fegyim. Mok mexui [Фегым. Мок мехуи]." This imprecise transliteration in turn corresponds to the Quranic statement: *fahum muqmahūna* [فَهُمْ مُقْمَحُونَ] (their heads are forced up)." In Gatuev's rendering, *muq* [мок] is inaccurately severed from *mahū* [мехуи], generating two separate words from a single word, the final *na* of *muqmahūna* is omitted, and, as elsewhere, numerous unwarranted vowel changes are introduced. In its Cyrillic iteration, the Arabic is almost incomprehensibly garbled, but since we know that the text in question is sura Yā Sīn, verse 8, the point is clear. Zelimkhan acts on behalf of God, vindicating the truth of the sacred word against the unbelievers.

In the very instant of his martyrdom, the abrek extracts testimony to his spiritual victory from the officers. Zelimkhan's Browning may indeed be the only modern equivalent Gatuev could conjure for the shackles that function in the Quran as a synecdoche for the infidel's condemnation to hell. Armed with his Browning, Zelimkhan carries out an ancient act of vengeance: he shoots down his enemies, before falling to the ground himself.[67] The impact of Gatuev's polylingual stylistics on the subsequent Chechen literature is made evident in Aidamirov's representation of Zelimkhan reciting the same sura Yā Sīn, this time in Chechen rather than Arabic, as he approaches death.[68] As seen already, this motif of the abrek singing Yā Sīn as he lunges toward death was first established in Chechen literature by Vara, the first abrek.

More Frightening Dead Than Alive: Mamakaev's Colonial Uncanny

To a greater extent than in Gatuev's text, Mamakaev's narrative is driven by the abrek's dream of redeeming his people. (His idealism contrasts sharply in this respect with the shrewd but jaded intelligence of Imam Shamil, who is represented here and elsewhere in the Caucasus literature of anticolonial insurgency as a corrupt demagogue.) Troubled by his increasing proximity to death, Zelamkha retreats to the forest with his *chinar*. For the first time in his life, the abrek realizes the "incredible, unbelievable weight that lies on the shoulders of anyone who tries to transform the sad and miserable existence of [the Chechen] people." Always eager to transgressively sanctify the Chechen abrek, the narrator enumerates Zelimkhan's paternal genealogy. Zelamkha remembers "that even his grandfather went to the grave without overcoming even a fraction of the evil that rules the world." "Who is strong enough," he wonders to himself, "to annihilate evil? Could he do it on his own? Could such a feat be accomplished by a single human being?" (179C).

Unsurprisingly for a figure gifted with uncanny perceptual capacities, Zelamkha prophesies his death through a dream that he relates to his wife, Bitsi. Bitsi refuses to believe her husband, but Zelamkha knows better. He interprets nature's songs, learns the language of the cosmos, and discerns from the stars' configurations that his days have reached their end. "The stars looked down on Zelamkha from their sky-blue heights, and stood guard over his destiny," the narrator writes. "The moon's sickle hovered above him in the sky . . . birds chirped restlessly from their arboreal perches, immersed in ominous dreams" (225R, 285C).[69]

Zelamkha's spiritual gifts and artistic talents converge most profoundly in the hours leading up to his death. The abrek softly sings an *illi*—the archetypal ballad of Chechen folklore—about a hero named Balu whose fate parallels his impending death.[70] Balu vanquishes a Circassian prince who attacks Chechen territory. Like the abrek, Balu dies in battle. The *illi*, we are told in a suggestive comparison, reverberates within Zelamkha "like the Argun River between a rock and a cliff" and rustles like "the wind on the tall mountains" (286R). In two respects, the comparison of the abrek's inner life to the region's most poetically resonant river recasts him from his precolonial role as a social outcast into a transgressively sanctified abrek. First, the comparison situates Zelamkha within a chronology of mythical heroes, of which Balu is but one example. Second, it reinforces the kinship between Zelamkha's fate and the cosmos. In comparing Zelamkha's recollections of his mythical predecessors to a river's current, the abrek is figured simultaneously as a violator of the colonial order and as a participant in a cosmic process.

As Mamakaev's text demonstrates, transgressive sanctity, the ethical system that emerges from within the colonial encounter, and for which the abrek serves as the penultimate symbol, is at once rooted in an indigenous order and a product of a radically new social arrangement. While achieving Chechens' political liberation is one element in his spiritual mission, violence is intrinsic to Zelimkhan's vocation. Through the pursuit of violence, the abrek aspires to two different freedoms, which are dialectically related but necessarily distinct. The first is political and pertains to the social realm. The second is sacral and extends into the cosmos. The abrek's symbiotic relation to the cosmos is evinced in a Chechen folk poem entitled "Abrek's Song":

> If suddenly I
> wept mountains
> if my tears fall
> to the lake's bottom,
> know that my sadness could scorch the earth
> so that on the plains no grass would grow.
>
> If I spread my grief
> into my songs
> if my tears merge with the river,
> from these salted tears and from this grief
> the river will flow into a sea.
>
> In the place where I wander,
> there is no sustenance.
> In the place where I hide
> there is no moistness.
> I get by on the oak leaves.
> I staunch my thirst on the dew.[71]

As in this folk poem, so in both Mamakaev's and Gatuev's accounts does nature participate in the abrek's grief. Additionally, as if responding to the abrek's grief, the rain falls heavily in both accounts, just as it did historically, on that fateful September day in 1913.

In both Mamakaev's and Gatuev's narratives, when Zelimkhan knows he will die, he begins to sing Yā Sīn. Without naming the prayer as did Gatuev, perhaps because he assumes greater intimacy with Islam on the part of his readers and therefore cannot use such references as a defamiliarizing device, Mamakaev writes that Zelamkha "sang the prayer [*duʿā*] loudly and passionately. There was something terrifying in his singing; even the officer felt the goose bumps run down his neck" (227R, 287C). Singing figures into both Mamakaev's and Gatuev's narratives as the language most suited for the elaboration of insurgency. Both authors evoke the loud *dhikr* (*dhikr jahrī*) famously practiced by Kunta Ḥājjī and his disciples. From Gatuev to Mamakaev, these recitations sanctify the abrek's violence. Zelamkha's singing in a language he only half understands registers the incapacity of the novel's secular speech to accommodate the language of transgressive sanctity, which inevitably introduces an epic dimension into mundane narratives. Notwithstanding the fanaticism ascribed to him in colonial sources, when he sings, the abrek does not contemplate revenge. His sanctity is realized through his suspension of the profane laws that govern everyday human affairs and through his opposition to the legal norms of a violent system that he nonetheless appropriates.

Zelamkha's melodic mysticism contrasts with the deracinated rationalism of the Russian soldiers, who, although well armed, are spiritually impotent. As the soldiers' first priority is their own safety, they are afraid of attacking the abrek. Their cowardice impugns their integrity within the moral economy of Mamakaev's narrative. "In spite of all the officers' bluffs," writes the narrator, "the number of officers who were eager to fight to the death turned out to be quite small" (227R, 287C). The cross fire between Zelamkha and the Russian officers—the soldiers have ceded the battlefield to their superiors—dies down. Hours pass, and the officers imagine that Zelamkha has died. They soon learn that Zelamkha is no ordinary enemy. An abrek whose body has been sanctified by transgression cannot be killed with a single bullet.

Troubled by the abrek's merger of the sacred with the profane, the soldiers refuse to approach his body and decide to wait until morning to remove his corpse. Zelamkha's uncanny power reasserts itself when he rises from the dead. "In the clouds that enclosed the earth in the pre-dawn hour," writes Mamakaev, "a new world began to appear; it was as if Zelamkha was rising from beneath the earth" (227R, 287C). By this point in the narrative, Zelamkha's body has been penetrated by hundreds of bullets. The material evidence for Zelamkha's death is overwhelming. And yet their fear remains. Far from being unique to Zelamkha, the abrek's oscillation between animacy and inanimacy, death and life, develops transgressive sanctity under the sign of colonialism, and newly inflects it with his body's uncanny materiality.

Only a few years following the capture of Zelamkha, Freud composed his famous essay "The Uncanny" (1919). This work explicates the violence of modern existence, albeit in more ontological terms than in the Chechen literature of anticolonial insurgency. After the collapse of religion, Freud remarked in this essay, "The gods morph into demons."[72] Zelamkha's body bears the traces of this spiritual transformation, whereby what is sacred for certain spectators morphs into an instrument of torture for the uninitiated who are external to the covenant between the abrek and the indigenous legal order. Not unlike the automaton that so haunted Freud and subsequent commentators on the uncanny, Zelamkha's body induces discomfort as it traverses the liminal space between life and death, a borderland Botiakov has analyzed as the abrek's native terrain.[73]

Three aspects of Freud's account merit closer investigation in a discussion of the aesthetics of transgressive sanctity: repression, inanimacy, and reason as an epistemic framework from which to narrate the miraculous. In outlining his theory of the uncanny and distinguishing his views from those of his predecessor Jentsch, Freud aligns the uncanny with that class of things in which "the frightening element can be shown as something repressed which *recurs*" (254). Freud's recurring uncanny is "nothing new or alien, but something that is familiar [*heimlich-heimlisch*], is long-established in the mind and becomes alienated from it only through the process of repression." In hovering at length over the border between life and death, Zelimkhan reveals his uncanniness as a repressed force, directed against the colonial officers who are epistemologically unequipped to face their spiritual impotence.

The battle between the abrek and the soldiers traverses a space desacralized by war and, even more devastatingly, by colonial violence. Resisting the totalizing narratives of colonial historiography, the abrek's aura infuses the battlefield with sanctity. In place of the war waged by the officers, which is driven by boredom and greed, the abrek's battle is *ghazawāt* (Chechen *gʿazot*; Russian *gazavat*), a holy war that, like its cognate, *jihad*, is conceptualized in Islamic thought as both just and sacred. The abrek's *ghazawāt* entails a "moral obligation that no adult male believer may shirk without extenuating reason."[74] In Freud's account, the very act of substitution—what Freud in different iterations calls repetition—constitutes the uncanny. In the mountains near Shali, which half a century earlier had been the site of the Battle of the Daggers, the disappearance of the abrek from the soldiers' field of vision renders his presence all the more uncanny.

Soon to be transformed into a corpse, and already redolent with the deaths of the hundreds of Chechens who had been killed while peacefully protesting Kunta Ḥājjī's arrest, Zelamkha's body becomes a vessel for the sacred. The abrek's acquisition of supernatural powers likewise bathes him in an aura suffused equally with the sacred and the profane. This conjuncture of sacred and profane, spiritual and material, is the physical expression of anticolonial insurgency and the origin of transgressive sanctity. This conjuncture entails the aestheticization of violence, which explodes "traditional boundaries of subjectivity and identity by overwhelming the subject with a plethora of stimuli" and configures war as a "mass escape not from but into modern technology and terror."[75]

Every detail of the novel's conclusion anticipating Zelamkha's return to life forecasts the abrek's resurrection from the dead. Offering his sanctified body as testimony, Zelamkha announces to the stunned officers: "My body doesn't take your bullets!" (227R, 287C). He then begins to pray. Terrified by Zelamkha's unworldly movements after he has come back to life, the officers freeze "in terror, unable to believe their eyes" (227R, 287C). Named but uncited here, verse 12 of sura Yā Sīn offers an apposite commentary on Zelamkha's final moments: "It is We who will bring the dead back to life," states God in Muḥammad's transcription. "We record whatever they send ahead, as well as the traces they leave behind. We keep an account of all things in a clear record" (36:12). Quṭb's commentary on this verse elucidates the theological implications of the resurrection (*al-qiyāma*). "Nothing is forgotten," Quṭb explains, "It is God Almighty who brings the dead back to life, records their actions and reckons everything."[76] As it links the resurrection of the dead to the eternal accountability of all creatures before God, sura Yā Sīn brings the abrek's sanctity together with his transgressive violence.

Freud's apt invocation of suppression as the force driving the uncanny is counterbalanced by his desire to avoid invoking the numinous (an impulse that recurs in the Soviet historiography discussed in chapter 2). This impulse emerges most explicitly in Freud's contestation of Jentsch's premise that the source of the "uncanny feeling [*Gefühl des Unheimlichen*]" is "doubt as to whether an apparently living being is animate and, conversely, doubt as to whether a lifeless object may not in fact be animate."[77] Freud finds merit in Jentsch's contention but modifies it on two grounds.[78] In the first instance, Freud perceives a deeper substratum of meaning operative in the borderline phenomena evoked by the uncanny, with doubt concerning animacy constituting only one subset of a more profound psychic event. Probing beneath the surface of mere doubt, Freud suggests that the uncanny is "often and easily reproduced when the distinction between imagination and reality [*Phantasie und Wirklichkeit*] is erased, as when something that we have hitherto regarded as imaginary appears real, or when a symbol assumes the full functions of what it symbolizes" (258). So far, Freud's suppression thesis as well as his suggestion that the uncanny arises from the impossibility of attaining certainty helps clarify the officers' terror of Zelimkhan's corpse. The officers are possessed by the uncanny because the abrek's corpse communicates their own complicity in injustice. Nor can they know the extent of the abrek's capacity to withstand their bullets.

The second ground for Freud's objections to Jentsch's thesis suggests the epistemic limits of the secular norms that buttress colonial governance. Freud regards the fear evoked by dubious animacy as a product of the primitive mentality that humans have suppressed without being able to overcome. Freud reasons: "Since almost all of us still think as savages [*Wilden*] do on this topic, it should not occasion surprise that the primitive fear of the dead is still so strong within us and always ready to rise to the surface on any provocation" (256). For Freud, the aspect of the uncanny associated with the return of the dead belongs to a form of thinking surmounted by the Enlightenment. "Our primitive forefathers [*primitiven Urahnen*]—once believed that these possibilities were realities and were convinced that they actually happened," writes Freud. "Nowadays, we no longer believe in them; we have surmounted [*überwunden*] these modes of thought" (262).

Freud's rationalizing prejudices are immanent already in Jentsch's earlier text, from which the later theorist drew more heavily than most subsequent commentators have recognized.[79] Notably, these same prejudices against the miraculous characterize many secular accounts of anticolonial resistance, including in the Caucasus.[80] While this suspicion toward the miraculous persists in contemporary anthropologies of resistance, it is strikingly absent from Chechen sources.[81] This hermeneutic divide is suggestive of the tension between epistemologies of the numinous that characterizes many literatures produced amidst colonial conflict.

Freud's refusal to incorporate the miraculous into his account of the uncanny prevents him from assimilating non-secular worldviews on their own terms. As Ranajit Guha notes with respect to peasant insurgency in colonial-era Bengal, anticolonial agency is often associated with divine intervention. In spite or perhaps because of his nominal rejection of secular historiography, Guha views divine agency in the context of peasant insurgency through the Marxian paradigm of self-alienation.[82] And yet Guha operates within the same secular framework that underwrites colonial *zakon*, acknowledging as objective only miracles that can be explained with reference to material conditions. Thus, while Guha accepts divine agency as a psychological factor driving peasant anticolonial insurgency, he follows modern historiography in rejecting it as a primary cause of action in history.

Much the same can be said of Freud, for whom the uncanny in its more "primitive" forms, including the form stimulated by doubt concerning animacy, is a remnant of ancient animisms. Himself the greatest theorist of the suppressed, Freud suppresses his own uncanny when he claims that "anyone who has completely rid himself of animistic beliefs will be insensible to this type of the uncanny."[83] While the colonial uncanny is articulated through a secular-religious axis, Freud's account privileges the former over the latter. Freud's analytical framework requires modification when used to elucidate the encounter between an ethos driven by transgressive sanctity and a colonial apparatus that coercively severs religious life and the political imagination.

The reader may at this juncture wonder whether Freud's taxonomy does not conceal the basic terror that lies at the heart of all modes of the uncanny and which Jentsch alluded to when he referenced the universal compulsion to project one's own animacy onto the external world. Like Freud, Jentsch sees this manifestation of the uncanny as a sign of the retarded intellectual development he associates with "primitive" societies. Hindsight reveals the extent to which these psychoanalytic prejudices were shaped by rationalist worldviews that bore family resemblances to colonialism's secular norms, and which are brought into relief by tensions among *sharīʿa*, *ʿādāt*, and *zakon*. Rather than domesticating anticolonialism's uncanny, the literature of Chechen insurgency documents vernacular contestations of a legal order that exercised a monopoly on violence but which transgressive sanctity prevented from acquiring hegemony.

The co-presence of the demonic and the sacred in Zelamkha's resurrected body terrifies the soldiers. If God sides with a fanatical Muslim bandit, then, even within the framework of secular law, the officers cannot justify the murder they have been tasked to perform. Like Qazbegi's deracinated soldiers, Mamakaev's officers inhabit the sphere of the canny, where bureaucracy rules and secular laws prevail. Zelamkha transports both the officers and the soldiers to the realm of transgressive sanctity, from which they are unable to extricate themselves. Obeying their superiors, the soldiers respond to the haunting image of Zelamkha's pacifist resistance in the only way they have been trained to respond: with violence. Like the officers at Shali who fired on Kunta Ḥājjī's unarmed followers, the soldiers apply their aggression to a peaceful enemy: they pour bullets into an already-fallen corpse. This imbalance of power between an armed aggressor and a peaceful abrek inaugurates the aestheticization of violence within the literatures of anticolonial insurgency. Had the abrek been the aggressor in the confrontation with the officers, his sanctity would have wielded less power. In colonial contexts, disempowered subjects are more readily available for sanctification.

Freud's hypothesis concerning the uncanny's double suppression—first of fear and then of the desire to erase the experience of fear—suggests that what is repressed when the officers are overcome by the abrek's uncanny presence is "the violence brought on by the Russians themselves, not simply by the Chechens in response to Russian incursions."[84] And yet, intriguingly, the paradoxical deflection of the uncanny is rendered most powerfully from a Chechen point of view. Whereas Gatuev was interested primarily in emphasizing (as well as sensationalizing) the abrek's alterity for a non-Chechen readership, Mamakaev defamiliarized the colonial fetishization of violence when he rendered it in Chechen. Mamakaev's double vision, which aestheticizes violence through the lexicon of transgressive sanctity, was shaped by an anticolonial agenda. The abrek's uncanny status figures the officers as bandits whose consciousness of their transgression drives their demonization of the abrek-bandit, as well as, ironically, the Chechen appropriation of it.

In a vain attempt to interrupt the abrek's morning prayers (*namaz*), one officer screams: "Don't listen to him! That bandit has no God!" (227R, 287C). This officer orders his soldiers to fire at the risen Zelamkha, to kill the creature whose proximity to the sacred generates anxieties with which no Russian, soldier or officer, is prepared to contend. At long last, after a violent battle, the soldiers manage to suppress, if only provisionally, the uncanny, as Zelamkha approaches death's threshold. Mamakaev writes: "Everything was over. . . . Zelamkha fell to his knees. The blood flowed from his wounds so copiously that he resembled a red vision. Still, Zelamkha stood up at his full height and, loudly reciting Yā Sīn, lunged toward the soldiers running toward him" (228R). Revising Gatuev's sensationalized rebel, Mamakaev offers an abrek sanctified by his Chechen audience. The "red vision" into which the soldiers transform Zelamkha is a synecdoche for his bleeding corpse and an index of the soldiers' stained consciences, drenched in the blood shed by their own violence.

Finally, in the middle of his prayer, Zelamkha falls to the ground. The soldiers remain unpersuaded of the death of the magical creature they have unsuccessfully tried to kill for so many years. From 1901 to 1913, over the course of his twelve-year career as an abrek, Zelamkha robbed banks and trains.[85] He ambushed the entourages of high-ranking tsarist officers. To the many who tried to kill him, Zelamkha seemed invincible. And yet, on 27 September 1913, after a long struggle on Shali's hallowed ground, the sanctified body of the most famous abrek in the Caucasus was vanquished by bullets. Whereas the newspaper reports issued immediately after the event describe it as a military victory, literary accounts render the event as a spiritual desecration of epic proportions.[86] Whose?

Rather than approaching the corpse to remove it, as would have been appropriate for a body that had been shot many times over, the soldiers in Mamakaev's narrative lodge ten extra bullets in the abrek's body for good measure. Through this superstitious act, they reveal their cowardice. Mountaineer customs forbid the firing of gratuitous bullets into the body of a vanquished enemy. As Baisangur warned Shamil, Chechen traditions scorn those who shoot their enemies from behind in battle. According to Chechen custom, the body of the dead enemy must be treated with respect.[87] Anticolonial resistance has its own *ʿādāt*, distinct from the *zakon* that the Russian soldiers and officers observe at the expense of local law.[88] The final words of Mamakaev's novel (before the epilogue) explicate the soldiers' cowardice in terms of an uncanny aesthetics of violence: "To his enemies, even when he was dead, Zelimkhan was alive" (228R, 288C). The abrek's turbulent death compelled the colonial regime's proxies to confront their own mortality.

In concluding his narrative, Mamakaev offers a nuanced aestheticization and sanctification of violence. In rendering Zelimkhan's body as uncanny, Mamakaev's vision of the impact of colonial violence evokes much more than a social bandit who steals from the rich and distributes to the poor.[89] While the abrek has been compared to Robin Hood, transgressive sanctity offers a more comprehensive and interdisciplinary account of the political and aesthetic consequences of proliferation of anticolonial violence across the Caucasus. In contrast to more familiar social bandits, the transgressively sanctified abrek actively intervened in a dominant legal order, or at least was believed to have such an effect by those who crafted his posterity.

While the abrek undoubtedly and even definitionally defies colonial law (*zakon*), equally fundamental to his character is his conformity to indigenous law (*ʿādāt*). Although they were originally opposed to each other in Islamic history, in the Chechen literature of insurgency, *sharīʿa* and *ʿādāt* jointly contested colonial legal norms. Rendering the abrek through the paradigm of transgressive sanctity, Mamakaev elevates Zelimkhan beyond his historical context and inscribes him into an ethical system that conflicts sharply with colonial governmentality.

Whereas Hobsbawm's social bandit fights the feudal ruling class, the abrek fights against an even more coercive legal order. While both the Hobsbawmian social bandit and the abrek violate external legal norms, the abrek is distinctive in two respects. First, because of his precolonial past as a violator of indigenous law and an antisocial outcast, which was radically inverted in the modern period. Second, because of colonial law, which dominates a population from which it does not seek consent, while feudal law remains deeply embedded in a social context. The anticolonial abrek's evolution set in motion the legal modulations traced over the course of this book. This trajectory is most destructively iterated in chapter 4's female martyr (*shahidka*) who kills herself along with her antagonists.

In his early Soviet incarnation, particularly in Gatuev's novel, the abrek is primarily a renegade against the tsarist order. In the later Soviet period, the abrek's struggle, particularly in Mamakaev's work, is embodied in the Islamic concept of *ghazawāt*. While across the Islamic ecumene, *ghazawāt* signifies a form of holy war cognate with *jihad*, in the Caucasus the term acquired a signification distinct from its better-known counterpart. Colin Imber gestures toward this distinctiveness when he notes that, in Ottoman Sufi literature, the *ghāzī* (person who wages *ghazawāt*) "is not someone who fights to acquire booty: he is someone who gives his life on earth in return for eternal life . . . in the highest sense of the word, [a *ghāzī*] is a spiritual warrior who kills his own carnal soul."[90] A fourteenth-century Ottoman Sufi hagiography similarly reinforces this alliance between the spiritual and the material embedded in the person of the *ghāzī*. "When the carnal soul is destroyed," writes the author Shams al-Dīn Aḥmad-i Aflākī, "he becomes both a martyr [*shāhid*] and a *ghāzī*."[91] The spiritual paradoxes that attended the *ghāzī* in premodern Ottoman borderlands also shaped the abrek under colonialism. In Islamic jurisprudence, the word *jihad* refers to holy war in general, whereas *ghazw* refers to a "specific campaign against the infidels."[92] But as with so many Islamic traditions, when these concepts were appropriated for modern ends, and incorporated into colonial governance, their meanings were internally transformed.

Classical Islamic jurisprudence distinguishes between two kinds of jihad, the first being offensive warfare and obligatory on the entire Muslim community, and the second, defensive form, obligatory only on specific individuals.[93] The Soviet Chechen scholar A. D. Iandarov inverts this relation. Where jihad implies "attack," for Iandarov, *ghazawāt* implies "defense." Even more than jihad, *ghazawāt* came to form the basis for Iandarov's "ideology of national liberation," as formulated from Kazakhstan following the Chechen deportation of 1944. Whereas, according to Iandarov, jihad can be declared "only by an iman or khalif in the name of the entire government,"[94] *ghazawāt* is suited to the low-intensity warfare that anticolonial insurgency entails. Meanwhile, for Musaev, a Daghestani scholar of Islam, *ghazawāt* is jihad, "understood from within."[95] Rather than attempting to convert non-Muslims to Islam, *ghazawāt* preserves the faith for believers.[96] Iandarov's and Musaev's understanding of the relation between jihad and *ghazawāt* graft onto classical Arabic sources, which regard *ghazw* as an act of raiding rather than of spiritual sanctification, new meanings informed by an emergent anticolonial nationalism.

Zelimkhan is victorious over his enemies in that he exercises agency until the end of his life, even to the extent of bringing about his own death, at least in Mamakaev's rendition. The officers cannot kill him. After Zelimkhan's second return to life, the officer Kibirov shrinks back in fear from his archenemy, hides behind a bale of hay, and screams "hysterically," requesting that Zelimkhan fall to the ground and return to the realm of the dead. Even in his death, the abrek maintains his liminal identity. The specter of an officer commanding his enemy to die while his subordinates hide far away in comparative safety infuses this scene with irony. Refusing to submit to the officer's command, Zelimkhan lunges toward the officer, reciting Yā Sīn. By reciting Yā Sīn as he rushes at the imperial proxies who stand waiting passively, their triggers poised to kill their antagonist for the third time, Zelimkhan sanctifies his own death. Suicide, Gushmazuko had taught his son, is condemned by God, but a noble death that sanctifies the Chechen quest for political autonomy is a respectable way to end one's life.

Zelamkha's transgressive sanctity led to the aestheticization of violence in Soviet Chechen literature in two distinct but intimately related spheres, each addressed to a different audience. For a Chechen readership, the abrek's violence was glorified by combining an aesthetics of defeat with an ethics of sanctity. For a Russian readership, the abrek's uncanny sanctity was deployed to instill fear. The abrek's capacity to instill fear elevated his status within his community and facilitated his transformation from a precolonial object of ostracism, driven from one village to the next, to the sanctified epic hero in Soviet Chechen literature.

This sanctification of transgression is the logical outcome of colonial laws that made crime controvertible with sanctity. Conceiving of the abrek through the colonial uncanny contextualizes his power within the war the Russian empire waged against the native Muslim population, and inverts the paradigm of jihad that figures the Muslim as the aggressor. As he dies, the abrek reminds the officer Kibirov and his soldiers of the suffering their actions have inflicted on the Chechen people. When the soldiers back away from the abrek's corpse, their reflex is due less to their physical aversion than to the light in which this uncanny corpse places their own actions. Here, the Muslim is an aggressor only in the sense that he compels his interlocutors to reflect within themselves.

The hierarchical distinction between soldier and officer further nuances the abrek's uncanny power to evoke the colonial repressed. The soldiers are sent out into the field to confront the abrek while the officer Kibirov hides behind a bale of hay. The officer's conscience is troubled neither by the risk his actions pose to his subordinates nor by the battle that he and the officers who preceded him have initiated. This chain of complicity, which links one colonizing generation to the one preceding it, is manifested in the officer as hysteria. The officer is himself the source of the terror that causes him to hysterically command the abrek to die. As elsewhere in the Chechen literature of insurgency, the officer's material power dissipates in the face of the abrek's spiritual authority. In his violent death, Zelimkhan attains the freedom for which he has given his life.

The Abrek after Soviet Rule

Like Balu's *illi*, the abrek's feats were transmitted from generation to generation. The stories and texts they generated gave Chechen writers a framework within which to teach themselves and their Georgian and Daghestani neighbors about their history of anticolonial insurgency as refracted by literature. In the context of contemporary Chechen culture, the abrek has significantly shaped Chechen identity. Witness the role played by music in mobilizing the Chechen population around war, and in particular the circulation of bootleg recordings by Timur Mutsuraev and Imam Alimsultanov, Chechen bards whose most popular songs are renditions of *illi* about abreks. Also indicative is a recent anthology of contemporary North Caucasus literature for which the Chechen contribution is a story about Zelimkhan.[97]

During the first post-Soviet Russo-Chechen war (1994–1996), the Chechen writer Musa Bakarov returned to his homeland after thirteen years of Central Asian exile following the 1944 deportation. He found his favorite childhood picture, a portrait of Zelimkhan that had hung in Grozny's art museum, hidden from view. None of Bakarov's inquiries after the lost portrait led to a satisfactory answer. This incident marked the beginning of what Bakarov calls his new "education," during which the "studied amnesia" of a Soviet regime that had aggressively propagandized the abrek's image decades earlier was fully exposed.[98] "I learned," writes this everyday believer in the abrek's transgressive sanctity, "that there used to exist a street in Gudermes [eastern Chechnya] named in honor of Zelimkhan, and that a film was made about his life, and that folk songs played on the radio dedicated to his memory, [singing] 'Chechen-Ingush men don't forget Zelimkhan.' . . . When I asked who this hero was, I was told, 'Forget him! What does that criminal have to do with you?'"[99]

As these variegated testimonies suggest, the abrek is as central now to contemporary Chechen identity as he was a century ago. Inevitably, the abrek's significations have changed, and he now indexes multiple defeats in the realms of war, politics, and masculinity. In his current idealization, the abrek evokes nostalgia for a world that was in many respects annihilated by the 1944 deportation. Abreks continued to haunt the mountains after the deportation, engaged in a struggle they were fated to lose. If one quality defines the abrek in his contemporary Chechen incarnation, it is his association with defeat.

Death itself is the moment when the abrek's true task is fulfilled. The post-Soviet Chechen writer Musa Geshaev tells the story of "the last abrek," Khasukha (1905–1976), one of the few Chechens who escaped the deportation and stayed behind in the mountains to wage war with the Soviet authorities for more than thirty years.[100] Although Khasukha hid from the KGB, ultimately he was engaged in a cat-and-mouse game that he could never win. In an echo of Mamakaev's *Zelamkha*, when Khasukha is caught and killed, Geshaev states that "although he was already dead, the soldiers waited two days" before they gathered the courage to "approach his body: so intense was their fear in the presence of this abrek."[101]

The anxiety that the dead Chechen's body repeatedly evokes in the tsarist and later Soviet soldiers offers one clue to the abrek's resonance in Chechen culture. When the officers are numb with fear, the victories of Zelimkhan and Khasukha are conditioned more by their spiritual authority than by their military prowess. Just as transgressive sanctity troubles the relation between indigenous and colonial law, these texts reveal the dead abrek's uncanny power to haunt the living. The officer Kibirov and his soldiers dread the dubious animacy of the abrek's corpse because it literally expresses the corruption that has resulted from their spiritual impotence.

From the colonial encounter, Mamakaev, Gatuev, and Geshaev crafted an aesthetics and ethics of transgressive sanctity. Their dialectic fluctuates between the moral degradation brought about by colonial law and the sanctity attained through that law's transgression. Whereas colonial law conflates the abrek with the bandit, transgressive sanctity showcases the ethical limits of colonial law. Generated from the tension between indigenous and colonial norms, transgressive sanctity demonstrates that resistance can be "truly creative and transformative, if one appreciates the multiplicity of projects in which social beings are always engaged, and the multiplicity of ways in which those projects feed on as well as collide with one another."[102] Even as it enriches anticolonial resistance, however, transgressive sanctity leaves a complicated ethical legacy through its aestheticization of violence.

Chechen representations of the abrek coincide with the words of a White Guard officer, Sergei Berdaev, who was entrusted with the task of capturing Zelimkhan during the seven years (1907–1915) he spent in the Caucasus. "The Chechens never fought with the goal of acquiring the territory of any other nation," wrote Berdaev admiringly. "They were not warriors; they merely courageously [*muzhestvenno*] protected themselves, defending their sovereign rights."[103] Another high-ranking officer, Lieutenant General Polozov, who also served in the Caucasus, similarly distinguished common criminals from abreks like Zelimkhan. Polozov noted that "abrek and *kachak* outlaws do not resemble Russian criminals, namely thieves and robbers."[104] Polozov went on to explain that abreks became outlaws while "living in the criminal underground in remote woods and mountains of the old Caucasus" and facing imminent deportation to Siberia. Berdaev's and Polozov's accounts illustrate how the abrek inflected external perceptions of Chechen heroism, even among tsarist officers. For Chechens in the diaspora, transgressive sanctity enabled them to cultivate sanctity while also asserting agency. The abrek enabled militant insurgents to accept defeat without relinquishing their reputation for courage. One unfortunate condition for the maintenance of this reputation was their death, for the true measure of courage in this context was one's willingness to die.

Alongside his profuse deployment in Chechen sources, the abrek has entered into the other anticolonial literatures of the Caucasus, including the diverse literatures of Daghestan, as discussed in chapter 2, and Georgia, as discussed in chapter 3. Even when these literatures possess their own rich archive of indigenous abreks, Chechen examples frame their own narratives of resistance and defeat. The same year that Mamakaev published *Zelamkha*, Daghestani scholar A. A. Akhlakov drew on Zelimkhan's symbolic capital in his study of Avar folk ballads and epic poetry.[105] The Georgian folklorist Akaki Shanidze cited similar stories decades earlier in his anthology of Khevsur folklore.[106] In the Georgian context, the Mokhev (mountaineer Georgian) poet Gabriel Jabushanuri (d. 1969) dedicated a poem cycle to an Ingush village on the Georgian border named Ghilgho. Ghilgho's Ingush population was deported to Central Asia in 1944. The opening poem in the Ghilgho cycle, "Lonely Aul" (1948), concludes by appealing to the depopulated village's dead souls to sing Zelimkhan's song (*saga zelimxanisa*) for the sake of an unknown future:

მიმიღე, როგორც მქვიდრი ღელღველი
და ვყაროთ რამლი ჩვენი ხვალისა,
კვლავ თუ მოგვაშთობს მაინც ნაღველი
ვიმღეროთ საგა ზელიმხანისა.[107]

Accept me, as an heir of Ghilgho.
We'll shed tears for our tomorrow.
If our hearts give birth to sadness
We'll sing the saga of Zelimkhan.

Colonial Law as a Generative Principle

This chapter's survey of the Soviet Chechen literature of anticolonial insurgency has sought to reconstruct the conceptual terrain traversed by the abrek on one particular colonial borderland. A literary anthropology of anticolonial insurgency must attend to state-generated as well as indigenous narratives, for it is through the former that the abrek was interpolated into history. To acquire transgressive sanctity, the abrek had to violate a normative code that had been coercively imposed. While *zakon* shared with *sharīʿa* the status of an external law, it lacked what *sharīʿa* possessed in amplitude: hegemony. Because *sharīʿa* was nearly as hegemonic as *ʿādāt*, and both were accepted by the community, the violation of either could not be a wholly sacred act, and hence the precolonial abrek was destined to remain a mere outcast. The violation of colonial law altered the equation. Transgressive sanctity presupposes the violation of a legal code that has not yet been internalized within the community. In the nineteenth- and twentieth-century Caucasus, the most pervasive such code was colonial law.

The relations among *ʿādāt*, *sharīʿa*, and *zakon* centrally inform the literatures of anticolonial insurgency, for the aesthetics, metaphysics, and politics of the colonial encounter are all equally entailed in the conflicts among indigenous, religions, and colonial legal norms. More than any other writer discussed here, Gatuev understood the centrality of legal norms to the elaboration of transgressive sanctity. In introducing the village of Kharachoi in the opening to his documentary novel, Gatuev distinguished *ʿādāt* and *zakon*, and added to this mix Islamic law (*sharīʿa*). Personifying the native village of Chechnya's most famous abrek and merging Soviet politics with Islamic values, Gatuev wrote: "Kharachoi knew that every evil, every violence, has its limits [*predel'*], set by *ʿādāt* and *sharīʿa*. [Kharachoi] knew that *ʿādāt* and *sharīʿa* are the acts and words of truth [*pravda*] and justice [*spravedlivost'*] in the forms instituted by tradition. Tsarism brought its own forms, which contradicted Kharachoi's norms."[108] Gatuev's contrast between a truthful and just indigenous law and an unjust colonial law resonates with Sheripov's account of the colonial abrek as the result of the "incompatibility of Russian justice and the local law of the mountaineers."

Both Gatuev's and Sheripov's distinctions supplement older legal interventions within the Caucasus literatures of anticolonial insurgency. One earlier example is the chronicle of Shamil's quarter-century-long jihad against Russian rule by his secretary al-Qarākhī, whose memorialization of the 1859 surrender was mentioned earlier. In this work, al-Qarākhī inserts the Russian term *zakon* into his Arabic text. According to al-Qarākhī, in a speech delivered to his *nā'ibs*, Imam Shamil said that the Russians "worked night and day [*laylan wa nahāran*] to establish themselves and promote their authority" (*Bāriqat*, 170–171). "They obey their *zakon*," the imam continued, mixing admiration with contempt, "with their arms, legs, and teeth" (*Bāriqat*, 171). *Zakon* is figured by al-Qarākhī as simultaneously negative, affiliated as it is with colonial governance, and generative, inasmuch as its power contrasts with and thereby helps redefine *sharīʿa*.

The tensions among colonial *zakon*, local *ʿādāt*, and transregional *sharīʿa* generated transgressive sanctity, a new way of aestheticizing violence that was most fully realized during colonial rule, and which helped validate anticolonial insurgency for a pious constituency. Locating subaltern agency in colonial archives, Guha reveals how colonial legal discourse traps crime "in its specificity" and reduces "the range of its signification to a set of narrowly defined legalities" by "assimilating it to the existing order as one of its negative determinations."[109] While the colonial state silenced multiple ways of making meaning and grounding ethics in the Caucasus, it also brought into being a new range of significations, among which transgressive sanctity arguably had the longest-lasting legacy.

Like much of postcolonial theory's repertoire, the center-periphery paradigm needs to be reconfigured for the Caucasus. The abrek entered literary modernity through colonial violence, and vernacular intellectuals turned to the Russian language to rework the images of anticolonial resistance that circulated locally across the Caucasus. The chain of creation, re-creation, and contestation that the abrek set into motion confounds endeavors to distinguish between derivatives and originals, and suggests the impossibility of deriving the culture of the colonized axiomatically from the dominant culture, or of reducing colonial rule to the mere imposition of external norms. Within the legal entelechy encompassed by transgressive sanctity, both colonial and local law were internally recalibrated.

The Georgian Soviet Orientalist Nikolai Marr, himself a living instance of one of the Caucasus's many cultural palimpsests, and Gatuev's intellectual collaborator, once claimed that, when it comes to cultural influence, the receiving side matters more than the source from which influence derives.[110] Marr maintained that the truth of a phenomenon is most richly revealed in the process of its adaptation.[111] The foregoing account of the abrek's aesthetic, spiritual, and political lifeworlds in the Chechen literature of anticolonial insurgency resonates with Marr's dialectic of cultural influence as the process through which objects attain their destiny. The polymorphic history of transgressive sanctity also places in a new light the Hegelian master-slave dialectic that, from Frantz Fanon to Susan Buck-Morss, has long figured into efforts to theorize the colonial encounter.[112] The abrek's coming into being partakes as much of the colonizing process as it does of the indigenous response to coercive power.

In contemporary discussions of violence in the Caucasus, it is often argued that the popularity of the abrek, and the embrace of violence this popularity implies, attests to the incapacity of these societies for government, civil society, and other institutions of modern political life.[113] A similar premise attends Hobsbawm's category of the prepolitical: the assumption that political consciousness is attainable only through participation in secular civil institutions. Habermas indirectly underwrote this dichotomy between a civilized Europe and a barbarian non-European order with his classic account of the emergence of a liberal public sphere in European coffee houses and through the proliferation of serial journalism.[114] As against Hobsbawmian and Habermasian visions of liberal harmony, transgressive sanctity expresses in literary form the political agency of nonliberal forms of organizing political life, which are grounded in the dialectics of various community-based legal systems. Rather than vindicating an autonomous self striving for personal freedom, the abrek is intimately connected in the Chechen literature of anticolonial insurgency to his community and to the cosmos.

Colonial violence caused the *aparag*, a social outcast within the indigenous social order, to become a cipher for a new anticolonial ethics of transgressive sanctity that incorporated the colonial order's violence into its own teleology. As anticipated in Hegel's slave-master dialectic, the demonization of the abrek in colonial sources is dialectically related to the transgressive sanctity this figure acquires in the literatures of anticolonial insurgency. Relatedly, Bobrovnikov has argued that the abrek is less the end result of traditional practices such as the blood feud, raiding, and the warrior cult than of interaction between "the state, local highland communities, and their military leaders" during the colonial period.[115] More than *ʿādāt* or *sharīʿa*, the colonial encounter situates the abrek within a legally plural anticolonial insurgency. By criminalizing banditry together with other traditional legal norms, the colonial legal order introduced a new form of sanctity into the metaphysical and moral economies of Caucasus cultures. Like colonial governmentality itself, this sanctity was premised, irrevocably, on the aestheticization of violence.

In the context of a colonial governmentality that used new technologies to perpetuate forms of coercion the world had not seen before, the path to sanctification had to be transgressive in ways unthinkable within the context of liberal societies that regarded the state as a source of ethical grounding and as a bulwark against chaos rather than, as it came to be in colonized societies, a stimulus to anarchy. To reference only the most influential liberal theorist of political modernity, Hegel, the state was conceived within Hegelian political theory as "the actuality of an ethical ideal," founded on expression of freedom rather than the exercise of coercion.[116] In contrast to the Hegelian alignment of the modern state with freedom, the literature of anticolonial insurgency testified, and perpetually testifies, to coercive forms of governance that inform the colonial legacy.

The abrek was at once outlaw and saint, criminal and hero. His anticolonial militancy codified transgressive sanctity's mandate. This book contends that the aestheticization of violence that was introduced by the colonial order and further developed by transgressive sanctity both anticipated and made possible the sanctification of violence against the state in postcolonial and post-Soviet modernity.[117] As Lauren Benton notes, legal pluralism occurs when there is "an implicit (mutual) recognition of 'other' law but no formal mode for the structure of the [other] legal order."[118] The colonial order is legally plural inasmuch as "the formal extension of legal jurisdiction" creates "a clear cultural boundary between the colonizers and the colonized."[119] This unequal but dynamic equilibrium gave rise to the anticolonial abrek in the literatures of anticolonial insurgency because, in a context where legal systems are multiple rather than uniform, the fulfillment of any given legal system necessarily presupposes the transgression of another.

As colonial governmentality generated a resistant jurisprudence that aligned transgression with sanctity, the sacred was deployed as transgression and transgression became controvertible with sanctity. This clash of epistemologies—rather than of civilizations—explains in part how Sufi piety came to be profoundly implicated in anticolonial jihads across Islamic Eurasia, from Algeria to the Caucasus, during the middle of the nineteenth century.[120] Although the aestheticization of violence in modernity is not confined to colonial contexts, as so often in world history, colonized peripheries reveal social transformations less legible in metropolitan centers. Having studied the evolution of transgressive sanctity within the Chechen literature of anticolonial insurgency, I now turn to the impact of this new aesthetic, ethical, and legal norm on the memorialization of anticolonial resistance in Daghestan, Chechnya's neighbor to the east. I then examine the appropriation of the Caucasus literature of anticolonial insurgency in Georgian poetry while also documenting one Georgian poet's indictment of his own culture's perpetuation of colonial violence, and his proposal for a new alignment between violence, poetry, and the sacred.

T·W·O

Regulating Rebellion

Miracles, Insurgency, and Daghestani Modernity

Notwithstanding the divergences between these neighboring traditions, Chechen idioms of insurgency exerted a powerful hold on the Daghestani imagination. This influence is reflected in vernacular representations of Ḥājjī Murād (d. 1852), Imam Shamil's *nāʾib* who defected to the Russians in hopes of reclaiming his ransomed family, only to be betrayed by the tsarist administration (figure 5). Ḥājjī Murād's legacy in Georgian literature is explored in chapter 3. Most relevant to this chapter is Ḥājjī Murād's representation in Avar and Arabic sources. The most important in the former category is a memoir chronicling Ḥājjī Murād's life and exploits and narrated by his grandson Kazanbii, known primarily in its Russian version.[1] Kazanbii's oral account was rendered into literary Avar by a Daghestani named Gamzat Iasulov (b. 1888), and subsequently translated into Russian under the title "Legends about Ḥājjī Murād" by Koisubulinets Katsarilov. In this multiauthor iteration, this memoir appeared in 1927 in the short-lived *Dāghistān mejmūʿasï*, a journal that was published from Makhachkala by Alibek Takho-Godi. Like the Chechen anthology *Concerning those who were called abreks* that was published the same year in Grozny, *Dāghistān mejmūʿasï* included a diversity of genres: historical memoir (*istoricheskie memuaryi*), folklore (*narodnaia slovestnost'*), and indigenous law (*obychnoe pravo*) (figure 6).[2]

ДАГЕСТАНСКИЙ

СБОРНИК

III

داغستان مجموعه‌سی

(علمی مقاله‌لری)

МАХАЧ-КАЛА

1927

Figure 5. Title page of *Dāghistān mejmūʿasï* (Makhachkala, 1927). Dagestan State Union Historical-Architectural Museum.

Figure 6. Ḥājjī Murād, as depicted by G. G. Gagarin (1847). Courtesy of Khadzhi Murad Donogo.

Alibek Takho-Godi was an influential intellectual and political activist.[3] A "classic technocrat" who graduated with a degree in law from Moscow State University in 1916, Takho-Godi worked as a lawyer in Vladikavkaz before founding the local Russian newspaper *Golos Dagestana* (*Voice of Daghestan*, 1917–1920), which was published from the administrative capital of tsarist-era Daghestan, Temir Khan Shura.[4] *Dāghistān mejmūʿasï* marked a new turn in Takho-Godi's editorial endeavors in the direction of literature and ethnography, and laid the groundwork for his introduction to Dzakho Gatuev's anthology of Caucasus mountaineer poetry.[5]

In the third volume of *Dāghistān mejmūʿasï*, Takho-Godi included a brief preface to "Legends about Ḥājjī Murād" that explained how he obtained the text. Iasulov probably had at his disposal no-longer-extant Arabic manuscripts pertaining to Ḥājjī Murād when he incorporated Kazanbii's words into his "Legends."[6] Supplementing legend with history, *Dāghistān mejmūʿasï* includes along with the semifictional biography of Ḥājjī Murād images of objects that belonged to the historical Ḥājjī Murād, and that were in the collection of the Daghestan State Museum, founded by Takho-Godi in 1923, in his capacity as commissar of enlightenment (*komissar prosveshcheniia*).[7] Among these objects was the banner he used during battle (figure 7).

In chronicling the tensions between the third imam and his *nāʾib* from the perspective of someone who was closely involved with the life

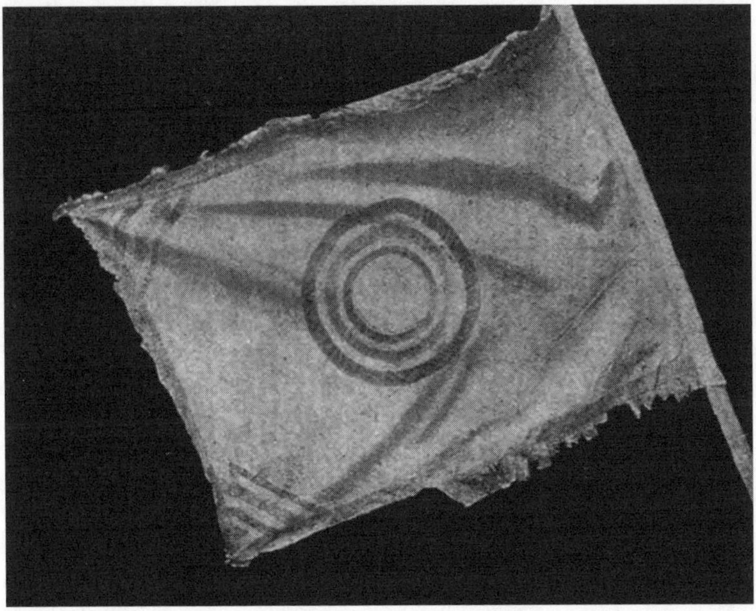

Figure 7. Ḥājjī Murād's Banner, in *Dāghistān mejmūʿasï*. Dagestan State Union Historical-Architectural Museum.

of his subject, Iasulov lays bare the contradictions within Daghestani idioms of insurgency, some, though not all, of which closely aligned with transgressive sanctity. "Legends" draw numerous revealing contrasts between Imam Shamil's authoritarian mode of governance and Ḥājjī Murād's more democratic politics. Less learned than Shamil in the traditional Islamic sciences, Ḥājjī Murād was literate, according to his grandson, "only in the Avar language, that is *ʿajam*" (7). Also in sharp distinction from the socially striated imamate, Ḥājjī Murād raided the higher social estates. Kazanbii affiliates his grandfather's raiding with that of the abrek. After the murder of the second imam Ḥamza Bek, Kazanbii reports, his *murīds* went their separate ways. Substantiating the argument adduced in the preceding chapter that the abrek (and thus transgressive sanctity) proliferates in vacuums of centralized political authority, Kazanbii notes that within a year of the murder of Ḥamza Bek, "there was no power, neither imamate nor khanate nor Russian" (15). Amid this vacuum of authority, "organized youth groups . . . called '*aburikzabi*' armed themselves." As Takho-Godi notes in a footnote, *aburikzabi* is the plural form of *aburik*, the Avar word for abrek. These abreks broke with the traditional clan organization, for the groups into which they formed themselves "were not comprised of members of any specific family group [*odnogo roda*]" (15). Far from being sanctified, the Avar abreks "followed their own impulses, inflicting violence on whomever they wished, stealing oxen, horses, and bread" (15).

Instead of going on raids, Ḥājjī Murād entered into the service of Imam Shamil, becoming the *nāʾib* of the village of Tlokh, on the border dividing Avaria from Andi. As Kazanbii recounts, even though Ḥājjī Murād "couldn't get along either with Shamil or with the Russians," he was welcomed by the villagers of Tlokh, who "submitted to him obediently," and other villages in the Hindalal region voluntarily agreed to obey him (19). Within this expanded domain of the region over which he was *nāʾib*, Ḥājjī Murād welcomed fellow Daghestanis who had escaped Shamil's surveillance (20).

Although Ḥājjī Murād was not directly affiliated with any of the abrek groups, his cousin Khedaras Ḥasan Oghlı was an abrek (16). Once he attained to a high level of power, Ḥājjī Murād engaged in raids himself. Midway through his narrative, Kazanbii offers a detailed account of Ḥājjī Murād's raids. The account demonstrates the distance between Chechen transgressive sanctity and the precolonial idioms of raiding, recently grafted onto an Islamic ethos, that remained dominant in colonial-era Daghestan:

> Because the population in his domain was impoverished, and he wished to improve the living conditions [of its residents,] Ḥājjī Murād deemed it necessary to carry out a raid [*nabeg*] twice a year. He didn't kidnap anyone [during these raids], and he issued warnings concerning his plans to raid in advance, and invited anyone who wanted to join him. . . . After completing the raid, Ḥājjī Murād gave a portion of his booty to orphans and widows, and visited the grave of sheykh Abū Muslim. After returning he would give a fifth of his war booty (the so-called *khums*) to the poor. He would also send some of this *sharīʿa* portion to Dargo, to the imam [Shamil] (25).[8]

Iasulov's reference to the raids that Ḥājjī Murād carried out twice a year suggests that the population he raided were the Georgians of the Alazani Valley, who harvested their crops twice a year. Hence, the targets of Ḥājjī Murād's raids were Christian.

Kazanbii concludes this paean with yet further praise, and by implicitly contrasting his grandfather to the reputedly arrogant Shamil. "Ḥājjī Murād was neither proud nor rough with his companions," he writes. "Of [the booty] he obtained during raids, he used no more than his companions did. He shunned wealth and was content with what he had inherited from his parents" (25). Ḥājjī Murād's own criticisms of Shamil's rapacity intensify the contrast between the two figures. On the day after a public argument between himself and the imam, Ḥājjī Murād complains to one of his acquaintances that Shamil "wishes to give the imamate to his son while he is still alive." "But did the imamate ever belong to [Shamil's father] Dengau?" Ḥājjī Murād asks. In what may have been an expression of his own claim to leadership, Ḥājjī Murād continues: "After Shamil's death, the imamate will pass to one of the brave ones, to he with the sharpest sabre" (38).

The distinction underscored by Ḥājjī Murād between power based on courage and power based on force broadly indexes one of the basic tensions separating Chechen and Daghestani idioms of anticolonial insurgency, albeit with substantial overlap between the two groups, given that Ḥājjī Murād was himself Avar. The abrek—who is paradigmatically Chechen but can also be Daghestani—is poor, of humble origins, and an outsider who has been impoverished or otherwise disenfranchised through unpropitious circumstances.[9] Across the Caucasus literatures of anticolonial insurgency, including in the narrative of Kazanbii, insurgency that lacked institutional backing appealed in ways that the more organized resistance of figures like Imam Shamil did not.

Although Ḥājjī Murād was himself a *nā'ib* of the imam, his efforts to distinguish himself from Shamil are noteworthy in this regard. Ḥājjī Murād's refusal to enter Russian service (in Iasulov's account) adds another dimension to our understanding of the Daghestani variant on transgressive sanctity. When Ḥājjī Murād is arrested by Russian soldiers and confined to the fortress Sunj in Grozny, he is invited to enter Russian service on highly favorable terms. The official (*namestnik*) offers to employ him "here [in Grozny] if you want, or in your Daghestan. Choose for yourself" (45). While two of Ḥājjī Murād's companions agree to serve the tsar, all the others, Ḥājjī Murād included, refuse, and prefer to instead undergo surveillance from the authorities in the village of Iaksai in the Tersk district.

The ethical force of Ḥājjī Murād's resistance is reinforced at the end of Iasulov's narrative, when he attributes to Imam Shamil a public concession that his harsh treatment of his gifted *na'īb* had been a mistake. According to this narrative, when Shamil was preparing to surrender from his last refuge in Ghunib, he declared: "If only I had cut the head of those who mocked Ḥājjī Murād, and kept him by my side, then I would never have found myself besieged on all sides in Ghunib" (49). More significant for our purposes than the question of whether the imam actually uttered these words are the thoughts this Daghestani text ascribes to the imam and the ways his concession complicates the discourse of anticolonial jihad within Daghestani culture.

While vernacular sources in Avar and Chechen portrayed Shamil negatively in relation to Ḥājjī Murād, many Daghestani Arabic sources stayed with the narrative that was generated from within the imamate. Shamil's official historian al-Qarākhī goes out of his way to portray Ḥājjī Murād in a negative light and to insist that the *nā'ib*'s desertion to the Russians was an act of cowardice, springing from flaws intrinsic to his character (*Bāriqat*, 179). Al-Qarākhī quotes Shamil reproaching Ḥājjī Murād for betraying the Islamic faith. "You fool [*aḥmaq*]!" says Shamil (in al-Qarākhī's narrative) when Ḥājjī Murād requests that his family accompany him into exile: "You have truly betrayed Islam! I am no fool like you, that I would permit your family to betray Islam as you have done" (179). Al-Qarākhī's harsh judgment of Ḥājjī Murād's conduct (conveyed through Shamil's words) categorically condemns those who compromise with the Russians. And yet this judgment was an ironic one for al-Qarākhī to make, given Shamil's eventual surrender.[10]

Other Daghestani sources, including by authors closely affiliated with Shamil, were more ambivalent concerning Shamil's nemesis. One of the most ambivalent, as well as most nuanced, such sources, is the record of Shamil's imamate by the imam's son-in-law ʿAbd al-Raḥmān al-Ghāzīghumūqī (1837–1901): *Tadhkira*, a title that signifies "recollection," while also denoting its membership within an Islamic genre of historiographic reflection. (Although he is known in Daghestani literature as ʿAbd al-Raḥmān, I refer to him by his *nisba*, which denotes his place of origin, Ghāzīghumūq, to avoid confusion with an older ʿAbd al-Raḥmān, ʿAbd al-Raḥmān al-Thughūrī, who is introduced later in this chapter.) Al-Ghāzīghumūqī finished his *Tadhkira*, one of his two major works, during a sojourn in Tbilisi in 1869, following the death of his wife.[11] Although he was connected through marriage to Shamil, al-Ghāzīghumūqī's report of Ḥājjī Murād's tragic defeat is more nuanced than that of al-Qarākhī and less partisan in its support of Shamil.

In his more sympathetic version, al-Ghāzīghumūqī makes special mention of the high regard in which Ḥājjī Murād was held by Imam Shamil, who remarked on his reliability and honesty (*Tadhkira*, 50a). According to al-Ghāzīghumūqī, Ḥājjī Murād first attempted to escape Shamil's domains only after reports reached him from jealous rumormongers that the imam intended to kill him (47a–48a). Although Shamil vehemently denied the charge, rumors continued to circulate, causing Ḥājjī Murād to flee (51b). Whereas al-Qarākhī blamed Ḥājjī Murād's tragic demise on his desertion of Shamil's camp, al-Ghāzīghumūqī interprets Ḥājjī Murād's story from a less partisan angle. Rather than portraying him as a traitor to Shamil's imamate, al-Ghāzīghumūqī suggests that ill-intentioned machinations against the *nā'ib* turned him into a renegade and forced him to seek peace far from home, on the Russian side. Al-Ghāzīghumūqī was joined in this sympathetic reading by his near contemporary Ḥasan al-Alqadārī, who described Ḥājjī Murād as "an usually brave and heroic person" in his history of Daghestan.[12] The diversity in Daghestani idioms of insurgency traced throughout this chapter is already discernable in two of the most significant texts of Daghestani Arabic literature, which narrate Ḥājjī Murād's desertion in terms that reflect the values the authors place on loyalty and infidelity, respectively, to Shamil's jihad.

Chechen Inflections to Daghestani Insurgency

Daghestani idioms of anticolonial insurgency were in constant dialogue and debate with Chechen transgressive sanctity. The life and writings of Ḥājjī Tashaw, who was encountered in the preceding chapter as Kunta Ḥājjī's teacher, offers one of the earliest testimonies to the tension between Daghestani and Chechen approaches to anticolonial insurgency.[13] A *nā'ib* in Shamil's service who ultimately defected for political reasons, Ḥājjī Tashaw's conception of the forms of religiosity most appropriate to the jihad state sharply diverged from that of Shamil. As part of the "competition in religious authority" that marked the mutual interactions of these two figures, Ḥājjī Tashaw claimed to have received an endorsement directly from the most influential sheykh in Shamil's imamate, Muḥammad al-Yarāghī, to rule over Chechnya and the northwestern Caucasus, all the way to the Black Sea.[14] Shamil was thereby prevented from appointing anyone in this region other than him. Ultimately, Ḥājjī Tashaw's claim to sovereignty was undermined by the preference of the influential sheykh Jamāl al-Dīn al-Ghāzīghumūqī (d. 1866) for Shamil as imam, and the *nā'ib* was compelled to accept Shamil's supremacy in 1837.[15]

Yet even after his submission, Ḥājjī Tashaw's legacy endured, as a subterranean revolt against a legalistic Daghestani discourse of insurgency and as an idiom of transgressive sanctity that entered the world following Shamil's surrender and the enfeeblement of *sharīʿa* that resulted from it. The small amount of scholarship that exists on this figure suggests that Ḥājjī Tashaw systematically privileged vernacular forms of religiosity over those that structured Shamil's jihad state.[16] Anna Zaks, the only Soviet scholar to study Ḥājjī Tashaw in depth, states that even though Ḥājjī Tashaw was actively opposed to tsarist rule, he dedicated most of his attention exclusively to Chechnya while neglecting the imamate that linked Chechnya with Daghestan. As for the booty obtained from conquest, Zaks states that Ḥājjī Tashaw "divided it among those who were connected to him by virtue of their origins [*proizkhozhdeniem*]" and adds that he protested the confiscation of their land and "communal property [*obshchino-rodovaia sobstvennost'*]."[17] As was shown in the preceding chapter, this preference for local over transregional idioms of governance, for *ʿādāt* over *sharīʿa*, and for forms of political life grounded in loyalty to the *taip* (clan), is more characteristic of Chechen transgressive sanctity than of its Daghestani counterpart, which turns to *sharīʿa* to transcend vernacular political loyalties.

Among the writings of Ḥājjī Tashaw that reveal the *nāʾib*'s divergence from Shamil is a short Arabic text titled "His Many Questions from a Faraway Place." As the title suggests, this work consists of a series of questions on mystical matters addressed to Ḥājjī Tashaw's spiritual preceptor, Jamāl al-Dīn. "His Many Questions" demonstrates that, in addition to cultivating a vernacular over a transregional political agenda, Ḥājjī Tashaw was also inclined, very much in keeping with the spirit of Chechen religiosity, to combine book learning with mystical experience.[18] In this text, Ḥājjī Tashaw revealingly situates himself within a lineage of Sufi saints. Responding to an accusation that he considered himself the equal of the ninth-century Iranian mystic Bāyazīd (Abū Yazīd) al-Bisṭāmī, Ḥājjī Tashaw boldly declares that his proximity to God is equal to that of the great Sufi, even though in other respects they cannot be compared. "By God!" states Ḥājjī Tashaw, "I don't consider myself his equal. However, I exceed him in terms of presence [*ḥaḍra*] to God the sublime. If [Bāyazīd] shows himself when the capacity for *ḥaḍra* is still latent within him, then he would see that I am made of the same material."[19]

Bāyazīd, the figure to whom Ḥājjī Tashaw compares himself, has been credited with about five hundred sayings and ecstatic utterances (*shaṭaḥāt*), which have earned him a preeminent place within the Naqshbandī *silsila*.[20] By incorporating such revered figures into his own spiritual lineage, Ḥājjī Tashaw demonstrated his debt to the affective dimensions of Muslim piety. This embrace of experiential knowledge did not, however, prevent Ḥājjī Tashaw from reproaching those among his fellow mountaineers whom he felt failed to adequately uphold *sharīʿa*.[21] Rather than occupying one side of the spectrum, Ḥājjī Tashaw mediated between Chechen transgressive sanctity and Daghestani legalism. Ḥājjī Tashaw's mystical leanings ceased to inflect the imamate's political-theological landscape at the height of Shamil's power. The Chechen *nāʾib* disappeared in 1843, but his endeavors to connect anticolonial resistance to mystical experience acquired new life with the imamate's decline.[22]

Following in the footsteps of Ḥājjī Tashaw, the Chechen ʿAlībek Ḥājjī played a pivotal role in the 1877 rebellion that swept through Daghestan and Chechnya. Chechens were also active in most Daghestani movements to overturn tsarist, and later Soviet, regimes. Spanning the northeastern Caucasus, these movements were either directed or heavily influenced—and, some would say, compromised—by Chechen actors. Alongside Chechens' direct participation in anticolonial resistance movements, Chechen idioms of insurgency proved formative to subsequent Daghestani history when Daghestanis emulated or explicitly rejected them.

When anticolonial insurgency became a factor in Daghestani history, it differed from its Chechen counterpart in several respects. First, whereas Chechen insurgency was suffused by indigenous culture and folklore, and was fully textualized only with the advent of Soviet modernity, the Daghestani encounter with colonial rule was textualized from its inception and deeply rooted in a preexisting Arabic literary tradition. Hence the greater preponderance of (nonvernacular) Arabic in the Daghestani literature of anticolonial insurgency. These divergences had implications for Daghestani and Chechen literary history. Daghestani idioms of resistance were articulated through the learned discourse of *uṣūl al-fiqh* (Islamic jurisprudence) that undergirded the legal institution of the imamate. While transgressive sanctity inflected nearly every aspect of Chechen insurgency, the Daghestani discourse pertaining to jihad was modulated by other legal norms. That, grounded as it was in rules, regulations, and codified law, Daghestan *fiqh* was also more adept than Chechen transgressive sanctity at accommodating the colonial legal order in part accounts for Daghestan's comparatively less traumatic encounter with colonial modernity.

Across a wide array of local and foreign sources, Chechens earned a reputation as a people with a democratic ethos. For the Georgian writer Qazbegi, who was on intimate terms with the Chechen mountaineers, "Chechens have never known slavery [*batonqmoba*]," because "they consider each other equal."[23] A colonial source reinforces this perception with the description of Chechens as a "democratic people, with no princes, nobility, peasants, or even clerical class," for whom the kinship relations enshrined in the institution of the *taip* were paramount.[24] More recently, the Russian ethnologist Jan Chesnov introduced the phrase "Vainakh democracy."[25] According to this consensus, Chechnya is one of many highland cultures wherein "political equality, not hierarchy, [was] the vision of social relations in the tribal community."[26] In Daghestan, by contrast, civic ties took precedence over ties of kinship. Far from denoting common ancestry, clans in precolonial Daghestani society were "consensual groups of those who agreed to share certain legal responsibilities."[27] In terms of Caton's anthropology of mountaineer societies, the Chechen social order approximates to the tribal culture of highland Yemen, which emphasizes honor over piety, and the Daghestani social order approximates to the culture of the *sayyids* (descendants of the prophet), which prioritizes piety over honor.[28]

With greater flexibility came increased social hierarchy as well as more possibilities for maneuvering among hierarchies. Concomitantly with the extensive networks of learning that flourished throughout Daghestan, Daghestani anticolonial insurgency was inaugurated as a movement of the learned and articulated as a jurisprudential discourse before it entered popular consciousness. Chechen insurgency by contrast was articulated through the transformation of ʿ*ādāt* norms which pertained to all members of society. My engagement with Daghestani attitudes to anticolonial violence begins with the intersection of

Chechen and Daghestani insurgency in local accounts of the 1877 rebellion. By way of reading Daghestani literature within as well as outside the framework of militant resistance, I examine Daghestani Arabic texts lamenting the aftermath of the 1877 rebellion from the vantage point of personal mourning.

Immersed as it is in traditional Islamic learning that extends back for nearly a millennium, Daghestan's textual culture offers new ways of reading the colonial encounter. Whereas Chechen piety called on insurgents to act according to their individual consciences as well as their indigenous ethics, Daghestani piety was heavily codified and legally elaborated. In almost all Daghestani uprisings against colonial rule from 1877 to 1920, scholars contributed decisively to their ideological justification by engaging with the nuances of Islamic law.[29] A consequence of this divergence between the two cultures was that many Daghestanis, including Imam Shamil, were able to engage with the colonial administration in ways that eluded their Chechen counterparts.

Consider, for example, the following account by Shamil's overseer Runovskii, made while the former was already in exile but recalling an earlier age, when the third imam sought to dissuade his contemporaries from embarking on jihad. Runovskii reports that Shamil initially tried to persuade the first imam, Ghāzī Muḥammad, to follow the advice of their spiritual leader Jamāl al-Dīn and desist from jihad. "All of Shamil's attempts at persuasion," wrote Runovskii, "all of his requests, and even his threats to end their friendship were in vain. Ghāzī Muḥammad was inflexible. His final words were 'Gazavat! Gazavat!'"[30] The son of this same Jamāl al-Dīn, ʿAbd al-Raḥmān al-Ghāzīghumūqī, shared his father's skepticism toward the jihad. Al-Ghāzīghumūqī emphasized his father's aversion to war and bloodshed, and he noted that, from the very earliest days of the imamate, his father "disagreed with [Ghāzī Muḥammad's] actions against the Russians, and with the disturbances he caused the people of Daghestan."[31]

Ghāzī Muḥammad is remembered in Daghestani biographical dictionaries as an intelligent if impractical leader, who "loved to read books on *sharīʿa*" and who was particularly familiar with Quranic exegesis (*tafsīr*) and "the biography of Muḥammad" (ʿAbd al-Raḥmān,

Tadhkira, 3a; compare al-Durgilī, *Nuzhat*, 76–77/56). By contrast, Shamil is eulogized in Daghestani historiography for his success in maintaining order. In his chronicle of Daghestan's pasts, the polymath Daghestani intellectual Ḥasan al-Alqadārī (1834–1910) praised the third imam, Shamil, for bringing about a political order regulated by just laws (*inṣāflū niẓāmlarī*) and complete civil governance (*tamām-i siyāsatī*) (*Āthār*, 202).

The social hierarchies that shaped the Daghestani social order also shaped the forms of its anticolonial insurgency, and distinguished it from Chechen transgressive sanctity. When Daghestani scholars rebelled, they justified their actions in terms of the legal traditions in which they had been trained. And yet divergences in legal practice and rhetorical justification coexisted alongside the profound congruencies that resulted from centuries of contact and exchange. Kunta Ḥājjī, often seen to epitomize Chechen conceptions of sanctity, brought together Islamic law and Sufi piety when he reportedly insisted that "*sharīʿa* and *ṭarīqa* are the core of religious teachings."[32] While *ṭarīqa* referred to the groups into which Sufis organized themselves. *sharīʿa* referred to the legal system whereby these groups were governed. Although Kunta Ḥājjī's insistence on keeping *sharīʿa* and *ṭarīqa* together was not always observed by his followers, Chechen and Daghestani idioms of insurgency were nonetheless in dialogue during his life and after. Nowhere do these two insurgent idioms interface more richly than in the 1877 rebellion, to which I now turn.

A New Insurgency

The 1877 rebellion occurred eighteen years after Shamil's surrender and eighteen years before the first Russian revolution. In contradistinction to the northwestern Caucasus, where the insurgency did not subside until five years after Shamil's surrender, the years immediately following Shamil's surrender saw limited conflict compared to the prior decades of violence that had ravaged the northeastern Caucasus during the Russo-Caucasus war. With the war officially over, large-scale battles gave way to small-scale insurgencies. Although the scale of violence underwent a fundamental alteration, it was never replaced by peace. The years intervening between 1859 and 1877 witnessed eighteen different revolts throughout Daghestan.[33]

Chechen transgressive sanctity introduced new ways of conceptualizing existing legal norms. Soon after the outbreak of the Russo-Turkish War (1877–1878), a group of Daghestani ʿ*ulamā*ʾ gathered in the home of ʿUmar al-Thughūrī, near the square of Anada, in central Daghestan. It was the second day of Ramadan, and these scholars wished, in the words of the Daghestani historian ʿAlī Qāḍī of Salṭa (a village not far from Ghunib), to "demonstrate their love for the *sharīʿa*."[34] During this meeting, these scholars also planned a rebellion against Russian rule. It was concluded that, although the jihad had nominally been halted by Shamil's surrender, it had never in principle ceased, because it had not attained its goal. At this meeting, Ḥājjī Muḥammad was declared their new imam, and those assembled celebrated the event by placing a turban on his head.

The jihad that the Daghestani scholars sought to revive when they gathered together on the first day of Ramadan had been sanctioned decades earlier by their predecessors. Ghāzī Muḥammad first approached sheykh Jamāl al-Dīn in 1828, soon before he became Daghestan's first imam, to request his blessing to engage in jihad against the Russians. When Jamāl al-Dīn refused to bless Ghāzī Muḥammad's war, he approached Jamāl al-Dīn's teacher, Muḥammad al-Yarāghī (d. 1838), who had just been expelled from his native village by a prince in the service of the colonial administration. Ghāzī Muḥammad informed al-Yarāghī of Jamāl al-Dīn's refusal to endorse his jihad and asked whether he was duty bound to obey his teacher's wishes. Unlike his student, al-Yarāghī agreed to bless Ghāzī Muḥammad's jihad, and Jamāl al-Dīn finally followed suit.[35] Al-Yarāghī soon afterward developed a conception of jihad as the application of *sharīʿa* to the problem of Russian rule.[36]

Under the imamate, which after the death of Ghāzī Muḥammad was headed briefly by Ḥamza Bek and finally, for the lengthiest period, by Shamil, the meaning of the Sufi term *murīd* ("seeker") underwent a transformation. In classical Sufism, a *murīd* is an adept in training to become a Sufi sheykh. In the context of the anticolonial jihad, however, *murīd* came to signify a more self-consciously political role. A marginal gloss found in a manuscript of al-Qarākhī's *Bāriqat* dated shortly after the completion of the final version in 1872, defines the *murīd* as someone who "subjects himself to a form of governance [*siyāsa*]" in keeping with the *sharīʿa*.[37] That this definition was given in a gloss rather than in the body of the text suggests that scribes writing after Shamil's surrender recognized that *murīd* had recently undergone a resignification and that its new meaning required explication.[38]

Another definition of *murīd* produced during this period by a *nāʾib* in Shamil's service, Ḥājjī ʿAlī al-Chūkhī, similarly underscores the code of conduct with which the *murīd* was newly inscribed under the imamate. Ḥājjī ʿAlī states that "to be a *murīd* is to believe deeply in God, and to submit oneself to Him; also to try to do good to all people; to obey the imam . . . to not deceive him in anything; to not take bribes from people; to not steal anything and to ask for what is needed; and to carry out as rapidly as possible all the imam's requests."[39] This resignification of *murīd* (which attains yet another meaning in Georgian literary modernism, as documented in the following chapter) generated a distinction between *ṭarīqa murīds*, who were traditional Sufis and did not necessarily support the jihad, and *nāʾib murīds*, who laid the political and infrastructural foundation for Shamil's jihad state.[40] Most *murīds* within Shamil's imamate were not *ṭarīqa murīds* but rather *nāʾib murīds*: they were elite warriors loyal to Shamil and lacked formal Sufi training.[41] As Sufi practices were redefined, Islamic idioms of resistance became politicized. In Daghestan, following Shamil's surrender, these idioms came into increasingly intimate contact with Chechen transgressive sanctity to constitute a veritable literature of anticolonial insurgency.

At the Ramadan gathering in 1877, the authorization given half a century earlier by al-Yarāghī and Jamāl al-Dīn for Ghāzī Muḥammad's jihad rendered superfluous the preparatory steps required by *sharīʿa* prior to an official declaration of war. The custom of sending a message to the enemy and awaiting a response could be foresworn, as the war was already in effect.[42] ʿAlī Qāḍī, whose account of the 1877 uprising was referenced earlier, notes that legal deliberations similar to those that he recorded for Andalal also occurred in the villages of Tsudakhar and Akusha.[43] In each location, the deliberations concluded in collective decisions to break covenants with nonbelievers. These agreements were deemed invalid because they had been formed under duress.

There were internal inconsistencies in both the means and the aims of the insurgency inaugurated in Andalal. A group of fighters, led by Muḥammad Ḥājjī (whom the group had named their imam), Nika Qāḍī, ʿAlībek Ḥājjī, and Uma Duev wanted to continue fighting even after the others had decided to surrender.[44] Some of these figures, including Uma Duev and Muḥammad Ḥājjī, had also served as Shamil's *nāʾibs.* Some, including Uma Duev, had participated in earlier rebellions, such as one in Shatoi (southern Chechnya) in 1860.[45] Others, such as Muḥammad Ḥājjī, combined experience as *nāʾibs* in Shamil's service with family lineages bearing distinguished Sufi credentials. After everyone surrendered, only ʿAlībek Ḥājjī managed to escape. In the more corrupt of the two extant manuscripts of his chronicle, ʿAlī Qāḍī claims that ʿAlībek Ḥājjī was "the only one involved in the rebellion who disappeared forever, not leaving a trace."[46] The other insurgents, so claims this manuscript, were either arrested or surrendered of their own accord. By contrast with this account, which was copied in the middle of the twentieth century, most sources state that ʿAlībek Ḥājjī surrendered to Prince Avalov, the tsarist governor of Vedeno.[47]

On the eve of an attack from the tsarist army, Uma Duev connected insurgency to both political exigency and sanctity in a speech he delivered to his fellow villagers in Tsudakhar. "We must be prepared to die," Duev proclaimed. "We are obliged to undertake a sacred *ghazawāt* on our land in order to prevent the infidels from invading."[48] Such statements anticipate Chechen transgressive sanctity as a form of resistance distinct from Daghestani insurgency. While among Chechens, through institutions such as the abrek, *ʿādāt* offered a living tradition that could structure anticolonial insurgency, in mid-nineteenth-century Daghestan, indigenous law had been codified by an imperial administration that aimed to divide northern Caucasus peoples into "powerless clans."[49] Having become an object of scholarship, Daghestani *ʿādāt* ceased to be a living tradition for Daghestani Muslims. At the same time, *sharīʿa* played a much more significant role in shaping daily life than in Chechnya; *sharīʿa* was the medium through which the Daghestani elite established its power and authority. As a corpus of legal precepts,

ʿ*ādāt* was too dispersed and unsystematized to underwrite a sovereign an anticolonial state such as Shamil's imamate.

Furthermore, ʿ*ādāt* lacked what both *sharīʿa* and *zakon* had in amplitude: "the motivation force of a new system."[50] ʿ*Ādāt* aimed to preserve the past and to maintain the integrity of traditional social structures. By contrast, both *sharīʿa* and *zakon* introduced new political orders into the fabric of Daghestani society. Although *sharīʿa* has long been established in Daghestan, it acquired the force of a singular legal code to which all other laws were subordinate only with the anticolonial movement. Colonialism, in other words, strengthened the authority of Islamic law in Daghestan. The newness introduced through the jihad was not *sharīʿa* per se but its singular status among many different legal options. In this newly singular iteration, *sharīʿa* brought with it "the idea of salvation that a faith-based ideology provides."[51] For apologists of colonial rule, *zakon* performed similar work, albeit for a different constituency and to different political ends. ʿ*Ādāt* by contrast lacked a salvific dimension, even for those who lived according to its law.

Although, as noted earlier, transgressive sanctity was originally inspired by ʿ*ādāt*, it ultimately worked towards ʿ*ādāt*'s subversion. This new insurgent idiom therefore required the infusion of a new legal order in order to become actionable. When transgressive sanctity was encountered in Daghestan, the role of the new legal order was fulfilled by *sharīʿa*, a positive discourse that the ʿ*ulamāʾ* harnessed to their political agenda and to which they adapted an originally Chechen concept. In Chechnya, the role of the new legal order was fulfilled by *zakon*, a negative discourse against which the abreks rebelled by transforming the meaning of ʿ*ādāt*. It is reflective of the changing fortunes of *sharīʿa* and ʿ*ādāt*, as well as of the influence of Chechen insurgency on Daghestani resistance generally, that the rebellions that reverberated throughout Daghestan during the second half of the nineteenth century are known collectively as the *sharīʿa* movement or, locally, as the "short *sharīʿa*" (*k'ok'ab shariʿat* and *x'anda shariʿat* in Avar).[52] Transgressive sanctity was in other words a factor in Daghestani insurgency even when it gave way to a different, *sharīʿa*-based legal norm. In both Daghestan and Chechnya, the role of transgressive sanctity in presiding over the disappearance of ʿ*ādāt* testifies to how this form of militant resistance was constituted by, and constitutive of, colonial modernity in the Caucasus. The fact that, along with the normalization of *zakon*, transgressive sanctity helped to bring about the disappearance of Chechen ʿ*ādāt* also underscores its distance from precolonial ethnology.

ʿAlī Qāḍī distinguishes between the Chechen ʿAlībek Ḥājjī and the Daghestani leaders of the rebellion in relatively minor ways, for example by occasionally attaching to ʿAlībek Ḥājjī's name the epithet *Chachānī*.[53] The Soviet scholar Rasul Magomedov similarly promoted a fluid understanding of Chechen-Daghestani differences when he noted that the 1877 uprising attained the greatest intensity along western Daghestan's Chechen border because "proximity to Chechnya doubled the [Daghestani] mountaineers' power by enabling them to unite with the Chechens."[54] Mountaineers from Andalal, a confederacy in central Daghestan, entered into "direct collaboration with the rebellion and with their leaders ʿAlībek and Uma Duev."[55] One of the Daghestani rebellions in the village of Titl was even led by the Chechen Uma Duev and his cohorts from Argun and Ichkeria (southeastern Chechnya). Finally, Sogratl in central Daghestan was a center of both the Chechen and the Daghestani opposition.[56]

The total number of Daghestani and Chechen participants in the rebellion has been estimated at around thirty thousand. This figure pales in comparison to the number of tsarist soldiers deployed to crush this minor insurgency. The subsequent suppression of the rebellion was followed by the extermination of auls as tsarist emissaries scoured the roads, killing everyone in sight. "These actions," writes Anchabadze, "aimed to crush by means of total terror even a thought of resistance."[57] With the important exception of ʿAlī Qāḍī, most accounts agree that eleven participants, including ʿAlībek Ḥājjī and his two sons, were hung in the center of Grozny on 9 March 1878. Other insurgents, including Muḥammad Ḥājjī, were hung in Ghunib, the site of Shamil's surrender, and hence a geography already marked by defeat. The claim in one of the two extant manuscripts of ʿAlī Qāḍī's chronicle that ʿAlībek Ḥājjī disappeared without a trace may reflect a Daghestani desire to assert that this Chechen insurgent could partake of immortality by offering more spiritual and longer-lasting resistance to colonial rule than that available within the discourse of the Daghestani imamate or its related post-Shamilian iterations.

An Avar folk song memorializes the public executions in verse while associating the tragedy with the persecutions of mountaineers across Daghestan and Chechnya, as their loved ones were killed in the crossfire and their homes were burned:

> Bad news comes from their fathers' *auls*.
> The best have been taken away and sent to Siberia.
> The poor villagers of Sogratl had a bad business of it.
> The learned ʿ*ulamā*ʾ have all been hung.
> The old *auls* have all been burned.
> The new buildings have all been destroyed.[58]

ʿAlī Qāḍī additionally differs from other sources in that he does not mention the thousands of Daghestanis who had either participated in the rebellion or were retroactively associated with it by colonial officials and were exiled to Siberia and Saratov Province in northern Russia.[59] His focus is rather on the small group of insurgents who masterminded this rebellion.

Many of the five thousand exiled Daghestanis and Chechens were incriminated merely by virtue of their place of birth, as when entire villages, including women and children, were uprooted.[60] Casualty rates were high, especially in the winter. To take merely the example of those exiled to Novgorod Province, there were 429 casualties during the first winter, including 311 women, out of a total of 1,625.[61] Although administrators were at pains to conceal the arbitrariness of officially sanctioned punishment, they could not mask the brutal logic of colonial rule, which was unfavorably compared by the mountaineer literary elite to the harsh but just strictures of *sharīʿa*. The worries of one official, A. Rudinovskii, of the Caucasus Committee, that the state's failure to deport a group of Chechens in the Terek region would make Russian rule appear arbitrary and accidental (*sluchaino*) illustrates the pressure felt by the Russian administration to practice a coercive form of governance. The state should punish as many people as possible, Rudinovskii argued, not to enforce justice but to demonstrate its consistency.[62]

The complex equilibrium between *sharīʿa* and ʿ*ādāt* in Daghestani culture could be neither suppressed nor surpassed by colonial law's arbitrary violence. Further nuancing the picture, colonial officials believed that "the conflict [*razlad*] between indigenous legal consciousness [*pravosoznaniem*] and [colonial] law [*pravo*], between custom [*obychai*] and law [*zakon*] . . . inevitably leads to . . . crime [*prestupnost'*]."[63] Chapter 1 traced the development of transgressive sanctity from within the tension between colonial *zakon* and an indigenous Chechen ethics that prioritized *ʿādāt* over *sharīʿa*. This tension generated a form of political life that colonial officials perceived as mountaineer criminality. It also transformed internal legal codes. However, these officials could not but recognize the fragility of their position, for if colonial laws were arbitrarily imposed, then the Russian regime could not claim legitimacy superior to either *sharīʿa* or *ʿādāt*. Like violence generally, crime (*prestupnost'*) became a matter of perspective.

This chapter supplements chapter 1's account of the genesis of transgressive sanctity within Chechen culture with arguments and examples from Daghestani archives. As I have noted, transgression was only partially sanctified in Daghestan, which differed from Chechnya due to the deeper penetration of Islamic law. Transgressive sanctity did, however, develop here as elsewhere throughout the Caucasus, in part because of the widespread influence of Chechen culture in the mountains and well as the plains. When Daghestani and Chechen insurgencies intersect, it is in the discourse of transgressive sanctity, which brings together Islam, political mobilization, and many forms of vernacular piety. Transgressive sanctity in Daghestan coexisted with equally deeply rooted nontransgressive sanctities, as well as with a diversity of attitudes to Russian rule broader in scope than the range of views that were openly articulated within Chechen culture. Among this plurality of pieties, many Muslim groups, including especially the Maḥmūdiyya brotherhoods, openly advocated peace with Russian rule following Shamil's surrender.[64]

Like the insurgencies that preceded it, the 1877 uprising resulted from the "actions of its spiritual leaders," particularly those trained in *uṣūl al-fiqh*.[65] Emphasizing the continuity between the imamate and the political order that underwrote the 1877 uprising, Musaev contends that the infrastructure that the insurgents of 1877 aspired to establish across the northeastern Caucasus "reproduced theoretically the system of Shamil's imamate and must have been its organic confirmation."[66] As under Shamil, an imam presided over a council of jurists. Comparable administrative and taxation systems, and methods of military engagement, characterized both political orders.

Notwithstanding these congruencies, much separated jihad under the imamate from its post-Shamilian iterations. Shamil's movement was united by a single purpose and vision, which he as imam embodied as well as created. Additionally, and partly as a consequence of the success with which this leader was able to implement his vision, Shamil's imamate generated a considerably less democratic political theory and praxis than that envisioned by the 1877 insurgency. Murtaḍā ʿAlī al-ʿUrāḍī, a jurist in Shamil's service, and a teacher of ʿAlī Qāḍī, produced a text that Michael Kemper calls "a *carte blanche* for autocracy."[67] Al-ʿUrāḍī's *al-Murghim* (*The compeller*) fell short of classical *fiqh* injunctions to circumscribe the power of the imam and even to rebel against rulers who had become tyrants. In traditional *fiqh* of the Shāfiʿī school of law that prevailed in Daghestan, when Muslims subjects give their allegiance under compulsion, they are "not obligated to support the ruler against the rebels."[68] Shamil's legal code, by contrast, made no provision for rebellion against the imam.[69]

Another difference between the highly regulated structure of the imamate and the chaos that prevailed during the 1877 insurgency is the former's internal stability. For all its frailty relative to the Russian state, the imamate and the jihad that was articulated from within its domain far exceeded in stability and duration any political form that was generated by Chechen transgressive sanctity. As a result of its astonishing duration and strength, Shamil's imamate attracted considerable international interest from the Ottoman empire and Europe during the years of its flourishing.[70] By contrast, the 1877 insurgency, faced with insurmountable challenges, was consigned to oblivion almost from its inception and failed to attract significant international attention. (The Russian administration's claims concerning Ottoman "interference" as the stimulus for this uprising is unsupported by evidence, although the expectation of help from the Ottomans no doubt encouraged the mountaineers to rebel.)

Before initiating the rebellion, ʿAlī Qāḍī informs us, ʿAlībek Ḥājjī gathered the best of his men and informed them of the onset of war between the Ottoman *hünkar* ʿAbd al-Ḥamīd II (r. 1876–1909) and the "Russian *padishāh*" Aleksandr II (r. 1855–1881).[71] After announcing this new war, ʿAlībek Ḥājjī declared that "the compact [*ʿahd*] Shamil had made with the unbelievers should be destroyed."[72] Denominating his work a history of the "*sharīʿa* uprising," ʿAlī Qāḍī maintains that ʿAlībek Ḥājjī wanted to return his people to the time when *sharīʿa* had the force of law. Persuaded that an Ottoman victory over Russia was imminent, ʿAlībek Ḥājjī advised breaking the pact before the Ottoman "imam-*hünkar*" and his army arrived in Daghestan to rescue the mountaineers from infidel hands. The mountaineers acted on ʿAlībek Ḥājjī's suggestions and agreed to break the agreement that had been "signed with the non-believers."[73]

Although his participation in a Daghestani insurgency set him apart from transgressively sanctified abreks like Zelimkhan, ʿAlībek Ḥājjī also shared much in common with his fellow Chechens. The Chechen leader who was regarded as Shamil's nemesis in local historiography was viewed by contemporary observers as someone "made to suffer for the sacred religious undertaking [*sviatoe delo religii*]."[74] ʿAlī Qāḍī's narrative reveals a similar faith in ʿAlībek Ḥājjī's exceptional spirituality, which transcended his material conditions and neutralized the consequences of his inevitable defeat. Because of his sacralized status, it was the duty of all Muslims to support ʿAlībek Ḥājjī's endeavors. The validity of the Chechen insurgent's endeavor to restore the *sharīʿa*-based legal order of the imamate was a function of his transgression of *zakon.*

Miracles and Insurgency: ʿAlī Qāḍī al-Salṭī

On 12 April 1877, ʿAlībek Ḥājjī was elected imam (a title that, as noted by Aslanbek Sheripov, was later ascribed to Zelimkhan) by the Chechen residents of Samsir, a village not far from the Daghestani border, on the mountain of Zigenoi-Dukh.[75] Within weeks, the rebellion had swept through Chechnya and Dagestan. Whereas colonial-era historiography (including some Daghestani sources discussed later) presents the 1877 rebellion as a deception inflicted by a ruling elite on a beguiled populace, Chechen (and some Chechen-inclined Daghestani) sources regarded the threat the tsarist regime posed to Islam as the primary factor motivating the rebellion.[76] The Daghestani literature of anticolonial insurgency is divided between these two conflicting relationships to violence.

Like Zelimkhan and Kunta Ḥājjī, in his capacity as both a spiritual and a worldly leader, ʿAlībek Ḥājjī was credited with miraculous powers. ʿAlī Qāḍī makes this nuance explicit when he states, during a revealing pause in his narrative, that he had been informed by "reliable people" that the leader of the 1877 uprising had been "granted the gift of foresight by God."[77] One anecdote in particular, narrated at length by ʿAlī Qāḍī, sheds light on the Daghestani Arabic historiographic impulse to ascribe miraculous powers to the leader of the 1877 uprising. ʿAlī Qāḍī tells of how a tsarist official named Prince Nakashidze sent one of his emissaries to ʿAlībek Ḥājjī. The emissary was to gain access to ʿAlībek Ḥājjī by pretending that he wished to immigrate to his territory. Although Nakashidze was instructed to simulate solidarity with the *sharīʿa* movement, his actual task was to kill the Chechen insurgent. Before he departed on his expedition, the emissary was promised in writing that if he returned to the Russian side with the murder accomplished, he would be awarded an illustrious title and a generous salary. Greatly tempted by such rewards, Nakashidze set out to fulfill his mission.

When Nakashidze arrived in the insurgent's territory, he discovered that ʿAlībek Ḥājjī was endowed, as the abrek would come to be endowed, with supernatural perceptual capacities. "Why did you come?" ʿAlībek Ḥājjī asked his visitor. "What reward were you given to come here? Tell me, what do you plan to do? Just what does that document in your pocket say?" When they heard these questions addressed to a guest who had arrived in the guise of peace, ʿAlībek Ḥājjī's companions were astonished. Terrified by his prospective victim's uncanny perceptive capacities, Nakashidze handed over the document that betrayed the true purpose of his mission. "ʿAlībek Ḥājjī killed him immediately," recounts ʿAlī Qāḍī.[78]

ʿAlī Qāḍī's version of these events ascribes the same truth value to miraculous occurrences as to the narration of battles transpiring in secular time. His pluralistic approach to historical causality contrasts with the monocausal narratives that inform later histories of anticolonial insurgency, particularly from the Soviet period. As if wishing to stress the sacral underpinnings of his version of history, ʿAlī Qāḍī adds that the rebels "depended on the mercy of God and dreamed of the heavenly paradise [that awaited them], and the mercy of great Allah, who knows better than anyone else what they said to each other."[79] Elsewhere, making God the grammatical subject of his narrative in ways that typify Islamic historiography, ʿAlī Qāḍī notes that "Allah covered the guard's eyes," thereby enabling ʿAlībek Ḥājjī to escape the grasp of the soldier who had been commissioned to kill him.[80] While such turns of phrase are standard within ʿAlī Qāḍī's Muslim historiographic tradition, they jar against colonial historiography's secular norms. This cognitive dissonance partly explains the divergent accounts of the 1877 uprising specifically and of transgressive sanctity generally.

Strikingly, the events in ʿAlī Qāḍī's chronicle that are most closely connected to miracles tend to occur when the actors are Chechen. In narrating Zelimkhan's death, Gatuev and Mamakaev associated Chechen insurgency with transgressive sanctity and distinguished it from the anticolonial legal discourse that drove the Daghestani jihad. By contrast, ʿAlī Qāḍī's narration of the 1877 rebellion interweaves Chechen and Daghestani idioms of insurgency while underscoring their respective differences. Incorporating as it does Chechen transgressive sanctity into a Daghestani legal understanding of anticolonial rebellion, ʿAlībek Ḥājjī's attitude toward normative forms of Daghestani piety and social conduct parallels Ḥājjī Tashaw's relationship to the political theory of Shamil's imamate.

ʿAlībek Ḥājjī's command of the miraculous is as distant from Daghestani jurisprudence as is the colonial uncanny that suffuses the corpse of Zelimkhan. Unlike the abrek, whose actions were informed by transgressive sanctity to the end, ʿAlībek Ḥājjī surrendered before the fight was over (or, as one manuscript of ʿAlī Qāḍī's chronicle has it, disappeared).[81] As Shamil had done eighteen years earlier when he surrendered to Bariatinskii, ʿAlībek Ḥājjī surrendered to the governor of Vedeno once victory receded from the horizon. He was transported along with his fellow insurgents to a prison in Grozny.

Even more than distinguishing between Chechen and Daghestani idioms of insurgencies, the miracles that puncture ʿAlī Qāḍī's chronicle configure sanctity in a manner that diverges from a European historiographic epistemology that resists being "rent by the interference of supernatural, transcendent powers," and which structures tsarist and Soviet accounts of anticolonial insurgency.[82] Thus, while chapter 1 suggested the Soviet-era contribution to transgressive sanctity, it is also worth stressing how some colonial-era contributions to this discourse diverged from Soviet secular norms. Even though transgressive sanctity is not equivalent to jihad or to religious resistance as such—for these movements do not necessarily subvert indigenous law—the sacred is constitutive of its persuasive power. Hence, transgressive sanctity exceeds the secular paradigm into which it was channeled during the Soviet period. Attention should be paid to the forms of piety and worship that persist throughout the literature of anticolonial insurgency. Retroactively, ʿAlī Qāḍī challenges secular history by treating miracles as valid evidence. Even more important, the sanctification of a Chechen insurgent within a Daghestani Arabic chronicle reveals the intimacy between these two related but distinct cultures in constituting a discourse, a literature, and ultimately, an aesthetic of insurgency.

In his death as in his life, ʿAlībek Ḥājjī's surrender diverged sharply from that of his Avar predecessor, Shamil. The oldest extant manuscript of ʿAlī Qāḍī's chronicle contradicts the more recent version's claim concerning ʿAlībek Ḥājjī's disappearance. According to this earlier version, when ʿAlībek Ḥājjī was being escorted to the scaffold in Grozny where he was to be hung, he pulled out a knife and stabbed the soldiers standing next to him. Only then was ʿAlībek Ḥājjī finally killed. "May Almighty Allah forgive ʿAlībek Ḥājjī!" exclaims ʿAlī Qāḍī as he commemorates his protagonist's death.[83]

Insurgency as Allegory: Poetry and Hadith

At the conclusion (*khātima*) to the chronicle on which he worked for several decades, al-Qarākhī cites an ode (*qaṣīda*) by ʿAlībek Ḥājjī's Daghestani counterpart, Muḥammad Ḥājjī, whose election to the office of imam by Daghestani ʿ*ulamā*ʾ took place at the same time that ʿAlībek Ḥājjī received this title from his Chechen followers. Al-Qarākhī's preceding remarks indicate that he reads this poem as an exegesis of the 1877 insurgency. Calling it an "elegant verse [*naẓm*]," al-Qarākhī alludes to his motives in incorporating it into his text. "May these verses," al-Qarākhī writes, "compare with the prose [*nathr*]" that preceded them (209). In narrating jihad, Muḥammad Ḥājjī in this *qaṣīda* also aestheticizes violence. Although Muḥammad Ḥājjī could not have anticipated his poem's afterlife, its significance in the Daghestani literature of anticolonial insurgency was reinforced through its publication, as part of a collection of poetic extracts from *Bāriqat*, in Istanbul in 1909, by the Daghestani Ṭāhir ibn ʿAbd al-Raḥīm Rukkālī.[84] Midway through his poem, Muḥammad Ḥājjī declares:

فكم من مسعر في الحرب اضحى
صريعا فى قتال الاضطرام
فاآلاف التحية و السلام
على الشهداء في دار السلام
قد ابتغوا الثواب و وجه ربٍّ
و قد غضوا عن الاهل الكرام
قد اختاروا على طيب الحياة
بدولة كافر سكر الحمام
و ما للمرء أن يختار موتا
على عيش بسلّ الانفصام

(Al-Qarākhī, *Bāriqat*, 212, vv. 10–15)

How many fighters enflamed by war streamed
into the flames of the fight [*al-iẓṭirām*]!
May the martyrs in the abode of heaven [*al-shuhadāʾ fī dār*
al-salām]
receive thousands of greetings and welcomes [in paradise]!
They get their recompense and [see] the Lord's face,
without heeding the noble ones [*al-ahl al-kirām*].
They preferred death to living well
in the state of an infidel [*al-dawlat kāfir*].
What is a man who does not prefer
death to a broken life [*bisall al-infiṣām*]?

Like his Chechen counterparts, Muḥammad Ḥājjī glorifies those who sacrificed their lives in the jihad. Unlike his Chechen counterparts, Muḥammad Ḥājjī links rebellion to Islamic teachings pertaining to the resurrection of the dead, the martyrdom of believers, and the legal injunction to resist infidel rule. These allusions reflect the institutionalization of anticolonial militancy, as its political agenda allied with a learned tradition that was shaped by centuries of reflection on the legal status of rebellion. This sanctity too was transgressive, but it was also institutionalized in a way that Chechen sanctity was not. Chechen writers were less influenced by the learned discourses that shaped the political thinking of Daghestani *ʿulamāʾ*. This divergence partly accounts for other differences between Chechen and Daghestani anticolonial insurgency.

The inflection of Islamic learning within the Daghestani discourse of insurgency enabled many Daghestani authors, including al-Qarākhī, to critique the extreme forms of rebellion that predominated among the Chechens. By contrast with other writers favorable to insurgency, al-Qarākhī's cautious approach to militancy is articulated from within prior Islamic discourses. Its primary idiom is *fitna*, the Islamic term for civil war. *Fitna* was strategically applied by some of the Daghestani authors discussed in this chapter to question the legitimacy of the violent rebellions that swept through the Caucasus following Shamil's surrender, but the term receives its most extended application in al-Qarākhī's history.

Within Islamic political thought, *fitna* literally means "putting to the proof," or testing, in the way that gold is tested in fire.[85] In historical terms, *fitna* refers to the struggles for political legitimacy that led to the founding of the first Islamic dynasty, the Umayyad caliphate (662–750), in Damascus, and which are at the origin of the political rift between Sunni and Shīʿa political theologies. *Fitna* is particularly central within early Shīʿa eschatology, and the Shīʿa belief that "it is obligatory to nominate an *imam* in the event of *fitna*, but not if peace is prevailing" is reflected in Sunni political theology as well.[86] In classical works of Islamic political theory, such as Niẓām al-Mulk's *Conduct of Kings* (*Siyyar al-mulūk*), the ruler (*sulṭān*) is obliged to guard against "corruption [*fasād*], insurgency [*āshūb*] and civil war [*fitna*]."[87] Finally, *fitna* can refer to the struggle within an individual Muslim to overcome temptation.

Muḥammad Ḥājjī first introduces *fitna* toward the end of his *qaṣīda*, when he narrates the rise and fall of Shamil's imamate and describes how he has borne witness (*shahadatu*) to the treacheries of his age (*ṣurūf dahr*) and reported (*khabartu*) on its events (219, v. 2). In this concluding section of his *qaṣīda*, Muḥammad Ḥājjī uses *fitna* to describe the tensions within the imamate, and in particular to suggest divergences between the political program of Shamil and his *nāʾibs*. Cryptically, he states that the *fitna* of pleasure (*fitna al-aḥlās*) is followed by the *fitna* of darkness (*fitna al-dahīāʾ*) (216, v. 2), without specifying the events to which he refers.

Although the purpose of Muḥammad Ḥājjī's digression into the different types of *fitna* is left obscure, the details that follow can be mapped allegorically onto specific moments in Daghestani history. As with any allegory, there is more than one legitimate interpretation; clearly, however, these verses refer to the period between 1825, the beginning of Shamil's imamate, and 1877, when Muḥammad Ḥājjī was elected imam. One possible reading would have the main actor in these verses be Shamil. Whereas Shamil appointed his *nāʾibs* to be like "shepherds protecting the people," they became in actuality like "wolves [devouring] a flock" (217, v. 17). Whereas Shamil taught his *nāʾibs* justice (*ʿadl wa inṣāf*), they practiced injustice and tyranny (217, v. 18) and incapacitated the people, refusing to grant permission to engage in jihad (*ʿijazūhum ʿan jihād*, 218, v. 1). Also apparently referencing Shamil's surrender in 1859, Muḥammad Ḥājjī states that Daghestani natures were altered (*taghiyrat al-ṭabāʿu min al-ānām*, 218, v. 7) when they were abandoned by their imam. Through such negative assessments, Muḥammad Ḥājjī delivers a surreptitious critique of the imamate, particularly in its later phases, without directly criticizing Shamil. Perhaps more to the point, he also creates a space for his own authority and political legitimacy. Shamil's imamate failed, this poetic and allegorical exposition suggests, because Shamil was betrayed by his chosen *nāʾibs*. Hence the real objects of critique in this poem are Daghestanis who turn away from jihad when they lack the courage to fight.

After incorporating the full *qaṣīda* into his history, al-Qarākhī proceeds to offer a commentary, albeit one not authored by himself. He follows Muḥammad Ḥājjī's *qaṣīda* with the hadith to which Muḥammad Ḥājjī's discussion of *fitna* had alluded. Found in the hadith collection of Abū Dāwūd (817/8–889), this hadith is attributed to ʿAbdullāh ibn

ʿUmar (614-693), the son of the second caliph ʿUmar ibn Khaṭṭāb.[88] In this hadith, ʿAbdullāh ibn ʿUmar sits by the side of the Prophet while the latter reflects on the many different varieties of *fitna*. The Prophet begins describing a specific kind of *fitna*, *fitna al-aḥlās*, which prompts someone in the audience to ask for elaboration. "The *fitna al-aḥlās*," responds the Prophet, entails "fleeing [*harb*] and plunder [*ḥarb*]. It is followed by the *fitna al-sarrāʾ* [prosperity], which is . . . produced by a man from my house [*ahl bayt*], who will assert that he belongs to me, although he does not, for my friends all fear God."

By this point, the relation of this hadith to Daghestani history is so obscure that the *form* of exposition—and specifically al-Qarākhī's choice of hadith as a genre of commentary—comes to appear as interesting as its *content*. Why did al-Qarākhī incorporate a hadith from early Islamic history into his account of the jihad? Why did he turn to allegory when other authors relied on straightforward exposition? In examining al-Qarākhī's choice of genres, we must keep in mind the context within which he penned his history: after Shamil's surrender, following the collapse of the regime for which he had been appointed the official historian, and now in the employ of the Russian administration, which had offered him the position of a provincial *qāḍī*. Al-Qarākhī had many reasons to be circumspect with regard to his actual views, given the source of his income and his precarious position. Hence, although the incorporation of this hadith into his text cannot easily be correlated with a fixed political position, either with regard to the Daghestani insurgents or the Russian administration, it is possible to appreciate the plurality of readings generated by this narrative strategy, and to infer that his hermeneutic ambiguity was part of a deliberate authorial strategy.

The hadith then broaches a theme that resonated profoundly across the Caucasus in the aftermath of Shamil's surrender: the power wielded by charismatic leaders, be they abreks or insurgents, to mobilize the populace. "Then the people [*al-nās*] will unite under the rule of a man like a hip bone on a rib," states the Prophet. A manuscript gloss reveals al-Qarākhī's readers struggling to extract meaning from the text: "This saying is neither accurate [*lā yastaqīm*] nor authentic [*lā yuthbat*]," states the glosser, because of the physiognomic mismatch between ribs and hip bones. "It is therefore necessary," continues the gloss, to express this meaning by a saying (*mathāl*): "like a palm on the hand and a hand on a palm." But what if the disjuncture was precisely the point of the hadith: that the charismatic leader who induces political catastrophe is as ill suited to guide his followers as are two bones intended for different parts of the body?

In the eschatology conveyed through this hadith, the *fitna* of prosperity is followed by a third *fitna*, of darkness (*al-dahīā'*), which leaves no one untouched. Concerning this third *fitna*, the Prophet states: "When it is affirmed that it has reached an end, it drags on. During this [*fitna*], a man who appears pious will turn into an infidel [*kāfir*] with the arrival of twilight, and then the people [*al-nās*] will divide into two camps: the camp of faith [*īmān*], which has no hypocrisy, and the camp of hypocrisy [*nafāq*], which has no faith." While the hadith condemns rebellion as *fitna*, the *qaṣīda* sanctifies jihad as martyrdom. Whereas the hadith warns of the dangers of revolution, the *qaṣīda* celebrates violence as a prelude to the day of resurrection (*yawm al-qiyām*). Considered together, in the way al-Qarākhī juxtaposes the two texts within his history, the hadith and the *qaṣīda* comprise a highly nuanced commentary on the recent jihad. Faced with this juxtaposition, it is impossible to extract the author's own position with regard to anticolonial violence. Given that al-Qarākhī was surely aware of the hermeneutical difficulties posed by his text, the best we can do is comment on his stylistic opacity and on the literary effects of his montage.

Also left obscure within the hadith's threefold typology is *fitna*'s relevance to Daghestani history. If the hadith is read as allegory, which Daghestani leads the second *fitna*? One candidate for the charismatic leader who appears during the third *fitna* is Shamil, but the interpretive possibilities do not stop here. Al-Qarākhī offers no clarification, and leaves it to his readers to extract their own sense from the text. Even though Muḥammad Ḥājjī could have not foreseen his impending execution, his *qaṣīda* anticipates a violent denouement for the jihad. From his position within the Russian administration, al-Qarākhī might well have regarded the 1877 rebellion as a *fitna*, as indeed the hadith he cites suggests, but it is also significant that he does not openly condemn jihad in the fashion of colonial sources. Al-Qarākhī's nuanced approach to this event suggests that he understood *fitna* in its subsidiary sense of "personal temptation," and that he saw jihad "as a condition in which you prove your faith."[89] On this reading, both *fitna* and jihad were tests of character that strengthened the moral fiber of the Muslims who engaged in them, rather than manifestations of political anarchy. Muḥammad Ḥājjī would not of course have called the jihad he led a *fitna*, but al-Qarākhī used this term allegorically, and undermined its negative connotations. At the conclusion to the anticolonial jihad in Daghestan, al-Qarākhī's use of *fitna* thereby introduced a new Daghestani discourse concerning insurgency that paralleled, while also allegorizing, its Chechen counterpart.

The distinctions adduced thus far, between Daghestani insurgency, underwritten by an hierarchical legal discourse grounded in *sharīʿa*, and the populist piety driving Chechen insurgency, grounded in an aesthetics of defeat and directed toward the transformation of *ʿādāt*, are broadly reflected in Chechen forms of worship and belief. "Islam among the Vainakh remained centered around the holy men," Anna Zelkina writes, "whose almost exclusive source of legitimacy was the ability to perform miracles. In contrast to Daghestani *ʿulamā'*, the Vainakh mullahs taught that the prophet had spread Islam by performing miracles."[90] Whereas Daghestani legal engagements with insurgency treated power as a force achieved through victory over the Russian enemy, Daghestani texts that were informed by transgressive sanctity turned to Chechen insurgents such as ʿAlībek Ḥājjī in their efforts to articulate an earthly immortality that exceeded the framework of secular existence.

A modern Chechen scholar renders this distinction between Daghestani militancy and Chechen insurgency by comparing Imam Shamil and Kunta Ḥājjī. Unlike his Daghestani counterpart, Kunta Ḥājjī was "a saint [*sviatoi*] and a peacemaker [*mirotvorets*] who . . . performed no military feats [*podvigi*]. . . . Because his feats were spiritual, Kunta Ḥājjī could not be vanquished by the secular powers of this world [*mira sego*]."[91] In terms of this distinction between material and spiritual power, the representation of ʿAlībek Ḥājjī in the literature of insurgency descends more directly from Kunta Ḥājjī than from Shamil. With respect to its popular basis in the miraculous, the Chechen-inspired literature of insurgency diverged from the legalistic discourse of Daghestani *fiqh*.

The sanctification of anticolonial abreks like Vara occurred simultaneously with the appearance of Chechen leaders such as ʿAlībek Ḥājjī, who was memorialized in historical chronicles as an insurgent who effected a merger of spiritual and secular realms. Ultimately, the imamate's military defeat drove abreks to participate in the "anti-Russian revolts" that culminated in the 1877 uprising.[92] As an Avar spiritual and political leader who displayed his power through military prowess and by promulgating a series of legal regulations, Shamil reinforced the distinction, and indeed the dichotomy, between Daghestani jurisprudential reasoning and Chechen populist piety. This does not mean of course that transgressive sanctity was exclusively Chechen and that *uṣūl al-fiqh* was exclusively Daghestani, for ʿAlī Qāḍī's chronicle demonstrates the considerable crossover between these two traditions, which ended by altering them both.

That ʿAlībek Ḥājjī was granted the title imam by his followers demonstrates his links to Shamil and his predecessors Ghāzī Muḥammad and Ḥamza Bek, each of whom bore this title. As noted in the introduction, after the death of the Prophet, the word *imam* came to signify the supreme leader of the Muslim community. *Imam* later acquired even more fluid significations that were creativity deployed throughout the Caucasus literature of anticolonial insurgency. ʿAlībek Ḥājjī became associated with Chechen religious figures such as Kunta Ḥājjī through their shared title, *imam*. Unlike Shamil and other Daghestani leaders who proclaimed themselves imam, Kunta Ḥājjī protested against the title when it was conferred on him, on the grounds of his "sinfulness." He claimed that he wasn't even worthy to accept the humbler title associated with his name: teacher (*ustadh*). Kunta Ḥājjī's authority as a religious leader did not detract from his mystical proclivities, for this Chechen was popularly believed to have the gift of performing miracles, healing the sick, and magically circumambulating the globe, from Mecca to the Caucasus and back again, just in time for daily prayers.[93] Kunta Ḥājjī was also considered one of the 356 saints (*abdāl*) whose existence, according to Sufi teachings, sanctifies the earth, transmitting blessings (*baraka*), and performing miracles (*karāmāt*).

In the annals of Daghestani literature, ʿAlībek Ḥājjī oscillated among the three insurgent idioms that proliferated throughout the

Caucasus in the wake of Shamil's defeat. As an imam, ʿAlībek Ḥājjī epitomized the militant idiom of anticolonial jihad. As a miracle worker in the lineage of Kunta Ḥājjī, ʿAlībek Ḥājjī epitomized the pacifism promulgated by Qādiriyyian and Maḥmūdiyya Sufism. Finally, as ʿAlībek Ḥājjī's charisma was incorporated into the new political dispensation of colonial rule, he helped transform Qādiriyyian Sufism into what, in the person of Vara, the first abrek, would become the transgressive sanctity.

Critiquing Insurgency: ʿAbd al-Raḥmān al-Ghāzīghumūqī

Notwithstanding the religious dimensions of the 1877 uprising, normative Soviet accounts tended to explain this event as a peasant revolt against the feudal class. The Daghestani scholars whose pioneering philology made ʿAlī Qāḍī's text available in print also voiced the residue of Soviet orthodoxies when they asserted that one purpose of the rebellion was to "free the peoples of the Caucasus from the feudal yoke [*ugneteniia*]."[94] In an earlier generation, the influential Daghestani scholar Khadzhi-Murad Khashaev made much the same point. According to Khashaev, the "leaders of the rebellion aimed to restore the Khan's power and clerical privilege."[95] While Khashaev acknowledged that the "hardworking peasants who participated in the uprising were engaged in a battle against the colonial yoke," his overall assessment of the 1877 rebellion as reactionary is one-dimensional, yet sadly typical of much scholarship on this subject. By eliding the aesthetic and spiritual dimensions of insurgency, Soviet historiography replaced the tension between the colonial legal order and the authority of Islamic law with a static understanding of class conflict.

Most recently, a new generation of Daghestani scholars is pioneering an alternative to the Soviet approach. Having come of age in a post-Soviet environment that is more receptive to Islamic learning than Soviet institutions were, these scholars emphasize the spiritual dimensions of the 1877 rebellion. One such scholar, Makhach Musaev, who has worked extensively on Daghestani Arabic literature from the early modern period to the present, replaces the Soviet focus on class conflict with a focus on Islamic piety by demonstrating that the 1877 uprising transpired "under the sign of jihad (*ghazawāt*)" stimulated by *sharīʿa*.[96] As one of the first post-Soviet accounts of anticolonial rebellion in Daghestan to examine insurgency from within the framework of Islamic piety, Musaev usefully moves beyond the Soviet narrative while suggesting further areas of investigation.[97]

If class conflict did not drive the 1877 rebellion, what motivated thousands of mountaineers to risk their lives for a cause that stood little chance of victory? Were the mountaineers simply "deceived," as the Avar poetry collected by Akhlakov (as well as the Arabic and Azeri texts discussed later in this chapter) suggests? Soviet historiography was justified in assuming that religion was not the only factor. The Qumuq author Yirchi Qazaq (d. 1879), who witnessed the 1877 rebellion from Daghestan's comparatively quiescent lowlands, addresses the question of motive in one of his lyric poems. For Qazaq, tensions between ruler and ruled framed the insurgency even more than religion. The poet contrasts the infidels into whose hands the peasants have been betrayed with the pious Muslim masses:

> Tying our hands and feet, our khan betrayed us
> to the pale-faced Russian.
> Betrayed by our khans,
> we have hardly anyone on our side.
> We will suffer in infidels' hands
> until Azrael takes our souls.[98]

Although Qazaq is attuned to the friction between the aristocratic khans and their disgruntled subjects, the last two lines of this poem articulate tensions internal to the sacralized juxtaposition of colonial oppression to religious eschatology.[99]

Whereas much of the literature discussed in chapter 1 celebrates the abrek as an inaugurator of a new political order, most Daghestani accounts of the 1877 uprising offer a more guarded engagement with anticolonial violence. With the significant exception of ʿAlī Qāḍī, Daghestani sources concur that the rebellion was an exercise in futility. The only point of contention is with regard to the assignation of blame. Although Qazaq and Avar folk songs present the insurgents as having been betrayed by their leaders and deceived by foreign powers, other Daghestani authors apportion blame more evenly across the class divide.

ʿAbd al-Raḥmān al-Ghāzīghumūqī and Ḥasan al-Alqadārī, to whose reading of the rebellion the remainder of this chapter is dedicated, were born in 1834 and 1837 respectively, only three years apart. In equally parallel fashion, both passed many of their adult years within Russia, and under conditions of exile. ʿAbd al-Raḥmān remembered his years in Russia more fondly than Ḥasan. I first consider a brief essay on the subject of the 1877 uprising by ʿAbd al-Raḥmān, composed in 1892, before turning to a contemporaneous representation of this event in a major historical narrative by Ḥasan al-Alqadārī, composed just a year prior.

Like his father, sheykh Jamāl al-Dīn, but perhaps to an even greater extent, and until the end of his life, al-Ghāzīghumūqī was opposed to jihad. Given his immersion in Daghestani culture, it is not surprising that al-Ghāzīghumūqī was also a major Arabic author in his own right. Two contemporary Daghestani philologists call him "one of the best-known representatives of nineteenth century Daghestani spiritual culture."[100] The centrality of al-Ghāzīghumūqī's oeuvre, and especially its critique of violence, to the Daghestani literature of insurgency is indicated, among other ways, by al-Qarākhī's incorporation of large sections of his second major historical work, *Epitome of the details of Shamil's time* (*Khulāṣat al-tafṣīl ʿan ahwāl al-imām shāmwīl*) into his *Bāriqat* (223–230). It is also attested by a little-known and recently discovered essay written in the aftermath of the 1877 rebellion that adds an important Daghestani perspective on anticolonial violence, to which I turn after reviewing the author's biography.

To an even greater extent than the other authors introduced over the course of this book, al-Ghāzīghumūqī's life traversed multiple worlds. Born into the village of Ghumūq, al-Ghāzīghumūqī received a traditional Islamic education and attained a high level of fluency in Arabic, the language of all of his extant compositions.[101] And yet al-Ghāzīghumūqī was also one of the first Daghestani intellectuals to have a presence in the Russian public sphere. His work first appeared in Russian 1862 in the journal *Kavkaz*, when he was only twenty-five.[102]

Al-Ghāzīghumūqī was also acquainted with important figures in the colonial administration, such as the Russian officer Apollon Runovskii, who was later assigned the task of looking after Imam Shamil in his exile in Kaluga.[103] Although al-Ghāzīghumūqī does not engage in his work with Russian sources as copiously as did his Persophone counterparts in southern Daghestan, familiarity with Russian writing on the Caucasus permeates his oeuvre, including in his account of Shamil's kidnapping of Princess Orbeliani (*Tadhkira*, 63b; *Khulāṣat*, 32a).

Combining in his person a Naqshbandī as well as an imamate lineage, al-Ghāzīghumūqī reflected extensively on the 1877 uprising, which he participated in quelling while in the service of the tsar. Written fifteen years after the events it describes, "The Defeat of Daghestan and Chechnya as a Consequence of Ottoman Incitement in the Year 1294" treats the 1877 rebellion as an act of futility and judges the rebels as traitors. Discovered in a Tbilisi archive in 1975, this brief work sheds significant light on al-Ghāzīghumūqī's position between the colonial administration and his native Daghestan, while also evoking the tensions among mountaineer lifeways, Islamic values, and the nascent modernities with which this book opened.[104] Without mentioning the thousands of innocent mountaineers who had been banished from their homeland following the suppression of the uprising, and concerning whose fates he was certainly aware, al-Ghāzīghumūqī implicitly justifies the punishment inflicted by the tsar.[105]

In terms of the relation between Daghestani and Chechen idioms of insurgency, the most notable aspect of al-Ghāzīghumūqī's account is his treatment of the role of Chechens as compared to Daghestanis in shaping the course of the insurgency. Al-Ghāzīghumūqī starkly contrasts the stupid mountaineers (*jabalī*) who rebelled with the wise mountaineers who remained faithful to the Russian government (*al-dawla al-rūssiya*), "thereby avoiding pollution from war and rebellion" (55). Al-Ghāzīghumūqī's testimony in favor of the colonial regime and against the insurgents differentiates Chechen from Daghestani communities. Al-Ghāzīghumūqī stresses that the primary instigator of the rebellion, ʿAlībek Ḥājjī, was Chechen. He accuses ʿAlībek Ḥājjī of accepting bribes from the Ottomans and adds to this accusation a general assessment of the Chechen character. "Not only did the Chechens, who are rebellious by nature [*fiṭra*] submit to [ʿAlībek Ḥājjī]," he writes, "so too did the hapless [Daghestani] mountaineers" (55).

Several formal and thematic aspects of ʿAbd al-Raḥmān's account of the 1877 insurgency are striking. First, there is the linguistic tendency that al-Ghāzīghumūqī shares with Daghestani Arabic writers of the nineteenth century to refer to Chechens not by any of the many indigenous ethnonyms in local circulation in Caucasus languages (*vainakh, ghalghai, malkh*), but by an Arabization of the Russian usage, *Chachān* (چچان).[106] As noted by the first Chechen ethnographer, Umalat Laudaev, the term *Chechen* was attached to the Nakh (as Chechens call themselves) as a result of some of them having taken up residence in a village named Chechniia, in the lowlands by the Terek River, during the colonial period.[107] Prior to their resettlement, the Nakh resided primarily in the mountains rather than in this village by the Terek.

Colonial resettlement had the effect of reifying the Nakh, who resided in the mountains, into "Chechens" who resided on the plains. While based in modern geography, *Chechen* encompasses only one portion of the territory that the Nakh call *daimohk* ("homeland") and represents a Russian simplification of a more complex indigenous reality. Modern Daghestani Arabic literature generally follows Russian rather than vernacular precedent in naming the Chechens. Like al-Ghāzīghumūqī, al-Qarākhī follows Russian linguistic norms (for example in *Bāriqat*, 21). By contrast, ʿAlī Qāḍī's Arabic chronicle is marked by "the heavy influence of Avar grammar," including its case system, which differs sharply from Arabic.[108] It is no accident that the text most heavily suffused with vernacular registers is also the one that, from among its Daghestani peers, was most favorably inclined to transgressive sanctity.

Of even greater interest than his lexical choices is ʿAbd al-Raḥmān's view of ʿAlībek Ḥājjī as the primary agent in the 1877 rebellion. In contrast to many secondary sources, ʿAbd al-Raḥmān hardly mentions Muḥammad Ḥājjī, although he also received the title *imam* and was also hung by the colonial administration. Some Daghestani sources portray Muḥammad Ḥājjī less favorably than his charismatic Chechen counterpart, and even represent him one-dimensionally as a deceiver. This contemptuous attitude is well illustrated in an Avar folk song, collected by Akhlakov, which mocks Muḥammad Ḥājjī's appointment as imam and associates him with a pretentious aristocracy:

> Ever since this man emerged from his mother's womb,
> he has not walked with weapons in his hands.
> He who never accomplished a feat
> since he matured and saddled his horse
> arose to speak and pronounced loudly:
> "I am a Daghestani prince [*bek*]."[109]

Arguably, one reason for this differing representation of the Daghestani leader of the uprising as compared to his Chechen counterpart in the folkloric record is that Chechen abreks did not cultivate alliances with the ruling elite. Their aestheticization in folkloric, and subsequently literary, texts emphasized miracles, vernacular idioms of worship, and personal piety over formal learning and hierarchical social structures.

ʿAbd al-Raḥmān's brief discussion of Muḥammad Ḥājjī and his father, sheykh ʿAbd al-Raḥmān al-Thughūrī (1792–1882), is of particular interest given his close personal connections (via his kinship to Jamāl al-Dīn) to the scholarly elite—a social class derided in Avar folklore and Soviet historiography.[110] Al-Thughūrī was the father of Muḥammad Ḥājjī, author of the *qaṣīda* discussed earlier, and a disciple (*khalīfa*) of the same Jamāl al-Dīn who was al-Ghāzīghumūqī's father.[111] The high price al-Thughūrī paid for his son's insurgency—a price that included the public execution of his son—doubtlessly influenced his final assessment of 1877. Toward the end of his essay, al-Ghāzīghumūqī describes how a group of Daghestani villagers carried the old Sufi sheykh, who, already in his eighties, was too weak to stand without support, to see Cavalry General Loris-Melikov. In the presence of Loris-Melikov, al-Thughūrī publicly renounced the insurgents, including his son. He was later sentenced to house arrest in the town of Nizhnee Kazanishche, where he lived until his death four years later in 1882, the same year that saw the death of al-Qarākhī.[112]

Although the evidence is inconclusive, the text suggests that Muḥammad Ḥājjī had yet to be executed at the time of his father's renunciation of him.[113] Al-Ghāzīghumūqī says that, prior to renouncing the *fitna*, sheykh al-Thughūrī had been the reason (*sabab*) that his son, "later [*baʿd dhalika*] hung in Ghunib," was granted the title *imam* (57). Al-Ghāzīghumūqī's shrewd, and mildly sardonic, dissection of the contradictions in the sheykh's behavior also serves an ancillary function. The author's suggestion that Muḥammad Ḥājjī could only have become imam with a sheykh's blessing indicates the intimate relation between the imam's political authority and the sheykh's spiritual power that permeates this literature.[114] Further, the phrasing in al-Ghāzīghumūqī's text—*walada imāmā al-makhnawq fī ghunib baʿd dhalika*—suggests that sheykh al-Thughūrī renounced his son prior to his execution. The timing is significant, suggesting as it does that this sheykh's aversion to transgressive sanctity caused him to renounce his son while he was still alive.

Thus, while transgressive sanctity is more in evidence in Chechen and Chechen-inspired texts than in Daghestani sources, both textual traditions engaged creatively and productively with this insurgent ideology. Both traditions also turned to transgressive sanctity in their quests for political agency under colonial rule, and in their engagements with colonial violence. While transgression is given material force through the violation of colonial norms, sanctity is made manifest in literary form. This productive nexus of transgression and sacralization is the guiding principle of transgressive sanctity.

The *qaṣīda* discussed earlier, by sheykh al-Thughūrī's son, was redolent with grief, but nowhere in that poem does Muḥammad Ḥājjī explicitly reject rebellion. To the contrary, Muḥammad Ḥājjī consistently links martyrdom to militancy. Invoking the "truth [*ḥaqq*] of jihad" (*Bāriqat*, 214, v. 15), the poet and describes how the hearts of the insurgents "open for *ghazawāt* [*anshraḥat ṣadūrhumʾl-ghazw*]" (*Bāriqat*, 213, v. 3). Nowhere else in his essay does al-Ghāzīghumūqī mention Muḥammad Ḥājjī, notwithstanding that some sources—and most modern historiography—consider him the leader of the rebellion. As for Muḥammad Ḥājjī's father, sheykh al-Thughūrī, al-Ghāzīghumūqī reports that Loris-Melikov determined that the old man, armed with the sword of Imam Shamil, was slowly losing his mind and let him go home.

From sheykh al-Thughūrī's sardonic perspective, Muḥammad Ḥājjī's claim to the title *imam* is spurious and ironic. The illegitimacy of Muḥammad Ḥājjī's claim to power is reinforced with the phrase "*their* imām [*imāmahum*]," which suggests that Muḥammad Ḥājjī's leadership was not universally recognized, least of all by the author. Al-Ghāzīghumūqī's displacement of the Daghestani role in organizing the 1877 rebellion onto Chechens is also worth noting. Opposed as he was to the uprising, al-Ghāzīghumūqī was more willing to discredit Chechens than his fellow Daghestanis, and therefore to blame the event on a people to whom he was less kindred. Like many of his fellow Daghestanis, al-Ghāzīghumūqī regarded transgressive sanctity, which he equated with *fitna*, as excessive, gratuitously violent, and needlessly destructive. Even more than the ruthless destruction of colonial conquest, 1877 was for al-Ghāzīghumūqī a year of apocalypse, comparable with the bloodiest *fitnas* in Islamic history.

In introducing al-Ghāzīghumūqī to a modern Daghestani readership, Shikhsaidov remarks on the contrast between al-Qarākhī's *Bāriqat*, where the chronicle of battles "occupies a dominant role," and al-Ghāzīghumūqī's memoirs, which are more interested in biographical narrative than in glorying in violence.[115] This same aversion to violence is evident in al-Ghāzīghumūqī's essay on the 1877 rebellion. While openly identifying with the Russian administration, al-Ghāzīghumūqī also voices at multiple junctures his affective identification with his homeland (*waṭan*), and his grief at its recent traumatic past. "As I left [Temir-Khan]-Shura and headed in the direction of my hometown Ghumūq," al-Ghāzīghumūqī laments, "my heart contracted [in thinking of] my loved ones left behind [*ahalī bāqayn*], as well as of my relatives [*al-aqārib*], who had also been deceived and drunk from the source of foolishness [*min ʿayn al-aḥmāqiyya*]" (56).

Al-Ghāzīghumūqī echoes al-Qarākhī (who claimed to have been quoting Shamil's words to Ḥājjī Murād), when he refers to rebellion as foolishness (*Bāriqat*, 179). At the same time, he anticipates al-Alqadārī by referring in four places to the 1877 rebellion as *fitna* (56, 57). Soon afterward, as if the mere evocation of the landscape filled him with nostalgia, al-Ghāzīghumūqī recalls how he approached his home village through a gorge that ran alongside the tall mountains. While al-Ghāzīghumūqī's powerful identification with his native land made it difficult for him to accuse his fellow Daghestanis of rebelling against the tsar, which he regarded as a crime, no such scruples constrained him with respect to the Chechen insurgents.

From the very beginning of the Daghestani jihad, "generational tensions" affected relations between imams and their sheykhs.[116] Al-Ghāzīghumūqī participated in crushing a rebellion that aimed to restore the political form of the imamate that his father-in-law, Shamil, had institutionalized in the Caucasus more thoroughly than anyone before him. He was also actively involved in fashioning his father's legacy and worked to foster an image of sheykh Jamāl al-Dīn as a proponent of peace, partly to contest more militant ideologies promoting violence.[117] Finally, Ḥasan al-Alqadārī's son and translator Ali Gasanov was more favorably inclined to Russian—by his time Soviet—rule than was his father, who, notwithstanding his interest in modern knowledge, continued to turn for answers to the Islamic past. In his notes to his translation of his father's chronicle, Gasanov announces his preference for "European ways [*evropeiskii byt*]" to the values of his "sharīʿa-inclined [*shariatist*]" father (168).[118] Such generational tensions shaped the dialectic between resistance and accommodation across the Caucasus, and profoundly inflect the contours of Daghestani literary history.

Further examples can be listed of insurgents active in the jihad who were born to men who served the tsar. Nor were all sons more radical than their fathers. There was also a cross-generational movement in the opposite direction, from rebellion to accommodation. The family of Bolshevik leader Said Gabiev (1883–1963), one of the most active proponents for replacing Arabic as the language of learning by Russian, had been punitively exiled following the 1877 uprising. During the same period during which Daghestani society was internally riven by generational conflicts among sheykhs, militants, and government functionaries, Georgian poets staged a battle between fathers and sons in verse that also inflected subsequent Georgian idioms of anticolonial insurgency. These are discussed in the following chapter.

As with the abrek's transgressive sanctity that occupied the preceding chapter, the narration of the 1877 uprising as a miraculous event was shaped by the social contexts from within which it was generated. Having examined the impact of Chechen insurgency on the trajectory of a rebellion that was initiated in Daghestan, I bring this chapter to a close with the literary texts that were composed in the aftermath of the 1877 defeat, often in the throes of exilic grief. Of particular interest to this literary exegesis are the ways in which the Daghestani poetry of defeat reconfigured classical Arabic poetics. Like so many other aspects of modern Islamic culture, classical genres were given new life when temporal horizons shifted. A more extended engagement with these literary dialectics will help clarify in formal terms the ways in which the Daghestani literary engagement with insurgency propagated its own unique modernity.

The Aesthetics of Defeat: Ḥasan al-Alqadārī

One of the outstanding products of Daghestani literary modernity, *Vestiges of Daghestan* (*Āthār-i Dāghistān*), composed in Turki (Azeri) in 1891 by the polymath poet-jurist Ḥasan al-Alqadārī, has already informed this account of Daghestani engagements with insurgency. As the author is gradually becoming a familiar figure to readers of this book, I refer to him as he referred to himself in his writings: Ḥasan Affandī. Ḥasan was born in the Lezgi village of Alqadar in southern Daghestan five years prior to the death of his grandfather Muḥammad al-Yarāghī, who, as noted earlier, authorized the initial jihad against the Russians in 1828. Best known in the Russian translation of Ḥasan's son (figure 8), *Āthār* is one of Daghestan's last major historical chronicles. Although much of the text narrates Daghestan's history after Nāder Shāh's attack on the khanate of Ghāzī-Ghumūq (1741), al-Alqadārī situated his contribution to Daghestani historiography within a long multilingual tradition that included the multiple versions of the *Darbandnāma* discussed in the introduction, as well as the Persian-language *Garden of Paradise* (*Gulistān-i Irām*) by ʿAbbās Qulī Āqā Bākīkhānūf. From his location on a relatively obscure periphery of the Russian empire, Ḥasan creatively interwove Arabic, Persian, and Turkic traditions throughout his oeuvre.

Unlike ʿAlī Qāḍī, who rarely mentions the Ottomans, but similar to ʿAbd al-Raḥmān al-Ghāzīghumūqī, Ḥasan places the bulk of responsibility for the 1877 uprising on Ottoman interference in the Caucasus. As Ḥasan's son and translator Ali Gasanov suggests, his father had a special stake in the historiography of the 1877 rebellion, in part because

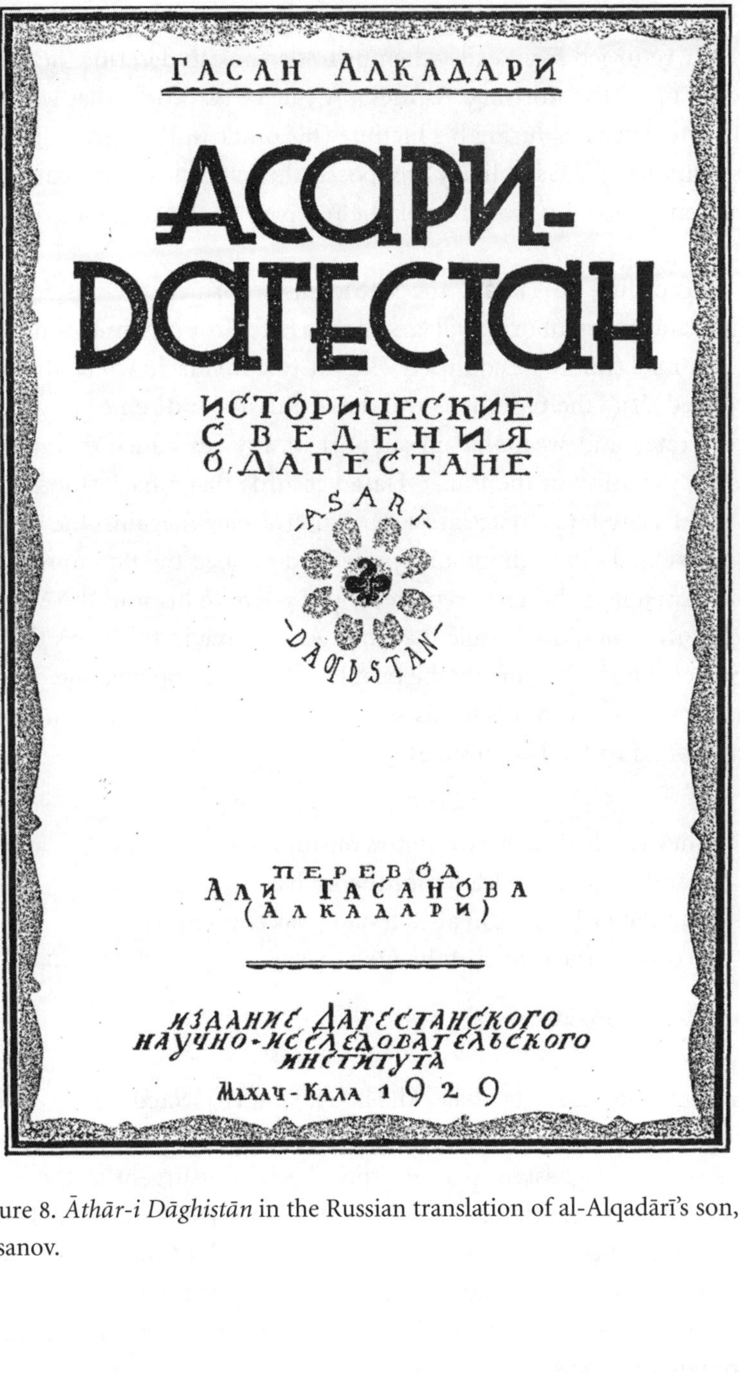

Figure 8. *Āthār-i Dāghistān* in the Russian translation of al-Alqadārī's son, Ali Gasanov.

he was unjustly persecuted following its suppression.[119] Ḥasan had only recently returned from exile when he undertook to describe the events leading up to the uprising. As the only one of his works that was submitted to a censor during his lifetime (his other works were published posthumously), Ḥasan likely composed this chronicle with particular attention to how his words would be received by the colonial administration.

According to Ḥasan, the Ottomans informed the residents of Sogratl and of neighboring villages about a letter from Shamil's son Ghāzī Muḥammad (not to be confused with the first imam) in which the latter predicted that "the Ottomans will defeat Russia [and] enter Daghestan with money and weapons" in support of any resistance they wished to offer the army of the tsar.[120] Ḥasan records that Ghāzī Muḥammad advised Daghestanis to declare a rebellion (*al-baghī*) against the tsar.

Just as al-Ghāzīghumūqī repeatedly described the 1877 uprising as *fitna*, Ḥasan uses this term repeatedly in a poem to his son Abū Muslim (1861–1911), composed while the latter was serving in the Tsar's Guards in St. Petersburg. "Suddenly the people of Thughūr opened the door to evil [*sharr*]," he recounts to his son in one verse (216, v. 16). And then, even more directly, Ḥasan states:

> They reached such extremities of stupidity
> that they elected a leader for themselves.
> The son of Ḥājjī ʿAbd al-Raḥmān [was chosen]
> to occupy the center of the *fitna*.
>
> (*Āthār*, 216, vv. 21–22)

Ḥasan's poem suggests that ʿAlībek Ḥājjī was elected imam before Muḥammad Ḥājjī (v. 13), but like other sources, this poem lays more stress on the Daghestani than on the Chechen insurgent as the agent driving the violence that ensued. This letter in verse is far from Ḥasan's only poetic reflection on the events of 1877; much of his poetic oeuvre responds in one way or another to the uprising's aftermath.[121]

An Avar folksong from Thughūr echoes Ḥasan's imputation of Ottoman influence:

A letter arrived from the *hünkar*.
They have done these things deceitfully.
Instructions came from the *pasha*.
They wanted to betray us treacherously.[122]

Ḥasan is more equivocal than this folk poem in assigning blame for the 1877 uprising, but his assessment of these events is just as negative.

Finally, the list adduced so far of Daghestani writers who portrayed the events of 1877 in a negative light should include Nadhir al-Durgilī (d. 1935), the author of a biographical dictionary that has been cited throughout this chapter for its details concerning Daghestani literary history, as well as a contributor to the polemics surrounding *ijtihād* (independent legal reasoning) in early twentieth-century Daghestan.[123] Al-Durgilī writes from both sides of the ideological divide. On the one hand, he follows al-Ghāzīghumūqī and Ḥasan by referring to the uprising as *fitna* (*Nuzhat*, 85/121). On the other hand, al-Durgilī charges the tsarist regime with brutally repressing the rebellion and with perpetuating injustices (*ẓulmat*) that no reasonable person could justify as an appropriate punishment for the uprising (*Nuzhat*, 85/121).

Alongside his activity as an historian, Ḥasan composed two books in Arabic under the *takhalluṣ* (pen name) Mamnūn ("grateful one"). These two works, *Jirāb al-Mamnūn* and *Dīwān al-Mamnūn* (figure 9), were distributed by Mavraev, the publisher and critic whose conflictual relation to Islamic learning was discussed in the introduction.[124] Unlike *Āthār*, *Jirāb al-Mamnūn* and *Dīwān al-Mamnūn* bear no trace of having been submitted to a censor for approval.[125] That Ḥasan assembled a *dīwān* on his own initiative reflects his position as a writer lacking patronage who has undertaken to fashion his posterity alongside his verse. That his *dīwān* merged poetry and prose, exegesis and narrative, self-reflection and historical reasoning, into a single cogent, and unprecedented in Arabic, literary form attests to the ambition and originality of his Arabic poetics. Yet even as he innovated through form and genre, Ḥasan situated his genre innovations within the classical Arabic tradition, as is demonstrated by his references to al-Ḥarīrī's *Maqāmāt* (*Assemblies*), a twelfth-century work that blended poetry and prose (*Dīwān*, 42).

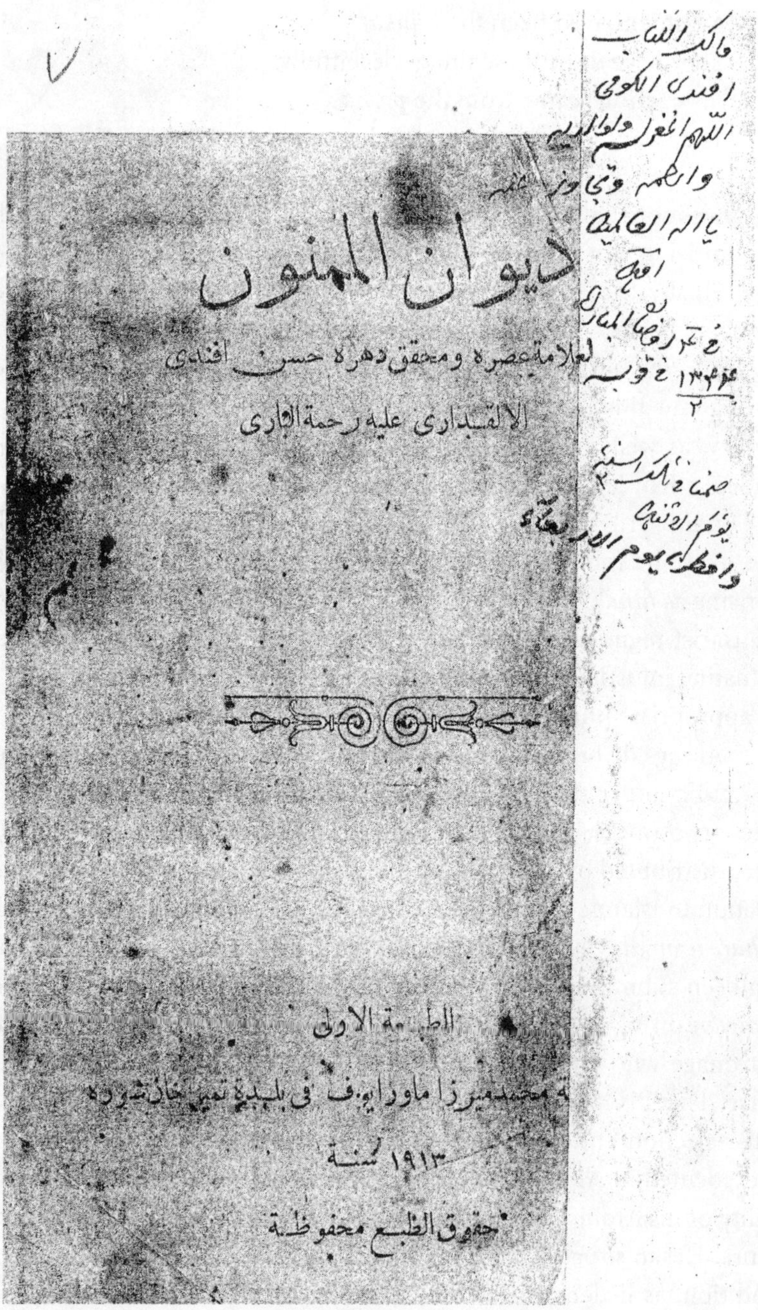

Figure 9. *Diwān al-Mamnūn* (Temir Khan Shura: Mavraev, 1913).

Ḥasan's *dīwān* is interspersed with poems honoring acquaintances, celebrating friendship, and lamenting recent historical upheavals. Once, when Ḥasan composed a poem (*qaṣīda al-mawlid*) honoring a friend whose son who had reached the age of maturity, the dedicatee hung a calligraphic transcription of the text over his guest room so that anyone entering the house would see it (*Dīwān*, 180). Ḥasan evidently took great pride in the prominent place given his poems in his friend's home. A poet as well as a jurist and an historian, Ḥasan accorded his poetry the same importance as his historiographic and legal writings.

One of *Dīwān al-Mamnūn*'s most striking poems is an elegy (*marthīya-zuhdiyyāt*) for the scholar Ḥājjī Dibīr al-Qarākhī, known as a teacher of many of the writers discussed in this chapter, including Muḥammad Ṭāhir al-Qarākhī and Ḥasan himself (see *Bāriqat*, 54n9; *Nuzhat*, 90–91/65–66). Ḥasan's poem emphasizes the depth of his teacher's learning:

لقد عاش مرضيا ومات مكرما
والزمنى دمعا عليه مذرفا
فجعت الطلاب يادهر جملة
وأوحشت علم العربي و قد عفا
حزنت علوم الدين ايضا بفقده
ولا سيما غربت هذا التصوفا

(*Dīwān*, 67; also *Nuzhat*, 90–91/65–66)

He lived nobly and died honorably.
His death stirred in me a wave of tears.
With his death, you have instilled fear in all students
and stalled the progress of Arabic sciences.
You have made the religious sciences suffer through his loss.
Sufism especially has become estranged.

By contrast with these inward-looking poems that situate the poet's self within his Daghestani milieu, in his *Āthār*, aside from the autobiographical digression that concludes the text, Ḥasan narrates the 1877 uprising as an event that transpired among strangers. It is only when the history ceases to function as a chronicle, and turns to the author's self, that Ḥasan alludes to his own exile. After recalling how he served for twelve years as a *nāʾib* of the southern Tabasaran district for the Russian administration, Ḥasan tells of how "justly or unjustly [*ḥaqq na ḥaqq*], I was included within the group who had been found guilty of the [1877] uprising, and the Russian state [*dawlat rūssīya*] decided to exile me from Daghestan, to the Tambov district" (*Āthār*, 249).

By contrast with the laconic treatment of this exile in his chronicle, Ḥasan's rendering of its aftermath in his *Dīwān* is fraught with the memory of the unjust fate he and his family suffered far from their homeland. "Towards the end of Rabīʿ al-ʿawwal 1296 [1879]," Ḥasan begins his recollection in a prose interlude of *Dīwān*, I was summoned by the *nachalnik* [a Russian term for a local official] of the Kura region, mayor Ivan Moiseevich Asaturov" (144). This official informed him that a law (*firmān*) had been issued by Grand Duke Mikhail Nikolaevich, referred to here as *sardār al-aʿẓam* (a Persian term for "great ruler"). Mikhail Nikolaevich had requested the officials under his command "to send into exile [*taghrīb*] certain . . . leaders [ʿ*umarāʾ*] who, due to groundless rumors, were viewed with suspicion by the tsarist officials during the events that [afflicted] the people of Daghestan in 1294 [1877]" (*Dīwān*, 145). This was not the first time that Grand Duke Mikhail Nikolaevich, who served as viceroy (*namestnik*) of the Caucasus from 1862 to 1882, had organized the banishment of the mountaineers under his rule. Even more infamously, Mikhail Nikolaevich had directed the deportation of the Circassians (Shapsugs, Adyghe, Abaza, and Abkhaz) to Ottoman territories in the preceding decade.[126]

Daghestanis who were implicated in the rebellion were placed under police surveillance (*al-naẓārat pulīsīyyat*) and ordained to be scattered throughout Russia. "On the list of those to be exiled," Ḥasan continues, "was my name. I had to prepare for departure" (145). After narrating the events leading up to his exile, Ḥasan documents his journey aboard a steamship, his imprisonment in Kharkov, traveling under police surveillance from Tambov with his family, and finally, his struggles to adjust to the "cold Russian winter, alien to our nature" where he settled near Spassk in provincial Russia (169). In a *qaṣīda* addressed to Ḥājjī Faḍl Allāh Akhund of Derbent, Ḥasan complains that fate (*dahr*) has been cruel to his alter ego (*takhalluṣ*) Mamnūn, "exiled to a foreign land and disgraced" (167).

The second work in the sequence denominated by Ḥasan's *takhalluṣ*, *Mamnūn's Knapsack* (*Jirāb al-Mamnūn*), gathers together the *fatawā* (legal rulings) addressed to his Daghestani constituents.[127] More systematically than his other works, *Jirāb al-Mamnūn* examines the proper regulation of Muslim life under the conditions of modernity. Al-Alqadārī touches in this volume on topics ranging from the appropriate use of the gramophone and the telegraph to geography textbooks (*Jirāb*, 234). Additionally, he looks beyond the Shāfiʿī school of law that predominated in Daghestan and incorporates into his legal rulings teachings from the Ḥanafī rite, a step made feasible by his greater access to Tatar Islamic learning while in exile.[128] Ḥasan's blending of the different schools of Islamic jurisprudence is a legal corollary to his polyphonic engagement with Arabic literary genres. Ḥasan's multifaceted oeuvre further testifies to the textual and disciplinary plurality of modern Daghestani literature, which included poetry, lexicography, and historiography.

Far from being an exception, exile was the norm for the nineteenth-century educated Daghestanis. The writers, historians, poets, and jurists who contributed most to Daghestani literature passed a substantial portion of their lives far from their homeland, usually in the Russian heartland. For those among this group whose ambivalent attitudes toward insurgency have been examined here, exile afforded new ways of seeing themselves and their others, and of understanding this history of interaction. Ḥasan Affandī and al-Ghāzīghumūqī both saw the official link with Russia that was formalized with Shamil's surrender as an opportunity for positive change. For both writers, life in exile intensified their belief in the futility of transgressive sanctity and the virtues of peaceful reconciliation. In concluding this tour through the Daghestani literature of (and against) insurgency, I turn to the last figure who made his mark on history by uniting an ethic of transgression with an aesthetic of sanctity.

Dressing the World in Grief: Najm al-Dīn al-Ḥutsī

Although al-Ghāzīghumūqī and Ḥasan were persuaded that the 1877 rebellion was a mistake, by no means did all Daghestanis regard rebellion against the tsar as a crime, or as a modern *fitna.* Some Daghestanis were as inclined to aestheticize transgression as were their Chechen counterparts. Najm al-Dīn al-Ḥutsī (d. 1925), the Avar leader of the first major anti-Soviet rebellion to sweep through Daghestan and Chechnya, and a prolific Arabic poet, is a case in point (figure 10).[129] As the leader of the fourth imamate (1918–1925), Najm al-Dīn was as

Figure 10. Photograph of Najm al-Dīn al-Ḥutsī (1918). Courtesy of Khadzhi Murad Donogo.

respected for his learning as for his militancy, but it is in the latter domain that he figures most frequently into the historical record.[130] Just as the first imamate was marked by dissent within Daghestan concerning the desirability of jihad, so too when Najm al-Dīn seized the revolutionary moment to establish a fourth imamate modeled after Shamil's jihad state, did the Sufi sheykh Ḥasan al-Qaḥḥī (d. 1937) criticized the new imam for embracing *fitna*.[131]

Like all the other Daghestani writers discussed in this chapter, Najm al-Dīn's literary language was Arabic, a language that Naqshbandī scholars cultivated more extensively than their Chechen Qādirī counterparts.[132] Najm al-Dīn writings constitute a third—and for the purposes of this chapter, final—lineage within the Daghestani discourse on insurgency, a lineage situated midway between Ḥasan's preference for peace and Muḥammad Ḥājjī's eschatological glorification of violence.

As with other Daghestani authors, especially Ḥasan, elegiac genres such as the *marthīya*, predominate in Najm al-Dīn's oeuvre.

Daghestani authors' interest in crafting a Daghestani poetics of mourning is also found among Georgian, Azeri, Chechen, and Russian writers. At the same time, Daghestani Arabic literature presents the most sophisticated and articulate critique of violence in the literatures of the Caucasus. Amid their vast internal differences, the texts cited in this chapter collectively constitute a Daghestani critique of violence which parallels while also subverting Chechen transgressive sanctity. Whether they supported or opposed insurgency, for Muḥammad Ḥājjī, Ḥasan, al-Ghāzīghumūqī, and Najm al-Dīn, as for their Chechen counterparts defeat was more poetically generative than victory. Yet for at least some of these Daghestani authors the suffering induced by violence was not redeemed by transgressive sanctity.

Najm al-Dīn's most notable elegies commemorate the Naqshbandī sheykh al-Yarāghī, who initially opposed jihad, and Ḥājjī Murād. A third significant poem, widely cited in Daghestani anthologies, is a satire for the poet and religious thinker Yūsuf al-Yakhsāwī (1795–1871), who was, in the words of al-Qarākhī, "a learned and a seasoned opponent" of Imam Shamil (*Bāriqat*, 199). The popularity of elegy and satire—both genres with strong affiliations to biographical narrative—in this scholarly milieu speaks to the complex role of poetry in a culture that regards the ability to compose verse as a sign of the highest cultivation. In his biographical dictionary, al-Durgilī cites two of Najm al-Dīn's lengthy poems, concerning al-Yakhsāwī and sheykh al-Thughūrī respectively.[133] The first poem, concerning al-Yakhsāwī, seeks to discredit Shamil's rival through satire. The poet writes:

تراب آرض من الحمرآء ألبسها
ما خاطه السيف لا ما خاطه الابر
يا يوسف الذم كذب ما تقول ولا
بالهجو قولك فى الاقوال يعتبر
لذكره اسنتك وبسمل لن يحلّ و لو
ثناؤه لمعاد فمّه قذر

(Al-Durgilī, *Nuzhat*, 64/88)

This land was dressed in red [from the warriors' blood].
This clothing was sewn by a sword, not a needle.
Yusuf, cursed man! What you say is a lie.
Your speech is no reproach.
Before you mention [Shamil], clean your teeth and recite
the *basmala*
An enemy with a dirty mouth has no need to praise [Shamil].

In the process of defending Shamil against his detractors, Najm al-Dīn also reveals his own intellectual genealogy.

The second poem included by al-Durgilī in his biographical dictionary, a *qaṣīda* for sheykh ʿAbd al-Raḥmān al-Thughūrī, reveals the imam's devotion to this sheykh, who, as seen earlier, renounced both the jihad and his own insurgent son. Sheykh al-Thughūrī was widely praised in Daghestani literature, and Najm al-Dīn's *qaṣīda* is just one among many poems composed in his honor.[134] Like Ḥasan in his elegy for Ḥājjī Dibīr al-Qarākhī, the poet begins by describing the calamity ushered in by sheykh al-Thughūrī's death, and then dwells on his learning, the depth of which surpassed the knowledge contained in seven seas (*sabʿa min baḥr*):

تزعزعت الأكوان و اضطرب الدهر
ولم أدر هل خير هنالك أم شرّ
الى أن أتانى بغتة نعى مرشد
همام وهجيراه مذ بلغ الذكر

هوى سبعة من أبحر العلم والذى
حواه سواه فهو من بحره قطر

(Al-Durgilī, *Nuzhat*, 81/116)

The world was compressed and the epoch shaken.
I didn't know if it was good or evil,
when suddenly I was told of the death of this *murshid.*
He surpassed the seven seas of learning.
Those who had contact with him
could glean only a drop of his learning.

The figures of speech used by Ḥasan to lament the death of his teacher Ḥājjī Dibīr al-Qarākhī suggest an obvious intertext. In Ḥasan's poem, Ḥājjī Dibīr was compared to a "light of guidance [*sirāj al-hadī*]" (*Dīwān*, 67). In Najm al-Dīn's elegy, sheykh al-Thughūrī figured as a guide (*al-hadī*) for the Daghestani people.

Nowhere in this lengthy *qaṣīda* does Najm al-Dīn allude to the well-known divergence between his jihadist commitments and that of the quietist sheykh. To the contrary, the poem appears motivated by an unalloyed desire to praise the sheykh. His learning, Najm al-Dīn stresses, penetrated deeper than seven seas, and his courage and fortitude are comparable only to the eagle (*al-ʿanqā'*). The *qaṣīda*'s concluding image, which calls the sheykh the "*murshid* of the birds [*al-ṭayr*]" further intensifies the majesty of his avian imagery. Although Najm al-Dīn's promotion of anticolonial jihad would seem to contradict sheykh al-Thughūrī's renunciation of the 1877 uprising, this *qaṣīda* attests to the fourth imam's desire to bask in the glory of the revered sheykh.

Najm al-Dīn's engagement with transgressive sanctity is distinct from later Chechen versions, in part through its Islamic inflection and its pre-Soviet conception of community. Like Chechen idioms, however, and especially in his verse, Najm al-Dīn's engagement with insurgency is thoroughly inflected by an expectation of defeat. This expectation is fully on display in one of the last poems Najm al-Dīn wrote before his death, in which he laments:

What can I do, if the enemy was victorious,
if the lion was sacrificed and the pig triumphant?

Their power is great and I am weak,
but they did not conquer me.[135]

Najm al-Dīn wrote these lines in 1925, after he had been captured by the Red Army that was establishing Bolshevik rule in the Caucasus and while he was awaiting execution.

One of Najm al-Dīn's most striking poems was omitted from al-Durgilī's dictionary. This is a *qaṣīda* in honor of Ḥājjī Murād, whose conflicts with Imam Shamil were detailed by al-Qarākhī. According to the Russian Arabist Krachkovskii, the *qaṣīda* was composed when political conditions made it possible "to erect a memorial on Ḥājjī Murād's grave."[136] Krachkovskii introduced Najm al-Dīn's *qaṣīda* to the scholarly world in one of a series of groundbreaking essays on modern Daghestani Arabic literature. Writing in 1948, prior to the rehabilitation of Shamil in Soviet historiography, Krachkovskii could not name the author.[137] Instead of attributing the poem to the still inflammatory name of the fourth imam, Krachkovskii stated that it had been composed simply by "an Avar." The verses construct an eloquent ekphrasis for the fallen *nā'ib*, making of his grave a testimony to his courage:

Here is the grave of a lion—Ḥājjī Murād.
In the field, he responded to everyone who called.
He died, after killing many enemies in battle.
He left behind a blessed memory at all gatherings.
May the rain fill his grave as it envelops the lion's bones.
His loss has dressed the world in grief.
This hero's blows shook his enemies' earth
and deprived the infidels of the taste of sleep.
He never died. He lives in his people's memories.
His glory has remained behind in his country.
Tormented by loneliness, his life passed
to Allah as he fought for his faith.[138]

Having described his Avar predecessor as a lion who died fighting for his faith, Najm al-Dīn later imagined his own life through this same imagery, in the verses cited here, which were composed just prior to his death. Like so many authors within Caucasus literary modernity, Najm al-Dīn was persuaded that captivity could not neutralize the politics—and the permanence—of memory.

Even as he laid claim to Shamil's legacy by styling himself the fourth imam, when he glorified his nemesis Ḥājjī Murād, Najm al-Dīn joined his voice to the subterranean critique of Shamil that permeates the Caucasus literatures of insurgency. Indirectly yet forcefully, he judges the third imam for surrendering to Bariatinskii and for renouncing jihad. Najm al-Dīn's attraction to Ḥājjī Murād, whose legacy traverses multiple Caucasus literatures, reveals the ambiguous legacy of Daghestan's original jihad, even and especially among for those whose political careers were fashioned in the image, and under the tutelage, of the third imam. While some Daghestani authors marshaled the Islamic discourse of *fitna* to critique Chechen transgressive sanctity (and its Daghestani variants), proponents of anticolonial militancy countered this critique by invoking the hopeless heroism of Ḥājjī Murād against that of Shamil. Other than the indirect respect Najm al-Dīn evinces for Shamil in his satire on al-Yakhsāwī, Najm al-Dīn did not in any of his extant writing praise Shamil directly.

Sheikhizm, or Transgressive Sanctity as Parody

As he traveled through Chechnya collecting materials for his novel about Zelimkhan, Dzakho Gatuev also embarked on a second project, concerning the relation between a movement he called *sheikhizm* and the phenomenon of the abrek in the early Soviet Caucasus. This second project never saw the light of day. Shot in 1938 for un-Soviet activities, Gatuev died before he was able to bring it to fruition. All that remains of his research is an undated typescript stored in the Daghestani branch of the Russian Academy of Sciences in Makhachkala.[139] Crisscrossed by the author's steady hand, the manuscript is signed: "Dzakho Gatuev . . . Dormitory of the Institute for the People of the East, Moscow," as if, by identifying his domicile, the author hoped to preserve his text for posterity.

Although Gatuev, an Ossetian writer, was strangely silent about the reasons for his interest in Chechen insurgency, he left behind a rich deposit of interviews, ethnographies, and impressions of Chechen modernity in "Sheykhism in Chechnya," an unpublished essay that I found in a Daghestani archive during my first extended visit to Makhachkala in 2006. One of the most detailed narratives in Gatuev's essay revolves around a figure he calls "Deni sheykh Arsanov." As Gatuev explains, Deni sheykh Arsanov descended from a long lineage of Chechen Sufi saints. Deni's story, which was relayed to Gatuev by the Chechen Djenar Ali Mullah, implausibly merges Soviet realities with traditional Chechen values. "Sheykhism in Chechnya" is Gatuev's possibly fictional paraphrase of the account of Deni's life related to him by Djenar Ali Mullah.[140] The text is incomplete, and its contents raises more questions than answers. Although its purposes and design are far from transparent, it is clear that Gatuev's story complicates the account of transgressive sanctity that has been introduced thus far. In particular, the text's parody of nineteenth-century idealizations of anticolonial violence makes it a fitting work for concluding the examination of Chechen and Daghestani engagements with anticolonial militancy that has consumed this book so far.[141]

Deni was born in 1850 in the village of Alkhan-Yurt to the Ingiloev clan (*taip*). He hated the Cossacks from his earliest days. Deni's father, who served in the tsar's army, was a friend of Prince Bekovich-Cherkasskii, who led the first Russian military expedition into Central Asia.[142] Deni tried to persuade his father, who had won medals and even crosses for his military service, to leave the army that had as its mission the conquest of the Caucasus. While still a child, Deni buried his father's military decorations below the ground. After his father's death, Deni dug up the treasure and divided it among his children.

During the 1877 rebellion, Deni fought alongside ʿAlībek Ḥājjī. After ʿAlībek Ḥājjī's defeat, Deni killed a Cossack. He then deserted to the village of Umakhan-Yurt, where he spent a year and a half working as a blacksmith. In Umakhan-Yurt, Deni formed a secret (*podpolnaia*) organization with the support of which he raided neighboring Cossack villages. From the start of each raid, Deni knew whether or not it would be successful. As a result of this talent, Deni was honored with the title *sheykh*.

Deni then moved to Kizliar (in northern Daghestan, on the Chechen border), where he worked in the fields. Finally, he relocated to Moscow, where he worked as a blacksmith with Daghestanis residing there. Because he was an excellent craftsman, his coworkers grew jealous. One day they invited him to dinner. His boss tried to persuade him not to go, but Deni said that if he did not accept the invitation he would be a coward. So he went to the dinner, knowing that his coworkers intended to poison him. Deni drank the wine that was served him but did not swallow. The liquor slid from his throat to the corners of his lips, at which point it was absorbed into his beard.

Eventually, Deni's boss arranged for him to return to Chechnya. Deni heard of a sheykh named Alikhan Chanti, who resided in Shedi-Yurt and was renowned for his hostility to Russians. Soon after Deni became Alikhan Chanti's *murīd*, his sheykh was arrested for robbing the officer Elumurzaev and punished with exile to Siberia, where he died. After Alikhan's death, this same Elumurzaev was murdered, which naturally gave rise to an investigation. It turned out that Deni had organized that murder as well. Deni was arrested but freed soon after. He then moved to a small village named Maken, where he built a home for himself and a stone bridge for the village. Although it was the height of the Russo-Japanese War, Deni predicted that the monarchy would be overthrown and that the Chechen people would be freed from the tsarist yoke. A revolution was on its way, he promised, a revolution in every country of the world. When these predictions were fulfilled, they enhanced Deni's reputation as a sheykh.

In 1905, Deni purchased a plot of land in Grozny, where he began to build a second house for himself. Other *murīds* soon joined him. Then he built a third home in Gekhi (the town where, perhaps not coincidentally, Vara, the first abrek, had been born a few decades earlier). Deni's house was permanently open to the poor, who received bread anytime they visited. The populace rallied behind him as a result of his service to the community, and he made peace with his enemies. The rich hated him and tried to get him in trouble with the authorities. The poor believed in him and chose him as their leader.

Djenar Ali Mulla then explains that, in 1915, when the Grand Duke Nikolai Nikolaevich was appointed commander (*namestnik*) of the

Caucasus, he was visited by a delegation that included Deni and Djenar Ali Mulla himself.[143] Their purpose was to complain about abuses of power by local officials. At this point, Gatuev launches into a verbatim citation from his informant:

> We traveled to Tiflis [Tbilisi]. The *namestnik* was absent and engaged in a campaign in Erzerum. Every night, the delegation gathered together to discuss what life would be like after the [Russo-Japanese] war. Deni said to the group: "You're worrying in vain about the future, and about your beloved officers. After the war, there won't be any tsar. He'll be destroyed." The delegation laughed. Colonel [*polkovnik*] Aduev and Jamal al-Din responded: "You speak in vain. Say those things to your *murīds*." Then Deni turned to me [Djenar Ali Mulla] and said: "Write: On this day and in this year, Nikolai will be deposed."[144]

After Nikolai was deposed, Deni traveled around Chechnya, informing people of the new future awaiting his people.

Deni's teachings were as unorthodox as his behavior. He was known for saying to his followers: "Rather than wasting money on pilgrimages to Mecca, it's better to invest in building a home. No one is saved by prayers." This Chechen sheykh further violated the teachings of his predecessors by valuing piety over industry: "One should pray only to the extent that [the Prophet] Muhammad advised. It's better to build your home than to waste time in prayers." Most provocatively of all, Deni insisted that "no one becomes a sheykh by sitting in a pit. You can become crazy in this way, but not a sheykh." Djenar Ali Mulla concludes his account of Deni's life in a conspicuously bourgeoisie idiom by affirming that "Deni was a good businessman [*kommersant*]" who built bridges for the villagers "at the bidding of his *murīds*." Although in many respects this story reads like pure entertainment and Gatuev's intent is obscure, his narrative of Deni Arsanov marks an important turning point in the history of anticolonial insurgency. The story signals a moment when war could be narrated as a joke and when jihad could be satirized to the point of absurdity. With "Sheykhism in Chechnya," history was repeating itself, but in the idiom of farce. This is the moment of Soviet mimicry, when a dark and difficult legacy is turned into a pastiche.[145] The reification of the tsarist past is also a feature of transgressive sanctity.

The ethical inversion entailed in transgressive sanctity did not transform Daghestan as thoroughly as it refashioned Chechen culture. Sayings such as "He who thinks about consequences lacks courage [*min tafkar fī al-aʿwāqib al-āmwar lam yashajaʿa*]" feature widely in Daghestani literature and are inscribed on a silver medal that Shamil received for courage in battle, and which he proudly displayed in his Kaluga home (al-Qarākhī, *al-Bāriqat*, 235; ʿAbd al Raḥmān, *Khulāṣat*, 93b).[146] Another banner of Shamil declares, "Cowardice will not save him and boldness will not kill him" (figure 11).

Such slogans reflect a general ethos of sacrifice for the common good and do not treat transgression as the *source* of sanctity. While some

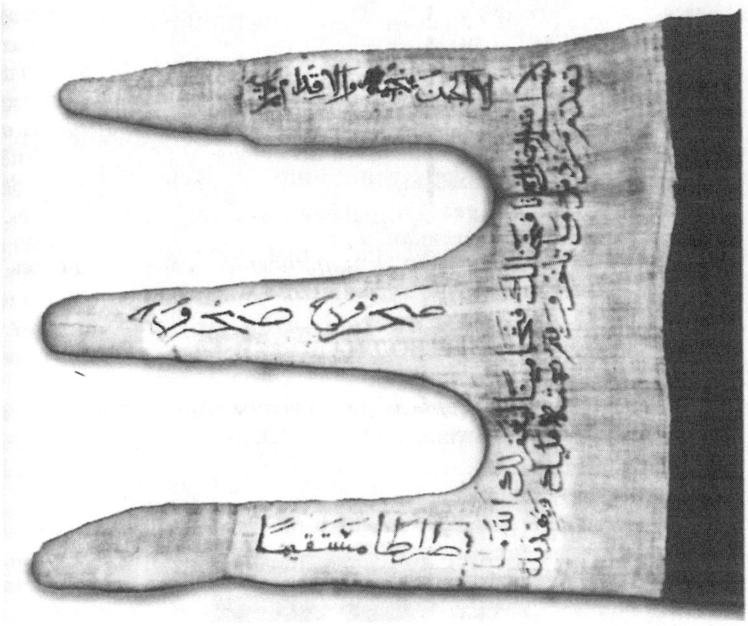

Figure 11. Banner of Imam Shamil. Courtesy of Khadzhi Murad Donogo.

Daghestani writers, including ʿAlī Qāḍī, Muḥammad Ḥājjī, and Najm al-Dīn, articulated an ethos of rebellion for rebellion's sake, others, including al-Qarākhī, al-Ghāzīghumūqī, Ḥasan, and al-Durgilī, criticized those who rebelled against the colonial regime, fraught as such acts were with violent consequences for the entire Daghestani community. Even among authors who were inclined to aestheticize violence, no writer was entirely insensible to the losses entailed in the pursuit of anticolonial militancy. Amid Chechen and other vernacular engagements with anticolonial violence, Gatuev was keenly attuned to its dark side, but he lived in a world of secret purges and public punishments that could conceive no alternative to rule by terror, and that was therefore susceptible to transgressive sanctity's apocalyptic allure.

Had he been born in Daghestan, Deni could not have maintained the precarious balance between criminality and sanctity that he cultivated as a Chechen sheykh. Rich in paradoxes and ironies, Deni's life story could only have unfolded as it did in early Soviet Chechnya. The combination of miracle-working powers and doctrinal heterodoxy is characteristic of Chechen piety, which differentiates it from its Daghestani counterpart. Equally an outlaw and a sheykh, Deni's life story epitomizes the intimacy between transgression and colonial modernity, whereby the transgressor, be he an abrek or another type of outlaw, ceases to be reviled by the community and is elevated into a hero on the basis of his violation of colonial laws. And yet that Gatuev's essay found its final resting place in a Daghestani archive, where it exists in a unique copy, attests to the close links between Daghestani and Chechen literatures, and to the necessity of studying these two sometimes opposed and at other times convergent discourses together.

That, aside from the story of Deni Arsanov, this chapter has been more densely populated by scholars, jurists, and historians than by folk heroes and abreks, as was the case in chapter 1, attests to crucial differences between Chechen and Daghestani idioms of insurgency and to the diversity of the anticolonial idioms that have informed Caucasus literary modernity. Far from being the expression of an unmediated collective will, or of a feudal peasantry, rebellion in Daghestan was regulated by the legal and textual authority of *fiqh* and the political authority of the imamate, even after Shamil's surrender. Hence the quasi-magical status accorded to the title *imam*, even after the imamate had ceased to exist as a viable political form. While examining the role of miracles in shaping Daghestani historiography, my discussion has oscillated between elite critiques of violence and populist conceptions of sanctity. Whereas idioms of resistance were popularized in the Chechen imagination and widely disseminated across genres and media, the richest articulation of the Daghestani relation to anticolonial insurgency is its texts, which traverse the disciplines of historiography, poetry, and jurisprudence.

In his classic study of the discourse of anticolonial jihad as it developed among the Daghestani *ʿulamāʾ*, Michael Kemper argues that "the key to the imamate's long success" lay in Shamil's deft balancing act between Sufi sheykhs, such as Jamāl al-Dīn, who wielded authority among the Daghestani populace, and his project of constructing a *sharīʿa* that would bind his followers legally to one another, in a new legal and social order.[147] As Shamil set about institutionalizing this equilibrium between political and spiritual authority in his jihad state, he inevitably came into conflict with many *nāʾibs* who felt they knew how to organize the imamate better than did their nominal leader, whose authority they contested in substantive ways. Ḥājjī Murād was one such figure. Ḥājjī Tashaw was another.

Building on Kemper's pioneering thesis that the key to Shamil's sovereignty was the relation the imam instantiated between Islamic law and Sufi piety, this book considers the forms of power that arose within the vacuum of legal authority that was inaugurated in the northeastern Caucasus with Shamil's surrender, with particular attention to their refraction in literature. By way of supplementing Kemper's conception of the imamate as based on an equilibrium between *sharīʿa* and Sufi networks, I have proposed transgressive sanctity as a heuristic tool to describe the circulations of power that were reflected in the Caucasus literatures of insurgency, when this equilibrium was rendered defunct by Shamil's surrender.

Kemper notes that the Sufism that Shamil endeavored to bring under his fold, and which he associated with Naqshbandī sheykhs such as Jamāl al-Dīn, incorporated "subjective experiences [*Erlebnissen*], emotions, and the encounter with the sacred [*Erfahrung von Heiligkeit*]."[148] Once Shamil exited the scene of political power in the Caucasus, new forms of sanctity came to be expressed, and contested, in Daghestani literature. These new sanctities privileged unmediated encounters with the sacred, and contributed directly to the formation of the anticolonial abrek, as well as to his aestheticization. Having viewed the aestheticization of violence amid its progressive divergence from historical actuality, it is now possible to understand how transgressive sanctity acquired authority following the decay of local structures of power and their replacement by colonial governmentality.

Kemper has demonstrated that the key to the success of the imamate was the balance Shamil maintained between law, a political form compelling obedience, and the sacred, an affective force inspiring worship. Political sovereignty, on this account, was underwritten by Shamil's highly strategic merger of legal and pietistic religious norms. Transgressive sanctity was stimulated by the dissolution of the Shamilian equilibrium. To become legitimate, transgressive sanctity had to oppose itself to the law that aimed to cancel its existence. It could do so successfully only in a political context wherein the law had relinquished its authority and was coming to be replaced by new legal norms. Compared to earlier legal systems, these new norms were less grounded in local idioms of governance and bore the traces of external coercion. This situation in the postconquest Caucasus accounts in part for Chechnya's having become a breeding grounds for the abrek and for Daghestan's having served as the site from which the 1877 anticolonial rebellion was launched.

Given my interests in the political aesthetics of literary form, I have examined these complex modulations in the foundations of political sovereignty in the northeastern Caucasus through textual, and, especially poetic archives. I have conducted this investigation in the belief that the literary can at times anticipate the historical, as well as place the historical in a new perspective. This possibility is activated in transgressive sanctity, which mediates between historical events and processes and their aesthetic re-creation. More than the political discourse of the jihad state so astutely analyzed by Kemper, transgressive sanctity is a product of the imagination. Articulated most forcefully in literature, transgressive sanctity acquires its fullest reality in the imaginations of authors and their readers. That resistance continues to be understood as an event in time and space rather than as an act of the imagination that transcends time-space barriers, accounts for the relative neglect of transgressive sanctity in the global study of anticolonial insurgency.

When scholars unilaterally privilege the historical over the literary, as they typically have done in the case of war-torn regions such as the Caucasus, then we are all, collectively, compelled to endlessly narrate, as well as to naturalize, the narratives generated by the victors, which, in the words of Walter Benjamin, "owe their existence [*sein Dasein*] to the anonymous labor of their contemporaries."[149] These documents of culture, Benjamin famously adds, are also documents of barbarism (696). Brushing against the grain of the historical record, transgressive sanctity is an ideology promulgated by those who are compelled to express their politics through their aesthetics and their aesthetics through their politics. Like Benjamin's historical materialism, transgressive sanctity contests the structural barbarism, and the historical determinism, that is all too frequently inscribed into the colonial encounter. Contesting the secularist reductionism that is entailed in certain forms of modern historiography, my account of anticolonial insurgency argues that political aspirations grounded in the imagination are not lacking in value by virtue of their aesthetic content.

Whereas Shamil's imamate has hitherto been studied through the historical method, transgressive sanctity inculcates an approach attentive to literary form. As noted in the introduction, literary anthropology counters the customary privileging of event-based history and refuses to naturalize the stories of the victors. This method strategically deploys texts that displace received histories by cultivating defeat. These texts, by Ḥasan, al-Ghāzīghumūqī, Najm al-Dīn, and others, variously articulate loss—of one's homeland, one's family, and one's own self. Using the vantage point of mourning to reflect on Daghestan's historical predicament, they articulate their own distinctive critiques of violence.

By outlining the alternatives to normative historical narratives that have been cultivated by the literatures of anticolonial insurgency, literary anthropology becomes entailed within a global postcolonial project. Within this global framework, it is necessary to reconceive postcoloniality for a post-Soviet modernity that, by virtue of its geography, will likely pertain to the Russian ecumene for many centuries to come. Colonialism in the Caucasus cannot be conceived of as the domination of faraway lands and distinct peoples, for Russia is contiguous with the territories it has dominated. A postcolonial aesthetics of Caucasus cultures will need to factor in this cartographic distinction. It will also need to recognize the historical impossibility, within this literary modernity, of severing the colonial from the colonized. Such severance has more salience for contexts that conform more precisely to the normative model of imperial governance from afar.

Having studied the interface of Chechen transgressive sanctity and Daghestani *fiqh* in the context of colonial modernity, the following chapter turns to Georgian, the third literature that grounds this book's excavation of the poetics and politics of anticolonial insurgency, and the literature that most radically aestheticizes transgressive sanctity for an avant-garde literary modernity. Positioned at equal distances from Chechen and Daghestani literatures, Georgian intellectuals had ample space to reflect on what made them both similar to and different from their Muslim counterparts to the north.

Transgressive sanctity entered literary history when Shamil ceased to be relevant to northeastern Caucasus politics. Notwithstanding the long shadow he casts over the history of insurgency in the Caucasus, transgressive sanctity highlights the progressive displacement of Imam Shamil's jihad by other forms of resistance in Chechen and Daghestani literatures. The Georgian case suggests a relation to Shamil's legacy even further alienated from history and even more grounded in the literary imagination. By way of better delineating the differences between northern and southern literary engagements with anticolonial violence in the Caucasus, the following chapter documents Georgian attempts to combine the radically distinctive insurgencies of Imam Shamil and Ḥājjī Murād into a unified anticolonial poetics. I then explore in detail how one Georgian Soviet poet, Titsian Tabidze, made such appropriations the crowning achievement of his literary career and how he paid for his creative interventions with his life. As the final installment in this study of transgressive sanctity in the colonial and Soviet-era Caucasus, chapter 3 chronicles transgressive sanctity's literary apotheosis while paving the way for the final chapter's documentation of how transgressive sanctity inflected the perception and performance of violent acts that originated in sources other than the literary artifact.

T·H·R·E·E

The Georgian Poetics of Insurgency

Redeeming Treachery

During most of Georgian literary history, the inhabitants of Daghestan were categorized into a single quasi-ethnic group—known as *leki* (ლეკი)—while the inhabitants of Chechnya and Ingushetia, as well as Pankisi and Tusheti, both on Georgian territory, were referred to by the term *vainaxi* (ვაინახი, meaning "we people" in Chechen and Ingush).[1] Distinctions were rarely more nuanced than this. While the relatively quiescent *vainaxi* were regarded as closely related to mountaineer Georgians, *leki* were tainted by association with the raids that bedeviled Georgia from the sixteenth to the nineteenth centuries, which are collectively referred to in Georgian history as *lekianoba*.[2] When the narrative poems of Vazha Pshavela (1861–1915), often regarded as Georgia's greatest modern poet, touch on relations between Georgian mountaineers and their Muslim counterparts to the north, they invariably compare Georgians to Chechen-Ingush *vainaxi*, rather than to Daghestani *leki*.[3] *Vainaxi* were, at least potentially, friends; *leki* were enemies. The appearance of *daghestani* as an ethnic denominator in Georgian literature is tied to Georgian Romantics such as Nikoloz Baratashvili (1817–1844) who were deeply immersed in European, and especially Russian, aesthetic canons.[4]

Amid this complex web of cross-cultural misunderstandings, this chapter examines the trajectory of anticolonial insurgency in

Georgian literary history. Composed at a relative distance from the epicenter of conflict, the Georgian literature of insurgency aestheticizes the Daghestani-Chechen discourse of *ghazawāt* by way of intensifying the relation between politics and literature. Unsurprisingly, Georgian accounts of *ghazawāt* are shaped by Georgian historical experience, and there is a marked tendency within Georgian literature to simplify, and even to obliterate, differences among different Daghestani peoples. Whereas Chechen insurgents disowned Shamil for surrendering to the tsar, Georgian poets and critics were less likely to distinguish Daghestani efforts to manage colonial incursions from the Chechen sanctification of anticolonial rebellion. A brief overview of Shamil's legacy within Georgian cultural memory will better enable us to track the Georgian poetic refashioning of his insurgency.

Shamil and Georgian Insurgency

When Shamil entered Georgian literary history, it was in a guise somewhat different from his Daghestani persona. The imam's Avar origins were replaced by a legend that he was the son of the Georgian prince Aleksandre Batonishvili (1770–1830), the illegitimate son of the Georgian king Irakli II (r. 1744–1798), who was sheltered by Daghestani mountaineers for many years after leading a rebellion from Kaxetia (eastern Georgia) against the tsar in 1812.[5] After he left Daghestan, Batonishvili mysteriously disappeared into Iran, and the circumstances of his death remain unknown to this day.[6] It is further believed that Batonishvili cooperated with Shamil in leading more insurrections against Russian rule while he was in exile in Daghestan.

The 1812 rebellion inspired a rich literature, mostly in prose, centered on Shamil's exact contemporary, the Georgian abrek (*abragi*) Arsena Odzelashvili (1797–1842). The most important poet to incorporate the legendary genealogy linking the Avar warrior to the Georgian prince into his verse was however Titsian Tabidze (1895–1937).[7] In "Poem, a Mongol King" (1926), composed in the middle of his brief career, Titsian invoked Shamil together with Batonishvili, thereby linking Georgian and Daghestani insurgencies. "Shamil surrounds me when I remember," the poet declares while constructing an urban panorama that strategically incorporates the Caucasus mountains into its background:

> სულ რაღაც ათი გავიდა წელი,
> სულ რამდენჯერმე მობრუნდა მთვარე
> რაც დასტიროდა მტკვარს ალექსანდრე
> და მთებს შამილის სული მშფოთვარე.
>
> ("poema—chaghatar," 3:131)[8]
>
> Ten years have passed. Yet the moon
> still turned as it did when Aleksandre
> cried on the banks of the Mtkvari River,
> when Shamil's soul swept through these mountains.

Even in this relatively early poem, Titsian connects the anticolonial insurgencies led by Shamil and Aleksandre Batonishvili to poetic labor. He asks rhetorically:

> რა შეედრება პოეტის სახელს?
> გმირის სახელი უფრო მეტია,
> მიყვარს ქართული მიწა მართალი
> რაც ვაჟკაცებით მინახვეტია . . .
>
> ("poema—chaghatar," 3:132)
>
> To what can the poet's name be compared?
> Even more than the hero's glory
> I love my true Georgian earth,
> hallowed by these brave young warriors.

The "brave young warriors [*vazhkatsebi*]" are of course Georgians who have died in a Georgian version of jihad. The incipient Georgian-Daghestani alliance is fully fleshed out in the closing lines, which connect the figure of the *murīd* (მჲრიდი) with the most famous Georgian insurgent, Aleksandre Batonishvili:

ამ საშინელ და უიღბლო ღამეს
მე მრჩება მხოლოდ ერთი ანდერძი:
რომ არ ამოშრეს ხალხში ნაღველი
ბატონიშვილის ალექსანდრესი.
და როგორც ერთი ურჩი მჲურიდი,
ვფიცავ საყვარელ ვაჟკაცთა წვერებს,
შამილის ფაფარს და თეთრ ჭაღარას,
ალექსანდრეს წვერს დროშათ ნაკერებს,
რომ მე დავტოვებ პოეტის სახელს,
თუ ვაჟკაცობას შენთვის ვერ ვამხელ . . .

("poema—chaghatar," 3:132)

On this terrifying and unlucky night
only one wish remains to me:
That Batonishvili's sadness
won't vanish with the *murīds.*
I swear by my warrior's fading beard,
By Shamil's mane and grey hair
and Aleksandre's beard, tied to the banner:
If I cannot speak to you these words of bravery,
I will cast aside my poet's name.

In addition to its thematic originality, Titsian's spelling of *murīd* (მჲურიდი) is noteworthy. The second letter of this transliteration (ჲ) corresponds to the long *i* in the Old Georgian alphabet and has no equivalent in modern Georgian. Titsian's archaic lexicon resonates against his modernist free verse form while also attesting to the poet's wish to incorporate Daghestani insurgency into Georgia's cultural heritage. Further compounding this effect is the poet's deployment of an originally Arabic word in the Georgian script. While Titsian's contemporaries were actively modernizing the Georgian language, Titsian was occupied, at least in this poem, with archaizing his native tongue so as to enable it to accommodate the Daghestani experience of war. (This linguistic nuance further makes it appropriate to italicize *murīd* when rendering Titsian's Georgian into English, so as to underscore its foreignness in the Georgian original.)

Six years later, the poet used the word *muridi* again in "The Land Slides" (1932). Titsian opened this poem, which elaborates a series of increasingly bold comparisons, by comparing streaks of lightning (*elva*) to rays emanating from Shamil's white beard (*tetri papari*). This beard features in many images of Shamil, particularly in his old age and during his Russian exile (see, for example, figure 12).

In "The Land Slides," Titsian asserts his identity as a living *murīd*, with an emphasis on "living" (*cocxali*). He then invokes the idiom of holy war in an idiom typical for a writer from the Caucasus, through *ghazawāt* rather than jihad:

ვარ დაფრენილი ორბისგან გნოლი
და არ იკარებს გული სალავათს,
ხევსურის ჯაჭვის ნაგლეჯი რგოლი—
ერთი ვაცხადებ მარტო ჰაზავატს.

("mecqeri mecqers," 3:78)

I, the partridge, escaped the vulture's nest,
And now I won't accept your prayers.
I, piece of a Khevsur's armor,
Declaim my lonely *ghazawāt*.

The final line in this stanza reproduces the same turning point within the Georgian aesthetics of transgressive sanctity that was encountered in connection with Chechen literature in chapter 1. Unlike the *nā'ibs* of an earlier era, the abrek acts alone. His transgressive sanctity is determined in part by his solitary status. The abrek violates legal norms that are coercively imposed by a powerful majority on a less powerful minority. In the process of such violations, he inaugurates a new, and uniquely modern, relation between violence and sanctity. Titsian's use of *ghazawāt* as a generator of poetry reveals the relation between aesthetics and politics within his literary modernism.[9] In this poem, Titsian figures his poetic persona through an analogy to the abrek embarked on

Figure 12. Imam Shamil in old age, in exile in Russia. Courtesy of Khadzhi Murad Donogo.

ghazawāt. (While Titsian uses only the term *muridi*, his resignification brings it into alignment with the abrek.) The poet's lonely vocation is analogous to the loneliness of the abrek, who fights for a cause doomed to defeat.

In the next stanza, the poet compares his body to a Lezgi cloak (*lekis nabadi*) trampled by the feet, presumably, of tsarist soldiers. He gives voice to his desire to become one of these mountaineers, by merging his poetics of insurgency with their battle-tested courage:

ვარ გათელილი ლეკის ნაბადი,
ყველა სახსარი მაქვს დალეწილი,
მაგრამ ვაჟკაცმა მხოლოდ გაბედე
და მეც ვაჟკაცის დამიდე წილი.

("metsqeri metsqers," 3:78)

I am the Lezgis' trampled cloak.
My joints have been bruised.
Only you dared to be brave.
I too want courage as my fate.

As will soon be seen, Titsian mobilized these insurgent idioms even more ambitiously in the final years of his life. Poems such as "Poem, a Mongol King" and "Land Slides" are early installments of a lifelong vision that was to culminate in "Gunib," a poem that stages a dialogue between the poet and his predecessors at Gunib, the site of Imam Shamil's surrender to the tsarist army (the Daghestani "Ghunib" is henceforth referred to as "Gunib," in keeping with Georgian and Russian spelling). As a prelude to examining this late period in Titsian's poetics, it is worth pausing over the figure who, alongside Shamil, was situated at the other end of the Georgian engagement with Daghestani insurgency. The historical Ḥājjī Murād was encountered in the preceding chapter in connection with his critique of Imam Shamil. Now it is time to consider Ḥājjī Murād's place in literature, and specifically in the Georgian and Russian literature of insurgency.

The Georgian *Haji-Muradi*

While Shamil's every word and movement have been studied meticulously, poets and prose writers have drawn from the full arsenals of their imaginations to craft a figure who belongs as much to myth as to history. Rather than representing a story of successful assimilation between Christianity and Islam, and Russia and the Caucasus, for many of the works considered in this book Shamil's story exemplifies an insurgent's betrayal of his people for the sake of self-preservation. This archetypal narrative of the Russian encounter in the Caucasus epitomizes the victory of the side with the largest military, but with the least integrity, and confirms the impotence of spiritual greatness when faced with military might. For Tolstoy, Shamil's *nāʾib* Ḥājjī Murād differed from his leader by epitomizing a courage that contrasted with Shamil's accommodation to defeat.[10]

As the most important literary modernist to reflect on Georgia's entanglement in colonial conquest, Titsian's amalgamation of the legacies of Shamil, Ḥājjī Murād, and other Daghestani insurgents into a rhetoric of anticolonial insurgency dominates this chapter. Titsian translated Tolstoy's novella about Ḥājjī Murād during the summer of 1929, shortly before composing his greatest poem on the conquest of the Caucasus (examined in detail later in this chapter), "Gunib."[11] In addition to his poetry and translations, Titsian composed an essay on the occasion of Tolstoy's jubilee, titled "Tolstoy's Days" (1928).[12] Although it was published after "Gunib," Titsian's account of his travels in his essay suggests that the two works were composed simultaneously. The links among "Gunib," "Tolstoy's Days," and the lost Georgian translation of *Hadji Murat* reveal Titsian's debt to the Russian anticolonial imagination while also making evident the new inflections the Georgian poet infused into his predecessor's anticolonial critique. In terms of this book's thesis, transgressive sanctity enabled the poet to redeem what Titsian termed his fellow Georgians' treachery (*ghalati*). Although Tolstoy's sympathetic portrayal of Chechens and other Caucasus mountaineers has been narrated many times before, a brief engagement with Tolstoy's Caucasus narratives will help to clarify their influence on subsequent

Georgian literature while also adding one more dimension to this book's plurilingual genealogy of the literatures of anticolonial insurgency.

Tolstoy's and Titsian's empathetic engagements with the 1859 defeat helped to constitute a literary sensibility grounded in the same aesthetics of transgressive sanctity that founded modern Chechen literature. These writers' deep knowledge of the Caucasus compelled them to recognize that the colonial legal regime conflicted with the legal codes that had structured mountaineer societies for centuries. Indigenous rulers who were at first favorably disposed toward Russian rule soon discovered that sovereignty on colonial terms was "more restrictive than the traditional patterns of dominance in the region" and that "rulers who openly opposed the Russians were ousted" while "even those who agreed to Russian terms lost most of their power and their territories were eventually annexed."[13] The clash was not of cultures but rather of legal systems that could not accommodate the existence of other, conflicting codes. In the Caucasus, as elsewhere in the legally hybrid Islamic world, "the superiority of one body of laws was affirmed at the expense of the other."[14]

Like many of Titsian's masterpieces and also like the works of Ḥasan al-Alqadārī that circulated primarily in manuscript form, Tolstoy's *Hadji Murat* was never published during the author's lifetime. Ever since its publication two years following the author's death, Tolstoy's novella has served as the primary channel through which the Avar *nā'ib* became known to world literature. Tolstoy's text is also important for its critical portrayal of Shamil, and for its suggestion of future directions in the Chechen ideology of transgressive sanctity. Beyond its importance for the world it reflects, the text is important for its impact. More than any other Russian text, Tolstoy's novella informs vernacular Caucasus narratives of anticolonial insurgency. Although much studied as a landmark intervention in Russian literature, the reception history of Tolstoy's novella in the vernacular literatures of the Caucasus remains wholly unassayed, as does the biography of the historical Ḥājjī Murād.[15] Just as the historical figure deserves closer scrutiny, particularly with respect to indigenous Caucasus sources, so has Tolstoy's text acquired an afterlife its author could hardly have foreseen.

When placed in dialogue with other texts in the literatures of anticolonial insurgency, this textual afterlife makes it possible to rewrite the history of the colonial encounter through literary sources. Both Tolstoy's own deep engagement with Caucasus cultures, particularly with the Chechens he came to know during his military service in the 1850s, and the influence his work has had on subsequent literary production in the region, could substantially revise the master narrative of colonial conquest.[16] Tolstoy's legacy is so prized by Chechens today that over the course of two Russo-Chechen wars, the Tolstoy Museum in Starogladkovskaia, a village on the Chechen-Cossack border where the author lived from 1851 to 1854, remains fully intact despite many years of war. In 2003, this museum hosted a conference that explored the relation between Kunta Ḥājjī and Tolstoyan pacifism.[17] While the monument to Shamil on the border between Azerbaijan and Daghestan (discussed in the epilogue) was destroyed by Azerbaijani officials, and a memorial to the 1944 deportation was destroyed during the Russian bombing of Grozny, Starogladkovskaia's monument to Tolstoy survived both wars unscathed.

Tolstoy used his youthful encounters with local Chechens while serving in the tsar's army to enrich his literary representations of colonial atrocity through Chechen eyes.[18] As noted by Paul Friedrich, the uses Tolstoy made of his ethnographic experiences in works such as *Hadji Murat* "raise in acute form the issue of just where the boundary line between ethnography and literature lies."[19] The novella's salience to subsequent Georgian and Chechen literatures owes much to a passage that Titsian later cited in his essay on Tolstoy's jubilee. "No one said anything about hating the Russians," writes Tolstoy after narrating a brutal raid by Russian soldiers on a village in the mountains near Vedeno in southeastern Chechnya, a well-known center of anticolonial resistance:

> The feeling that all Chechens, from the youngest to the eldest, experienced, was stronger than hate. . . . So intense was their repulsion, disgust, and incomprehension when confronted with the cruelty of these Russian creatures, that the desire to destroy them as they would destroy a rat, a poisonous spider, or a wolf was simply a matter of self-preservation [*samosokhranenie*].[20]

Engaging with the existential response to an unjust massacre, Tolstoy uses this graphic imagery to cast doubt on the legitimacy of colonial rule. In addition to attracting the attention of the most important Georgian poets to pick up Tolstoy's mantle, this incendiary passage was the most heavily censored among the chapters of *Hadji Murat* when the novella was finally published posthumously in 1912.[21] The year of *Hadji Murat*'s publication coincided with that of Ḥasan's *Jirāb* and preceded that of his *Dīwān* by one year. (Ḥasan and Tolstoy also died in the same year, 1910, when the Chechen writer Magomed Mamakaev was born.)

Although Titsian's translation of *Hadji Murat* is no longer extant, fragments have remained through the poet's own citations from his Georgian version in his essay on Tolstoy. Titsian prefaces his self-citation with the comment, "I don't think that any other writer has such a deadly [*momakvdinebli*] description of tsarist politics [*mepis politika*] as does Tolstoy in *Hadji Murat*" (3:12). Titsian then proceeds to cite from his own unpublished translation:

> შადრევანი წაიბილწათ, ალბატ საგანგებოდ, წყალის ამოღება ჭიდან არ შეიძლებოდა, წაიბილწათ მეჩეთი და მოლა მუტალიმებით მიდგომოდნენ გასაწმენდად. გრძნობა, რომელსაც განიცდიდა ყველა ჩეჩენი დიდიდან პატარამდე სიკვდელზე ძლიერი იყო.
>
> The fountains were desecrated, probably intentionally, and water could no longer flow from the well. The mosque has also been desecrated, and the mullah and his assistants were busy setting it back in order. The feeling that every Chechen experienced, from the elderly to the young, was more powerful than death.

Titsian follows Tolstoy's original closely, with the exception of the concluding sentence. Whereas Tolstoy delineates the repulsion and disgust (*otvrashchenie i gadlivost'*) that Chechens felt for the soldiers who had destroyed their village as self-preservation (*samosokhranenie*), Titsian describes this feeling (*grdznoba*) as stronger than death (*dzlieri sikvdilze*). He connects Chechens' reaction not with self-preservation, but with its precise inverse. A sense of grief remains present in the life of a community long after those who first experienced it have died. Tolstoy's *samosokhranenie* refers to the lives of a specific set of individuals whose village was destroyed; Titsian's *grdznoba* implies an encounter of greater duration and intimacy.

Given that "Tolstoy's Days" lays the groundwork for Titsian's poetics of insurgency, it is worth pausing over the Georgian poet's skillful transmutation of Tolstoy's prose into a style all his own. Titsian's essay is suffused with poetic citations, from the Georgian poets Vazha Pshavela (9) and Rustaveli (29) to the Russian poets Pushkin (9) and Esenin (7). Although he is writing prose, Titsian does not hesitate to intersperse his prose with sentence fragments that read like verse. For example, Titsian breaks the prosaic flow of his syntax in one paragraph by exclaiming over the rivers he has traversed, in an intonation that could have been taken from one of his poems: "This Tergi [Terek], this Qurban, this Don" (3:11).

Decades earlier, in another incendiary passage that was deleted by the censor from his short story "The Raid" (1853), Tolstoy contrasted the mountaineer who has lost everything to war to a Russian officer who, having risen high in the ranks through his corruption, is a coward in battle. While the forsaken mountaineer is ready to "tear off his tattered jacket, drop his gun, and draw his sheepskin cap [*papakha*] over his eyes while singing his death song [*predsmertnaia pesnia*]," the Russian officer rushes into battle "singing French songs."[22] Whereas the Russian officer dramatizes his encounter with war through European fashions, the mountaineer, who is more courageous because he has lost everything and has nothing more to lose, cannot mask his corrupt soul in the mendacity of language.

After the raid on Vedeno, *Hadji Murat*'s narrative focus briefly shifts away from the Chechens to a young, dim-witted, but otherwise innocuous soldier named Butler, who professes to be deeply moved by "the poetry of war" (alternately referred to as *voennaia* and *voinstvennaia poeziia*). The sequence is revealing: the Chechens' boundless contempt for their Russian antagonists leads as if by the sheer logic of colonial violence to Butler's entry into the text. Decades earlier in "The Raid," Tolstoy had mocked Russian officers who sought to demonstrate their courage through "vulgar [*poshlii*], pretentious phrases that pretended to imitate antiquated French chivalry."[23] In *Hadji Murat*, Tolstoy carefully tabulated the collateral damage inflicted by these officers' pretensions to bravery.

Although Butler participated personally in the Vedeno raid, the young soldier is utterly oblivious to the suffering he has caused. "Butler gazed at the mountains," eulogizes Tolstoy with deep irony, "breathed in deeply, and rejoiced that he was alive, precisely that he was alive [*zhivyot imenno on*], in this beautiful world" (99). The parenthetically ironic "*he* was alive" lays bare the author's agenda: The Russian officer's joy stems less from the innocuous joy of living than from a toxic propensity to ignore the suffering his presence inflicts on his Muslim neighbors. That Butler's pleasure in his own virility immediately follows the gratuitous annihilation of innocent Chechen lives demonstrates that the real source of the soldier's joy is less life itself than the gratification of his ego. With respect to his obliviousness to his surroundings and to his deracination, Butler recalls the soldiers of Mamakaev's and Qazbegi's narratives encountered in chapter 1. At the same time, in his depiction of Butler, Tolstoy ironizes his own early romantic attraction to the "poetry of war" that is reflected in his early writings, including in his first novel, *The Cossacks* (1863).

Many years before he conceived *Hadji Murat*, while still serving in the Caucasus, Tolstoy confided in his diary sentiments as naive as those he later attributed to Butler, although Tolstoy's phrasing was more sophisticated. "I have begun to love the Caucasus," wrote the young Tolstoy, "even fatally, with powerful love. That wild region [*dikii krai*] where the two most contradictory things are strangely and poetically united—war and freedom—is breathtaking."[24] The young Tolstoy's vision of an ethos specific to the Caucasus that merges violence with freedom is shared by the protagonist of Tolstoy's first novel. This work introduces us to the world-weary Olenin, who arrives in the Caucasus from Moscow. Although Olenin's prejudice against the mountaineers is evident from the beginning, his character evolves as his contact with the Caucasus deepens, and the stereotypes that had originally blunted his perception are replaced by direct contact with the region. Until he encounters the Caucasus, Olenin regards mountains as a taste not worth cultivating. His attitude changes radically when he sees the mountains looming twenty paces away from him and is awed by the "pure white gigantic masses with delicate contours, the miraculous outlines of their peaks gleaming sharply against the far-off sky" (*Kazaki*, 13). Olenin's encounter with the mountains presages *Hadji Murat*'s alpine topography, the major difference in the latter work being that the mountains' sublimity is coupled with the author's recognition of their inhabitants' suffering.

Butler's toxic oblivion is laid bare more through irony than with the conscripts who populate Mamakaev and Qazbegi's texts, wherein the soldiers' ignorance is contrasted with the mountaineers' sense of moral purpose. *Hadji Murat* was one of the first Russian texts to foreground the Chechen encounter with colonial violence and to explore how that violence generates new hostilities. As with many of the texts discussed in this book, Tolstoy's identification with the Chechen perspective required the use of his imagination, but this does not dilute its historical implications. Formally, the text performed an ethno-exegesis on its native culture by subjecting the soldier's naive delight in the poetry of war to anthropological critique. Tolstoy offers less authorial judgment and more ethical ambiguity than either Qazbegi or Mamakaev, not to mention Gatuev. We are told only that Butler is happy to be alive and given to understand that his happiness depends on his ability to block out the suffering he inflicts on others. So long as Butler's oblivion dominates the scene, the purely selfish pleasure of being alive functions as a self-explanatory narratological device.

The reader does not share in Butler's irresponsible joy, however, for it is made clear that the soldier's pleasure comes with a heavy price: one man's happiness is purchased through an entire community's near annihilation. By juxtaposing the colonizer's oblivious delight to the grief of those targeted for destruction, Tolstoy explicates the moral calculus entailed in colonial governmentality, whereby an administrative class that rules through coercion prospers from the disempowerment of its colonial subjects. Tolstoy further enables us to perceive how this unrest is generated by a colonial legal system that, in contradistinction both to *sharīʿa* and indigenous law (*ʿādāt*), emphasizes power over justice, and maintains its authority through a Weberian monopoly on violence. Inasmuch as transgressive sanctity is generated by the imposition of a colonial legal system onto a precolonial social order, it is also irrevocably a product of colonial modernity and must be critiqued in these terms.

Grounded in injustice from its inception, the uneven distribution of goods that is a result of the colonial dispensation is sustained by the structural dependency of the colonizer's pleasure on the subjugation of colonial subjects. It is not only Chechens and Daghestanis who suffer from the moral calculus entailed in imperial governance. At least as much attention is devoted in *Hadji Murat* to the sufferings of impoverished Russians, most poignantly to the Russian soldier Pyotr Avdeev, whose death is relayed in a deadpan register that mocks the crude rhetoric of official pronouncements:

> Two companies of the Kura Regiment advanced from the fort on a wood-felling expedition. At midday a considerable number of mountaineers suddenly attacked the wood-fellers. The sharpshooters began to retreat, but the second company charged with the bayonet and overcame the mountaineers. In this affair two privates were slightly wounded and one killed. The mountaineers lost about a hundred men killed and wounded. (54)

Such is the death of the innocents, rendered in the language of colonial governmentality. This brief, staccato announcement of Avdeev's death demonstrates how the colonial glorification of violence trumps ethical respect for human life. Although it constitutes a major tragedy within Tolstoy's narrative, Avdeev's death is a mere footnote in the annals of imperial historiography. (This difference in scale is one aspect of literature's contribution to the study of anticolonial insurgency.) Tolstoy anticolonial critique also inspired Titsian Tabidze, forty years later, to flesh out in verse the formal contradictions between power and legitimacy, politics and ethics, and the transgressive aesthetic and colonial governance, that his Russian predecessor rendered so powerfully in prose.

Titsian's Poetics of Anticolonial Insurgency

As a poet who came of age during an era shaped by political horizons radically different from those faced by Tolstoy, Titsian wrote under the twin shadow of Soviet anti-imperial rhetoric and the Soviet construction of Shamil's historical legacy. The empire into which he had been born had collapsed, temporarily. A rhetorical brotherhood of peoples had replaced the trope of an Orthodox Christian Russia acting as savior to a Georgian nation besieged on all sides by Muslim enemies. Out of the new political alignments that arose from transgressive sanctity's recalibration of legal norms, a new set of aesthetic possibilities was generated. "Gunib"—a text that was excised from Caucasus literary history even more thoroughly than *Hadji Murat*'s critique of colonialism from a Chechen optic—is one major result of these new configurations. For the first time in Georgian literature, Titsian shifted into poetry a discourse of transgressive sanctity that had primarily transpired in prose.

In 1929, soon after returning from a pan-Soviet celebration of Tolstoy's anniversary in his ancestral home of Yasnaya Polyana in Central Russia, Titsian embarked on the first translation of *Hadji Murat* into Georgian.[25] Titsian recollected his translational endeavors in two different essays, "Lev Tolstoy and Georgia," extant only in Russian, and "Tolstoy's Days," versions of which are extant in both Russian and Georgian. The lengthier version of "Tolstoy's Days" is in Georgian, and the essay appears to have been first composed in that language. In the first of these essays, "Lev Tolstoy and Georgia," Titsian reports being possessed by "an inexplicable feeling of delight" while engaged in translating Tolstoy's text.[26] "In studying *Hadji Murat*," Titsian continues, "you become persuaded of the enchanted magic of [literary] language, and [come to believe] in the possibility of achieving anything on earth."[27] In the Georgian essay, Titsian's recollection of translating Tolstoy's book is more ambivalent. The summer after he first encountered the text, Titsian states that he undertook its translation immediately. "Every day," he recalls, "my work merged with the biblical Jacob wrestling with the Lord. Unsurprisingly, this battle culminated in my defeat."[28] The poet's allegory of his tortured relation to Tolstoy's text and of its significance for his understanding of colonialism offers the clearest explanation available concerning why his Georgian translation of Tolstoy's text never saw the light of day.

Calling *Hadji Murat* "a rare document" in the history of the confrontation between "the politics of violence and 'barbarian culture'"—while leaving ambiguous who the barbarians were—Titsian maintained that "rarely in world literature does one find works that compare with this text's power of poetic expression or intellectual honesty."[29] As he constructs an anticolonial literary canon, Titsian identifies the Georgian writer Aleksandre Qazbegi, whose "Eliso" was cited in chapter 1, as the closest Georgian counterpart to Tolstoy's anticolonial prosaics, and who also did the most, among Georgian writers, to celebrate Shamil's legacy. (Like other Georgian writers, Titsian does not acknowledge the ambivalence toward Shamil's legacy that animates Chechen and other northern Caucasus literatures of insurgency, and that Tolstoy incorporates into his *Hadji Murat.*)

In the context of praising Tolstoy, Titsian adds that, like his Russian counterpart, Qazbegi is "truly a progressive novelist."[30] A few years after affirming Qazbegi's aesthetic and political achievements in this essay, Titsian wrote to his wife, Nina, that he was engaged in creating a museum in Qazbegi's honor, in the author's native village of Stepantsminda.[31] Only two years after Gatuev's documentary novel concerning the exploits of the abrek Zelimkhan pushed the Ossetian literary imagination toward hitherto-untrodden terrain, Titsian credited Tolstoy and Qazbegi with inventing a prose literature of anticolonial insurgency. Titsian's next text was to fashion—from these authors' prosaics—a poetics that would revise the aesthetic representations of his predecessors, who had preferred the ephemeral stability of colonial governance to the chaos of rebellion.

Beyond the effusive praise Titsian offered for Tolstoy's achievement on the anniversary of his death, and his affirmation that the peoples of the Caucasus proudly regard *Hadji Murat* as "their own national creation,"[32] Titsian maintained a conspicuous silence about the text that inspired him more than any other work of Russian prose. A decade and a half after the collapse of the Soviet regime, the poet's daughter Nitka Tabidze recalled that her father had been working on a novel about Imam Shamil at time of his arrest by the NKVD.[33] As recorded by Tsurikova, whose biography of the Georgian poet was written in close collaboration with Titsian's wife, Titsian originally intended to write a play about Shamil, and only later determined that a historical novel was better suited as a medium for documenting Shamil's life and legacy.[34]

Neither the unrealized novel nor the manuscript of Titsian's translation of *Hadji Murat* is extant. Both works were destroyed when Titsian's writings were confiscated during his arrest in 1937, and the poet himself was "liquidated," to employ the standard Soviet euphemism. (Ironically, the first Georgian translation of *Hadji Murat* appeared in 1938, shortly following the poet's death.[35]) In his last public pronouncement on Tolstoy, delivered in 1937, Titsian declared that "no other colonial novel has described what Tolstoy described in *Hadji Murat*."[36] *Hadji Murat* casts a long shadow over Titsian's oeuvre, including in his literary-critical writings on Tolstoy, but even more strikingly in his poetic commemorations of Shamil and his *murīds*.

Titsian's fame outside the Georgian-speaking world pales in comparison to that of his Russian colleagues and collaborators.[37] And yet, when the Georgian poet was at the height of his power, in the late 1920s until his death in 1937, Titsian's poetry "travelled well beyond the boundaries of Georgia . . . in translations carried out by different, sometimes extremely different, poets" as it reached readers in languages ranging from Russian to Lithuanian.[38] Poets such as Boris Pasternak and Osip Mandelstam turned to Titsian's verse for inspiration and translated the Georgian poet profusely. Like Mandelstam who died in a Gulag one year after the execution of his fellow Georgian poet, Titsian's aesthetic lacked the propagandistic intonation that was necessary to placate Soviet administrators. Titsian faced an additional challenge beyond the aversion to praising the Soviet state that he shared with Mandelstam. Along with regarding the state skeptically, he was unwilling to pay tribute to Georgian nationalism. The poetic unfolding of Titsian's second refusal in the poem "Gunib"—which went beyond *Hadji Murat*'s critique of colonialism by critiquing the Georgian investment in colonial norms—occupies the remainder of this chapter.

"Gunib" is one of the greatest, and one of the most neglected, poems in Titsian's oeuvre. Named for the village near which Shamil surrendered to Bariatinskii in 1859, "Gunib" resembles earlier poems by Titsian such as "Ode to a Mongol King" ("poema, chaghatar," 1926), which eulogize the imam. Such poems take their place alongside other avant-garde engagements with Shamil's legacy, by, for example, the Russian modernist poet Osip Brik.[39] Perhaps because of their incendiary content, Titsian's poems on Shamil have been overlooked by later readers. Tsurikova is the only scholar to note how, in his later years, Daghestan "entered into [Titsian's] work, becoming a leitmotiv."[40] Titsian's few other critics, in Georgian, Russian, and English, have remained silent concerning this dimension to his anticolonial poetics, although the poet's general tendency to "translate political or religious terms into aesthetic ones" has been noted.[41] Anyone familiar with the visionary thrust of Titsian's poems on Shamil will understand why they were given so little attention during the Soviet era and why they continue to exist on the peripheries of the Georgian literary canon, as well as the Georgian literary imagination. Read closely, Titsian's aestheticization of Shamil's insurgency is a searing indictment of Georgian entanglements in colonialism, as well as an ambitious declaration of poetry's capacity to mobilize the aesthetics of insurgency.

When the Georgian modernist poet decided in 1927 to commemorate his recent excursion to the mountain village Gunib, it was not necessary to provide much context for his Georgian readers. Like many Georgian travelers to Daghestan during the Soviet period, who could cross currently sealed borders with ease, Titsian would also have had occasion to visit the precise site of Shamil's surrender, the so-called *besedka* (conversation hut), which has been memorialized, as well as reviled, by local Daghestanis, for decades (see figure 10).[42] Written in the year that inaugurated a Soviet campaign to liquidate local Muslim leadership throughout Central Asia and the Caucasus, "Gunib" was never published in Titsian's lifetime. The poem first appeared in print in an edition of Titsian's collected works published in 1966, two years prior to the publication of Mamakaev's *Zelamkha.*[43] Titsian was well aware of his poem's unpublishability under the conditions of Stalinist rule. The most articulate Georgian critique of colonial violence, and one of the few to acknowledge the contribution to this violence by the Georgian literary elite, thereby escaped the censor's gaze.

It is not known whether the Soviet authorities who organized Titsian's persecution were directly acquainted with Titsian's evocation of Shamil's defeat, although the poet's execution nine years after "Gunib" was written was certainly related to his failure to conform to the ideological status quo. Certainly the text never reached Moscow, for "Gunib" remained untranslated during Titsian's lifetime.[44] While the revival of interest in Shamil's legacy during the early Soviet decades is an important context for "Gunib" as well as for Titsian's other poems on Shamil, it should be borne in mind that "Gunib" appears to have had no immediate audience.[45] That this poem remained confined to Georgian is extraordinary, given the popularity of Titsian's works across the Soviet Union in the renderings of Pasternak and Mandelstam. Pasternak in particular helped to establish Titsian's reputation among readers of Russian, but even he remained oblivious to his friend's incendiary masterpiece. Indeed, "Gunib" appears to be the only major poem in Titsian's oeuvre that had to wait until the Khrushchevian thaw (1953–1964) to see the light of day.

Here is the text of Titsian's penultimate poem on Shamil's insurgency, "Gunib":[46]

I crossed Daghestan. I saw Gunib.
I, an infidel—now a *murīd.*
My sword is an arrow; it will not bend
though it may stab me.

The sky drowns the mountains in snow.
Their peaks stand tall as a scaffold.
When the deluge returns,
when the dinosaur roams,
the wind will utter its vengeful tones.

I see the ghost of an eagle's ravaged nest.
My eyes flow with memory's shame.
How could they exterminate this sky's glory?
Georgia, this mountain's grief belongs to you.
Our bones rot beside our swords and bayonets.

I pity my gangrened Georgian flesh.
Those who gave their lives are safe in paradise.
As for you who remain behind,
my Georgian brothers, memory has no mercy.
Tonight, the wind shudders. Shamil prays for his men.

You, who lost the fierce battle eternally,
The night won't weep for cowards under a foreign sky.
I never pulled the fatal trigger.
I never donned the fighter's armor.
But suddenly I too am moved into manhood.

I don't want to be a poet drunk on blood.
Let this day be my penitence.
Let my poems wash away your treachery.

Although he did not read Arabic, Titsian's poem significantly intersects with the Daghestani literature of anticolonial insurgency. One of the most notable texts within this corpus is Muḥammad Ḥājjī's *qaṣīda* cited in chapter 2. Among the qualities "Gunib" shares with Muḥammad Ḥājjī's *qaṣīda* is an emphasis on eschatology and an aesthetics of defeat. In Titsian's text this convergence is revealed in lines such as "Those who gave their lives are safe in paradise" which recalls Muḥammad Ḥājjī's allusion to the "martyrs in the abode of Islam [*al-shuhadā' fī dār al-islām*]" who "receive a thousand welcomes" when they attain to a victory that, judged according to the norms of secular historiography, is in fact a defeat (*Būriqat*, 212, v. 12).

Also like Muḥammad Ḥājjī, Titsian conceives of this battle in which the warrior poet is engaged as an eternal battle, which he describes as *samudamod brdzola medgari*, which literally translates as "eternal battle fierce." In Titsian's peculiar phraseology, *samudamod* is an adverb, modifying "lost" in the sense of defeat. The line I have rendered in English as "You, who lost the fierce battle eternally" constructs a grammatical parallelism between the Georgian fighters who lose the battle and the temporality of their defeat, which is destined to recur perpetually, as long as time itself. Finally, "Gunib" shares in common with Muḥammad Ḥājjī's *qaṣīda* an eschatological orientation, reflected in the allusions to a second deluge (*meore mosvlit*), the sky drowning the mountains in snow, a scaffold (*eshapoti*), the wind (*kari*) that screams vengeance, and dinosaurs roaming the earth.

The impact of Shamil's surrender on modern Caucasus literatures helps shed light on the place of "Gunib" in Georgian literary history. Titsian's own contrarian reading of Georgia's past is clear from "Gunib." In Titsian's work, as in the texts of many of his Chechen and Daghestani counterparts, Shamil's surrender represented a capitulation to colonial governmentality. More directly than his Muslim counterparts, Titsian exposed the Georgian contribution to the conquest of the Caucasus. The complicity of the Georgian literary and military elite in the colonial project had already been well documented for literary history by the searingly ironic portrayal of Georgian officers at the Tbilisi residence of Mikhail Vorontsov (1782–1856), Russian proconsul to the Caucasus, in *Hadji Murat*.[47] But whereas Tolstoy exposed the corruption of a colonial administration by mocking Georgian aristocratic women like Manana Orbeliani, Titsian places his own masculinity (*vazhkatsoba*) into conflict with a cohort of male officer-poets, and links the courage required for battle to the courage inculcated by poetry. In privileging the vatic utterance over the militant decree, "Gunib" also intensifies transgressive sanctity's aestheticization of violence, unmoored as it increasingly is from familiar ethical norms.

Other than Shamil, Titsian does not identify specific actors in the conflict. However, there is one figure in Georgian literary history who is unmistakably present in "Gunib," even though he is never mentioned by name. This is Grigol Orbeliani (1804–1883), the Georgian Romantic poet and military officer whose family name was synonymous with colonial conquest even for Tolstoy.[48] The poet suggests that, in forging the dominant aesthetic of Georgian literary culture, this elder statesman of Georgian letters also shaped its politics. When Titsian addresses his "brothers" in the vocative (*chemo dzmebo*, v. 17), an educated Soviet Georgian reader would have alighted on Georgia's entangled history of collaboration with the tsarist army. Such apostrophes prefaced many of the Georgian Romantic conquest odes that served as hallmarks for the literary style that has been called the "imperial sublime."[49]

The apostrophe initiated with the appeal to "my brothers" in v. 17 is intensified in v. 20, when the poet addresses these brothers as "you who lost the fierce battle eternally."[50] This apostrophe forms a pivot on which the poem's political aesthetic turns. Until this turning point, "Gunib" largely consisted of an indictment of past crimes with no concrete negotiation of religious difference. Titsian's appeal to his brothers viscerally injects the theme of religious difference into a contrast between the Muslim mountaineers' courage and Georgian Christians' cowardice. Ultimately, the poem's aestheticization of transgressive sanctity endows poetry with the capacity to redeem a century of treachery.

Alongside the elite aesthetics of literary modernism that formed Titsian as a poet, "Gunib" is grounded in the literature of anticolonial insurgency that honored Baisangur, ʿAlībek Ḥājjī, Vara, Zelimkhan, and a long lineage of other anticolonial abreks. Titsian's comparison of the mountain peaks to a scaffold (v. 6) can be read intertextually, in relation to the many insurgents who were publicly executed for rebellion against the colonial regime, such as ʿAlībek Ḥājjī and Muḥammad Ḥājjī. Specifically redolent of Daghestani spiritual hierarchy is the vision of the "eagle's ravaged nest [*artisvta sabudarit dangreul budes*]" (v. 10) that fills the poet with shame. Although Titsian was obviously thinking of Imam Shamil, who had been compared to an eagle two decades prior in a Georgian prose narrative on the conquest of the Caucasus, Najm al-Dīn drew on similar imagery when he called sheykh al-Thughūrī an eagle (*al-ʿanqāʾ*) and a "*murshid* among the birds" in his poem on the latter's death (*Nuzhat*, 81/116).[51]

Situating himself against Georgian Romanticism and within avant-garde Georgian literary modernism, Titsian's anticolonial poetics aestheticized jihad as a striving for spiritual liberation. "There is even a jihad for poetry," argues the Daghestani scholar Musaev in his book on the 1877 uprising, "that requires the poet to refrain from writing even one dishonest line."[52] In this literary context, transgressive sanctity stimulated Titsian to poetically redeem Georgian treachery through verbal exploits that performed in words the feats that the abrek was said to perform in deeds.

By first translating *Hadji Murat* into Georgian, reflecting on the text in prose, and transmuting these lessons into the verses of "Gunib,"

Titsian aestheticized transgressive sanctity. He gave literary form to a political discourse that concerned the relation between law and legitimacy in colonial modernity. We have traveled quite a distance from the precolonial abrek alluded to in chapter 1 to the poet-as-*murīd* who redeems his brothers' treachery by writing poetry. In certain respects, Titsian's aestheticization of violence, as well as his ignorance of many important details concerning Shamil's jihad, might seem to dilute the political force of his transgressive sanctity. But Titsian's own execution, in which tragedy his fate was joined to that of many other authors discussed in this book, gives the lie to view that an anticolonial agenda is divested of political salience once its ethics and aesthetics is transmuted into poetry.

Poetry as Militancy

The late 1920s witnessed a rapid shift among the Georgian intelligentsia from bright hopes of revolutionary equality to a Soviet regime that perpetuated tsarist disparities. Titsian turned to poetry to channel the despair experienced by the best poets of his generation. In 1926, on the occasion of the suicide of his friend the Russian lyric poet Esenin (d. 1925), who had been driven to the brink at the age of thirty by his fear of impending Soviet terror, Titsian evoked a world of camaraderie that was rapidly becoming a figment of the past. Titsian wrote:

არ გამოცვლილა ხომ პოეზია—
მუზები ცისკრის კარებს აღებენ,
ხოლო ჩვენ სხვა დრო წამოგვეწია,
ჩვენც ალბათ სადმე ჩაგვაძაღლებენ.

("sergei esenini," 1:131)

Poetry cannot be replaced.
At dawn, muses overtake the gates.
That other time has caught up with us.
Somewhere we will be slaughtered like dogs.

Even as he lamented his friend's untimely end, Titsian also prophesied his own violent death:

ამხანაგებო, თუ ღრმა ღელეში
ჩვენი თავებიც სადმე დაგორდეს,
ყვლამ იცოდეს—სხვა პოეტებში
ესენინ ჰყავდა ძმად ცისფერ ორდენს!

("sergei esenini," 1:131)

My friends, when our heads roll
somewhere into a deep pit, I want
the world to know that among the poets,
Esenin was the king of us all.

In the context of a regime that consolidated its power by persecuting poets, it is unsurprising that Titsian's aesthetic would take a turn different from that of his predecessors. Unlike his Romantic antecedents, Titsian did not conceive of poetry as either autonomous from, or as coterminous with, its political context.[53] Instead, for this Georgian modernist, poetry was a contestation of prior political hegemonies. Titsian's contestation of the colonial project is one dimension of the Georgian poet's literary modernity, which is distinct from the literary modernism that Titsian also helped to fashion. Verses 22–23 of "Gunib" compare the exaltation of a soldier arming himself for battle to the ecstasy of poetic creation. And yet the comparison between war and poetry entails more opposites than similarities. Rather than reduce poetry to war, Titsian distinguishes between the warrior's goals and the poet's aims. In this respect as in others, the modernist poet's militant pacifism contrasts with—even as it borrows from—the militant aesthetics that informs much of the Georgian and Russian Romantic canon.

The poet's denials of having "pulled the fatal trigger" or "donned the fighter's armor" would seem to suggest his unpreparedness for the violence that has swept through the Caucasus. The denials might, on a superficial reading, connote total innocence of any encounter with war. However, the closing four verses suggest an even more radical divergence between the poet and his Georgian and Russian predecessors. Unlike his fellow Georgians Baratashvili and Orbeliani, unlike also Lermontov, Pushkin, and other Russian Romantics with whom Titsian was in active and often polemical dialogue, this Georgian modernist account of poetry's mediation of civilizational conflict aestheticizes violence to critique imperial conquest. Whereas Russian and Georgian Romantics implicated their poetics within the imperial sublime, Titsian countered the Romantic aesthetic of conquest with an anticolonial sublime. *where is the sublime, since this book is all about aesthetics*

"But suddenly I too am moved into manhood [*vazhkatsoba*]," the poet declares in verse 24, infusing a traditionally masculine idiom with the rhetoric of anticolonial insurgency. It is not the shedding of blood, Titsian implies, that makes a man a poet—or a poet a man—but rather the quality and integrity of his verse. *Shemashpota*, the verb governing Titsian's statement that he is "moved into manhood," can also be translated as *incited* or *stirred*.[54] *Moved* suggests the physicality of his transformation, which conforms to the poem's literal engagement with violence, and is also supported by the modifier *suddenly* (*uetsrad*). To be *moved* into manhood is to stand in judgment on one's ancestors, and to categorically reject their authority, implicated as it is within colonial logics of power. Appropriating the putatively Islamic language of holy war that animated early twentieth-century Soviet accounts of resistance to colonial rule and that have been most memorably displayed in this book in Sheripov's anticolonial rhetoric, Titsian develops his Romantic genealogy to a point of total disintegration.

As figured in "Gunib," the poet's courage derives from an Islamic tradition of insurgency that was inevitably regarded as inimical to Georgian Christian culture. And yet Titsian did not propose a break with a Christian past. Instead, and much more subtly, speaking in the voice of Imam Shamil but with a pathos reminiscent of the Chechen *nā'ibs* who rejected their leader's autocratic methods of governance, the poet folds a colonial tradition of conquest into militant Islamic anticolonial resistance. Titsian styles himself as a *murīd* to demonstrate that poetry overcomes cowardice. While Titsian borrows from stereotypical alignments of Sufism and anticolonial militancy that emerge from a Soviet refashioning of colonial rule (under the banner of the "*murīd* movement"), he resignifies these imaginary constructions in his poetry. Beyond romanticizing the militant freedom fighter, as his Romantic predecessors had done, Titsian merges his voice with that of his putative enemy. Simply put, the Georgian poet becomes a *murīd*. The originality of "Gunib" lies less in its deployment of Soviet Orientalist tropes than in the way the text uses these worn images to rewrite the history of colonialism.

Perhaps because Shamil was more central to his anticolonial poetics than was Ḥājjī Murat, Titsian reserved his discussion of Ḥājjī Murat for literary criticism and prose translation, while consecrating his poetry to invocations of Imam Shamil. Another Georgian modernist by the name of Nikolo Mitsishvili (1896–1937), who, like Titsian, belonged to the avant-garde Blue Horns movement, chose a different path. Mitsishvili dedicated one of his most important poems, "Haji Murad's Severed Head," composed in 1935, two years before his own execution, to a poetic re-creation of the events that followed Ḥājjī Murat's death. The poem describes the procession of Ḥājjī Murat's head along the road leading to Shemakhi in northern Azerbaijan near the border with Daghestan, and afterward to Tbilisi, as the victors narrate Ḥājjī Murat's defeat.

Midway through "Ḥājjī Murat's Severed Head," an Englishman in the service of the Russian administration boasts that "that barbarian was killed cleverly [*chkuam daghupa eg barbarosi*]."[55] The text however interprets this event differently. The concluding three stanzas of Mitsishvili's poem are devoted to evoking the scene through the eyes of Vorontsov, on whose behalf Ḥājjī Murat was executed. Comparing Ḥājjī Murat the Khunzakh warrior to Hamlet, Vorontsov speaks to the severed head of the Avar warrior whom he briefly took under his protection, and whom he ultimately betrayed. Unwittingly echoing the poet's declaration in "Gunib," Vorontsov announces to the dead warrior that "blood is treachery [*moghalatesi*]." He then proceeds to compare Ḥājjī Murat's head to a mountain trapped within its own cliffs:

მაშ ვინ იყავი? რა იყავი? მაშ, რალა გქვიან,
აქაც და იქაც დალუპულო, მოჭრილო თავო.
ხუნძახელ ჰამლეტს რად გინდოდა, რომ გაჩნდი
    გვიან
გაორებულო, უფსკრულებში ჩაშლილო მთაო.

Who were you? What were you? They're speaking about
you.
Severed head, taken captive, you are fettered on all sides.
You who appeared too late wished for the Khunzakh
Hamlet,
you bifurcated, cleft cliff, sunk in the mountain's cracks.

In the stanza that follows, Ḥājjī Murat's head assumes a more passive role, as it delivers a series of moral lessons comprehensible only to Vorontsov. "I see from here," Vorontsov says while gazing on Ḥājjī Murat's head, that as "[the head] says . . . if you fight, then you must forever know that the fate of a divided soul [*gaorebuli katsis bedi*] ends in defeat [*martsxit*]" (vv. 51–54). Deploying different historical frameworks, Titsian and Mitsishvili both concluded their poems by contrasting the nobility of the Khunzakh spiritual warrior—who functions as a metonym for the poet—with the cowardice of the ethically compromised officer, fighting for the tsarist regime. Like "Gunib," "Ḥājjī Murat's Severed Head" hinges on definitions of manhood and virile glory. Although Titsian's poem is declaimed in the voice of a poet and Mitsishvili's poem is declaimed in the voice of a colonial officer, both texts explore the many varieties of courage while extending the meanings of transgressive sanctity. Equally, both poets sharply distinguish the colonial regime's military success from the sanctification of defeat enshrined in the anticolonial literary imagination.

Redeeming Treachery

While Titsian's polemic was inspired by the Tolstoyan tradition, it also drew on a literary genealogy situated far beyond the pale of Russian literature. In modern Caucasus literatures, this genealogy is realized by Qazbegi, Gatuev, Mamakaev, Aidamirov, ʿAlī Qāḍī, Muḥammad Ḥājjī, and Najm al-Dīn. Looking beyond any single ethnicity, articulated in Arabic, Georgian, Russian, Chechen, Avar, and other Caucasus vernaculars, transgressive sanctity is arguably the dominant theme of Caucasus literary modernities. The examples of Gatuev, an Ossetian writer who dedicated his life to exploring and celebrating Chechen and Ingush culture, and Titsian, a Georgian writer obsessed with glorifying the Daghestani Shamil, attest to the cosmopolitan poetics that animated transgressive sanctity as a poetic and political agenda. More than generically global, this cosmopolitan was intimately engaged with vernacular literatures and local literary genres. Aesthetically, politically, and intertextually, the Chechen, Georgian, Arabic, and Ossetian texts introduced in the preceding chapters use transgressive sanctity to engage with violence.

Looking beyond the commonplace dichotomy between the colonizing army and the colonized mountaineers, Titsian elaborates a tripartite colonial encounter as he traces the Georgian oscillation between collaboration and accommodation. Rather than contrast an aggressive imperial army and the courageous mountaineers this army aims to destroy, Titsian delineates the many levels of complicity that contributed to the everyday functioning of the colonial state. Tolstoy projects the guilt associated with conquest outward, onto Russian society. The Georgian poet supplements Tolstoy's indictment of colonial violence with a troubled interrogation of the poetic self. He projects the guilt associated with conquest inward, onto his fellow poets, and ultimately onto himself.

By affiliating and then distancing himself from the Georgian officers who are also his "brothers," Titsian implicates himself and his poetic vocation in the civilizational ambitions that inspire his scorn. In one of the first studies of Tolstoy's writings on the Caucasus, L. P. Semenov wrote that the "empathy experienced by Russian war historians for Ḥājjī Murād was expressed by Tolstoy, who penetrated more deeply than anyone, and gave poetic life" to his tragedy.[56] The empathy that Semenov discerned in 1927 in Tolstoy's portrayal of Ḥājjī Murād attained an even deeper articulation in the Georgian "Gunib" that same year. When he declares, or rather demands, that his poems "wash away your treachery" (v. 27), Titsian stages the ultimate confrontation between the aesthetics of anticolonialism and the violence of conquest. Although it is clear which side wins, the mountaineers' defeat wields a power that makes the victory of the colonizer appear hollow by comparison.

Among the many miraculous aspects of "Gunib" is its simultaneous penetration into two distinct literary traditions: Georgian and

is this the same sense as in chpt. 2?

Russian, alongside its more mediated engagement with Daghestani idioms of insurgency. Within Georgian literary history, Titsian's poem constitutes the third installment in a long polemic that pitted Georgian literature's elder statesmen against a new generation of poets. As with the intergenerational conflict among Russian intellectuals immortalized in Turgenev's *Fathers and Sons* (1861), the ideological battle that raged between the generations during the same decades in Georgian literature revolved around the question of the utility of art. The "sons" maintained that art had to serve a higher social goal, while the "fathers" insisted on the autonomy of art from politics. Art for the second group was the domain of the aristocracy; its cultivation required leisure and presupposed military service to the tsar. The greatest poet among the "fathers" was Grigol Orbeliani, who polemicized in verse with Ilya Chavchavadze, the most famous among the "sons."[57]

The first volley in the debate was launched by Chavchavadze, who circulated a series of satires under the title *Riddles* ("gamotsanebi," 1871), mocking the Georgian nobility. Orbeliani replied to this attack with his poem "Answer to My Children" ("pasuxi shvilta"), in 1874. Chavchavadze replied again, this time with the poem "Answer to the Answer" ("pasuxis pasuxi"). As Paul Manning notes, this debate between Georgian fathers and sons, which touched on "emergent intelligentsia notions of publicness," transpired exclusively in manuscripts, and thereby excluded from its ambit nonaristocrats, who are in these texts "spoken of savagely in the way that one might speak of someone who cannot talk back."[58] For Titsian, the debate between fathers and sons therefore provided a foil for the debate that animates "Gunib," wherein both generations of aristocrats are confronted with the language of their enemies.

Asserting the primacy of the Georgian people (*eri*) and their faith, Orbeliani's "Answer to My Children" laments Georgia's seemingly perpetual propensity for defeat. Orbeliani juxtaposes the old generation's clinging to past traditions to the new generation's relentless thrust into the future. Labeling them "false [*tsru*] Rustavelis" to mark their perverse inversion of Georgia's greatest medieval poet and author of the most widely read Georgian epic poem, Orbeliani evokes a progressive history of defeat and despoliation that, with respect to its sense of being written from the vantage point of defeat, parallels Muḥammad Ḥājjī's verse history of the jihad:

უწყალოდ წახდა უწმინდურთ ხელში!
ერის ცხოვრება,
მისი დიდება,
მის ისტორია დაცულ არს ენით:
რა ენა წახდეს,
ერიც დაეცეს . . .
წაეცხოს ჩირქი ტაძარსა წმინდას![59]

Mercilessly defeated, cruelly despoiled!
A people's life,
its glory,
its history, is crushed in speech:
when a language is lost
its people are vanquished . . .
and its holy temple is filthily defiled!

In the published version of the poem, Orbeliani added to these verses a footnote instructing the reader to read Chavchavadze's newspaper *Droeba* in order to "observe the corruption of the Georgian language." Although much separates Orbeliani's text from the Islamic literature of insurgency, "Answer to My Children" is linked to this literature through its emphasis on defeat. Like his Daghestani and Chechen counterparts, Orbeliani too writes from within a history of perpetual conquest by hostile foreign powers, during the course of which his native land (*mamuli*) was, more frequently than not, on the losing side. Although his aristocratic calling dictated that he would fight on the side of empire, Orbeliani was, like his Muslim opponents, invested in poetry as a means of sacralizing violence.

While the first verse cited here from "Answer to My Children" makes mention of *tsaxda*, meaning "defeated," to describe contemporary Georgia's desecrated condition, the final verse in this citation ends with *tsaretsxos*, meaning "washing away," or "cleansing," as well as "despoilment." Only the second meaning of *tsaretsxos* is active in

Orbeliani's verse, but in Titsian's "Gunib" the second meaning becomes primary. Inverting the closing lines of Orbeliani's famous poem, Titsian links desecration and purification, insisting that the Georgians who eternally lost the great battle (*tsaxda samudamod brdzola medgari*) will be overtaken by a poet who writes poems "to wash away [*rom tsarecxos*]" his brothers' "treachery." The concluding verse of "Gunib" thus invokes Orbeliani's lamentation from half a century prior while inverting its political implications.

The political orientations of the two poets were not so different in their early lives. In his youth Grigol Orbeliani was exiled from Georgia for his participation in an uprising that attempted to end Russian sovereignty in Georgia in 1832, only two years before Shamil became imam of Chechnya and Daghestan.[60] He soon made peace with the colonial regime. Orbeliani rose to a high rank in the tsarist army, attaining power not only over his fellow Georgians but also over the Muslim mountaineers. Meanwhile, another Georgian Romantic, Aleksandre Chavchavadze (1786–1846), rose to "almost supreme power in the Caucasus" under Bariatinskii, the viceroy to whom Shamil surrendered.[61] Among the Georgian aristocrats who most actively facilitated the colonization of the Caucasus, the Orbelianis and Chavchavadzes are the most prominent names. The Orbelianis belonged to a class of Georgians that has led scholars to see Georgia as "the real partner of Russia in the conquest of the Caucasus in the nineteenth century," even through, prior to this period, Georgia's literary and cultural ties were more fully vested in Iran and Byzantium than in Russia.[62] The divided loyalties of Grigol Orbeliani and Aleksandre Chavchavadze were paralleled in Daghestan by figures like al-Ghāzīghumūqī, who lashed out against the 1877 insurgents even as he grieved over their suffering, and Ḥasan al-Alqadārī, who regarded the uprisings as another *fitna*, even when he was sympathetic to their aims.

The benefits he derived from the imperial project confer on Orbeliani's "answer" to his children an additional layer of irony. Just as Georgian poets looked to the Safavids for protection and patronage in the sixteenth and seventeenth centuries, Orbeliani's generation courted the Russian administration because this was the surest means of securing the conditions most favorable to literary production. Georgian

Romantics were raised on the texts of Pushkin, Lermontov, and Krylov. They translated Racine, Corneille, Voltaire, Hugo, Lamartine, and Rousseau.[63] Yet if any figure in Georgian history understood the price of colonial conquest, that person was Grigol Orbeliani. Late in life, Orbeliani praised the same Qazbegi whom Titsian had singled out as the only Georgian writer to rival Tolstoy for his aesthetically persuasive critique of colonial rule.[64] Orbeliani's onomatopoeic obsession with *tsaxda*, the most powerful word in the Georgian lexicon to denote the many varieties of defeat, has been noted. The verbal pyrotechnics of "Gunib" stem in large measure from its deployment of a similar set of consonantal clusters (specifically *ts* [წ], *x* [ხ], and *gh* [ღ]). When Titsian accuses his brothers of losing the great battle, Orbeliani is his likeliest addressee. Orbeliani is also a likely subject for Titsian's rhetorical question, "How could they exterminate this sky's glory?" Indirect references to Orbeliani and his cohort perforate "Gunib" each time Titsian incites his readers and himself to insurgency.

Orbeliani concludes "Answer to My Children" by lamenting the destruction of the holy temple (*tsminda tadzari*), which in this context signifies Orthodox Georgian sanctity and cultural purity. This lament appeals to his "children," the younger generation of poets led by Ilya Chavchavadze whom Orbeliani believed had, through their infatuation with 1860s radicalism, become aligned with a political movement that would compel them to betray Georgia's aristocratic past. In "Gunib," the modernist "son" stands in judgment of his aristocratic "fathers," and with a conviction as deep as Orbeliani's opposition to his youthful antagonists. For Titsian, Orbeliani is the elder poet for whom memory has no mercy, who contributed to Shamil's defeat and helped the imperial army win a war that ended by corrupting both parties to the conflict.

Given his youthful attempts to overthrow the colonial regime, Orbeliani's position was anomalous. Culturally, Orbeliani was an aristocrat, a believer in noblesse oblige and in the virtues of tradition. As the author of poems inspired by Persian genres, and modeled in particular after the *muxambazi* (the Georgian term for *mukhammas*, a Persian strophic poem comprising five rhyming distiches), Orbeliani believed that Georgia could preserve its Persianate cultural heritage while benefiting from the political ascendancy of European and Russian power.[65]

The subservience of culture to power proved more insidious than he imagined.

While Orbeliani's generation worked out a provisional existence in both the Persianate and European traditions, his was the last generation to navigate this transition with any measure of success. At Orbeliani's funeral, Ilya Chavchavadze made peace with his elder antagonist, describing him as a "master of the Georgian language, and a poet, distinguished by the highest degree of talent."[66] Orbeliani's stature was in part a result of his transmutation of Persian and European literary norms into Georgian literary form. While the last Georgian Romantic remained invested in Georgia's literary pasts, modernizing Georgian poets looked to Europe and turned away from Georgian's historically deeper Persianate and Islamicate pasts. Their aesthetic preferences were to prove decisive for Georgia's experience of colonial modernity.

By articulating in "Gunib" a literary modernity that was neither wholly European nor unreflexively Christian, Titsian substantively diverged from the Georgian avant-garde's adulation of European modernism. We find articulated in this late poem a dialectics of insurgency that contrasts starkly with the civilizational antinomies that sustained and legitimized the colonizing process and that isolated Georgia from the north Caucasus by severing Christian from Islamic pasts, and by elevating *zakon* over *sharīʿa* and *ʿādāt*.[67] "Gunib" was Titsian's answer (*pasuxi*) to his literary progenitor, a parallel to Orbeliani's response to his literary "son." At the same time, particularly in its penultimate line ("Let my poems wash away *your* treachery"), Titsian's *pasuxi* replaces the value system animating his predecessor's text with a Georgian modernist iteration of transgressive sanctity.

When he stated that Georgia's holy temple had been defiled (*tsaretsxos*), Orbeliani evokes an image of a believer whose faith has been desecrated. Titsian's *tsaretsxos* induced a comparable sense of sacrilege in his audience. Unlike the first sacrilege that was associated with the younger generation's rejection of tradition, the second sacrilege was generated by colonial violence. The angst induced by this violence had less to do with an external enemy in Titsian's case than with the enemies in his literary past, specifically with his predecessors' prior complicities with the invading army against the Muslim mountaineers. Amid an emergent literary tradition wherein the most politically engaged works by Chechen and Ossetian Soviet writers such as Gatuev were in prose, Titsian inaugurated vernacular anticolonial insurgency in a specifically poetic mode. At the same time, he continued a tradition that had been given most forceful expression in the Daghestani Arabic literature of insurgency a several decades prior. By translating literally as well as figuratively Tolstoy's and Gatuev's documentary narratives into verse, Titsian further aestheticized transgressive sanctity's relation to violence. He also introduced into Georgian modernism forms of poetic critique that until then had been confined to prose fiction and documentary journalism, such as the stories and novels of Qazbegi.

Poetically, "Gunib" demonstrates the deep entanglements between violence and colonial modernity in the Caucasus. "I, an infidel [*giaouri*]," Titsian states, just before contradicting himself with a provocation punctuated by a dash, "now a *murīd*" (v. 2). Although Titsian is obviously referring to Shamil's surrender by titling his poem "Gunib," he could not have been unaware that the same purges he faced in Georgia were under way during those very years in Daghestan. During the year that "Gunib" was composed, two influential spiritual leaders in the northern Caucasus, sheykh Solsa Ḥājjī Yandrov of Urus-Martan and Najm al-Dīn's rival sheykh ʿAlī Akusha of Daghestan, were executed in their capacity as *murshids* (teachers of *murīds*).[68] In calling himself at once an infidel and a faithful *murīd*, Titsian overcomes the self-other dyad that structured Georgian metropolitan discourse about Georgian-Muslim difference for much of the modern period, since the poetry of Davit Guramishvili (1705–1792), if not earlier.[69]

Were "Gunib" a work of history, one might take the poet to task for essentializing the jihad movement under the rubric of militant Sufism. The conflation of religion and insurgency has impoverished the contemporary understanding of anticolonial resistance in the Caucasus, while also preventing the recognition that most Sufi orders in the Caucasus were prepared to accept Russian rule. By no means all, or even most, religious or literary actors in the northern Caucasus embraced anticolonial violence. Rather than homogenizing all vernacular responses to colonial violence under a monolithic conception of transgressive sanctity, I have been engaged by the many ways in which the anticolonial literary imagination reshapes history in politically salient and aesthetically productive ways. From the perspective of Caucasus literary history, the most revealing paradox is not Titsian's romanticization of the *murīd*; rather, it is his deployment of a stereotyped and aestheticized version of mountaineer resistance to deconstruct even more deeply entrenched stereotypes concerning Georgia's Muslim others.

In his poetry, Titsian mobilizes clichés while subverting their significations. Far from enabling the essentialist reduction of anticolonial militancy to fanaticism, in calling himself a *murīd*, and even more powerfully, a *murīd* who is also a *giaour*, Titsian appropriates the religious warrior stereotype to implode it from within. He blows it apart as only poetry can do, by at once acknowledging a stereotype's discursive force and then shifting the terms of its signification. Titsian figures the *murīd* and the *giaour* as agents who, like Zelimkhan, act outside the framework of secular law. Poetry for Titsian involves self-accusation, but even more fundamentally, it requires the courage to speak the truth without fear. As Musaev says: poetry is a jihad, requiring that every word speak the truth. The purge of Georgian intellectuals that transpired within a decade of the writing of "Gunib" demonstrates that even poetic jihads reverberate politically.

Titsian's proposal to wash away a prior generation's treachery and his politicization of a poetic tradition reoriented Georgian literary history. Granted, the reorientation was more aesthetic than historical, and other poems in Titsian's oeuvre, such as "Bandits Killed Me on the Banks of the Aragvi" (1926), suggest a less sympathetic orientation to the mountaineers.[70] Indicting Orbeliani's and Chavchavadze's generations, the modernist poet shaped his vocation in light of an anticolonial aesthetic that reclaimed poetry as a political force. Revitalizing but also moving beyond the Romantic imperial sublime, Titsian also rejected nineteenth-century realism's prosaic understanding of the relation between history and the imagination to propound an avant-garde aesthetics of transgressive sanctity in verse. Rather than subordinating the aesthetic to the political, or the political to the aesthetic, he made the two categories constitutive of each other.

Shamil's grip on the Georgian literary imagination reaches well beyond Titsian's poetry. Another Georgian writer who was executed by the

Soviet regime, Mixeil Javaxishvili, in his historical novel on the Georgian abrek (*abragi*) Arsena Odzelashvili, alluded to the popular Georgian belief that Shamil was Aleksandre Batonishvili's son.[71] Javaxishvili's allusion to Shamil's reputed Georgian paternity was censored from later Soviet editions of Javaxishvili's novel, with the result that the Georgian claim to genealogical affiliation with Shamil has been systematically erased from the Soviet record. More than his deeds, which were controversial in their own day and not unilaterally supported by his fellow Muslims, Shamil's most lasting legacy in the Georgian literature of insurgency is the example he offered for critics of the imperial project. Shamil's resonance across Chechen, Daghestani, and Georgian literatures is yet one more illustration of how the modern literatures of the Caucasus were constituted and canonized by the specter of insurgency.

Poetic Relations, False Accusations

The majority of Georgia's most talented poets did not survive the regime that had risen to power by the time Titsian's Shamil cycle came to an end. Titsian's fellow poet and literary collaborator Paolo Iashvili killed himself in 1937 with a hunting rifle during a session of the Writer's Union that had been convened to authorize his arrest. Titsian's cousin and fellow poet Galaktion Tabidze drowned his sorrow in alcohol for decades before killing himself in 1959 by jumping from the window of the psychiatric hospital where he had been confined.

Also in 1937, Mixeil Javaxishvili, arguably the greatest Georgian novelist of the twentieth century, was executed on the charge of espionage. Labeled a spy by Lavrenty Beria, the notorious first secretary of the Georgian Communist Party, Javaxishvili was accused of campaigning to "separate the autonomous Republic of Ajaria from Georgia."[72] Among Georgia's greatest twentieth-century writers, only Konstantin Gamsaxurdia was spared persecution.[73] Gamsaxurdia had earlier paid his dues to the Soviet state by penning a thick trilogy that compared Stalin to the twelfth-century Georgian king David Aghmashenebeli. That the text had pleased Stalin likely enabled Gamsaxurdia to live, and to die, in peace.

To gain a deeper perspective on the still largely untold story of Titsian's death, I sought out an interview with his daughter Nitka. I first located her in 2006 at 18 Griboedov Street, near Tbilisi's elegant Music Conservatory, where she had passed her childhood. Nitka recalled that her father was about to embark on his novel about Shamil when the NKVD arrived to take him away. Titsian had been asked to sign a document incriminating Paolo Iashvili as spy. Knowing that the document would result in his friend's execution, he refused to sign.[74] Titsian refused to incriminate any fellow poet, let alone his best friend. In a rare moments of stasis amid the chaotic terror that pervaded the Writer's Union meetings during that period, Titsian pleaded with both the accusers and the accused. "Let everyone look into his own heart," he said, alluding to the New Testament (John 8:7), "and see who is without sin."[75] These bold words, uttered in the presence of those empowered to order his execution, decisively influenced Titsian's own fate.

Like most major Georgian poets and novelists of his generation, Titsian was arrested by the NKVD during Beria's term as first secretary of the Georgian Communist Party (1934–1938). His arrest followed immediately after Iashvili's suicide. Because he refused to incriminate his deceased friend, Beria accused Titsian of spying for the United States of America. When asked to name his accomplices, Titsian declared with characteristic irony that he had been assisted by the Persianizing poet Besiki (d. 1791). Predictably ignorant of Georgian literary history, Titsian's interrogators assumed that Besiki was a living person and scoured all Tbilisi for the putative conspirator before executing Titsian.[76] The "Protokol" announcing his execution gives the reasons as follows: (1) membership in a "nationalist-fascist" organization; (2) having engaged in harmful work [*vreditel'skuyu rabotu*] on the literary and cultural fronts; and (3) having engaged in espionage to benefit French intelligence-gathering efforts (*razvedka*).

Titsian was killed in 1937, half a year prior to the execution of Dzakho Gatuev, who, like Titsian, had composed his most incendiary work a decade earlier. Titsian's death was kept secret from his family, including his wife, Nina, who awaited her husband's return from the Gulag, where she was told he had been sent, throughout the 1940s and into the 1950s. The documents pertaining to Titsian's execution were made public only in the late 1950s. Only when the documents had been released to the public, and made available in the Georgian Literature Museum a few blocks away from Titsian's home, did Nina discover that her husband had been summarily executed within days of his arrest.[77]

The only specific poem mentioned in the official accusations against Titsian was one he had written to another major Georgian modernist, Grigol Robakidze, after the latter had fled the Soviet Union and settled in Nazi Germany.[78] (Robakidze was incidentally also the author of a German short story concerning Imam Shamil.[79]) Even though it would be erroneous to draw a direct line from "Gunib" to the poet's execution, his poetry and novel in progress about Shamil surely did not help his case. Few poets were as outspoken as Titsian was in his verse concerning the family resemblances between Russian imperialism and the Soviet "brotherhood of peoples." Titsian was one of the most talented Georgian poets to be persecuted for his views, but he was far from the only one.

Twelve years after publishing his fictionalized life of Zelimkhan, Gatuev paid for his literary brilliance with his life. He was arrested on 13 November 1937 and transported to Ordzhonikidze (present-day Vladikavkaz).[80] Gatuev's wife Fatima Borisovna was arrested the following day. Like many who met this fate, Gatuev was accused of participating in an armed uprising organized by Ossetian nationalists. Declared guilty on 13 July 1938, he was executed the same day. Gatuev's execution, one in a long chain of purges that depleted the northern Caucasus intelligentsia of its most brilliant representatives and that reached deep into Daghestan, has generated a lacuna in Caucasus literatures that persists to this day.[81] Formally rehabilitated in 1955, Gatuev's works were not republished until the 1970s.

Entrusted with the delicate task of reintroducing his father's work to the Ossetian and Russophone reading public in 1971, Gatuev's son Soslanbek Gatuev, who barely had the chance to know his father before he was executed, wrote of how, in 1937, a year prior to his death, the writer hung over his son's bed a picture of children who had been murdered in Franco's Spain. When his aunt (Dzakho's sister) asked why he had decorated his son's wall with such a horrific picture, Dzakho explained that he wanted his son to know "what fascism is."[82] In this same volume and even while failing to mention the causes of his death, Gatuev's editor V. Shalepov acknowledged that "Dzakho's life was cut short when he was at the very height of his poetic powers."[83] Aside from these cryptic references to a life cut short by terror, the circumstances of Gatuev's death were not made public until after the fall of the Soviet Union. As with Titsian's insurgent modernism, Gatuev's delineation of transgressive sanctity necessitated his execution. For both writers, their outspoken views generated the silence that surrounded their death in subsequent decades.

This chapter has examined the Georgian aesthetics of insurgency as an internal critique of Georgian participation in the conquest of the Caucasus. On the basis of his discomfort with Georgia's colonial past, Titsian Tabidze elaborated an aesthetics suited for an anticolonial literary modernity. Working at the intersection of aesthetics and politics, Titsian and Tolstoy cultivated distinctively poetic strategies for challenging colonial rule. Particularly in the case of Titsian, whose intervention was shaped by a contemporaneous revival of Shamil and the northern Caucasus jihad in Soviet historiography, their literary contributions cannot be read as unmediated expressions of political solidarity.[84] Their mediated aesthetic broadly replicates the discourse of transgressive sanctity and speaks to the work of literary form in making violence legible.

The mobilization of literary form in the service of oppositional critique is one dimension of transgressive sanctity's modernity. Among the formal devices that composed this anticolonial aesthetic were irony (exemplified in Tolstoy's juxtaposition of Butler's joie de vivre with the brutal aftermath of the Vedeno raid), apostrophe (exemplified in Titsian's address to Orbeliani and his aristocratic-military cohort as "my brothers"), and double entendre, a poetic strategy uniquely suited for making evident the instability of meaning entailed in the politics of representation. When deployed by Titsian and Tolstoy, each of these three poetic devices served a broader political goal. In deploying irony to convey their messages, Tolstoy and Titsian drew attention to the literary imagination's unique capacity to intervene in the status quo through imagined possibilities. Through apostrophe, Titsian implicated his readers and himself in the colonial project. In undermining the stability of linguistic and thus social categories in his verse, Titsian's modernism inaugurated a new moment in Caucasus literary history, marked by a break with the historicizing modes of representation that dominate the Daghestani and Chechen literatures of anticolonial insurgency. By capitalizing on literature's compact with pure possibility, Titsian's aesthetics refused the identities into which Georgian poets had been coerced and cultivated in its place a dialectic of relation in the sense conceptualized by Édouard Glissant.[85]

In his brief memoir of Gatuev, written long after the Ossetian writer had been executed, the Chechen writer Khalid Oshaev (1898–1977) recollected how he had once asked the Ossetian poet Kaitukov why the Ossetians did not do more to commemorate the achievement of Gatuev in Ossetian literary history. Kaitukov's response was at odds with the stereotypes that plague the Caucasus today, and which construct it as a region haunted by ancient ethnic hatreds and narcissistic nationalisms. "It's you, Chechens, who neglect Gatuev," Kaitukov responded. "In essence Gatuev is a Chechen writer! He wrote most about the Chechens."[86] As simple as his response appears, Kaitukov's answer encapsulates the ethnographic imagination that Caucasus literatures sustain collectively when brought into comparison with one another. The literatures of insurgency in the Caucasus generate a network of relations that link politics, aesthetics, and transregional affiliations into a cohesive, yet still cosmopolitan, whole. Like identities in the account of Glissant, literatures are forged in the interstices of multiple superimposed and vernacular cultural formations. In the angle on Caucasus literary modernities afforded by insurgency, the salient literatures have been in Arabic, Georgian, Russian, and Chechen; other accounts could have added Turkish, Persian, Armenian, and other Circassian and Daghestani languages.

The literary Caucasus created by Gatuev, Mamakaev, Tolstoy, Qazbegi, ʿAlī Qāḍī, Muḥammad Ḥājjī al-Thughūrī, ʿAbd al-Raḥmān al-Ghāzīghumūqī, and al-Alqadārī conflates the monolithic views of cultural exchange that continue to characterize the areal taxonomies projected onto this region. Because most of these writers did not read one another's works, the comparisons that have been essayed here have involved parallels, juxtapositions, and convergences more than direct influences. And yet all the authors studied here deployed the ethics and aesthetics of transgressive sanctity to engage with colonial violence. Transcending both the valorization of rebellion for rebellion's sake and the Romantic worship of sublime power, transgressive sanctity distills both aesthetics into itself. Transgressive sanctity is the political aesthetic born of the void in political legitimacy created by the annihilation of a community's legal and ethical infrastructure. It is a form of political and aesthetic aspiration created by authors who oppose the claims to legitimacy promulgated by the ruling regime with alternative visions of vatic power. In part a social theory of the political life of aesthetic form, transgressive sanctity is also a literary praxis.

As a form of aesthetic and political life, transgressive sanctity generated multiple vernacular and cosmopolitan poetics. These culminated in what Terry Eagleton has called the aesthetic ideology's "powerful challenge and alternative to . . . dominant ideological forms."[87] Ultimately, Titsian's aestheticization of violence overcomes violence by transmuting it into poetry. Although his engagement with transgressive sanctity was not the dominant theme of his broader avant-garde literary modernism, Titsian's poetic identification with the *murīd*, and his endeavor through poetry to redeem his fellow poets' treachery is situated at the core of his poetic mission. Merging poetics with politics, Titsian's modernism enabled transgressive sanctity to forcefully, if elliptically, critique the Soviet state's coercive governmentality, as well as to demonstrate its continuity with colonial rule.

Beyond its impact on Titsian and Mitsishvili, Tolstoy's haunting image of Ḥājjī Murat's severed head has provoked many subsequent writers. The Avar poet Rasul Gamzatov (d. 2003) were inspired through his contact with Tolstoy's text to produce his own narrative of Ḥājjī Murat's gruesome death. In "The Head of Hadji Murat," a poem that bears (in translation) the same title as Mitsishvili's Georgian poem, Gamzatov stages a conversation between himself and Ḥājjī Murat's head that echoes Vorontsov's conversation with the head in Mitsishvili's poem. "Were you once famous in these lands," the Avar poet asks the head. "And whose were you, to meet with such a fate / And come to grief in alien hands?"[88] Acknowledging that it used to belong to Ḥājjī Murat, the head replies that it fell from its former owner "because I went too far astray." The speaker concludes: "Sadly I contemplate the erring head / Severed in the unequal fight." Like the pronouncements of Ḥasan al-Alqadārī and al-Ghāzīghumūqī discussed in the previous chapter, the words Gamzatov attributes to Ḥājjī Murat's head suggest not just that this specific warrior went astray but more generally that the entire anticolonial jihad was a mistake.

Although Gamzatov's questioning of the value of the jihad diverges from the insurgent aesthetics promulgated by Titsian, Qazbegi, Mitsishvili, and even Tolstoy, it too marks an important moment in the literatures of anticolonial insurgency. With Gamzatov, the idea of resistance was incorporated into mainstream Caucasus cultures and domesticated (and neutralized) into the fabric of everyday life. Just as the recurrence of the abrek across multiple languages and literatures helped foster a Caucasus literary modernity, so does Ḥājjī Murat's severed head, often in close proximity to Shamil's persistent and contradictory legacy in these same literatures, constitute the Caucasus literatures of anticolonial insurgency as a refraction of colonial modernity. Like transgressive sanctity broadly, this motif generates a vital literary canon for cross-cultural comparative poetics, and particularly for investigations attuned to the interface between aesthetics and violence.

The critique of violence that is entailed in this late Soviet iteration of transgressive sanctity gave rise to new forms of coercion. These new forms in turn necessitated a critique of the critique of violence, as pursued in chapter 4 and the epilogue. To make the conditions for such a critique more apparent, and to better understand what Walter Benjamin would call the philosophy of violence's history, it is necessary to shift briefly away from the literary engagement with colonial violence that has consumed this book so far. The chapter that follows turns to the ethnographic context where this book was first conceived, in wartime Chechnya and among the Chechen diaspora. While this anthropological turn parts ways with the literary forms taken by insurgency, my ultimate goal is to think these two ways of conceiving violence, the literary and the ethnographic, together.

The literary archive of anticolonial insurgency reveals the extent to which all forms of violence are socially and culturally constructed. The ethnography of violence within postwar Chechen society reveals how these constructs have deadly implications. While contemporary Chechen insurgents did not necessarily read the texts discussed here, their conceptualizations of the limits of peaceful action were cultivated within a milieu characterized by similar distributions of power. The constraints within which contemporary insurgents operate have generated aestheticizations of violence that are kindred in origin as well as content to Soviet and even tsarist precedents. While conditions vary radically, the belief that violence can bring about redemption has remained remarkably constant. Hence, a comparative account of these two iterations of violence, in literature and among Chechens traumatized by war, can significantly advance our understanding of the lives of texts beyond their immediate readerly communities.

F·O·U·R

Violence as Recognition, Recognition as Violence

Having dwelled on literary engagements with violence, I now transition to a different engagement with violence. Although the violence with which this chapter is concerned exists outside texts, it is no less mediated by representations than its textual counterpart. Here, I direct my attention to the aestheticization of violence that transpires among women traumatized by war, which I encountered during fieldwork in and around Chechnya, particularly from 2004 to 2006. This chapter turns to ethnography in a final effort to offer a more dialectical account of anticolonial violence. If, as Walter Burkert claims, "sacrificial killing is the basic experience of the sacred," an ethnography of anticolonial violence will touch on both sacrificial killing and the sacred.[1]

As I conducted research and interviews in and around Chechnya, I came into contact most frequently with men: fighters, politicians, citizens, fathers, sons, and writers.[2] When women figured into my fieldwork, it was only by way of accentuating a male-inhabited foreground. The more time I spent with Chechen families, however, the more apparent it became that women's activities had public implications. Although women shaped public consciousness well before the recent wars, decades of post-Soviet violence have increased the proportion of women who support themselves and their families through their own resources more than ever before. This transformation in social demographics has shifted, in subtle ways, the balance of power between genders.

While visiting refugee camps and seeking out those displaced by war, I met women who had acquired professional skills late in life to support themselves after having lost their husbands and extended families. These women, who became journalists, publishers, translators, and teachers, often succeeded in ways that had eluded their male counterparts. One particularly well-organized group of female Chechen refugees I met had survived for years by selling sunflower seeds on the streets of Nazran. (In many instances, of course, these women could not survive on their earnings alone and depended on extended social networks for survival.)

Every night, after a long and often fruitless day of waiting for customers, the sunflower-seed sellers of Nazran gathered together in a large room near the central bus station to exchange stories pertaining to the displacements of war and to trade memories of the beautiful city that Grozny used to be. It was here that they slept, thanks to the generosity of the owner of the home who had opened his doors to these refugees. Together they grieved in ways they could not have done alone. During one night I spent in Nazran, between my travels from Nalchik to Chechnya, I was shown postcards, family albums, and scrapbooks of the places where these women grew up. I was told of dreams that had been cut short by war, like marriage, children, and love, and of dreams the war had made necessary: education and careers, as doctors, lawyers, nurses, human rights advocates. I was told of the children, husbands, and parents they had lost to war, of their despair of ever repairing the voids war had created in their lives. Before I left Nazran, one of these refugees gave me one of the postcards she had shared with her fellow bedmates the night before. Tattered along the edges, and in bright colors that seemed to evoke a film from half a century ago, the postcard depicted a memorial to the 1944 deportation that had been destroyed during a recent Russian bombing campaign.

While the division of labor in Chechen societies is strictly apportioned according to gender, those who assess such divisions in terms of conventional gender politics neglect the power women wield over their own spheres. Under the conditions of war, domestic spheres have permeated the entirety of Chechen society, which has had the effect of making the personal political in hitherto unseen ways. In Chechnya and its border regions, the domestic sphere has been permeated by forms of violence that in times of peace, before the collapse of the Soviet Union, were restricted to the public institutions where, following Foucault, governmentality is understood to flourish: the asylum, prison, and hospital.

The first round of bloodshed in the post-Soviet period began in 1994, with a Chechen bid for independence and a violent Russian backlash. By the time I arrived in 2004, in the aftermath of a second war, years after the most intense bombing campaigns, any space that may have been untouched by politics prior to war was, when I first arrived, politicized by war. This politicization was reflected in the words of my Chechen teacher in Tbilisi who was widely esteemed among local Chechens. Each lesson began with her showing me pictures of armed Chechen boys from families with whom she was distantly acquainted and praising their heroism. When I asked her for her views on the conflict, she affirmed her preference for peace, but her pictures indicated a more ambivalent relation to violence. While this hyperpoliticization of domestic life intensified the trauma of war, it also created new roles for women, who enable society to live in war's aftermath, at times by sacrificing—literally and fatally—their lives.

Like the Chechen public sphere, transgressive sanctity is a predominantly male domain. The only instance of a woman proposing to take up arms in defense of her people encountered so far has been Zelimkhan's wife Bitsi, who offered to become an abrek to help her husband. The masculinist framing of anticolonial insurgency has thus far constrained the scope of this study, and predetermined its account of violence. This chapter implodes that orientation from within. From the premise that violence is integral to the social order, it follows that it is also central to the sexual contract.[3] Transgressive sanctity's spiritual ramifications are forcefully expressed in the specter of the female suicide bomber (*shahidka*). Her image has come to dominate the representation of violence in Chechen society, although, as I show, such representations date back no further than the past decade. Aiming to show how the sexual contract underlies a social order premised on violence, this chapter considers how transgressive sanctity shaped the life choices of a woman who, unlike the male authors considered in the preceding chapters, did not present her voice to posterity in a text. Instead, this woman left behind an unwritten message when she sacrificed her life in pursuit of what she called recognition. Although the form of her utterance was determined by those who remembered and refashioned her words, like the texts discussed in this book, this woman's message crystallized the ideology of transgressive sanctity, this time for a post-Soviet constituency.

On 29 November 2001, Aizan Gazueva of Urus-Martan, twenty-five kilometers south of Grozny and Chechnya's second-largest city, visited the barracks of Gaidar Gadzhiev, a Daghestani general who had killed her husband before her eyes. Shortly prior to killing her husband, Gadzhiev had kidnapped and killed Gazueva's brothers under secret circumstances. Gazueva addressed to the general a simple question in Russian: "Do you recognize me?" (*Vyi menya uznaete?*).[4] Gazueva wanted to know whether the general recognized her as the woman whose husband he had recently killed. Rather than acknowledge her gaze, Gadzhiev dismissed her. "Go away!" he said. "I don't have time to speak with you!" Then there was an explosion. "A young widow detonated the instrument hidden on her body," runs one journalist's account.[5] According to the human rights organization Memorial, two soldiers were killed, and Gadzhiev died the next day from his wounds.[6]

Although she was one of the first suicide bombers in post-Soviet Chechnya, Gazueva's attack diverges from the stereotypical case in multiple respects.[7] When she detonated the grenade, Gazueva did not take civilian lives with her into the grave. Instead, she aimed her life at a military target: the general who had killed her husband and kidnapped her brothers a few months earlier. While Gazueva's targeting of the military distinguishes her case from other suicide bombings, the posthumous reception of her act is also strikingly different from that of other suicide bombings. Among other distinctions, Gazueva was associated with transgressive sanctity to a much greater extent than any other *shahidka*. In its movement beyond exclusively literary domains within wartime Chechnya, transgressive sanctity becomes inflected with neocolonial violence.[8] Like its late tsarist and early Soviet counterparts, post-Soviet transgressive sanctity aestheticizes violence, albeit in images rather than texts. Echoing Walter Benjamin's account of the function of fascist aesthetics in Weimar Berlin, the post-Soviet aesthetics of violence through images can be seen as a degenerated version of the communist politicization of the abrek.[9]

Before surveying the circumstances of Gazueva's death and its memorialization by the residents of Urus-Martan, I briefly consider suicide bombing within the geography with which it was primarily associated prior to its appearance in Chechnya: Palestine. Like Chechens, Palestinian insurgents have commonly engaged with sacralized idioms of martyrdom that are often tied to, even when they are not subsumed by, religious motivations. Also in both contemporary geographies, the visual spectacle of violence takes precedence over its textualization. Both geographies shed light on the mediation of violence in the global public sphere beyond literary canons.

Everyday Violence

In her study of Palestinian modes of commemorating martyrdom, Laleh Khalili identifies three rhetorical modes through which Palestinians have framed their narratives for themselves and the world. The first, dominant during the Thawra ("revolutionary") period (1965–1982), foregrounds resistance through narratives stressing sacrifice for the nation. The second, fostered by international nongovernmental organizations (NGOs), foregrounds victimhood and suffering. The third rhetorical mode, which Khalili calls *ṣumūd* (steadfastness), traverses the extremes of heroic resistance and helpless victimization. Khalili's characterization of *ṣumūd* as an "infrapolitics of the powerless" that "neither demands self-sacrifice nor valorizes suffering," suggests the many parallels between Palestinian and Chechen responses to their dispossession.[10] Other anthropologists have contrasted *ṣumūd* with event-based narratives of conflagrations, structural shifts, and violent outbursts.[11] Generating a form of memory distinct from that generated by the event, *ṣumūd* characterizes war-torn societies so intimately acquainted with death and violence that they constitute part of the "totalitarian overcoding of social life."[12] In contradistinction to glamorous stories of heroic resistance and the passivity entailed in NGO-generated narratives of Palestinians' victimization, *ṣumūd* informs those "inconspicuous act[s] of resistance required to rebuild your house even after it has been destroyed for the fifth time" and to "once again have children even after your sons were butchered in front of you."[13] Whereas the literary violence that has been studied in the preceding chapters aestheticizes violence, the violence to which *ṣumūd* is a response is manifested in everyday spheres that impede the impulse to aestheticization.

These threefold trajectories of Palestinian memory converge with narratives that have framed and in certain respects overdetermined Chechen lives over the past half century. Chechen analogues to the Palestinian heroic narrative, which has "armed resistance as its central motif, the *fida'yi* guerilla fighter and his gun," are widely in evidence in contemporary Chechnya and among Chechen diasporas in the Pankisi Gorge on the Georgian border.[14] Like Palestinians, Chechens have oscillated between secular nationalist and sacralized redemption narratives for much of their modern existence while endeavoring to establish civil society on local terms. Additionally, both Palestinians and Chechens are intimately acquainted with the everyday violence that generates *ṣumūd.*

The same years that witnessed a turn to Islamic symbology in Palestinian refugee camps in the early 1990s, soon after the Oslo Accords and settler attacks on mosques, saw Chechen attitudes toward resistance transformed. After having been defined as an Autonomous Soviet Socialist Republic within the Soviet commonwealth for the better part of a century, suddenly, with Yeltsin's abdication in 1991, Chechens faced the possibility of full political autonomy.[15] After the Russian collapse, Jawhar Dudaev stepped forward to declare the first independent Republic of Ichkeria in world history. Although *Ichkeria* is a premodern Turkic name for Chechnya, its attraction for Dudaev and his followers had little to do with its historical meaning. As Derluguian writes, Ichkeria "sounded glorious, historical, unifying, and, moreover, it was much easier to pronounce than Nokhchi-Mokhk—which indeed was a sound consideration when attempting to put a new nation on a map."[16]

Ichkeria's claims to political autonomy did not go unchallenged for long, for Russia was unwilling to relinquish the oil-rich Caucasus. In 1996, Dudaev was assassinated when Russian military surveillance traced him through his satellite phone to his hideout in mountainous Chechnya. In the first popular elections that followed shortly after Dudaev's assassination, Ichkeria's first president was succeeded by his more moderate chief of staff, Aslan Maskhadov. Maskhadov signed the Khasavyurt Accords (1996), whereby the issue of Chechnya's territorial sovereignty was left undecided, although the Chechen Republic's mandate to defend Chechens' "rights to self-determination" was specified, and thereby implicitly recognized by the Russian state.[17] Notwithstanding the bloodshed that preceded this peace treaty, the Khasavyurt Accords seemed to many like a reasonably successful conclusion to a brutal war.

The peace, however, did not last long. Militancy trumped what some Chechens regarded as Maskhadov's policy of amelioration. In 1999, after a series of explosions in a Moscow apartment building, Shamil Basaev, a local Chechen rebel, and Amir al-Khattab (d. 2002), a Saudi-born Arab-Circassian, invaded Daghestan, hoping to drag the northeastern Caucasus into a war with Russia. In 2000, the year that marked the beginning of the second Palestinian Intifada (uprising), Russia responded to the Moscow bombings and to Basaev's Daghestan campaign with a second air strike on Grozny, far more brutal than the airstrikes of the First Chechen War (1994–1996).

The Russian state did not present any evidence that the Moscow apartment bombings that instigated the Second Chechen War were orchestrated by Chechens, and no Chechen group claimed responsibility for the attack. The absence of a culprit did not prevent Vladimir Putin in a famous campaign speech from vowing to "waste the bandits in the shithouse [*mol'chit v sortire*]."[18] Following Putin's reelection in 2000, this campaign promise soon translated into an aerial attack that reduced much of Grozny to ashes. Forever afterward, terrorist attacks in Russian metropolitan centers came to be inextricably linked to Chechen demands for political autonomy, notwithstanding that the initial linkage appears to have been based more in fiction than fact. Just as terrorism came to be associated with Chechen independence in metropolitan Russia, so did Chechen demands for sovereignty come to be seen as terrorist by implication. The Dubrovka Theater hostage crisis of 2002 was followed by Beslan in 2004, until it was no longer possible to extricate in the popular imagination the Chechen demand for political autonomy from innocent Russian casualties.

Outside the Caucasus, the typical response to such entangled histories has been to narrate the events of the Chechen war from the seemingly omniscient viewpoints of Washington and Moscow, as far removed as possible from the facts on the ground.[19] The majority of scholarly engagements with contemporary Chechnya have viewed this region from the point of view of the vested interests of foreign powers. This chapter moves beyond approaches attuned to the interests of the state through its ethnography of Gazueva's mediation of violence and its aftermath in local memory.

The proliferation of suicide bombing in wartime Chechnya exemplifies the degeneration of transgressive sanctity in everyday life.[20] Harootunian has identified how, in postcolonial contexts, the everyday breaks off from the exceptional "in order to negotiate the meaning of the modern." In wartime Chechnya as elsewhere, this postcolonial modernity is ungoverned by the nation-state.[21] Viewed within and against its geopolitical context, Gazueva's story, along with her place in local Chechen memory, merges the aesthetics of violence that this book has so far explored with the response to everyday brutality that Palestinians call *ṣumūd*. This everyday dimension is relatively new to the terrain of transgressive sanctity and stands in tension with its literary genealogy. More locally, if also more bleakly, Gazueva's story also resonates with a statement made by a victim of the massacre in the Chechen village of Novyi Aldy in 2000: "We do not live anymore. We merely exist."

Seeking Recognition, Engendering Insurgency

Over the course of many years of fieldwork in the Caucasus, I had not had occasion to reflect on suicide bombing until the subject reached me in the form of local memories pertaining to Aizan Gazueva. While based in Tbilisi from 2004 to 2006, I traveled north, across the Russian border, in spring 2006, to Nalchik, the largest and safest city with a proximate connection to the Chechen Republic and home to tens of thousands of Chechen refugees seeking to create their lives over again.

Chechnya was still a war zone in 2006 and barred to anyone without a Russian passport or a stamp issued by the military authorities. Following a brief and difficult visit to Grozny in 2004 along a back road leading from a refugee camp in Ingushetia that was soon after "liquidated" (to deploy a still-current Soviet euphemism), I decided to concentrate my attention on Chechen refugees.

My host in Nalchik was a Grozny-born Chechen journalist named Zeynap.[22] Zeynap had been forced to relocate to Nalchik in 1995 after her home in Grozny had been destroyed during an air raid. Like the Chechen refugees in Nazran who passed their daylight hours selling sunflower seeds near the bus station, Zeynap dedicated her every working hour to miscellaneous jobs, many of which she undertook to stay afloat financially. Every moment that was not invested in such menial labor was dedicated to bringing peace to Chechen society and educating her fellow Chechens.

The project in which Zeynap invested most profoundly during the months that I stayed with her in Nalchik was a multivolume Chechen translation of the Grimm fairy tales, that was to be published with lavish illustrations and distributed for free to Chechen children. Zeynap dreamed that every Chechen child would eventually hold one of these books in their hands and that access to such works would make literacy in Chechen possible for every Chechen child. When she was not raising funds for the publishing house she had founded in order to publish the Chechen translations of Grimm's fairy tales or engaged in secretarial work to stay financially afloat, Zeynap also worked as a journalist, documenting human rights violations.

A mutual acquaintance had put me in touch with Zeynap. Immediately after our first meeting, Zeynap invited me to reside with her in her two-room apartment on the outskirts of Nalchik for as long as I wished. Although she certainly could have used help with her rental payments, she refused to accept payment from me and preferred to look on our time together as a way of initiating me into the Chechen experience of war. A few weeks into my stay in Zeynap's apartment, a guest arrived unannounced. Zeynap introduced her visitor as Zarema, a close friend she had known since their high school days in Grozny.

Although she had attended high school in Grozny, Zarema was born in Urus-Martan, the hometown of Aizan Gazueva.

After we shook hands, Zarema sat down on a couch that fronted a wall covered with green and gray posters of wolves, symbols of Chechen identity. She opened a bag that had been tucked under her shoulder and began to sort through two packs of photographs. The first series of pictures were scenes from everyday life, against the background of war. Children played in courtyards riddled with glass shards, leaned smiling against walls crumbling from mortar attacks, and danced in streets filled with stray tires and uncollected trash. When the first pack of photos came to an end, Zarema turned to the second. She handled it more cautiously than she had the first, as though its fragile contents were already damaged. All the photos in the second pack were of a single woman. I asked for her name and was told: Aizan. It was a name, Zarema said, that deserved to be known to the world. I asked about the identity of this Aizan, whose face I had not seen before.

"Aizan," Zarema solemnly intoned by way of a response. She spoke of General Gadzhiev's pleasure in "making people suffer." In Zarema's reconstruction, the Daghestani general had forgotten that he had kidnapped Gazueva's brothers while he was killing her husband, so desensitized had he become by his own violence. Zarema added that Gadzhiev "forced Aizan to witness as he stabbed her husband. Then he pressed her head against her husband's wound." This final act was the greatest indignity of all that had been inflicted on her. In response, Aizan strapped a hand grenade around her waist a few days later, went to the *komendatura* (military authority), and asked him quietly, "Do you recognize me?"

For Zarema, the keynote of Gazueva's life (and death) was her demand for recognition, and her violent response to not having received it. In a world where to be recognized is to exist, recognition becomes a goal worth dying for and self-destruction acquires a halo of sanctity. Such sanctity, refashioned by modern technology and by mass circulation, is inherently transgressive. It transgresses against a corrupt legal system that cannot claim legitimacy. Unable to secure peace, a citizen's best hope is to wage their own private war. Jean and John Comaroff have discerned the "coincidence of democratization and criminal violence" within the contemporary postcolony, a rubric that for them encompasses "nation-states, including those of the former USSR, once governed by, for, and from an elsewhere; nation-states in which representative government and the rule of law, in their conventional Euro-modernist sense, were previously 'underdeveloped'; nation-states in which the 'normalization' of organized crime and brutal banditry" is the status quo.[23] In a world where violence is the norm, the suicide bomber's transgressive sanctity appears as the surest form of self-preservation. At the same time, Gazueva's transgressive sanctity marks an even fuller relinquishment of political agency than that experienced by Chechens under Soviet rule. The sacralization of transgression inevitably intensifies the cycle of violence.

Zarema was not alone in framing Gazueva's violence through the idiom of transgressive sanctity. Five years after Gazueva's suicide, a community leader of Urus-Martan and director of the organization *Materinskaia Trevoga* (Mother's Anxiety), described Gazueva's act with pride in an interview with *Radio Svoboda* (*Free Radio*), a subsidiary of the US State Department–funded Voice of America. "Until such grief reaches your house," Zeynap Mezhidova stated during the interview, "you never know how you will act. In my view, [Gazueva] is a hero. She acted courageously."[24] Back in Nalchik, Zarema echoed the praise that my Chechen teacher had bestowed on those who gave their lives for war: "Aizan, a brave *shahidka*, died as a warrior for her people." Zarema's comment exposes transgressive sanctity's ethical ambiguity, which some might call its duplicity: in resisting state coercion, the aestheticization of violence exacerbates the suffering it seeks to arrest. In its textual as in its visual iterations, the violence of transgressive sanctity is circular and self-perpetuating. Originating in the colonial encounter, transgressive sanctity has no identifiable end. Its logic reveals the persistence of colonial logics of governance within the postcolony.

The three of us gazed together in silence at the intense, searching eyes of the young woman who had become both the subject and the object of her tragedy (figure 13). Her hair was pulled away from her face in a scarf. She stared at the camera fearlessly, rays of light illuminating her blue silk dress that gleamed beneath the camera's glare. The remainder

Figure 13. Aizan Gazueva. Photograph by Rebecca Gould.

of our conversation was taken up with the request by my host and her friend that I distribute Aizan Gazueva's picture as widely as possible to the US media. CNN, NBC, ABC, FOX—they named all the networks. As a visiting American, I was marked as a journalist, although it was not my profession, and I was expected to have contacts with each of these networks. The aestheticization of Aizan's suicide, now through visual means, demonstrates how the postcolony domesticates violence in the aftermath of war.

What did the visitor from Urus-Martan and my host expect to gain by disseminating Aizan's photograph globally? Why did they want her to be known in the United States, where she had never traveled and where there were no ties to home? Their request implied that a sacrificial death could be redeemed through technology. Just as the aesthetics of violence is more appealing in its extreme than its everyday iterations, this episode taught me that transgressive sanctity is more persuasive in literature than in political life.

The parallelisms adduced earlier with respect to Palestine and Chechnya are more apparent than in the proliferation of suicide bombing as a political device. Suicide bombing first appeared in Palestine in 1994 in response to the attack by the American-Jewish settler Baruch Goldstein on the Ibrahimi Mosque in 1993.[25] This gender with which this practice was associated shifted in Palestine in 2002, when, in the first four months of that year, four Palestinian women (Wafāʾ Idrīs, Darīn Abu Aishah, Ayat Akhraṣ, and Andalīb Takatka) blew themselves up in organized attacks against Israeli military personnel or civilians.[26]

Palestinian female suicide bombers often take center stage in discussions of gendered violence.[27] Notwithstanding the preponderance of these women in the popular imagination, the proportion of female to male suicide bombers is even greater in Chechnya. Chechnya witnessed the first female-perpetrated suicide attack in June 2000. Whereas Hamas only reluctantly and belatedly allowed women to further its political goals through suicide bombing, the practice was embraced at an earlier stage in the Chechen conflict, allowing for an even greater number of Chechen *shahids* than in Palestine.[28]

In the Chechen case, in contradistinction to Palestine, there was no clear shift from the ethic of the *fidaʾyi* (secular, often nationalist, warrior) to the Islamic *shahid*. Chechen suicide bombers, women as well as men, situated themselves, and were situated by others, as religious martyrs from the war's inception. The distinction drawn by Palestinian religious leader sheykh Bassam Jarrar between a "martyrdom operation" that connotes "respect and honor for the bomber" and suicide, forbidden by the Quran (2:195, 4:29), has less traction in Chechnya, a society where Islamic practices reemerged only in the post-Soviet period.[29] The strategy of encouraging women to sacrifice their lives for the Chechen struggle was readily adopted by Chechen militants such as Shamil Basaev, who in other respects emulated the gender policies of Islamic organizations that attempted to keep women away from the battlefield.[30] Transgressive sanctity was the Chechen counterpart to more transparently Islamic forms of religiosity elsewhere in the Muslim world.

In the eyes of the neoliberal state, Gazueva's actions rendered her a criminal. And yet when compared with actions perpetrated by Russian officers, the connection between state legitimacy and justice appears quite arbitrary. One year prior to Gazueva's act, in March 2000, Elsa Kungaeva, an eighteen-year-old Chechen woman, was taken from her home in the village of Tangi-Chu, also in the district surrounding Urus-Martan. She was beaten, raped, and strangled to death by Yuri Budanov, recipient of the "Order of Courage" and one of Putin's star colonels prior to the crime. Three years passed before Budanov was brought to trial. When the trial finally transpired, many Russians sided with him against Kungaeva's family, regarding Budanov as "a valiant fighter who helped wage a bloody but necessary war against separatist rebels in Chechnya."[31] Budanov was finally sentenced to ten years of prison in 2003. On 15 January 2009, he was released on parole for good behavior, after only six years in prison. On 10 June 2011, Budanov was killed by unidentified gunmen in Moscow.[32] Although the Budanov scandal had yet to be sentenced when I encountered Aizan's story in Nalchik, Zarema was already persuaded, rightly as it turned out, that the verdict would be in Budanov's favor. She had seen enough, she said, to know that Russian courts refused to make criminals accountable for their crimes. She was convinced that the media would never reveal the full extent of his crimes. Zarema's distrust of media representations of Budanov stood in interesting tension with her desire to circulate Aizan's image across the global media.

When our conversation concerning Aizan came to a close, Zarema asked whether I had heard of Elsa Kungaeva. I told her I only knew what I had read in newspapers, which presented Kungaeva as a passive victim of Russian brutality. Just as *shahidki* are presumed by the media to be incapable of commenting intelligently on the legal codes that had come to overdetermine their lives, so were those among Kungaeva's family who survived her rendered silent through their reconfiguration in the media as victims. Zarema had a different story to tell.

Kungaeva, she explained, had been burned alive by the Russian army in Samashski, a village made famous by the massacre that occurred there in 1995, during the first war.[33] Kungaeva had been taken from her home by force, carried into the forest, raped, and then set on fire by a group of Russian soldiers. Budanov's soldiers confined her parents to their house until the crime was finished. When her body had become so charred that only the ashes remained, the soldiers released her parents, who promptly ran into the forest in search of their daughter. They could locate only a few shards of bone and a pair of earrings made of gold too pure to burn in the fire. According to Zarema, her parents recognized that the ashes covering the ground were the last embers of their daughter's body by the sparkle her earrings released under the sun's glow. Like the colonial uncanny that caused Zelimkhan to appear alive to his assassins even when he was dead, Elsa's earrings are metonyms for the soldiers' crime. That they did not burn even in the fire's white heat suggests how this narrative functioned in these Chechens' imaginations as an ethical indictment of Budanov's crime, an indictment grounded in a conception of justice that is both superior and inaccessible to the law of the state.

In June 2000, three months after Kungaeva's death and a little more than a year before Gazueva's attack, though still almost two years in advance of the first female Palestinian suicide bombers, Khava Baraeva and Luisa Magomedova drove a truck filled with explosives into the temporary headquarters of an elite OMON (Special Forces) detachment in the Chechen village of Alkhan Yurt.[34] Six years after this initial act of violence, it was possible to state that Chechen *shahidki* had been involved in "twenty-two of the twenty seven suicide attacks attributed to Chechen rebels."[35]

The widespread circulation of Timur Mutsuraev's song composed in honor of Khava Baraeva adds another layer to the sacralization of violence, that, judging from his lyrics, is grounded more in nationalist sentiments than in the Islamic faith.[36] Mutsuraev's tribute to Baraeva was one of the songs most frequently heard in cars traveling from Nalchik to Chechnya, and its influence reached beyond the young generation. A Kabardian taxi driver who drove me from Nalchik to the train station in Mineralnyi Vody ("Mineral Waters") played Mutsuraev in his cassette deck. Although he was not Chechen, the driver's profession of devotion to the Chechen bard recalled the conversation between Oshaev and Kaitukov concerning Gatuev cited in the preceding chapter. "I play this music because it helps me understand Chechen suffering," the driver explained, as we coasted forward along the highway's yellow ribbon. "Mutsuraev helps me understand Chechen pain."

Genealogies of Martyrdom

Although the concept of martyrdom is of ancient provenance, the logic that treats death as a contribution to a national liberation struggle is, like transgressive sanctity, specific to modernity. *Shahada*—the verbal noun from which the Islamic term applied to those who die in war, *shahid*, is formed—encompasses a sphere of action and experience beyond martyrdom. According to the classicist G. W. Bowersock, the martyrdom concept is a historical innovation that coincided with the advent of Christianity, and it was not immanent in ancient societies.[37] In Islamic and early Christian contexts, martyrdom means striving for a death capable of imparting earthly mortality. As Islamicist Ignaz Goldziher noted many years ago, martyrdom is not restricted to, or even epitomized in, the suicidal act. "He who dies in defense of his possessions," writes Goldziher, "or far from his home in a strange country; who meets his death in falling from a high mountain; who is torn to pieces by wild beasts . . . [is] counted in the category of *shuhadā᾿* [pl. of shahid]" in the Islamic tradition.[38] Internally various as are Muslim views regarding suicide at present, suicide was condemned by Islamic jurists from the eighth-century. One hadith reported by Ibn Ḥanbal, al-Tirmidhī, and others, states that the Prophet refused to say prayers over the body of a suicide.[39] Notwithstanding the legal consensus against suicide in classical *fiqh*, in modern times suicides have generally been accorded standard Islamic funeral rites.[40]

Inhabiting a territorial state that had short-circuited alternative forms of resistance and co-opted transgressive sanctity to refashion the social order, Gazueva responded to violence through her body, which was the only resource at her disposal. To adapt Hannah Arendt's description of the Greek polis, the manner of Gazueva's death evoked a world in which "men entered the public realm because they wanted something of their own or something they had in common with others to be more permanent than their earthly lives."[41] The major difference between the violence Gazueva perpetrated and the world Arendt describes is that Gazueva was working with a degenerated concept of transgressive sanctity that she could activate only by killing herself and others. This was the polis—the global public sphere—from which Zarema and Zeynap regarded me as an emissary. This is also the polis where, in postmodernity, violence is aestheticized and sanctity is instrumentalized.

While Gazueva's violence cannot be reduced to any single motivation, her quest for recognition was unambiguously foregrounded when she asked her victim and persecutor, "Do you recognize me?" Furthermore, the posthumous canonization of Gazueva by the inhabitants of Urus-Martan attests to a local belief, already evident in Chechen narrations of Zelimkhan's death, that bearing witness (*shahada*) through self-immolation confers immortality on the sacrificer's community. Musaev's reflection with respect to the 1877 uprising also elucidates Chechen insurgency as it has developed over the past two centuries, in the context of colonial violence. "Holy war," Musaev writes, "is a permanent condition."[42] This claim activates the circular logic of transgressive sanctity and foregrounds its dependency on violence as a source of (negative) meaning.

Agency and Judgment

Gazueva's example diverges from the suicide bomber stereotype. She created only two victims, a military officer and herself. Rather than pursuing a nationalist or religious agenda, her goal was the destruction of her family's murderer. Also unlike the stereotype, Gazueva's military target was Daghestani, not Russian. Gazueva's demand for recognition, together with her posthumous canonization by the residents of Urus-Martan, suggests a form of agency that privileges violence as the means through which meaning is made.

Although Gazueva's violence did not stop the circulation of violence, it did reveal the limits of the state's presumed monopoly on it. In light of Talal Asad's claim that the primary task of the state is "to exclude violence from the arena of politics and connect it to the domain of war" this post-Soviet act of insurgency blurred divisions between public and private, and placed war at the center of public life.[43] In reconnecting violence to the polis and the polis to violence, Gazueva's death and its reception in Chechen culture showed how, in postwar Chechnya, violence and politics implicate each other through war, thereby contributing to transgressive sanctity's proliferation.

Chapter 1 examined how sanctity is constituted in a colonial context through the transgression of colonial legal norms. In a similar vein, Indian historian Ranajit Guha's diagnosis of colonialism in India as a "domination without hegemony" provides a suggestive, if inadequate, framework against which to track the morphologies of colonial power and anticolonial resistance. Connecting hegemony to Marx's analysis of the political economy, Guha notes that, in precapitalist polities, "dominance neither solicits nor acquires hegemony."[44] Indeed, as Guha shows, following Gramsci, hegemony is generated by conditions specific to capital. Colonialism's relation to capital implicates this sociopolitical economy as the specific outcome of modern distributions of power. Guha also shows that viewing colonization as merely the imposition of coercive laws on a subject population means ignoring the persistence of indigenous legal norms.

Guha usefully distinguishes the workings of hegemony as experienced within colonized societies from hegemony as experienced within colonizing societies. Arguably, however, he goes too far when he suggests that some societies experience hegemony while others do not. Although unevenly experienced, hegemony was a persistent feature of colonized and colonizing societies alike. Guha writes against the secular historiography that "endows colonialism with a hegemony . . . denied to it by history" and ends by denying *any* hegemonic content to the colonized's negotiation of colonial power.[45] Vivek Chibber and others have objected that, in denying hegemony, Guha commits a category error similar to colonial historiography by denying the agency of the colonized.[46] Militating against the view that colonialism overdetermined all aspects of life in the colonies, the vernacular experience of colonial rule suggests forms of hegemony that never attained to dominance in the Gramscian sense.

Over the long course of Chechnya's encounter with colonial rule, numerous intellectuals served in the tsarist administration, as did al-Ghāzīghumūqī and al-Alqadārī, and otherwise facilitated the establishment of colonial rule in the Caucasus. Through the actions of Najm al-Dīn's father Donogo Muḥammad, who quelled the 1877 rebellion, and the involvement of many Caucasus intellectuals in constructing a new Soviet legal order, colonial law was variously consolidated, rejected, and transformed. As anthropologist Saba Mahmood has posited, agency emerges in contexts of war "not simply as a synonym for resistance to relations of domination, but as a capacity for action that specific relations of subordination create and enable."[47] Likewise, insurgency can be overdetermined, simultaneously as a locus of coercion and as a locus of resistance. In the first half of the twentieth century, the anticolonial abrek wielded political capital. He went from being the antisocial outcast of precolonial eras to the sanctified hero of high literary modernity. In the post-Soviet era, the abrek of Soviet memory degenerated into the *shahidka* who is socialized to sacrifice her life for the collective good. This shift entailed a turn away from the textual aesthetics of insurgency and toward a visual glorification of violence.

The dialectic of transgressive sanctity elucidates the relation between violence and externally imposed legal systems described for the postcolony by subaltern theorist Upendra Baxi. "If the violence of the law converts an act of insurgency into a series of crimes," writes Baxi, the law of violence that motivates both the abrek and the suicide bomber "valorize[s] 'crime' as a pathway to justice."[48] When crime is valorized, the law's violence "decriminalize[es] the rebel violence aimed at itself." That such decriminalization can lead to a situation wherein the indigenous legal "structuration of subalternity" becomes "no different in range and intensity" from "state-sanctioned death" reminds us that the violence of insurgency does not conduce to the social good.[49] Far from resolving the problem of violence, transgressive sanctity in its degenerated, post-Soviet iteration is one of violence's most attenuated symptoms.

The tendency of emancipatory legal systems to initially celebrate "popular illegalities" and then morph into systems that are "repressive of its own makers [and] participants" reverberates across the postcolonial world.[50] When postcolonies perpetuate colonial frameworks, vernacular polities that began life as "emancipatory" soon acquire "the fully repressive visage of hegemonic formations."[51] Like many of Guha's most brilliant students, Baxi contests his teacher's thesis that colonial rule was experienced in India as dominance without hegemony. For Baxi, if not for Guha, hegemony is the ultimate fruit of the colonial experiment, and the proof that colonialism has brought about a true revolution in legal norms. Baxi's equivalence between the violence of anticolonial insurgency and colonial coercion, on the one hand, and externally coercive law and internally coercive custom (ʿ*ādāt* in Islamic terms), on the other hand, suggests the limitations of transgressive sanctity as a political principle for regulating violence.

Zelimkhan entered the world when transgressive sanctity was in the process of being transmuted into literature. In this age of serial reproduction, violence was aestheticized by colonial officials and anticolonial writers alike in popular journals, mass circulation newspapers, and official communiqués. The relationship between literature and history was already problematic at this early juncture, for the fecundity of the narratives transgressive sanctity generated was inversely proportional to their historical realization. Gatuev's narrative of the implausible exploits of Deni sheykh Arsanov is a case in point, as is Mamakaev's of Zelimkhan's miracle working: lacking a clear basis in history, these stories generate transgressive sanctity from folklore, miracles, and the vernacular imagination.

With the progression of the Soviet project, as the state penetrated ever more deeply into private lives, or rather sealed off the private from the public imaginary, violence came increasingly to seem like a holdover from another, less civilized era, which predated the advent of communist rule, and permanent peace that was said to have been put in place. Transgressive sanctity was relegated to the literary past and expelled from quotidian domains, just as the violence of the Soviet experiment was systematically denied and suppressed through ideological conceits such as the brotherhood of peoples. As we know however, the Soviet experiment was only peaceful in the most superficial of senses: beneath the surface lurked prejudice, resentment, and mass deportations.

Only with the collapse of the Soviet Union, and the revival of violence on a scale not seen in the Caucasus since the beginnings of Soviet rule, did transgressive sanctity reemerge as a guiding principle of everyday life. This time, violence was entailed with new technologies of communication, with the digital photograph, and with the television screen, rather than with the old documentary histories, and journalistic profiles that writers such as Gatuev composed for Zelimkhan. As with early Soviet transgressive sanctity, post-Soviet violence generated a discourse fraught with contradictions. Otherwise peaceful civilians suddenly began to glorify violence, and the state predictably demonized these civilians as terrorists who merited punishment to the fullest extent of the law, and often beyond. Once again, transgressive sanctity wielded a paradoxical appeal for internal and external observers who did not customarily endorse violence.

At this juncture, however, it was less the literary aestheticization of violence that brought about this inversion in ethical hierarchies than the realignments that transpired in popular culture, and in mass technologies of representation, such as the digital image. The materials assembled in this book suggest that transgressive sanctity was more nuanced and denser with ethical complexity in the early Soviet period than in the post-Soviet present. Perhaps this difference is simply a function of the transvaluation of values that is afforded by any ideology that is radically new, and which is thereby capable of calling the most basic of received ideas into question. What is certain is that, by the end of the Soviet experiment, transgressive sanctity could no longer claim to be sacred. Having relinquished its capacity to persuade outside observers or to win converts to its cause, it degenerated into an expression of desperation, the type of wartime rhetoric engaged in by those who have no other options. In light of post-Soviet transgressive sanctity's failure to uphold higher ethical values, the lessons of the colonial era and Soviet-past, not to mention the precolonial period, have much to offer endeavors to understand contemporary violence in the Caucasus.

By the time of Gazueva's suicidal act, resistance had become a fiction, subject to the state's surveillance. While the brutal murder of her family itself explains Gazueva's action in human terms, many commentators have constructed the female suicide bomber as a victim, a robot, or a monster.[52] Such interpretations replace the study of social meaning with speculation about motives. Against the grain of such tendencies in the scholarship on insurgency against the state, Talal Asad disambiguates *motives* from *causes.* The social scientist, Asad maintains, learns more by studying historical causes than by analyzing motives, which are inevitably enmeshed in cultural prejudices.[53] Whereas considerations of motive may drive a psychoanalytic reading, a "process geography"—to borrow Arjun Appadurai's phrase—that examines the dialectical generation of violence from within imbalances of power situates individual acts within social infrastructures. Rather than objectifying Gazueva's motives, I have examined the relation between her insurgency and forms of violence implemented by the state.

Foucault understands biopower as a domain in which agency is eliminated in the process of securing protection.[54] Deriving from Foucauldian biopower his own concept of bare life, Giorgio Agamben characterizes sovereignty as the sphere in which "it is permitted to kill without committing homicide."[55] On both Agamben's and Foucault's readings, Gazueva endeavored unsuccessfully to act meaningfully within a terrain eviscerated by bare life. Agamben constructs sovereignty from within the framework of bare life. However, as Guha does with his conception of domination without hegemony, Agamben risks reinforcing the victimization that governs representations of female *shahidki.*[56] These thinkers are not alone. A prevailing consensus among policy analysts sees *shahidki* as predominantly "widows and rape victims," desperately in need of assistance from the state.[57] Contrary to these patronizing framings, Gazueva's violence, along with its memorialization, inverts Agamben's formulation: bare life appropriates the sovereignty of the state for nonstatist ends.

The second sense in which Zarema's narration undermines the governmental logic of the state, as well as the common sense we bring to the study of violence, was that she neither condemned nor victimized Gazueva. The pictures of Gazueva could have easily become embedded in feminizing stereotypes. But neither Zeynap nor Zarema mentioned Gazueva's beauty, even though women are as commonly assessed in terms of their physical appearance in Chechen society as elsewhere across the world. In contradistinction to the dominant social discourse that undertakes to "explain" the female suicide bomber with reference to the weakness of the female gender, my Chechen informants refused to depoliticize Gazueva's violence.[58]

For both Zeynap and Zarema, the point of disseminating Gazueva's picture was to sanctify her transgression. Even more than her body, her soul was to be immortalized through the peculiarly postmodern technique of digital circulation. In contrast to the Soviet anticolonial writers who propagated poetry's immortality to a select literary elite, this quotidian engagement with violence vested its faith in the efficacy of mass circulation. The more people Aizan's image reached, so Zeynap and Zarema believed, the more her cause would be served. Benjamin's insight that "technological reproduction places the copy of the original in situations the original itself cannot attain" reads as prophetic with regard to this event.[59] Similarly prophetic is Benjamin's insight into the difference made by mass circulation on the cultural aesthetic of a given age. "It might be stated as a general formula that the technology of reproduction detaches the reproduced object from the sphere of tradition," Benjamin writes. "By replicating the work many times over," he continues, "it substitutes a mass existence for a unique existence. And in permitting the reproduction to reach the recipient in his or her own situation, it actualizes the object of reproduction."[60] Although circulation rather than reproduction is the key dimension to this *shahidka*'s power, Benjamin's account of the power of the image broadly helps to explain transgressive sanctity's persistence within the post-Soviet digital landscape. When they requested that I publicize Gazueva's image to the world, Zarema and Zeynap embedded the image's afterlife within the "public realm" which Arendt recognized as "more permanent" than "earthly" life.[61] This permanent life was to be generated and sustained through the photograph, a technology that, as Benjamin points out, "emerged at the same time as socialism."[62] Appropriately for a post-Soviet context, Gazueva's photograph was to morph into a digital image on the television screen.

Zarema and I did not spend much time in Nalchik discussing the war. Our conversation focused instead on Gazueva's demand for recognition. Whereas political scientists and media gurus postulate a "clear distinction between the personal and the political" to separate suicide bombing from "political contexts such as occupation or civil war," Chechens tasked with representing their traumas to the world correlate political violence and personal suffering in quite different ways.[63] In seeking to secure Gazueva's afterlife in the public sphere, my interlocutors also constructed an aesthetic monument to violence. Whereas earlier contributions to transgressive sanctity, such as the novels of Gatuev and Mamakaev, politicized art, these post-Soviet engagements aestheticized political violence. Already in his 1935 essay on mechanical reproduction, Benjamin had gloomily passed judgment on this process, which he linked to the fascism of his age. "All efforts to aestheticize politics," he wrote, "culminate in one point. That one point is war. War, and only war, makes it possible."[64] While war aestheticizes violence, it also vindicates this aestheticizing process.

In one of the few studies of female suicide bombers that recognizes their agency, Hasso notes that recognizing these acts "as anti-colonial resistance in a situation of overwhelming subjugation does not negate patriarchal societal operations . . . or debates about the morality and short- and long-term implications of such a method."[65] The anthropology of transgressive sanctity differs from policy-oriented scholarship in suspending judgment and in viewing the state's violence from beyond the perspective of the state.[66] In the early decades of the twentieth century, Chechen poets and prose writers, together with their Ossetian sympathizers, evolved a literary canon grounded in the figure of the abrek. Their political aesthetic shaped a body politic that combined spiritual aspiration with ethical conviction. After the collapse of the Soviet Union, the political promise inherent in this vision had degenerated into an aesthetics devoid of any real political goal. No longer a part of a broader aspiration to overturn the colonial order, the post-Soviet insurgent was soon incorporated into criminal structures that defied, without transfiguring, the rule of law.

Andalīb Takatka, one of the four Palestinian female suicide bombers whose image clogged the international airwaves in early 2002, recorded before her death a video in which she questioned the gender hierarchies governing her society along with the norms that restricted political action to men. "I've chosen to say with my body what Arab leaders have failed to say," Takatka stated, unwittingly echoing Gazueva's method of demanding recognition through her body. "My body is a barrel of gunpowder that burns the enemy," she proclaimed.[67] Such women cultivate a self-immolating critique of bare life. Along with critiquing the cycles of violence that dominate their world, the persuasive force of their visceral critiques calls of recognition. Pathologizing the *shahidka* as the manifestation of merely personal suffering depoliticizes acts that are better read as social critiques.

Among those who have reflected on the political implications of self-immolating violence, anthropologist Iris Jean-Klein has crafted one of the most exemplary frameworks for conceiving of such violence against the state in vernacular terms. Similarly to Mezhidova's glorification of Aizan's violence, Jean-Klein contests commentaries on suicide bombing that focus exclusively on questions of motives. Under certain conditions, she observes, people's actions become "so utterly overdetermined by their objective historical forces that analysis can (or is it that it 'had better'?) dispense with 'actors' own' or with 'local' understanding."[68] In identifying the need for a critical space between the state and "local understanding," Jean-Klein anticipates the charge that indigenizing narratives (including my own) rely excessively on discourses of cultural authenticity. In a Benjaminian critique of suicide bombing, local explanations must be supplemented by critiques of transgressive sanctity. At this juncture in my account, the historical method becomes a means of shedding light on the political present.

What social forces and historical factors can ground our understanding of transgressive sanctity in an age of neocolonial governance? As with Elsa Kungaeva, and even Khava Baraeva, possibly the best-known Chechen *shahidka*, the paraphernalia of transgressive sanctity consists of pictures taken and stories told by others. Even the perpetrators' words are heavily mediated by the few who have made it their mission to remember. Like so many of her counterparts, Gazueva was memorialized in pictures alone. The ethnography of Chechen *shahidki* that this chapter has made its object of inquiry is faced with multiple representational challenges. Beyond the shadow over these proceedings cast by the ethical ambiguity of violence, the *shahidka* destabilizes liberal assumptions concerning our willing subordination to the laws of the state. Those who fear defeat more than death are oblivious to the rational self-interest that "undergirds capitalism and the power of the state."[69] Hence, suicide bombing destabilizes social categories.

What then is the ultimate meaning of Gazueva's question: "Do you recognize me?" If her query articulates a politics of resistance, what was she resisting? A Daghestani general, not a Russian officer, was the primary object of her aggression. It seems therefore that, although her act was entangled within a long history of violence that encompasses ethnography, literature, and history, she was not precisely resisting any specific political mandate. Rather, Gazueva's violence was a symptom of neocolonial violence, arising from the impossibility of coherently and viably resisting the logic of wartime governmentality. How did Gazueva inscribe her agency into *bios*, the "qualified life"—distinguished from *zoe*, "the simple fact of living"—that for Agamben references "the form or way of living proper to an individual or a group"?[70]

In the light of recent efforts to disentangle agency from mere resistance to the state, the argument that Gazueva's life and death were wholly overdetermined by sovereign power when she detonated her grenade seems all the more precarious.[71] Valid ethical judgment cannot be anchored in contextless, unchanging values. Moreover, the greatest analytical gains to be made from studying Gazueva's canonization in Chechen historical memory will come from understanding her role in the social praxis of everyday Chechen political life, not from moralizing.

Transgressive Sanctity beyond Violence

This book opened by suggesting that a literary anthropology of anti-colonial insurgency in the Caucasus can undo dichotomies between indigenous resistance and global circulations of power while also introducing new disciplinary relations within this intellectual labor. I began by showing how premodern archives, in particular literary production in Arabic, Persian, and Turkic, can lay the groundwork for a new way of understanding the Caucasus. Having traversed the colonial, Soviet, and post-Soviet periods, it is fitting to conclude by exploring how these conceptual revisions play out with respect to the contemporary moment.

"When no signs of the living body can be relied on, the ground that sustains the sense of being human—and therefore of what it is to be humane—collapses," writes Talal Asad.[72] In wartime Chechnya, human bodies were destroyed by agents acting on behalf of a state, including through rape and murder. Suicide bombing's unique capacity to instill terror, adds Asad, consists in its revelation of the ease with which the boundary between the living and the dead, "between the sanctity of a human corpse and the profanity of an animal carcass—can be crossed." We have already seen this slippage from life to death and back again activated in the abrek's uncanny animacy. But the capacity to fabricate death from life is clearly not the insurgent's prerogative. Indeed, the state's power over life and death often exceeds that of the insurgent.

The unequal distribution of power between the *shahidka* and her antagonist recalls the imbalance in power between the abrek and his colonial persecutors. In both cases, the conflict is preordained to result in defeat. The certainty of defeat in both instances complicates the ethics and aesthetics of their posthumous sanctification. Reflecting on how Palestinians who use themselves as ammunition against the occupation come to be considered martyrs (*shuhadā'*), Asad proposes a twofold explanation: "first, they have been struck by a catastrophe, and, second, their mode of death gives them immortality."[73] After its political potential has been eviscerated, transgressive sanctity can aspire only to see the fruits of its ideology realized posthumously.

Asad, similarly to Guha in his Marxian mode, sees this striving for immortality as an element in a kind of false consciousness. Indeed, the impact of the quest for immortality on the colonial legal order is provisional at best. As Asad notes, all strategies of modern warfare, from the soldier trained to kill and die to the suicide bomber who detonates a bomb, belong to a failed and deeply troubled secular project to "secure a kind of collective immortality" for the state and its constituencies.[74] And yet Asad also perceptively reminds us that to hunt for motives with suicide bombing is to fail to understand the cause of this violence.

More interesting and important than the question of why suicide bombers choose to die, argues Asad, is the issue of how willed self-immolation can instill in us a horror greater than the horror that attends ordinary descriptions of rape, murder, and pillage in war. What is so frightening, and so alluring, about violence? "Liberalism," Asad reasons, "disapproves of the violent exercise of freedom outside the frame of the law." Like the abrek of an earlier era, the suicide bomber archetypally enacts a "limitless pursuit of freedom" while cultivating an "interiority that can withstand the force of institutional disciplines."[75] Within this interiority lies concealed the appeal of a violence that transgresses secular law (*zakon*) for the sake of a higher ethical imperative.

Liberal theory (for example, the Hegelian philosophy of right referenced in chapter 1) teaches that there is no tribunal higher than the state: metaphysically and morally, the good of the state is the goal toward which all our actions are supposed to strive. Pace liberal political theory, the abrek and the suicide bomber bring the state's legitimacy into conflict with individual sanctity. This conflict is conveyed not through a vacuum of ethics but through an excess of ethics that so thoroughly exceeds the boundaries of the liberal discourse underwritten by the state that it can exist only as resistance to the state or not at all.

In acting outside coercive legal frameworks while also cultivating higher ethical codes, Zelimkhan laid bare the corruption of colonial law. Zelimkhan's interpreters used his legacy to reveal the corruption of Soviet law. Finally, Gazueva attempted to reveal the limits of post-Soviet law, but her self-immolation doomed her to failure. Neither liberalism of the colonial state nor the atheism of the Soviet order nor the secular violence of post-Soviet rule can accommodate transgressive sanctity as an ethical norm. One flaw endemic to legal systems violated by the abrek and the *shahidka* is that they make no provision for the agency of those who, whether through their birthrights or their convictions, have been excised from the civil-social order. These ostracized actors opt for the course of action proposed—though not endorsed—by Hannah Arendt nearly half a century ago in her reflections on violence. "Under certain circumstances," argued Arendt, "acting without argument or speech and *without counting the consequences*—is the only way to set the scales of justice right again."[76]

Like Arendt, Asad underscores the persuasive logic wielded by death. The logic of death, which centrally structures the aesthetics of transgressive sanctity, is one of the few means available to many Chechens and other disenfranchised peoples of preventing state coercion from encompassing the entirety of their lives. Particularly under wartime conditions, the state fails to secure its legitimacy. This failure stimulates the creation of a new value system by subjects whose needs the structures of liberal governance are constituted to ignore. Refusing to honor the law merely on the grounds of its normativity, practitioners and propagators of transgressive sanctity hold the law of the state to a higher standard than the state holds itself.

As the ethical system arising from the failure of the state to protect the basic rights of all its citizens, transgressive sanctity in post-Soviet society is constrained by two substantial limitations. First, it can never be translated into a viable political system. Having already been aestheticized during the early Soviet period, it is premised on the abdication of political life. Second, transgressive sanctity is all too frequently generative of new forms of social coercion. Over the course of such a transvaluation, "mortal vengeance" counters "death as loss with death as restoration, the former a brutal crime and the latter a just satisfaction."[77]

Such fantasies of restitution are inevitably short-lived. The scales of justice cannot be set right through murder, whether of oneself or of others. Nonetheless, it is evident that, for a society such as Chechnya, devastated by war, the most viable ethical system will be grounded in principles external to, and in certain cases, contrary to, the legal apparatus of the governing state. The task for the future is to determine how transgressive sanctity, as it has been cultivated across the literatures, cultures, and historical memories over the course of the nineteenth and twentieth centuries, can be used to short-circuit the cyclical violence it has most recently perpetuated. As a political theory of violence, transgressive sanctity is also an implicit program for peace. The endeavor to reach that moment of status, when the critique of violence merges with the object of its critique, animates this investigation.

Epilogue

Transgression as Sanctity?

What does it mean to protest suffering, as distinct from acknowledging it?
—Susan Sontag, *On Regarding the Pain of Others*

Three years after Aslanbek Sheripov assimilated the abrek's revolutionary violence to the Bolshevik rejection of tsarist rule, Walter Benjamin confronted the problem of violence in a context that, for all its seeming distance from Bolshevik Russia, similarly witnessed dramatic social upheavals, the decay of old political institutions, and newly emergent forms of social life. Although these thinkers could not have fully cognized what they shared in common, it is also no coincidence that they were both approaching violent deaths. The Weimar Republic had recently been established in the wake of Germany's wartime defeat. Benjamin's life, and financial prospects, had changed accordingly. New alliances were being forged between mutinying sailors, who had refused to risk their lives in battle for the sake of an elusive victory, and the newly emancipated proletariat, who united under the slogan *Friedon und Brot* (freedom and bread) to demand improved social prospects. A general strike loomed on the horizon, stimulating intellectuals whose lives were entangled in these transformations to rethink the foundations of sovereignty and to identify the new possibilities opened up by mass collective action.

Like the Bolshevik Revolution that preceded it by one month and from which it derived its inspiration, the November 1918 revolution that culminated in the creation of the Weimar Republic generated a ferment of discussions concerning the possibilities of dissent, the limits of state coercion, and the ethics of violence. One result of these new intellectual currents was a series of pioneering reflections on the foundations of political sovereignty by the legal theorist Carl Schmitt, whose "state of exception" anticipated the mentality governing the Third Reich, under which he later worked.[1] A second result of this ferment was Benjamin's "On the Critique of Violence," which set the tone for the discussion of violence at the beginning of this book. Benjamin was Schmitt's sometime admirer and trenchant, though subtle, critic.[2]

Benjamin regarded his "Kritik" as a chapter in what was to become an ambitious book-length study on the problem of violence in politics, a project cut short by his untimely death.[3] Far from simply judging violence negatively, as the English term *critique* imprecisely suggests, Benjamin aimed to systematically review the conditions for violence, to account for its efficacy, and to document the means through which violence attains hegemony in political modernity. In concluding this consideration of the literatures of anticolonial insurgency, I move from transgressive sanctity's variegated critiques of colonial violence, which the preceding four chapters have documented across Chechen, Russian, Daghestani, and Georgian literatures, to the critique of the transgressive sanctity's own forms of violence. While the concept of transgressive sanctity has driven this book, the relevance of its anticolonial ethos to politics as such remains unprobed.

Max Weber's definition of the state as a *Gewaltmonopol*, an entity that wields a "monopoly on the legitimate use of violence [*Gewalt*]," was one stimulus for Benjamin's "Kritik." Weber first described the state in relation to its dependency on *Gewalt* in "Politics as a Vocation," a lecture he delivered to the Free Students Union at the University of Munich in 1919. In the preceding year, Aslanbek Sheripov had used the abrek to legitimate revolutionary violence. Weber anticipated Benjamin by defining the modern liberal state in relation to violence (*Gewalt*) during a period of political upheaval when the governmental forms that were to replace the old political order increasingly ceased to compel obedience.[4]

When Benjamin incorporated Weber's alignment between the state and violence into his "Kritik," however, his focus on the conditions for the emergence of violence led to him to place the Weberian conception of the state's legitimacy in a different light. Following Benjamin's insight, the preceding chapters have shown that the Soviet refashioning of revolutionary violence, particularly by writers such as Gatuev, Titsian, and Mamakaev, developed a new understanding of the relation between the poet's vocation and political critique.

Benjamin subtly defamiliarized Weber's account of the state's legitimacy, arguing that "the law's interest in a monopoly of violence [*Monopolisierung der Gewalt*] . . . is explained not by the intention of preserving legal ends but rather by the intention of preserving the law itself" (183). Benjamin's formulation reproduces Weber's definition, but in a different affective register. In Benjamin, violence is the means through which the law, harnessed to the state, is justified. As Benjamin wrote in a fragment penned a year prior to his "Kritik," the law is fundamentally concerned "with self-preservation. In particular, with defending its existence against its own guilt."[5] Violence threatens the state until it is located within the law, for its extralegal location reveals the arbitrariness of the state rather than its legitimacy. Just as violence reveals the state's illegitimacy, so does transgressive sanctity expose the colonial generation of violence. A Benjaminian reading of this process suggests that the monopoly on violence that Weber considers intrinsic to the state's power is generated by highly contingent political relations. Weber perceived this contingency as well as Benjamin, but he lacked the latter's interest in undoing the state's claim to legitimacy.

The scope of Benjamin's actual intentions with respect to the critique of violence are set forth only at the end of his essay. "The *Kritik* of violence," Benjamin writes here in a famous line already cited in the introduction, "is the philosophy of its history" (202). Conceiving of this philosophy as a temporal unfolding along Hegelian lines, Benjamin adds that only by excavating violence's history can a critical, discriminating, and decisive (*kritische, scheidende, und entscheidende*) approach be articulated (202). Benjamin's critique of violence suggests how violence can function as a tool to resist the state. Historically prior to any given legal order, violence can, on Benjamin's reading, overturn any political regime. At the same time, Benjamin goes further than many of the writers considered in this book with regard to his critique of violence, for he aimed to use violence to overcome violence itself. One means of such political transcendence was the general strike, a form of mass mobilization that Benjamin regarded as "a pure means, a purified, immediate form of violence which deposed the whole legal order" even as it "diminished the incidence of actual violence."[6]

Transgressive sanctity took root in Caucasus cultures when a coercive legal order legitimized revolt. Similarly, violence for Benjamin is a reaction to the law. Praising the French philosopher Georges Sorel, whose *Réflexions sur la violence* (1908) pioneered a general theory of the strike, Benjamin notes that "in the beginning all right was the prerogative of kings or nobles—in short, of the powerful . . . *mutatis mutandis*, it will remain so long as it exists" (198). Alongside Benjamin's belief in the provisional efficacy of violence lingered an equally compelling understanding of the capacity of violence to inaugurate what months before his death he would call "the real state of emergency [*Ausnahmenzustand*]" that emerges from the "tradition of the oppressed."[7] Benjamin countered Weber's autopsy of the state's legitimacy by underscoring how violence becomes sacred in the act of transgression. Although they share in common a concern with the relation between power and sovereignty, Benjamin is more interested in the tradition of the oppressed than in Weberian legitimation theory.

Of the many forms of violence Benjamin discusses, only divine violence is intimately related to ethics. One purpose of Benjamin's "Kritik" is to trace how the state legitimates the arbitrary relation between ethics and politics. Whereas Weber locates the state's power in its control of violence, Benjamin locates the state's power in its ability to naturalize its arbitrary relation to violence. Guided by the belief that every political order is founded on violence, Benjamin aims to produce a taxonomy of its immanent power. He elaborates two non-isomorphic but occasionally overlapping rubrics to bring these differences into relief. In the first instance, Benjamin distinguishes between law-founding (*rechtsetzende*) and law-preserving (*rechtserhaltende*) violence (187). In the second instance, Benjamin contrasts mythic (*mythische*) to divine (*göttliche*) violence, a distinction Jacques Derrida correlates to the difference between Greek and Hebraic legal systems.[8]

Recapitulating the continuum leading from law-founding to law-preserving violence, transgressive sanctity proposes to replace the colonial order. As seen in chapter 4, it ends by producing a legal anarchy even more destructive than colonial rule. Transgressive sanctity draws on the affective power wielded by the great criminal (*grossen Verbrecher*, 183, 186), a paragon for the abrek, to contest the state's violence. In a legal domain that is maintained through coercion, the law is equally compelled to rely on force. Hence the appeal of violence, which functions as a surrogate for authority. By opposing anticolonial violence to the coercion of the state, transgressive sanctity throws into relief the oscillations between divine and mythic authority that are intrinsic to modern governmentality. As Benjamin recognized, the state's dialectical relationship to violence sanctifies transgression and makes sanctity transgressive.

As to the second distinction drawn by Benjamin, between mythic violence, based on Greek norms, and divine violence, epitomized by Hebraic law, Benjamin's examples have particular salience for the Caucasus. Endeavoring to retrieve a conception of divine violence from within the mythic violence he seeks to overcome, Benjamin invokes the archetypal rebel within Caucasus mythology, Prometheus. Known in Chechen as Pxarmat and in Georgian as Amirani, Prometheus epitomizes the struggle between the worlds of the gods and the human will.[9] Benjamin uses the story of Prometheus's attempt to steal fire from Zeus and his punishment for this act on Mt. Elbrus to distinguish between divine violence, which he admires, and the "law preserving violence of punishment," which he regards as a hallmark of tyranny. The legend whereby Prometheus "challenges fate with dignified courage" in the hopes of "one day bringing a new law [*ein neues Recht*] to men" (197), demonstrates how the mythic figures onto whom are projected the desire to rebel against unjust laws promulgate new legal codes through their transgressions. The global renown of Prometheus, which extends from the works of Aeschylus to Percy Bysshe Shelley, attests to the persistent appeal of rebellion against arbitrarily instituted legal orders within and outside Benjamin's political theology.[10]

Only at the very end of his essay does Benjamin pass negative judgment on the object of his critique: *Gewalt.* Here Benjamin states, in a clear yet nuanced allusion to Schmitt's state of exception, that "all mythic, lawmaking violence, which may be called executive, is pernicious [*verwerflich*]" (204). (Benjamin's more frontal attack on Schmitt would have to wait until 1940, for his "On the Concept of History," discussed in chapter 2.) For the majority of his "Kritik," Benjamin examines how violence is made efficacious in order to overcome violence as such. In the spirit of Benjamin's hermeneutics of ambivalence, this book has offered a double-edged critique of transgressive sanctity. Rather than seeking to dismantle the ideological constellations that hold transgressive sanctity together, I have examined the concept's visceral and verbal power. I have explored transgressive sanctity's literary genesis while attending to the elements of its aesthetic and affective form that compel and inspire insurgents to sacrifice their lives.

The heuristic usefulness of transgressive sanctity reverberates well beyond the Caucasus. More thoroughly than prior paradigms for understanding violence, transgressive sanctity captures the ethical ambivalence of violence in the service of justice. Responding to the aestheticization of violence that Benjamin considers a hallmark of fascism (and which unfolded in post-Soviet spaces in chapter 4), transgressive sanctity enacts a communist politicization of art. While the state claims a monopoly on violence to secure its legitimacy, poetry is sanctified in the process of performing the work of religion in a secular world.

As with the early Soviet aestheticization of violence, Benjamin's endorsement of revolutionary and messianic violence marks the limit of liberal ideologies of governance. At the site of this impasse, the literary imagination is alienated from history. For those who are tethered to historical necessity, the suffering entailed in revolutionary violence calls for critique (and not merely analysis). Transgressive sanctity acquires power at precisely this juncture, as a justification of literature's ambivalent relation to violence. Amid the many transformations in post-Soviet society, the shift from the Soviet aestheticization of violence to the sanctification of transgression within the postcolony has been by and large ignored. Meanwhile, literary critiques of violence have been drowned out by belligerent calls for war.[11]

While there is no single, unified critique of violence in Daghestani, Russian, Chechen, Georgian, and Ossetian sources, the heteroglossic literatures of insurgency collectively constitute a local literary canon. Soviet Chechen literature pioneered a pan-Soviet ideology that used anticolonialism as a means of uniting the disparate peoples of the Caucasus. The new literary discourse deployed what Benjamin called the communist politicization of art to integrate aesthetics, ethics, and politics for a post-theistic world.

Communism's revolutionary aesthetics are implicit in Judith Butler's conception of critique, which also derives from Benjamin. "To offer a critique," writes Butler, "is to interrupt and contravene law-preserving power, to withdraw one's compliance from the law, to occupy a provisional criminality that fails to preserve the law and thus undertakes its destruction."[12] The lawbreaker's "provisional criminality" is epitomized in the Chechen abrek and in the Georgian modernist *murīd.* While the critique of violence implicit in transgressive sanctity takes centuries to become manifest, Benjamin suggests that violence can be overcome through the "messianic power of language" itself.[13]

As with any aesthetic process, the dialectic between reality and representation is fluid in the case of transgressive sanctity. As the texts assembled here have shown, transgressive sanctity was generated by a confluence of aesthetic orientations across several Caucasus literatures during the colonial and early Soviet periods. With the progressive regimentation of the Soviet culture, and the silencing of earlier forms of critique, the aesthetics of transgressive sanctity was incorporated into a broader delegitimization of the tsarist regime. This phase was marked less by the politicization of art that Benjamin discerned in early communist aesthetics as by its subordination to political ends. Finally, during the post-Soviet period, transgressive sanctity came back to life within local cultures. But this time there was a difference: literature had become epiphenomenal, and civil society was becoming progressively obliterated by war.

Had this been a work of conventional historiography, greater weight would have been given to the disjuncture between the texts engaged and the worlds they reference. These disjunctures would have revealed new aspects of the undoing of violence and its refashioning according to changing political exigencies. However, such an approach would have risked obscuring the role of the literary imagination as an arbiter of political change. That political-aesthetic conjuncture of aesthetics and violence has been the theme of this book and is presupposed by its literary-anthropological method.

Rather than tracing the historical emergence of transgressive sanctity, this book has engaged with how Chechen, Daghestani, Russian, Georgian, and Ossetian literature from the late tsarist and Soviet periods intertextually reconstituted the anticolonial jihad in cultural memory. The literary history that was constituted by texts legislated its own realities. These literary realities subsequently brought into conversation forms of experiences, such as the miraculous, that were excluded by the historical method. While, as Benjamin discerned, history can assist in the task of critique, it is also problematically blind to violence as it is lived. By contrast with historicizing accounts of violence, literary texts expose the rawness of violence as an aesthetic experience, a reorganization of the sensory. As Claude Lévi-Strauss discerned, humans often work as bricoleurs, assemblers of seemingly random objects, rather than as historians, excavating causality from the archive.[14] Although they complement each other, the analytical tools that reconstruct the literatures of insurgency cannot be converted into weapons of resistance, because the historical formation of literature is nonsynchronous with the history it resists.

The changes this book has traced in the abrek's literary trajectory are conceptual as much as chronological, and discursive as much as they are temporal. They participate in a broader trajectory of communist violence, whereby the state neutralizes dissent by celebrating dissidence from an earlier dispensation. The genesis of the literary abrek from within the tension between indigenous legal norms and the forces of modernity demonstrates how colonial and postcolonial subjects are ineradicably transformed by modern governmentality.

Although post-Soviet transgressive sanctity perpetuates the violence to which it was originally opposed, it has not relinquished its hold on the postcolonial imagination. As Susan Sontag notes, "Violence can exalt someone subjected to it into a martyr or a hero" without resolving the basic ethical dilemmas of the sanctification of violence.[15] Sontag's account of how we regard the pain of others through the mediation of technology suggests that our desensitization to violence is specific to the experience of modernity and is particularly attenuated in colonial contexts. Sontag traces the aestheticization of violence to the proliferation of secular warfare in the seventeenth century, "when contemporary alignments of power become material" within the secular iconography of war.[16] Equally, the literatures of insurgency sacralize war under the rubric of jihad for a desacralized society.

To borrow from Benjamin's account of the aestheticization of violence as a facet of modernity is not to reduce modernity in the Caucasus to the colonial encounter. To the contrary, as I have argued, colonialism marks a relatively late moment in modern Caucasus literary history.[17] Even more than their Georgian and Chechen counterparts, Daghestani scholars cultivated forms of reflexivity now associated with modernity engaging critically with the Islamic tradition long before the normalization of colonial rule. Far from originating within colonialism, modernity's beginnings can be discerned during the eighteenth century. Transgressive sanctity emerged a century later. In between the beginnings of modernity and the emergence of transgressive sanctity, the colonial dispensation introduced the conflicted legal order that generated the abrek.

We Will Not Make War

During the summer of 2006, while on my way to Tbilisi after fieldwork with Chechen refugees in Nalchik, I stopped in northern Azerbaijan's former colonial outpost of Zaqatala, on the border of Daghestan and Georgia. Home to Shamil's fortress, Zaqatala also happened to be the former site of the only monument to Shamil in the southern Caucasus.

It was a July morning high in the mountains. The sun was already blistering overhead. Hoping to leave the run-down guesthouse where I had been staying for a week, I began asking passersby for directions to the nearest hotel. "Come inside and drink some tea with me," offered an elderly woman who happened to overhear my queries. "I have lived in this town all my life," she explained. "I have pictures to show you. I can tell you the history of everything." I followed her past the wrought iron gates opening onto her garden. A peach tree was in bloom, and white blossoms covered the ground, resembling snowflakes turned to stone.

My host closed the gate and extended her hand to greet me: "My name is Svetlana." She pronounced her Russian name as fluently as any native Russian speaker would have done. I determined that, clearly, Russian was her first language. She was a *pensionerka*, I speculated, an elderly woman surviving on a pension, stranded by some fluke of circumstance in northern Azerbaijan. Her ethnic origins turned out to be as mixed as that of nearly everyone local to this region. "My father was Lezgi," Svetlana explained, referencing the ethnic group of Ḥasan al-Alqadārī and Muḥammad al-Yarāghī. "He met my mother, a Russian Cossack, in Krasnodar. They traveled together to Zaqatala, fell in love with the place, and decided to stay here forever."

Svetlana then began sifting through her belongings, which were scattered over the table. The first item she showed me was a tattered copy of a newspaper published in Russia fourteen years earlier: the 12 August 1992 edition of *Literaturnaia Gazeta*. She pointed to a headline and nodded to me to as she read it aloud: WE WILL NOT MAKE WAR ON OUR TERRITORY. The headline referenced an interview with Jawhar Dudaev, soon to be assassinated by a targeted Russian missile in 1995. The message was obvious: Russia's literary elite were refusing to wage war with the self-proclaimed Republic of Ichkeria (although they were also apparently refusing to think of Chechnya as a territory other than "ours"). Similarly, Dudaev had embraced Russia during his career as a pilot in the Soviet air force. Fourteen years after its original publication, this text had been preserved, like a sacred scroll, on a decaying table in the garden of a provincial Azeri home. I asked Svetlana why she had kept the article for so long, and why she was showing it to me now.

"Dudaev was here for the monument's unveiling," she responded reverently.

"Which monument?" I asked, confused. No history or guidebook mentioned anything about a monument relevant to Dudaev. The streets of Azerbaijan's mountain outposts were still dense with Soviet war heroes, with women who had been the first in their family to ride tractors, and who had ripped off their veils in the name of gender equality following the revolution. I had yet to see a monument to any anticolonial insurgent in the Azeri mountains, or any other recognition of the long history of resistance to colonial rule that had ravaged this landscape.

"The monument to Shamil, of course," she said.

I asked her what monument to Shamil she was talking about. I had seen no such thing, and I had been in Zaqatala for over a week.

"It's in the park. Haven't you seen it?"

I had been to the park many times. It was after all the central site in downtown Zaqatala, and the most logical site for a monument. Impressed by Svetlana's conviction, I agreed to join her on the brief walk to the city's center. As it turned out, there was a monument in the middle of the park. It wasn't to Shamil, however, but rather to Heydar Aliev, Azerbaijan's recently deceased president, in whose honor the park had been renamed. In the 1990s Aliev, a former communist leader who had been refashioned by the state-backed media into the patron saint of Azeri nationalism, led his country from the chaos induced by the Nagorno-Karabakh conflict to a tenuous stability. In 2003, Aliev's son Ilham "won" the Azeri presidential elections with a landslide victory of 76 percent, thereby repeating a pattern common to post-Soviet and postcolonial states, whereby sons follow their fathers by right of lineage rather than by right of free elections.

Svetlana wanted to visit the park before going to the Shamil monument. We passed the regal black gates opening onto the idyllic Heydar Aliev Park. While the gates were still overhead, Svetlana pulled from her purse a packet of Soviet-era postcards, as picturesquely arranged as had been Zarema's pack of photographs from war-torn Chechnya. On the front side of every card was a severed head, the image of a war hero. On the obverse was an explanation of why every Soviet citizen was duty bound to honor this image. One of the postcards matched the severed head that stood in the corner of park, and we headed straight for the original. The statue, of graying limestone, was covered with graffiti and surrounded by refuse. Svetlana read to me from the back of the postcard: "In 1908, Zaqatala was stormed by a group of Russians who called themselves Potemkinites. They were rebelling against the tsar."

We finally reached the center of the park, where the Aliev monument stood. At that moment, I recalled how an Avar bus driver had told me just a few days prior that the monument to Shamil had been replaced by Aliev's bust. How could I have forgotten his words? "Cretins," the Avar had spat into the earth as he recalled the removal of Shamil's monument to the edge of the town: "Traitors." Only now, in Svetlana's presence, did I realize that the driver had been referring to this very spot, where Shamil had once proudly stood.

Svetlana froze reverently. "Let us stand silently and pray," she said finally, and closed her eyes. She rocked back and forth on her heels in a kind of trance. "Aliev was a great man," she finally said with a sigh and moved away.

As we basked in the aura of Azerbaijan's illustrious past president, Svetlana suddenly gave voice to the memory that had haunted me: following its destruction by Aliev, a new monument to Shamil had been constructed on the edge of the town, far from the center, near the border with Jar, a village inhabited by Avars rather than Azeris. The destruction of the Shamil monument on 17 August 2001 with four kilograms of explosives was the unuttered subtext of our conversation.[18] Following this explosion, the local Avar and Tsakhur community leaders addressed an open letter to Putin and Aliev in which they claimed that the "terrorist act" that destroyed a monument that had been erected by the Avar community in 1992 had occurred "with the participation of the local government, which relies on Baku for everything."[19] Their accusation was substantiated by the fact that the then mayor, Rafael Medjidov, had attempted to gain official support for the removal of the monument only a year prior, but his plans had met with too much opposition and had to be postponed. Although Shamil was himself Avar and local Avars had erected the original monument, the Azeri authorities blamed the monument's destruction on the local Avar community. By 2006, the case had reached a stalemate, with no group claiming responsibility.

Svetlana proposed an excursion to the new monument, which she had never seen. Although the statues to Shamil and Aliev were only a kilometer apart, I insisted on taking a taxi. The blistering sun had sapped my energy. I did not understand why Svetlana insisted on walking until we reached the park and I opened my purse to pay the driver. Svetlana thrust forward a five-manat bill—the equivalent of five euros—roughly her pension for an entire week. She protested that she had to pay because I was her guest, but I finally prevailed on the driver to accept my money instead of hers.

"This is the first time I have ever been here," Svetlana said reverently when we reached Shamil's bust. The stone effigy faced a Sunni mosque attended by Jar's Avar population. "All these years I suffered over the destruction of Shamil," Svetlana sighed, "and I never once visited this holy site." Then she kneeled down, scooped up a handful of earth, and pressed it to her chest.

While Zaqatala is remembered as a place of exile, nearby Jar has historically been marked as a site of resistance.[20] In this small village, on the Azeri border with Daghestan, Ḥājjī Murād lost his head in 1852. Along with the surrender of Shamil in 1859, Ḥājjī Murād's decapitation might be said to mark the beginning of transgressive sanctity, when it became obvious that traditional warfare could not prevail over the army of the tsar, and new forms of resistance had to be imagined into being. In the case of both Shamil and Ḥājjī Murād, transgressive sanctity originates in defeat.

Svetlana's account of Ḥājjī Murād's death paralleled in many respects the versions of Mitsishvili and Tolstoy: "They captured him here, not far from my home." Svetlana pointed to the mountains. "They cut off his head so they could display it in the center of the city." She stared at the mountains in the distance and breathed in the air that had been purified by the Avar warrior's sanctity. "Ḥājjī Murat was a good man," she finally said.

On the train from Baku to Zaqatala, I had heard a similar comment about another insurgent from a later period. I was discussing, with a young Azeri woman seated next to me, a Sufi sheykh who led a rebellion against the Soviet regime in 1930. The woman had asked about my visit to Bash Shabalid, the place from which Mullah Mustafa initiated the 1930 rebellion. On a particularly violent day in April 1930, ten thousand men and women, "farmers and tradesmen, Muslim clerics and Communist Party members" staged a violent rebellion that spread throughout the region of Sheki.[21] As soon as I finished recounting my visit, another woman in the seat across from me in the train interjected: "Mullah Mustafa was a good man."

Similarly to the circulation of Gazueva's aura, albeit in a radically different key, the migration of Ḥājjī Murat's severed head codifies one of the most persistent motifs in the literatures of insurgency. In Tolstoy's account, once the Avar warrior has been shot, "several policemen raced with triumphant shrieks towards the fallen body" (599). When they reached the murder scene, they found that "[the body] that had appeared dead to them suddenly moved" (599). The soldiers witness the ascension of Ḥājjī Murat's "bleeding, uncovered, shaven head," followed by his body, as his hands gripped the trunk of a tree. That Tolstoy's rendering of Ḥājjī Murād's death closely recalls Mamakaev's and Gatuev's narrations of the death of Zelimkhan illustrates the thematic coherence of the Caucasus literatures of insurgency.

Ḥājjī Murat's return to life from death also anticipates the abrek's uncanny body, which hovers over the ground while haunting the living. Tolstoy's description presages the terms through which Zelimkhan's death was rendered by Gatuev and Mamakaev. "He was so frightening," Tolstoy's narrator continues, "that the soldiers running towards him stopped short. But suddenly a shudder passed through him, and he staggered away from the tree and fell on his face, stretched out at full length like a thistle that had been mown down, and he moved no more." In the hands of Gatuev and Mamakaev, Tolstoy's thistle becomes the abrek's swan song. In the hands of Titsian, Tolstoy's thistle becomes the poet's dagger, which is then transmuted into his treachery-redeeming pen.

To note how these images were inspired by Tolstoy's text is not, to argue for the unilateral influence of colonial literature on the literatures of anticolonial insurgency. To the contrary, Tolstoy's account of Ḥājjī Murād's death was inspired by indigenous sources. Like Gatuev's Zelimkhan and Qazbegi's ethnographic fictions, Tolstoy's *Hadji Murat* is the product of ethnographic research that rivals the most rigorous scholarly treatments in its depiction of the Daghestani and Chechen experience of conquest and in its engagement with indigenous, primarily folkloric, archives.[22] The Russian text could not have been composed had Tolstoy not engaged with Chechen and Avar oral literatures. As with Zelimkhan's uncanny passing, Ḥājjī Murād's death inculcates guilt in those who observe it and compels readers to consider how to set matters right. When the dying insurgent is illumined by the halo of transgressive sanctity, death acquires creative force, and the poetics of insurgency enters into rivalry with the materiality of colonial rule.

Even when the head of the dying Ḥājjī Murād magically frees itself from the body as though it were a sentient object, its severance remains incomplete. Ḥājjī Murād's head still awaits the desecration that is carried out, ironically, by the Daghestani Ḥājjī Agha. Ḥājjī Agha steps "on the back of the corpse and cut[s] off the head with two blows" (599). Careful not to soil his shoes with blood, he rolls Ḥājjī Murād's head forward with his foot. "Crimson blood spurted from the arteries of the neck," the narrator recounts, as "black blood poured from the head, soaking the grass" (599). After Ḥājjī Murād's head has been completely severed from his body, the three soldiers who had chased Ḥājjī Murād to his death gather around the spectacle of his body and triumph in their victory "amid the smoke hanging over the bushes" (599). Tolstoy compares these tsarist spectators to "sportsmen round a slaughtered animal" (599). Anticipating Zelimkhan's uncanny red splotch, Ḥājjī Murād's head rises above the scene, shaven and bleeding, and then is cut with two blows of Ḥājjī Aga's sword, cut so carefully that the blood doesn't drip on his shoes. Notwithstanding this brutal attempt to extinguish the fallen hero's life, black blood continues to spurt "from the arteries of the neck" and to soak the grass.

Ḥājjī Murād's tragic fate intersects with that of Mullah Mustafa, who organized the 1930 rebellion from nearby Bash Shabalid. Serendipitously, the Avar warrior and the Sufi sheykh were both detained in the same city, old-town Sheki, although at a divide of eight decades. It is not known whether Mullah Mustafa was familiar with Ḥājjī Murād's life story. Mullah Mustafa's grandfather and Ḥājjī Murād's contemporary, Sheykh Baba, did however study under Shamil's father.[23] This study enabled Mullah Mustafa to receive an extensive Islamic education, while also cementing ties across these border regions. The intersecting life trajectories of these two figures who shaped anticolonial insurgency in the Caucasus converges in their shared dispossession and exile, a fate shared by many of the writers in this book.[24]

Svetlana's contradictory loyalties testify to the radical divergences that permeate and complicate the Caucasus literatures of insurgency when considered a literary canon unto itself. During the Soviet period,

Russian became a major language for many of these traditions, and the example of the Russophone Gatuev, who wrote in Russian and was Ossetian by birth, was repeated elsewhere within formerly vernacular literature. Notwithstanding the reduction in diversity that transpired during the mid-Soviet period, these homogenizing tendencies never fully displaced the heteroglossia of Caucasus literatures. Poetry, historiography, and folklore continued to be produced in Arabic well into the 1930s and in Avar, Georgian, and Chechen to the end of the Soviet period. The latter three languages remain major media for the literatures of the Caucasus today.

Viewed through a Braudelian *longue durée*, the colonial encounter in the Caucasus will eventually come to represent merely one episode in a deeper history. Viewed in terms of world systems theory, the Caucasus literatures of insurgency are only one of many significant literary canons that were forged in these interstices between Europe and Asia. What will remain when the geopolitical situation becomes irrelevant is the unique dialectic these power relations fostered between aesthetics and violence.

Transgressive sanctity generated an ethics of negation whereby disobedience to the state was perceived as intrinsically virtuous and the state was irredeemably corrupt. Under the conditions that made transgressive sanctity appeal to broad constituencies of mountaineers, writers, and civil servants alike, ethical life could be cultivated only outside the state apparatus, through a dialectic that brings *sharīʿa*, *ʿādāt*, and *zakon* into new relations. Transgressive sanctity was ethics for a world lacking legitimate modes of governance, and a religion for a society that had been deprived of its gods. It was a theory of violence for a polity that knew only the coercion of material force. Transgressive sanctity's ambivalent legacy is demonstrated by the proliferation of violence across the Caucasus over the past few centuries. That, notwithstanding its celebration of defeat, this concept has sustained thinkers, writers, and insurgents at the epicenters of violent conflict is demonstrated by the succession of intellectuals who have sacrificed their lives for the worlds they helped to create, and in the process intensifying the intertextuality of Caucasus literary history.

In his recent discussion of Mullah Mustafa's rebellion, Bruce Grant pointed to the work done by transgressive sanctity in shaping the terms through which sovereignty is articulated. "Man and mausoleum folded into one," writes Grant of Mullah Mustafa's self-rendering in a poem of complaint (*şikayət*) penned shortly before his death in exile, the insurgent's "status as the khan over angels, or as the shah of misfortune, placed him among sovereigns of a rather different order than those then ruling the state that aimed to confine him. [Mullah Mustafa] operated in realms that were entirely of, and yet equally beyond, the Soviet embrace."[25] As in mountainous Azerbaijan, so in neighboring Daghestan and Chechnya: Soviet atheism conditioned sacralized insurgency and created a space where transgressive sanctity could flourish and proliferate.

Whether enacted through the legal discourse of *sharīʿa* as in Daghestan, through the discourse of social banditry as in Chechnya, or through the poetics of insurgency as in Georgia, transgressive sanctity reinscribes sovereignty from the vantage points of the governed. In documenting the refashioning of violence by vernacular insurgency, Ranajit Guha has laid the groundwork for a form of dominance that is at once—if a Gramscian revision to Guha can be permitted—hegemonic *and* generated of freedom. As elsewhere in the world, in the Caucasus, transgressive sanctity calls on the subject to become the hero of his or her own existence, to authorize, and, as literature is so well equipped to do, to *revise* his or her own fate. If transgressive sanctity can assist in extracting from the violence of the colonial encounter a form of social life that substitutes for the state's coercion the agency of the colonized and violated, it will have fulfilled its function by rendering itself obsolete. At that moment, the early Soviet aestheticization of violence will come to life again, and replace the post-Soviet degeneration of the aura. A new postcoloniality will enter the world, now no longer subject to the constraints of colonial law. This new dispensation stands a better chance than any other of creating a framework for a provisional peace.

APPENDIX I

The Abrek in Caucasus Vernacular Literatures

Adyghe, Chechen, Ossetian, Kabardian, Georgian, and Turkic Sources

Encompassing all languages in which abreks have been discussed, this appendix aims for breadth more than depth. Items not personally seen are marked with an asterisk (*).

Among Zelimkhan-related materials not mentioned in chapter 1, Tarık Cemal Kutlu's Turkish translation of Mamakaev's Zelamkha should be mentioned: *Zelimhan: bir Çeçen halk kahramanının zulme karşı mücadelesinin gerçek öyküsü** (Istanbul: E Yayinlari; reprinted by Anka, 2002). Another source on Zelimkhan not incorporated in this study is Michel Pavlovitch, "Zelim Khan et le brigandage au Caucase," *Revue du monde musulman* 20 (1912): 139–162. Bakarov's Chechen-language memoir of Zelimkhan is partially available in Russian at the website www.chechenews.com. Finally, mention should be made of the many Chechen- and Russian-language songs about abreks by the popular Chechen bards Alim Imamsultanov and Timur Mutsuraev.

For the abrek in Avar, see the songs of the eighteenth-century bandit Khochbar in *Geroiko-istoricheskie pesni avartsev*, ed. A. A. Akhlakov, 163–179. V. O. Bobrovnikov's detailed study of Khochbar is found in his "Nasilie i vlast' v istoricheskoi pamiati musul'manskogo pogranich'ia (k novoi interpretatsii pesni o Khochbare)," edited by I. Gerasimov,

M. Mogilner, and A. Semyonov, *Imperiia i natsiia v zerkale istoricheskoi pamiati* (Moscow: Novoe izd-vo, 2011), 297–327. Khaibulaeva recently published several poems about Zelimkhan by the Avar poet and Zelimkhan's contemporary Magomed Chirkievskii. Khaibulaeva notes the same tendency I have identified in Chechen sources to sanctify the abrek in the Avar poems concerning social banditry: "[Zelimkhan's] ability to evade capture and the magical power of his weapons is connected with his supernatural powers, supported by the angels and by God, because his battle is endowed with religious significance" (Khaibulaeva, *Tvorchestvo Magomeda Chirkievskogo* [Makhachkala, 2003], 60).

In Ossetian, Kosta Khetagurov's epic poem *Fatima* tells the story of a love affair between an abrek who is, unsurprisingly, Chechen, and his beloved Fatima, whom he is unable to marry due to their different social estates: Khetagurov, *Izbrannoe* (Moscow: Goslitizdat, 1956), 153–86. For a later Soviet period, there is a play by Khadzhumar Tsopanaty [alt. spellings: *Tsopanov* and *Copanaty*] titled *Abyræg: Ærmæakton fondznyvon dram* (Ordzhonikidze: Ir, 1971). In the prerevolutionary period, the Estonian Ossetophile V. Ia. Ikskul' (b. 1860) composed the Russian short story "Abrek," 181–185. For a survey of the abrek in Ossetian folklore, see V. I. Bekoev, "Osetinskie istoriko-geroicheskie pesni s abrecheskoi tematikoi," *Zhurnal fundamental'nikh i prikladnikh isledovanii* 30.2 (2009): 155–160. Naira Taimurazovna Nakusova's *kandidatskaia* dissertation, "Khudozhestvennoe osmyilennie problemyi abrechestva v osetinskoi literature" (Vladikavkaz, 2009) examines the abrek in Ossetian literature.

In Adyghe, Tembot Kerashev's short story "Abrek" (1957) is found in his *Abrek: Povesti* [Moscow: Sovetskaia Rossiia, 1969], 3–46. A century earlier, the Adyghe enlightener Adil-Girei Keshev (pseud. Kalambiia) published "Abreki" (*Russkii vestnik* 30 [November 1860]: 127–90). More recently, Dzhambulat Koshubayev finished his experimental novel called *Abrag* in 1996 (*Abrag: roman povest'* [Nal'chik: Elbrus, 2004], 1–92).

Kabardian culture gravitated more toward the plains than the mountains, and therefore was less intensively connected to the mountaineer ethos that lies at the foundation of the abrek's paradoxical social status. The abrek is therefore less widely represented in Kabardian literature. The most detailed treatment is Alim Keshokov's *The Green Half-Moon*, a contemporary novel of a modern abrek, focused mostly on the glamour and rise in status that accrues to a young man who acquires the abrek label: Keshokov, *Zelenyi polumesiats* (Moscow: Izvestiia, 1969). Kerashev's Adyghe "Abrek" has also been translated into Kabardian as *Abredzh* (Nal'chik: K"ėbėrdeĭ-Bal"k"ėr tkhyl" tedzapȟė, 1963).

In Georgian, the paradigmatic *abragi*, Arsena Odzelashvili (1797–1842), was born the same year as Imam Shamil. Arsena's exploits inspired the Georgian folk poem known as "Arsenas lek'si" (Arsena's poem). This work is available in multiple editions: *Arsenas sruli lek'si xalxuri lek'si: shedgenili mest'viret'a da saxalxo leksebidan* (Tbilisi, n.p., 1913); *Arsenas lek'si* (Tbilisi: Nakaduli, 1966); and in Russian as *Pesn' ob Arsene* (Moscow: Khudozh. lit-ra, 1938). For a Georgian folk poem on Zelimkhan, see Akaki Shanidze, *Kartuli xalxuri poezia Xevsuruli* (Tbilisi: Saxelmtsipo gamomcemloba, 1931), 1: 246–248. Finally, two scholarly essays quote extensively from the western Georgian Firali Epic, which chronicles the exploits of a *qachagi* (Georgian abrek): N. Tskitishvili, "Piralis eposidan" [From the Firali Epic], *Matsne* 1.34 (1967): 152–171, and Mixeil Chikovani, "Piralis eposi guriashi" [The Firali Epic in Guria], *Marksisturi enatmetsnierebisatvis* (Tbilisi: Tbilisis universitetis gamomcemloba, 1934), 109–142.

Three novels stand out in Georgian literary history for their perspectives on the abrek: Mixeil Javaxishvili's *Arsena Marabdeli* (composed from 1925 to 1932; published from 1933 to 1936), concerned with the eponymous protagonist, Chabua Amirejibi's *Data Tutashxia*, composed in 1975 (Tbilisi: Merani, 1978), and Aleksandre Qazbegi, *Mamis mkvleli* [*Father-Killer*], composed in 1882 (Tbilisi: Sabchota sakartvelo, 1948). The Russian edition of Javaxishvili's novel, *Arsen iz Marabdy: Roman* (Moscow: Khudozhestvennaia literatura, 1935; reprint, Tbilisi: Gosizdat Gruzinskoi SSR, 1956), was published in a huge print run of half a million copies and was heavily censored in its translation. The story of Arsena's life would have been well known to Mamakaev. Even more concretely, the Chechen *Zelamkha* contains several passages that quote verbatim from the Russian translation of *Arsena*. The reader who compares the Russian edition of Mamakaev's *Zelimkhan* (pp. 129, 229, 227, respectively) with the Russian translation of Javaxishvili's *Arsen* (pp. 118, 396, 403, respectively) will conclude that *Zelamkha* was written under the influence of *Arsena.*

In Azeri (and sometimes Georgian), the term *qachag* is commonly used in the sense that abrek is used in the cultures of the northern Caucasus. The most famous abrek, Nabi (according to some sources of Kurdish background), has inspired multiple literary treatments in Azeri. Authors include Ähliman Ahundov, *Gachag Nabi: dastan* (Baku: Azärbajgan Dävlät Näsrijjaty); Azad Nabiiev, *Gachag Nabi* (Baku: Ganjlik, 1982); and F. Qasimzadah, *Qachaq nabi* (Iran: n.p., n.d. [c. 1970–1980]). That the abrek's impact reached beyond the Russian and Soviet empires is attested by Zubeydet Shapli's Turkish-language *Abrek: Roman* (Istanbul: Kuzey Kafkasyalilar Kültür ve Yardim Dernegi, 1977). This novel narrates events in the Caucasus from a perspective sympathetic to the mountaineers.

Given the centrality of the Caucasus to the Russian literary imagination, the extensive literature on the abrek in Russian should not occasion surprise. Although literary representations of the abrek by Pushkin, Lermontov, and Tolstoy have been treated by numerous prior scholars, serious tsarist-era scholarship remains underappreciated, in particular the pathbreaking essay by P. K. Uslar, "Koe-shto o slovesnyh proizvedeniiakh gortsev," *SSKG* 1 (1868): esp. 39–41. In Aleksandr Bestuzhev-Marlinskii's *Ammalat-Bek* (1832; St. Petersburg: A. S. Suvorin, 1887), the eponymous Qumuq hero is called an abrek by the author.

Finally, mention should be made of what is probably the first full-length European treatment of the abrek outside Russia: the anonymous *Aslan der Abrek: ein Lebensbild aus den Kaukasischen Gebirgen** (Miatu: Reyher, 1859), listed as having been authored by a German-Russian (*von einem Deutschrussen*). The Staatsbibliothek zu Berlin states in its online catalog (http://stabikat.de) that the item belongs to that group of materials that was lost in World War II ("Kriegsverlust möglich"), and the British Library catalog incorrectly transcribes the title as *Aolan der Abrek.* For a summary of the novel's plot, see *Blätter für literarische Unterhaltung* (Leipzig: Brockhuas, January–June 1861), 644.

Also omitted from this study are the many films pertaining to the abrek that were produced during the 1920s. Within the space of six years, at least four feature films produced in the Caucasus concerned the abrek. *Mamis mkvleli** (1923) was based on the novella by Aleksandre Qazbegi and directed by Amo Bek-Nazaryan. *Arsena Kachagi** (1923) was directed by Vladimir Barsky and concerned with the Georgian abrek immortalized by Javaxishvili a few years later. *Abrek Zaur** (1926), was directed by Boris Mikhin with the collaboration of Bej-Abaj and Esther Shub and produced by Goskino. Finally, mention should be made of O. Frylikh's *Zelimkhan** (1929), based on the novel by Gatuev discussed in chapter 1. The author of the novel on which the film was based was mistakenly listed as the famous Ossetian writer Kosta Khetagurov in a recent screening for the film festival "Tchetchenie criblee d'images" (2004). The billing summarizes: "Alors que les tsars étouffent le peuple, l'histoire de Zelimkhan, bandit d'honneur tchétchène (abrech) présenté comme . . . un bandit." The Moscow-based writer Zalpa Bersanova reports that her father Chechen writer Ḥājjī-Aḥmad Bersanov has written an unpublished Chechen screenplay based on Zelimkhan's life (personal communication, 2008).

These are the key titles in what could be a book-length bibliography of the social bandit in Caucasus cultures. With the exceptions of Keshokov, Adil-Girei Keshev, and Amiredjibi, scholarship has so far ignored these contributions to the Caucasus literatures of anticolonial insurgency.

APPENDIX II

Georgian Text of Titsian Tabidze, "Gunib," *Rcheuli natsarmoebi* 1:106

გუნიბი

1. გადავიარე დაღესტანი . . . ვნახე გუნიბი,
2. გიაური ვარ—და ვარ მაინც ეხლა მჲურიდი.
3. ხმალი—ლეკური ამხანადაც არ ილუნება,
4. ამ ხმალს მე ეხლაც სიხარულით გულს გავუყრიდი.
5. დაუთოვია სისპეტაკე ზეცას თეთრ თოვლით,
6. დგანან ზვირთების ეშაფოტად მაღალი მთები.
7. მოქუხს გრიგალი შურისგების მეორე მოსვლით,
8. იხტიოზავრიც წარღვნის ღამეს დაეფეთება.
9. ვხედავ არწივთა საბუდარით დანგრეულ ბუდეს
10. და მოგონების სირცხვილიდან თვალი მევსება.
11. ამ ცის სიმაღლის შეგინება როგორ გაბედეს,
12. ამის ტკივილი, საქართველოვ, შენც ხომ გედება.
13. ქართული ძვლები ალპებიან აქ ხმალს და ხიშტებს,
14. მეცოდებიან ამ საწყალთა გახრული ძვლები.
15. სული თან გაჰყვათ სამოთხეში მამაც ჯიგიტებს
16. და თქვენ კი დარჩით, ჩემო ძმებო, გაძარცულები.
17. და ამაღამაც, როცა ლეწავს ყველაფერს ქარი,
18. მჲურიდების სულს კვლავ ლოცავს მათი იმამი.
19. თქვენი კი წახდა სამუდამოდ ბრძოლა მედგარი,
20. არც დაგიტირებს უცხოეთში უცხოთა ღამე.

21. არ მისროლია მე არასდროს ჯერ კაჟის თოფი,
22. არც გალესილი მრტყმია წელზე ლეკური ხმალი,
23. მაგრამ უეცრად ვაჟკაცობამ მეც შემაშფოთა,
24. არ მინდა ვიყო მე პოეტი, სისხლით დამთვრალი,
25. და ამ ღამიდან დაწყებული დღე რაც კი გადის,
26. მე ვწერ პოემას: რომ წარეცხოს თქვენი ღალატი.

17 ივლისი, 1927 წ.

Chronology of Texts, Authors, and Events

1797—birth of Shamil (the third imam of Chechnya and Daghestan); birth of Georgian abrek Arsena Odzelashvili

1828—Ghāzī Muḥammad becomes first imam of Chechnya and Daghestan

1832—Ghāzī Muḥammad killed; Georgian nobility conspire to reject Russian sovereignty

1834—Shamil becomes the third imam of Chechnya and Daghestan; the Russo-Caucasus War begins in earnest; birth of Ḥasan al-Alqadārī

1836—Ḥājjī Tashaw acknowledges Shamil's claim to the imamate, disappears in 1841

1837—ʿAbd al-Raḥmān al-Ghāzīghumūqī is born to the sheykh Jamāl al-Dīn

1852—death of Ḥājjī Murād

1859—Shamil surrenders to Bariatinskii; resistance to Russian rule persists through the Caucasus

1861—uprising led by Baisangur and Sulṭamurād, both of Beno; Kunta Ḥājjī returns to the Caucasus to spread the Qādiriyya order

1864—northwestern Caucasus (Abkhazia, Kabardia, Balkaria) officially incorporated into the Russian empire; arrest of Kunta Ḥājjī; massacre of Kunta Ḥājjī's followers in Shali

1864—ʿAbd al-Raḥmān al-Ghāzīghumūqī (Shamil's son-in-law) finishes his *Khulāṣat* in Kaluga, continues to revise the text until 1883

1865—abrek Vara of Gekhi killed in Novi Atagi; uprising lead by Taza Ekmirzaev of Kharachoi

1869—ʿAbd al-Raḥmān al-Ghāzīghumūqī finishes his *Tadhkirat* in Tbilisi

1872—birth of Zelimkhan Gushmazukaev; al-Qarākhī completes his *Bāriqat*

1877—uprising against Russian rule in the eastern Caucasus led by ʿAlībek Ḥājjī; extensive forced deportations of Chechens to Ottoman territory

1878—ʿAlībek Ḥājjī hung, along with hundreds of other participants, in the 1877 uprising

1882—Qazbegi's "Eliso" published; death of al-Qarākhī; death of ʿAbd al-Raḥmān al-Thughūrī

1891—Ḥasan al-Alqadārī completes his magnum opus *Āthār-i Dāghistān* (Vestiges of Daghestan)

1893—ʿAbd al-Raḥmān finishes his essay on the 1877 uprising ("Suqūṭ dāghistān")

1897—Aslanbek Sheripov born

1901—probable death date of ʿAbd al-Raḥmān al-Ghāzīghumūqī

1910—Ḥasan al-Alqadārī dies; death of Tolstoy; birth of Magomed Mamakaev

1912—Tolstoy's *Hadji Murat* published

1913—Zelimkhan Gushmazukaev of Kharachoi killed by tsarist officers near his home in Shali

1919—Aslanbek Sheripov dies

1926—Gatuev publishes his *Zelimkhan*

1927—Titsian Tabidze writes "Gunib"

1935—Nadhir al-Durgilī, author of the Daghestani biographical dictionary *Nuzhat*, dies

1933—first publication of Mixeil Javaxishvili's *Arsena Marabdeli*, a historical novel about the famous Georgian *abragi* (composed from 1925 to 1932)

1938—execution of Dzakho Gatuev (July); execution of Mixeil Javaxishvili (September); execution of Titsian Tabidze (December)

1944—Deportations of the Chechens and Ingush to Central Asia (February); Soviet Union's Supreme Soviet abolishes the autonomous Soviet republic of Checheno-Ingushetia (March)

1957—Vainakhs officially pardoned by the Soviet Union's Supreme Soviet and allowed to return home; autonomous Soviet republic of Checheno-Ingushetia restored (January)

1968—Mamakaev publishes *Zelamkha* in Chechen

1971—death of Khasuhka, "the last Chechen abrek"

1973—death of Magomed Mamakaev

1994—beginning of First Russo-Chechen War (December)

1999—beginning of Second Russo-Chechen War (October)

2001—Aizan Gazueva carries out one of the first suicide bombings in Chechen history

Abbreviations

Archives

IIAE	Institut istorii, arkheologii i etnografii, DNTs RAN (Makhachkala)
IIILGT	Dagestanskii nauchno Institut Istorii, Iazyka i Literatury Im. G. Tsadasy (Makhachkala)
KSXI	Kekelizdis saxelobis xelnatsertʿa institutis (Tbilisi)
LXCA	Literaturis da xelovnebis centraluri arkivebi (Central Archives for Literature and Art, Tbilisi)
RGIA	Rossiiskii Gosudarstvennyi Istoricheskii Arkhiv (Russian State Historical Archive, St. Petersburg)
TsGA	Tsentral'nyi gosudarstvennyi arkhiv (Central Government Archive, Moscow)
TsVIA	Tsentral'nyi voenno-istoricheskii arkhiv (Central War-Historical Archive)

Manuscript Catalogs

KAXK 2	R. Gvaramia, N. Qanch'aveli, and L. Mamulia. *Kekelizdis saxelobis xelnatsertʿa institutis arabul xelnatsertʿa katalogi: L kolekʿtsʿia* (Tbilisi: Kavkazskii Dom, 2002)

Journals and Reference Works

AKAK	*Akty Kavkazskoi arkheograficheskoi komissii*
CAS	*Central Asian Survey*
CMR	*Cahiers du Monde russe*
CSSAAME	*Comparative Studies of South Asia, Africa and the Middle East*
CSSH	*Comparative Studies in Society and History*
WDI	*Die Welt des Islams*

EAI	*Encyclopedia of Arabic Literature*, ed. Julie Scott Meisami and Paul Starkey (London: Routledge, 1998)
EI²	*Encyclopedia of Islam, Second Edition* (Leiden: Brill, 1986–2004)
EI³	*Encyclopedia of Islam, Third Edition* (Leiden: Brill, 2007–)
EIrc	*Encyclopedia Iranica*
EWIC	*Encyclopedia of Women & Islamic Cultures* (Leiden: Brill, 2003–)
JAS	*Journal of Asian Studies*
JESHO	*Journal of the Economic and Social History of the Orient*
JHS	*Journal of the History of Sufism*
JIS	*Journal of Islamic Studies*
JMMA	*Journal of Muslim Minority Affairs*
JNES	*Journal of Near Eastern Studies*
JOAS	*Journal of the American Oriental Society*
JRAS	*Journal of the Royal Asiatic Society*
Lane	Edward W. Lane, *An Arabic-English Lexicon*, 8 vols. (London: Williams and Norgate, 1863–1893)
MCRCA 1	*Muslim Culture in Russia and Central Asia from the 18th to the Early 20th Centuries*, vol. 1, ed. Michael Kemper, Anke von Kügelgen, and Dmitriy Yermakov (Berlin: Schwarz Verlag, 1996)
MCRCA 2	*Muslim Culture in Russia and Central Asia from the 18th to the Early 20th Centuries*, vol. 2, *Inter-Regional and Inter-Ethnic Relations*, ed. Michael Kemper, Anke von Kügelgen, and Dmitriy Yermakov (Berlin: Schwarz, 1998)
MES	*Middle Eastern Studies*
PMLA	*Proceedings of the Modern Language Association*
SEER	*Slavonic and East European Review*
SSKG	*Sbornik svedenii o kavkazskikh gortsakh*
Vestnik IIAE	*Vestnik Institut istorii, arkheologii i etnografii* (journal of IIAE)
ZDMG	*Zeitschrift der Deutschen Morgenländischen Gesellschaft*

Publishers and Publication Terminology

AN SSSR	Akademii Nauk SSSR (Academy of Sciences, Soviet Union, 1925–1991)
DNTs	Dagestanskii nauchnyi tsentr (Daghestan Scholarly Center)
IS	*izbrannie sochineniia* (Russian for "collected works")
PSS	*polnoe sobranie sochinenii* (Russian for "complete collected works")
RAN	Rossiiskaia akademiia nauk (Russian Academy of Sciences, 1991–)
SS	*sobranie sochinenii* (Russian for "collected works")

Notes

Introduction

1. Muḥammad Ṭāhir al-Qarākhī, *Bāriqat al-suyūf al-dāghistānīyah fī baʿd al-ghazawāt al-shāmilīyah*, ed. A. M. Barabanov and I. Iu. Krachkovskii (Moscow: AN SSSR, 1946), 8.

2. See Michael Kemper, *Herrschaft, Recht und Islam in Daghestan* (Wiesbaden: Ludwig Reichert Verlag, 2005), 255–404.

3. See Moshe Gammer, "The Imam and the Pasha," *MES* 32.4 (1996): 340; id., *Muslim Resistance to the Tsar*, 233.

4. See A. Runovskii, "Kodeks Shamilia," *Voennyi sbornik* 2 (1862): 338–339.

5. *Araboiazychnye dokumenty epokhi Shamilia*, ed. R. Sh. Sharafutdinova (Moscow: Vostochnaia literatura, 2001), documents 127, 131 (letters 67, 68); *100 pisem Shamilia*, ed. Kh. A. Omarov (Makhachkala: DNTs RAN, 1997), 156, 198 (letters 65, 84).

6. See W. Madelung, "Imāma," *EI*^{2}.

7. Thomas R. Bates, "Gramsci and the Theory of Hegemony," *Journal of the History of Ideas* 36.2 (1975): 352. As the pages that follow suggest, my understanding of Gramscian hegemony in a colonial context has benefited substantially from Ranajit Guha, *Dominance without Hegemony* (Cambridge: Harvard UP, 1998).

8. The first iteration of this argument appeared in Rebecca Gould, "Transgressive Sanctity," *Kritika* 8.2 (2007): 271–306, and is developed in revised form in chapter 1 of this book.

9. This book uses the figure of the abrek to advance several theses concerning the aestheticization of violence in Caucasus literary modernity, but the task of producing a comprehensive study of the abrek as such is better left to historians. For an excellent account of the abrek that combines historical and anthropological methods, see Vladimir Bobrovnikov, *Musul'mane Severnogo Kavkaza* (Moscow: Vostochnaia literatura, 2002).

10. James C. Scott, *Domination and the Arts of Resistance: The Hidden Transcript of Subordinate Groups* (New Haven: Yale UP, 1992); Pierre Clastres, *Archéologie de la violence: La guerre dans les sociétés primitives* (New Haven: Yale UP, 1977).

11. Steven C. Caton, "Power, Persuasion and Language," *IJMES* 19.1 (1987): 77.

12. For thought-provoking engagements with the former question, see Jeremy Weinstein, *Inside Rebellion: The Politics of Insurgent Violence* (Cambridge: Cambridge UP, 2007).

13. Charles King, *Extreme Politics* (New York: Oxford UP, 2009), 4.

14. See chapter 4 and the epilogue, respectively, for further engagements with these methods. For other significant works at the intersection of anthropology and textuality, see Michael E. Meeker, *Literature and Violence in North Arabia* (Cambridge: Cambridge UP, 1979); Brinkley Messick, *The Calligraphic State: Textual Domination and History in a Muslim Society* (Berkeley: U of California P, 1993); and Steve Caton, *"Peaks of Yemen I summon": Poetry as Cultural Practice in a North Yemeni Tribe* (Berkeley: U of California P, 1991).

15. Fridrik Thordarson, "Dāğestān. ii. Linguistic Influences," *Encyclopedia Iranica.*

16. Amri R. Shikhsaidov, "Arabic Historical Studies in Twentieth-Century Dagestan," in Michael Kemper and Stephan Conermann (eds.), *The Heritage of Soviet Oriental Studies* (London: Routledge, 2011), 211.

17. Shikhsaidov, "Arabic Historical Studies," 210. On archeological expeditions, Shikhsaidov and his team have discovered more than three hundred previously unknown manuscript collections.

18. B. Miller, *Taty, ikh rasselenie i govori* (Baku: Obshchestva Obsledovaniia i Izucheniia Azerbaidzhana, 1929); and Yo'av Karny, *Highlanders* (New York: Macmillan, 2000), 116ff.

19. Given the close kinship between Qumuq and Ottoman Turkish, the boundary between cosmopolitan and vernacular in this instance is inevitably more porous than with other Caucasus vernaculars that lacked a genetic relation to cosmopolitan languages.

20. My source for this account is Mavraev's article, published in the journal *Musavat* (*Equality*) on 8 June 1917, and republished and translated into Russian as A. A. Isaev, *Magomedmirza Mavraev* (Makhachkala: RAN, 2003), 124–126.

21. Ismail Bey Gasprinskii, "First Steps towards Civilizing the Russian Muslims," trans. Edward J. Lazzerini, in "Čadidism at the Turn of the Twentieth Century," *CMR* 16.2 (1975): 250. For jadidism in Daghestan, see Amir Navruzov, "*Dzharidat Dagistan*" *Araboiazychnaia Gazeta Kavkazskikh Dzhadidov* (Moscow: Mardzhani, 2012).

22. See Mavraev, article dated 5 July 1917 in *Musavat,* in Isaev, *Magomedmirza Mavraev*, 130.

23. In addition to the essays in *The Heritage of Soviet Oriental Studies,* on this subject see Michael Kemper, Raoul Motika, and Stefan Reichmuth (eds.), *Islamic Education in the Soviet Union and Its Successor States* (London: Routledge, 2009).

24. For Arabic script publications prior to this period, see A. A. Isaev, *Katalog pechatnykh knig i publikatsii na iazykakh narodov Dagestana: dorevoliutsionnyi period*

(Makhachkala: Dagestanskii filial AN SSSR, In-t istorii, iazyka i lit-ry im. G. Tsadasy, 1989).

25. For Daghestani contributions to these areas of learning, see M. S. Saidov, "The Daghestan Arabic Literature of the Eighteenth and Nineteenth Centuries," *Papers Presented by the USSR Delegation, XXV Congress of Orientalists* (Moscow: Oriental Literature Publishing House, 1960), 1–13.

26. A. N. Genko, "Arabskii iazyk i kavkazovedenie," in *Trudy vtoroi sessii Assotsiatsii arabistov* (Moscow: AN SSSR, 1941), 85–86.

27. O. G. Bol'shakov and A. L. Mongait, eds., *Puteshestvie Abu Khamida al-Garnati v vostochnuyu i tsentral'nuyu Evropu. (1131-1153 gg.)* [=*al-Muʿrib ʿan baʿḍ ʿajāʾib al-maghrib*] (Moscow: Nauka, 1971), 26.

28. For this phrase, see, for example, Abū'l Fidā', *Kitāb taqwīm al-buldān*, ed. Joseph Toussaint Reinaud, Fuat Sezgin, and William de Slane (Frankfurt am Main: Johann Wolfgang Goethe Universität, 1992), 71.

29. Michael Kemper, "An Island of Classical Arabic in the Caucasus: Dagestan," in Françoise Companjen and Lia Versteegh (eds.), *Exploring the Caucasus in the 21st Century*, 73.

30. M. Kh. Neimatova, "Epigraficheskie pamiatniki i ikh znachenie v izuchenii sotsial'no-ekonomicheskoi istorii Azerbaidzhana XIV-XIX vv.," PhD diss., University of Baku, 1968, 57–59; A. R. Shikhsaidov, *Epigraficheskie pamiatniki Dagestana X-XVII vv. kak istoricheskii istochnik* (Moscow: Nauka, 1984), 384.

31. *IIILGT*, ms. f. 14, no. 189.

32. Ronald Wixman, *The Peoples of the USSR: An Ethnographic Handbook* (Armonk: M. E. Sharpe, 1984), 116.

33. For a lucid theorization of *ʿajam* as a modality of non-Arab Islamic identity, see Muzaffar Alam, *The Languages of Political Islam* (London: Hurst & Co, 2004), 7 and passim. Another locus classicus on this subject is Ignáz Goldziher, *Muhammedanische Studien* (Halle an der Saale: Max Niemeyer, 1889–1890), 1:10–146. For a concise overview, see F. Gabrieli, "Adjam," *EI*[2].

34. A. M. Barabanov first deciphered this system in his classic study "Poyasnitelnye znachki v arabskikh rukopisiakh i dokumentakh severnogo kavkaza," *Sovetskoe Vostokovedenie* 3 (1945): 193–214.

35. M. S. Saidov, "Vozniknovenie pis'menosti u avartsev," *Iazyki Dagestana* 1 (1948): 136–140.

36. *Jāmiʿ al-luġatayn* is available in *IIILGT* ms. f. 14 no. 535. For Dibīrqāḍī's other work, see the pioneering work of P. M. Alibekova, *Zhizn' i tvorcheskoe nasledie Dibir-Kadi iz Khunzakha* (Makhachkala: IIALI DNTS RAN, 2009).

37. For a recent analysis of this codex, see A. A. Isaev, "K voprosy o datirovke darginskikh zapisei na poliakh arabskikh rukopisei XV v.," *Istochnikovedenie istorii i kul'tury narodov Dagestana i Severnogo Kavkaza* (Makhachkala: Dagestanskii nauchnyi tsentr RAN, 1991), 85–89.

38. M. G. Magomedov and A. P. Shikhsaidov, *Kalakoreish* (Makhachkala: Iupiter, 2000), 164. *Qītāgh* is alternately spelled *Khidāq*.

39. Ibn Rusta, *Kitāb al-aʿlāq al-nafīsa*, ed. de Goeje (Brill: Leiden, 1892), 147–148. See also Vladimir Minorskii, *Istoriia Shirvana i Derbenda X-XI vekov* (Moscow: Vostochnaia literatura, 1963), 217–221.

40. A. N. Genko, "Arabskii iazyk i kavkazovedenie," 100.

41. See L. I. Lavrov, ed., *Epigraficheskie pamiatniki Severnogo Kavkaza na arabskom, persidskom i turetskom iazykakh* (Moscow: Nauka, 1966–1980).

42. Although a *Tārīkh al-Bāb* was attributed to Mammūs al-Darbandī as early as the fifteenth century in al-Sahāwi's *Iʿlān*, he has not been regarded by most modern scholars as the author of the original texts. Al-Lakzī's authorship of the original eleventh century *Tārīkh al-Bāb* was only recently demonstrated in A. K. Alikberov, *Epokha klassicheskogo islama na Kavkaze* (Moscow: Vostochnaia literatura, 2003), 309ff.; and *id.*, "Ob avtore istoricheskoi khroniki XI v. Tārīkh al-Bāb wa Shirwān," *Rukopisnaia i knizhnaia kultura v Daghestane* (1991): 119–121. Alikberov stipulates that the title by which the text is known in some redactions, *Tārīkh al-Bāb wa-Shirwān*, refers to a later supplement. Prior to Alikberov, al-Lakzī was assumed to be only one among many authors; see, for example, Minorsky, *A History of Sharvān and Darband in the 10th–11th Centuries* (Cambridge: Heffer, 1958), 3.

43. Only the date of Muḥammad Rafīʿ's chronicle has been provided by extant primary sources: 712/1313, according to ʿAbbāsqulī Āqā Bakikhānūf (*Gulistān-i Iram*, ed. ʿAbd al-Karīm ʿAlīzādah [Baku: Idārah-i intishārāt-i ʿIlm, 1970]). Minorsky casts doubt on the accuracy of this date (*A History of Sharvān and Darband*, 9).

44. A. K. Alikberov, *Epokha*, 314.

45. E. Daniel, "Historical Literature," *EAL*, 291.

46. None of these texts have been published in their original languages. Among the Russian translations, the most useful is *Dagestanskie istoricheskie sochineniia*, ed. and trans. Shikhsaidov, Aitberov and Orazaev (Moscow: Vostochnaia literatura, 1993). The first and only English translation (based on the Turkish version) of the *Darbandnama* is Mirza Kazem Beg's *Derbendnameh* (St. Petersburg: Imperial Academy of Sciences, 1851).

47. N. D. Miklukho-Maklai, "Opisanie tadzhikskikh i persidskikh rukopisei Instituta narodov Azii AN SSSR," *Istoricheskie sochineniia*, 3rd ed. (Moscow: Nauka, 1973), 396–399.

48. V. V. Bartol'd, "K voprosu o proizkhozhdenii Derbent-name," *Sochineniia* (Moscow: Nauka, 1973), 8:475.

49. Muḥammad-Ḥaydar b. Ḥājjī Mīrzā Āqāsī, *Derband-nāma-ye jadīd*, Akademiia Nauk, Institut Vostokovedeniia, St. Petersburg, ms. no. V4547.

50. Sheldon Pollock, "Cosmopolitan and Vernacular in History," *Public Culture* 12.3 (2000): 612. Although Pollock writes with reference to premodern South Asia, the cosmopolis concept is intended as a comparative rubric, on which see Rebecca Gould, "How Newness Enters the World," *CSSAAME* 28.3 (2008): 533–557.

51. Mitchell Dean, *Governmentality* (London: Sage, 1999), 46–47. The locus classicus for the governmentality concept is Michel Foucault, "La gouvernementalité," *Dits et écrits III* (Paris: Gallimard, 1994), 635–657.

52. For endeavors to reconceptualize Foucauldian governmentality in terms of colonial rule, see David Scott, "Colonial Governmentality," *Social Text* 43 (1995): 191–220; Gyan Prakash, *Another Reason* (Princeton: Princeton UP, 1999); Tania Murray Li, *The Will to Improve* (Durham: Duke UP, 2007); James Duncan, *In the Shadows of the Tropics* (Aldershot: Ashgate, 2012).

53. Umalat Laudaev, "Chechenskoe plemena," *SSKG* 6 (1872): 1–62.

54. W. E. D. Allen, *A History of the Georgian People* (London: Kegan Paul, 1932), 101.

55. Iu. I. Krachkovskii, *Izbrannye sochineniia* (Moscow: AN SSSR, 1960), 4:611.

56. For the complex genealogy of the Shirwānshāhs, see Bosworth, "Shīrwānshāh," *EI²*. Bosworth observes in the history of the dynasty a "progressive Persianisation of this originally Arab family . . . parallel to and contemporary with that of the Kurdicisation of the Rawwadids in Adharbaydjan."

57. Accounts of the Persian influence on medieval and early modern Georgian literature are available in Georgian, Russian, and Persian. The most comprehensive source is volume 5 of *Dānishnāmah-i adab-i Fārsī*, ed. Ḥasan Anūshah (Tehran: Mu'assasah-'i Farhangī va Intishārātī-i Dānishnāmah, 1996–).

58. See Titsian Tabidze, *Rcheuli natsarmoebi* (Tbilisi: Literatura da xelovneba, 1966), 1:106. This poem is discussed in detail in chapter 3.

59. I refer to Michael Kemper's groundbreaking study *Herrschaft, Recht und Islam in Daghestan* (Wiesbaden: Reichert Verlag, 2005), which surpasses earlier accounts through its philological rigor and engagement with Daghestani Arabic sources.

60. Although there are significant precedents in colonial historiography, the Soviet locus classicus for the "*murīd* movement" is N. A. Smirnov, *Miuridizm na Kavkaze* (Moscow: AN SSSR, 1963), a work that is eloquently critiqued in Alexander Knysh, "Sufism as an Explanatory Paradigm," *WDI* 42.2 (2002): 155. These views remain largely uncontested in Moshe Gammer, *Muslim Resistance to the Tsar* (London: Frank Cass, 1994); and Anna Zelkina, *In Quest for God and Freedom* (New York: New York UP, 2000).

61. In addition to Kemper's monograph cited earlier, see his "Khalidiyya Networks in Daghestan and the Question of Jihād," *WDI* 42.1 (2002): 41–71, and "Einige Notizen zur arabischsprachigen Literatur der jihād-Bewegung in Dagestan und Tschetschenien in der ersten Hälfte des 19. Jahrhunderts," *MCRCA* 2, 63–99.

62. On the marginalization of literary approaches within the study of the Caucasus, see Rebecca Gould, "The Death of Caucasus Philology," *Iran and the Caucasus* 17.3 (2013): 275–293.

63. Alexander Nazaryan, "Blood and Tragedy: The Caucasus in the Literary Imagination," *New Yorker*, April 19, 2013, http://www.newyorker.com/books/page-turner/blood-and-tragedy-the-caucasus-in-the-literary-imagination.

64. One locus classicus for such work within Russian studies is Harsha Ram, *Prisoners of the Caucasus* (Berkeley: Berkeley Program in Soviet and Post-Soviet Studies, 1999). More recently, the ongoing work of Nergis Ertürk and Leah Feldman point new directions for a Caucasus literature beyond Russian. Neither scholar, however, foregrounds the problem of violence that is the focus of this book.

65. Kemper's work on Ḥasan al-Alqadārī (discussed in chapter 2) and Ram's work on Titsian Tabidze (discussed in chapter 3) are two of the most important contributions to Caucasus literatures in contemporary Euro-American scholarship, and yet the richness of their work demonstrates just how much remains to be explored.

66. For a more detailed reflection on, and critique of, modern historicism, see Rebecca Gould, "Antiquarianism as Genealogy," *History and Theory* 53.2 (2014): 212–233.

67. The most significant studies of Russian representations of the Caucasus include Susan Layton's *Russian Literature and Empire* (Cambridge: Cambridge UP, 1995), Harsha Ram's *The Imperial Sublime* (Madison: U of Wisconsin P, 2003), and the volume edited by Daniel R. Brower and Edward Lazzerini, *Russia's Orient* (Bloomington: Indiana UP, 1997). These works offer, by their own self-estimations, accounts of Russia's engagement with her cultural others, rather than engagements with the vernacular literary cultures of the Caucasus.

68. See, respectively, Antonio Benitez-Rojo, *The Repeating Island* (Durham: Duke UP, 1997); Takeuchi Yoshimi, "Asia as Method (1960)," in Richard F. Calichman (ed. and trans.), *What Is Modernity? Writings of Takeuchi Yoshimi* (New York: Columbia UP, 2005), 149–166; and Ammiel Alcalay, *After Jews and Arabs* (Minneapolis: U of Minnesota P, 1992).

69. In addition to the work of James C. Scott (cited earlier), Clifford Geertz and Benedict Anderson have formulated arguments of transdisciplinary significance on the basis of Southeast Asian archives.

70. Stephen Greenblatt, *Renaissance Self-Fashioning* (Chicago: U of Chicago P, 1980), 4.

71. Paul Friedrich, "Tolstoy and the Chechens," *Russian History* 30.1–2 (2003): 116.

72. Friedrich, "Tolstoy and the Chechens," 129.

73. Friedrich, "Tolstoy and the Chechens," 123, referencing Layton, *Russian Literature and Empire.* Also see the important investigation of the interface of ethnography and the literary imagination by Friedrich's student Kevin Tuite, "Ethnographie et fiction en Géorgie," *Célébrer une vie*, eds. Kiven Strohm and Guy Lanoue (Montréal: Département d'anthropologie, Université de Montréal, 2007), 161–169.

74. See Valery Tishkov, *Chechnya: Life in a War-Torn Society* (Berkeley: U of California P, 2004). Meanwhile anthropologists such as Iu. Karpov, G. Charachidze, S. Makalatia, and N. Baliauri, and more recently, scholars such as Paul Manning, Kevin Tuite, Bruce Grant, and Florian Mühlfried, are actively elaborating more complex readings of Caucasus cultures, with an emphasis on Georgia.

75. For an illuminating study of these complex mediations in recent Chechen cultural history, see Georgi Derluguian, *Bourdieu's Secret Admirer in the Caucasus* (Chicago: U of Chicago P, 2005), esp. 29–64.

76. Matthew Hart, *Nations of Nothing but Poetry* (Oxford: Oxford UP, 2010), 38–39.

77. Jean Bodin, *On Sovereignty* (Cambridge: Cambridge UP, 1992), 86.

78. Clifford Geertz, *Works and Lives* (Stanford: Stanford UP, 1988); James Clifford and George Marcus, eds., *Writing Culture* (Berkeley: U of California P, 1986); James Clifford, *The Predicament of Culture* (Cambridge: Harvard UP, 1988).

79. Wolfgang Iser, *Prospecting* (Baltimore: Johns Hopkins UP, 1989), vii (for this and the following citation).

80. I refer of course to works such as *Kritik der reinen Vernunft* (1781), *Kritik der praktischen Vernunft* (1788), and *Kritik der Urteilskraft* (1790).

81. For the historical genesis of distance in modern historiography, see the recent important study of Mark Salber Phillips, *On Historical Distance* (New Haven: Yale UP, 2013).

82. Walter Benjamin, "Zur Kritik der Gewalt," *Gesammelte Schriften*, eds. Rolf Tiedemann and Hermann Schweppenhäuser II. Erster Teil (Frankfurt am Main: Suhrkamp, 1991), 202.

83. For an ambitious attempt at the former, see Robert Muchembled, *Une histoire de la violence: de la fin du Moyen Âge à nos jours* (Paris: Éditions du Seuil, 2008).

84. See Hans-Georg Gadamer, *Hermeneutik: Wahrheit und Methode* (Tübingen: Mohr, 1993), 2: 57–65, 184–198. For a defense of Gadamerian *Verständigung* within Islamic studies, see J. Van Ess, "From *Wellhausen to Becker*," in *Islamic Studies*, ed. Malcolm H. Kerr (Malibu: Undena Publications, 1980), 49.

85. In addition to Bobrovnikov, *Musul'mane*, see his "Abreki i gosudarstvo," *Vestnik Evrazii* 1.8 (2000): 19–46.

86. With respect to my insistence on plural modernities, my concept of modernity differs from Jameson's singular modernity, elaborated in *A Singular Modernity* (London: Verso, 2002), as well as from the modernity that is the object of Cooper's and Latour's important critiques (see *Colonialism in Question* [Berkeley: U of California Press, 2005], 113–152, and *Nous n'avons jamais été modernes* [Paris: La Découverte, 1991]), respectively.

87. See Nergis Ertürk, *Grammatology and Literary Modernity in Turkey* (Oxford: Oxford UP, 2011), 22.

88. Key texts in this scholarly project of reclaiming the modernity concept for non-Eurocentric ends include the essays in Sheldon Pollock, ed., *Forms of Knowledge in Early Modern Asia* (Durham: Duke UP, 2011); Sudipta Kaviraj, "An Outline of a Revisionist Theory of Modernity," *European Journal of Sociology* 46.3 (2005): 497–526; and Sanjay Subrahmanyam, "Connected Histories," *Modern Asian Studies* 31.3 (1997): 735–762.

89. See, for example, Rebecca Gould, "*Ijtihād* against *Madhhab*: The Meanings of Modernity in Early Modern Daghestan," *CSSH* 57.1 (2015): 35–66.

90. The literature on *ṣumūd* is richest with respect to Palestine; see, for example, Laleh Khalili, *Heroes and Martyrs of Palestine* (Cambridge: Cambridge UP, 2007), 94.

91. See Dipesh Chakrabarty, "Reconstructing Liberalism?" *Public Culture* 10.3 (1998): 457–481, esp. 460, 463.

92. I reference some of the most common approaches to the study of the Caucasus in light of postcolonial studies, for which see Adeeb Khalid, "Russian History and the Debate over Orientalism," *Kritika* 1.4 (2000): 691–699; Vera Tolz, *Russia's Own Orient* (Oxford: Oxford UP, 2011); David Schimmelpenninck van der Oye, *Russian Orientalism* (New Haven: Yale UP, 2010).

93. See Ranajit Guha, *Elementary Aspects of Peasant Insurgency in Colonial India* (Durham: Duke UP, 1999); and Ranjit Sen, *Social Banditry in Bengal* (Calcutta: Ratna

Prakashan, 1988). This subfield was arguably founded with Eric Hobsbawm's *Primitive Rebels* (Manchester: Manchester UP, 1959) and *Bandits* (London: Weidenfeld & Nicolson, 1969).

ONE The Abrek in Soviet Chechen Literature

1. For a classic discussion of the precolonial abrek across the Caucasus, see Yu. D. Anchabadze, "'Ostrakizm' na Kavkaze," *Sovetskaia etnografiia* 5 (1979): 137–144.

2. Jane Burbank, "The Ties That Bind," in Stefan B. Kirmse (ed.), *One Law for All?* (Frankfurt: Campus Verlag, 2012), 153.

3. Although my account of the anticolonial abrek begins with 1859, the abrek evolved in the northwestern Caucasus according to a somewhat different timeline, in keeping with this region's later incorporation into the Russian empire in 1864. For a collection of primary source documents on anticolonial resistance in the northwestern Caucasus, see *Mukhammad-Amin i narodno-osvoboditel'noe dvizhenie narodov Severo-Zapadnogo Kavkaza v 40-60 gg. XIX veka*, ed. G. G. Gamzatov et al (Makhachkala: RAN: Fond Shamilia, 1998).

4. Barabanov, the editor of al-Qarākhī's *Bāriqat*, notes that it was obvious that the author intended to conclude his chronicle with the surrender because of the way the author "asks Allah to come to the aid of the downtrodden residents of Daghestan" following his narration of this fateful event ("Vvedenie," 11).

5. Thomas M. Barrett, "The Remaking of the Lion of Daghestan: Shamil in Captivity," *Russian Review* 53.3 (1994): 353–366.

6. Moshe Gammer, "Collective Memory and Politics," *Caucasian Regional Studies* 4.1 (1999).

7. Magomed Gasanaliev, *Vosemnadtsat' let spustia: o vosstanii gortsev Dagestana i Chechni 1877 goda* (Makhachkala: Mezhdunarodnyi fond Shamilia, 2009), 27.

8. The text of this song is cited in Dalkhan Khojaev, *Chechentsy v Russko-Kavkazskoi voiny* (Grozny: Seda, 1998), 290–291.

9. I. L. Babich and V. O. Bobrovnikov, *Severnyi Kavkaz v sostave Rossiiskoi imperii* (Moscow: NLO, 2007), 138.

10. Khojaev, *Chechentsy*, 241; and Amjad M. Jaimoukha, *The Chechens* (London: Routledge, 2005), 49.

11. On *amān* as a social institution and its place in mountaineer Caucasus society, see M. B. Kandelaki, *Iz obshchestvennogo byta gortsev Gruzii—institut amanatstva* (Tbilisi: Metsniereba, 1987).

12. I borrow this phrase from Laleh Khalili, *Heroes and Martyrs of Palestine*, 217.

13. Iu. V. Khoruev, *Abreki na Kavkaze* (Vladikavkaz: Severo-Osetinskii Gosudarstvenii U, 2010), 15.

14. See Eric Hobsbawm and Terence Ranger, *The Invention of Tradition* (Cambridge: Cambridge UP, 1983). Paradoxically, Hobsbawm does not apply his concept of the invention of tradition to the social bandit he has helped to canonize. To the contrary, Hobsbawm refers to "classical banditry, which essentially belongs to the pre-industrial period" (*Bandits*, 138) as the ideal type for all social banditry.

15. For this body of literature generally (without specific reference to the abrek), see the collections edited by Vladimir Bobrovnikov, *Obychai i zakon v pis'mennykh pamiatnikakh Dagestana V—nachala XX v.* (Moscow: Mardzhani, 2009); and M. A. Ismailov, T. M. Aitberov, and A. S. Akbiev, *Antologiia pamiatnikov prava narodov Kavkaza* (Rostov-na-Donu: Severo-Kavkazskaia akademiia gos. sluzhby, 2010).

16. Cited in F. I. Leontievich's *ʿādāt* compendium, *Adaty kavkazskikh gortsev* (Odessa: Tip. P.A. Zelenago, 1881), 1:361, which provides an important summary of the abrek according to *ʿādāt* on pp. 360–363. Leontievich's definition is drawn from the *ʿādāt* of the Cherkess of the Black Sea region.

17. In Daghestan, the most important such source is the story of Khochbar, concerning which see V. O. Bobrovnikov, "Nasilie i vlast' v istoricheskoi pamiati musul'manskogo pogranich'ia," in I. Gerasimov, M. Mogilner, and A. Semyonov (eds.), *Imperiia i natsiia v zerkale istoricheskoi pamiati* (Moscow: Novoe izd-vo, 2011), 297–327.

18. One of the first such works is the fictional first-person account by the Adyghe enlightener Adil-Girei Keshev under the pseudonym Kalambiia, "Abreki (raskaz [*sic*] cherkesa)," *Russkii vestnik* 30 [November 1860]: 127–190. Further sources in this vein are cited in appendix I.

19. For example, N. Dubrovin, *Istoriia voiny i vladychestva Russkikh na Kavkaze* (Sankt-Petersburg, 1871), 1:215.

20. G. A. Vertepov, "Sektanstvo v Chechne," *Zapiski Terskogo obschestva liubitelei kazachei starini* (Vladikavkaz, 1914), 2:79.

21. Kh. Oshaev, "Muridizm v Chechne," *Revolutsiia i Gorets* 9 (1930): 50.

22. See V. V. Akaev, *Sheikh Kunta Hadji* (Grozny: Nauchno-Issledovatel'skii Institut, 1994), 61–73.

23. For the most recent scholarship on Kunta Ḥājjī, see R.-Kh. Sh. Albagachiev, *Sheikh, Ustaz, Ovliia Kunta-Khadzhi Kishiev* (Nal'chik: Tetragraf, 2013).

24. A. K. Alikberov, *Epokha*, 686.

25. For al-Jīlānī's biography and his influence on later Sufism, see Binyamin Abrahamov, *Ibn al-ʿArabi and the Sufis* (Oxford: Anqa Publishing, 2014), 151–155.

26. Gammer, *The Lone Wolf and the Bear* (London: Hurst, 2006), 76. For tsarist politics with respect to Chechen Sufism, see Christian Dettmering, *Russlands Kampf gegen die Sufis* (Oldenburg: Dryas-Verlag, 2011).

27. Although the dichotomy between jihadist Naqshbandīs and pacifist Qādirīs has been nuanced by the recent work of Michael Kemper, the general distinction is still recognized. For a valuable account of Kunta Ḥājjī's teaching by one of his disciples, see Anna Zelkina, "Some Aspects of the Teaching of Kunta Hâjjî," *JHS* 1–2: (2000): 483–507.

28. TsVIA, f. VUA, 1861 g, d. 6696, ll. 479–982, cited in A. I. Ivanov, "Natsional'no-osvoboditel'noe dvizhenie v Chechne i Dagestane v 60-70kh gg. XIXv.," *Istoricheskie zapiski* 12 (1941): 180. For another discussion of this movement by a colonial official, see A. Ippolitov, "Uchenie zikr i ego posledovateli v Chechne i Argunskom Okruge," *SSKG* 2 (1869): 1–17.

29. Ippolitov, "Uchenie zikr," 15.

30. Akaev, *Sheikh Kunta Hadji*, 59. This transfer is described by Kunta Ḥājjī's disciple ʿAbd al-Salâm, who accompanied his teacher to prison (as cited in Zelkina, "Some Aspects," 486).

31. Gammer, *The Lone Wolf and the Bear*, 78, citing an interview conducted in Eliskhan-Yurt in 1992. For such beliefs among the Qādiriyya in Daghestan, see Shamil Shikhaliev, "Sufische Bildung in Dagestan," in *Repression, Anpassung, Neuorientierung*, ed. Michael Kemper, Anke von Kügelgen, and Raoul Motika (Weisbaden: Reichart Verlag, 2014), 158.

32. Julietta Meskhidze, "Shaykh Batal Hajji from Surkhokhi," *CAS* 25.1–2 (2006): 181ff.

33. TsGA, f. 38. op. 7. d. 429. ll. 58, cited in Akaev, *Sheikh Kunta Hadji*, 74 and n163 (p. 123).

34. Abuzar Aidamirov, *Exa bu'sanash* (1972; Grozny: Kniga, 1990), 325. Further references to this work are given parenthetically.

35. For Vara's recitation of Yā Sīn, see Ippolitov, "Uchenie zikr," 15, and compare the discussion of Zelimkhan's recitation of Yā Sīn at the end of this chapter.

36. The phrase, from Abdurahman Avtorkhanov's rich (and unjustly ignored) exposition of Chechen history, *K osnovnyim voprosam istorii chechni* (Grozny: Serlo, 1930), 27, appears to echo Ippolitov, "Uchenie zikr," 15.

37. Aslanbek Sheripov, *Stat'i i rechi*, 2nd ed., ed. E. P. Kireev and M. N. Muzaev (Grozny: Checheno-ingushskoe knizhnoe izd-vo, 1972), 66–68. The words in quotations are taken by Sheripov from *Razboi na Kavkaze*, by P. Kozachkovskii (Vladikavkaz, 1913). A Chechen version of Sheripov's introduction can be found in Sheripov, *Stat'iash a, qʿamelash a sbornik* (Grozny: Nokhch-Ghalghain knizhni izd-vo, 1977), 71–77 (presumably the translation was done by the editors, although this is not stated).

38. Sheripov, *Stat'i i rechi*, 66.

39. Aslanbek Sheripov, *Iz chechenskikh pesen* (Vladikavkaz: Terskii Narodnii Sovet, 1918); reprinted in Sheripov, *Stat'i i rechi*, 157–160. This text is translated and analyzed in detail in Rebecca Gould, "The Lonely Hero and Chechen Modernity," *Journal of Folklore Research* 51.1 (2014): 199–222. For the *illi* in Russian verse (apparently from the field notes of Aslanbek Sheripov), see *O tekh kogo nazyvali abrekami* (Grozny: Chechenskogo otdela narodnogo obrazovaniia, 1927), 5–9.

40. For one such anthology, see Sh. A., Dzhambekov ed. *Nokhchin folklor* (Grozny: Kniga, 1990), esp. "Obarg Varin illi" and "Zelamxa Gıizlarex' lataran illi."

41. Sheripov, *Stat'i i rechi*, 66.

42. Sheripov, *Stat'i i rechi*, 66–67.

43. These are "Sheykh Mansur" (151–158), "Propavshee zoloto" (182–186), "O tom, kak var stal sheykhom" (194–196), "Satana" (197–199), and "Gairak" (200).

44. For Moritz Wagner's writings on the Caucasus, see Clemens P. Sidorko, "Nineteenth Century German Travelogues as Sources on the History of Daghestan and Chechnya," *CAS* 21.3 (2002): 283–299.

45. *O tekh kogo nazyvali abrekami*, 187.

46. There were, however, divisions within the ʿ*ulamā*ʾ regarding the source of the imamate's legitimacy, concerning which see Michael Kemper, "Daghestani Legal Discourse on the Imamate," *CAS* 21.3 (2002): 265–278.

47. Sherry Ortner, "Resistance and the Problem of Ethnographic Refusal," *CSSH* 37.1 (1995): 188, 190.

48. For Zelimkhan's epistolary legacy, see Khoruev, *Abreki na Kavkaze*, 493–505; and Lema Gudaev, *Abrek Zelimkhan* (Grozny: Knizhnoe izd-vo, 2011), 149–153.

49. Gatuev, *Zelimkhan* (Rostov: Severnoe Kavkazskoe izd-vo, 1926), 41.

50. See P. I. Kovalevskii, *Vosstanie Chechni i Dagestana v 1877-1876 gg* (St. Petersburg: M. I. Akinfiev, 1912).

51. Magomed Mamakaev, *Zelamkha* (Grozny: Nokhch-Ghalghain Knizhni, 1968). The Russian edition is Magomed Mamakaev, *Zelimkhan*, trans. V. V. Timofeev (Grozny: Checheno-ingushskoe knizhnoe izd-vo, 1981). Parenthetical citations from the Chechen edition are followed by the letter *C*; parenthetical citations from the Russian edition are followed by the letter *R*.

52. Mamakaev, "Dzakho Gatuev," 10. The impulse to distinguish the abrek from the bandit (*razboinik*) is evident in other literatures of the North Caucasus. See, for example, the account (c. 1957) of how the Adyghe abrek-protagonist Kaymet entered his vocation: "He hit the official and afterwards had no option other than to become an abrek. But Kaymet did not become a bandit [*razboinik*]," in Tembot Kerashev, *Abreki* (Moscow: Sovetskaia Rossia, 1969), 4.

53. Mamakaev cites from the textbook edited by N. A. Smirnov, the Soviet historian who did much to popularize the study of Shamil's "murīd" movement: *Ocherki istorii checheno-ingushskoi ASSR* (Grozny: Checheno-Ingushskoe knizhnoe izd-vo, 1967).

54. A. Qazbegi, *Txzulebani* (Tbilisi: Sabchota msterloba, 1948), 1:385–412, quotation on 401–402, translated in Qazbegi, *Prose of the Mountains* (Budapest: Central European University Press, 2015), 65.

55. A. Kazbegi [Qazbegi], *Kha'rzhinarsh*, trans. from the Georgian by I. Margoshvili (Grozny: Nokhch-Ghalghain knizhni izd-vo, 1961), reanthologized in the textbook edited by V. A. Dykhaev: *Nokhchiin sovetski literatura* (Grozny: Nokhch-Ghalghain knizhni izd-vo, 1978), 116–126.

56. Many Kists spoke of Qazbegi during my fieldwork in the Pankisi Gorge (2005–2006), documented in Rebecca Gould, "Secularism and Belief in Georgia's Pankisi Gorge," *JIS* 22.3 (2011): 339–373.

57. P. Chinskii, "Zelimkhan," *Rannee utro* 147 (1913): 2.

58. Sayyid Quṭb, *In the Shade of the Quran* (London: MWH Publishers, 1979), 14:193.

59. Devin J. Stewart, "Rhymed Prose," in *Encyclopaedia of the Qur'ān*, ed. Jane Dammen McAuliffe (Leiden: Brill, 2005), 4:478.

60. J. Burt, "Hypotaxis and Parataxis," in Roland Greene et al. (eds.), *The Princeton Encyclopedia of Poetry and Poetics* (Princeton: Princeton UP, 2012), 650.

61. Burt, "Hypotaxis and Parataxis," 650.

62. Gatuev, *Zelimkhan*, 174.

63. To take just one example, *fahum ghāfilūna* is transliterated into Cyrillic as *fsgim gi fil' lush* (Фсгим ги филь люш), which makes it unrecognizable to a reader who does not know precisely which text Gatuev is drawing from. Although he could have used the Cyrillic x as in (Зелимхан), Gatuev chose to render the Arabic *hā* (ه) by a hard *g* (г). It is equally hard to ascertain why the last sounds in the phrase are swallowed, such

that *lūn* (لُون) becomes *lush* (люш). In contrast, Gatuev correctly reproduced the Arabic *qāf* (ق) by the Russian *k*, as Cyrillic lacks a more precise equivalent. Given the highly volatile shifts from Arabic to Cyrillic to Roman script, for which Gatuev's imprecise translations are partly though not entirely responsible, I have reproduced the original scripts where necessary.

64. Gordii Semyonovich Sablukov, *Kalam sharif* (1907; Moscow: MP "Mif," 1991). This work, the product of thirty years of labor by a scholar less than favorable to Islam, has been well analyzed by Robert Geraci in *Window on the East* (Ithaca: Cornell UP, 2001), 87–88.

65. The verses cited here, 36:6–8, correspond to 36:5–7 (p. 825) in Sablukov's text.

66. The rendering "a people" is somewhat more justified with reference to the Arabic than to Sablukov's Russian. Whereas Sablukov has *liudi*, which can mean "people" in general rather than a specific people (*narod*), the Arabic has *qawm*, which specifically means *a* people in the sense of a delimited collectivity, not humanity in general. I believe the latter was the sense Gatuev most wished to evoke.

67. In keeping with the garbled Arabic style that characterizes this section, the final words of the text "va dzhaal pa," may correspond to 39:9, *wa jaʿalnā* [وَ جَعَلْنَا]. Accepting this reading, which seems the likeliest, would mean accepting that Gatuev confused the final *nā* in the Arabic for the *pa* in his transliteration. Other imprecisions, such as the missing *ʿayn* in Cyrillic and the rendering of *waw* [وَ] by *va*, can be explained through lacks inherent in the Cyrillic script. *Wa jaʿalnā* translates simply as "and we have done/created," and it introduces the punishment extracted by God: "put a barrier before them, and a barrier behind them, and We have covered them up, so that they cannot see."

68. Aidamirov, *Darts: roman* (Grozny: GUP, 2006), 234.

69. Whereas the Chechen and Russian versions coincide in most respects up to this point in the narrative, at this juncture the later Russian version offers a more detailed depiction of abrek's death than the original Chechen. The details here are therefore based mostly on the Russian version. Mamakaev's involvement in the translation of his novel is unknown, but it is significant that Zelimkhan recites Yā Sīn only in the Russian version.

70. For Balu's *illi*, see *Nokhchiin illesh, esarsh* (Grozny: Nokhch-Ghalghain knizhni izd-vo, 1973), 103. For an exegesis, see I. S. Vagapov, "Odinokii geroi v checheno-ingushkom *illi*," *Izvestiya voprosi checheno-ingushskoi literature* 5.3 (1968): 102.

71. *Antologiia checheno-ingushskoi poezii*, ed. Vakha Dykhaev (Grozny: Checheno-ingushskoe knizhnoe izd-vo, 1981), 55–56 (Trans. Naum Grebnev). The Chechen source for the Russian translation is not cited in the anthology.

72. Sigmund Freud, "Das Unheimliche [1919]," in *Gesammelte Werke*, ed. Anna Freud (Frankfurt: S. Fischer Verlag, 1986), 248. Future references are given parenthetically. As his source for this insight, Freud references here Heine's *Der Götter im Exil* (1853).

73. Iu. M. Botiakov, *Abreki na Kavkaze* (St. Petersburg: Petersburgskoe vostokovedenie, 2004).

74. Asma Afsaruddin, *Striving in the Path of God* (Oxford: Oxford UP, 2013), 65.

75. Lutz Peter Koepnick, *Walter Benjamin and the Aesthetics of Power* (Lincoln: U of Nebraska P, 1999), 75.

76. Quṭb, *In the Shade of the Quran*, 14:201.

77. Freud, "Das Unheimliche," 237; compare Ernst Jentsch, "On the Psychology of the Uncanny (1906)," *Angelaki* 2.1 (1997): 11.

78. For an alternative account of the reasons for Freud's qualified rejection of the animacy thesis, see Sarah Kofman, *Quatre romans analytiques* (Paris: Éditions Galilée, 1974), 131–176.

79. Consider, for example, Jentsch's claim that "It is all the more impossible to resist this psychical urge, the more primitive the individual's level of intellectual development" ("On the Psychology of the Uncanny," 13).

80. Ranajit Guha takes up this point with respect to the British historiography of India; examples from the Caucasus include P. I. Kovalevskii, *Vosstaniye*; and A. Ippolitov, "Uchenie zikr," esp. 1 and 12.

81. For further examples of resistance to the miraculous in contemporary ethnography, see Ortner, "Resistance and the Problem of Ethnographic Refusal," 181.

82. See Ranajit Guha, "The Prose of Counterinsurgency," *Subaltern Studies II*, ed. Ranajit Guha (Delhi: Oxford UP, 1983), 78.

83. Freud, "Das Unheimliche," 262.

84. I cite from the comments of Bruce Grant (New York University) to an earlier iteration of this argument.

85. For this dating, see Zaindi Shakhbiev, *Sud'ba checheno-ingushskogo naroda* (Moscow: Rossiia Molodaia, 1996), 436.

86. For a collection of newspaper reports of Zelamkha's death, see Lema Gudaev, *Abrek Zelimkhan*, 60–115.

87. See M. A. Musaev, *Musul'manskoe dukhovenstvo 60-70-x godov XIX veka i vosstanie 1877 goda v Dagestane* (Makhachkala: IIAE DNTs RAN, 2005), 106.

88. For an enumeration of the specific rules in Caucasus *ʿādāt* apportioned to thievery (*vorovstvo*), see Manai Alibekov, *Adaty kumykov* (Makhachkala: Dagestanskogo Nauchno-Issledovatel'skogo Instituta, 1927), 24–27.

89. For the former line of thought, enshrined above all in Hobsbawm's concept of the social bandit, which transgressive sanctity seeks to move beyond, see Mariel Tsaroieva, *Peuples et religions du Caucase du Nord* (Paris: Éditions Karthala, 2001), 339. Whereas the Chechen abrek diverges from the Robin Hood paradigm, the Georgian abrek (*abragi, qachagi*) Arsena Odzelashvili (see appendix I), approaches more closely to Hobsbawm's ideal type.

90. Colin Imber, "What does ghazi actually mean?" in Ç. Balım-Harding and C. Imber (eds.), *The Balance of Truth* (Istanbul: Isis Press, 2000), 174.

91. Shams al-Dīn Aḥmad-i Aflākī, *Exemplary Acts of the Mystics* [*Manāqeb al-ʿarefīn*] (Leiden: Brill, 2002), 334.

92. Imber, "What Does Ghazi Actually Mean?" 167.

93. Imber, "What Does Ghazi Actually Mean?" 171.

94. A. D. Iandarov, *Sufizm i ideologiia natsional'no-osvoboditel'nogo dvizheniia* (Alma-Ata: Nauka, 1975), 110.

95. Musaev, *Musul'manskoe dukhovenstvo*, 107.

96. The *ghazawāt*-jihad distinction was reiterated in multiple interviews with Chechen refugees in Nal'chik. When asked to explain the difference between jihad and *ghazawāt*, my interlocutors said that *ghazawāt* aimed to protect the homeland, whereas jihad looked beyond the homeland and to broaden the Islamic community of (*umma*).

97. Ziaudin Abdullaev, "Zasada," in *Mir domu tvoemy* (Nal'chik: Elbrus, 2003), 246–255. The story tells of an apocryphal—but, among Chechens, widely referenced—meeting between Zelimkhan and the Russian opera singer Fyodor Shaliapin on a Chechen road.

98. I conceive of the Soviet regime's "studied amnesia" in terms of the "learned ignorance" that for Pierre Bourdieu characterizes relations between the state and its subjects. See Bourdieu, *Outline of a Theory of Practice* (Cambridge: Cambridge UP, 1977), 19.

99. Musa Bakarov, *Obarg Zelamkhekh dagaletsamash* (Grozny: Kniga, 1990).

100. In light of Khasukha's example, it is difficult to agree that after the deportation of the Chechens, "the criminal situation in the area became more stable for half a century" (Bobrovnikov, "Bandits," 260).

101. Musa Geshaev, *Izvestnye chechentsy* (Moscow: n.p., 1999). Khasukha's story is presented by Geshaev as an account taken from history, and Khasukha is remembered by other Chechens as a historical figure.

102. Ortner, "Resistance and the Problem of Ethnographic Refusal," 191.

103. Sergei Berdiaev, *Chechnia i razboinik Zelimkhan* (Paris: Pascal, 1932), 15. Also see Berdiaev, *Razboi na Kavkaze* (Paris: Pascal, 1930).

104. V. Polozov, *V debriakh Zakavkaz'ia*, Bakhmeteff Archive, Columbia University, 1–2, cited in Bobrovnikov, "Bandits," 247.

105. A. Akhlakov, *Geroiko-istoricheskie pesni avartsev* (Makhachkala: AN SSSR, IIILGT, 1968), 164–180.

106. Akaki Shanidze, *K'artuli xalxuri poezia Xevsuruli* (Tbilisi: Saxelmtsipo gamomcemloba, 1931), 1:246–248, for a Georgian-language poem dedicated to Zelimkhan (poem no. 604 in other editions of Shanidze's text).

107. Gabriel Jabushanuri, *Hoi, ghilgos daghrubluri tsao* (Tbilisi: Gulani, 1991), 13. Also see the poem "Abragis natvra" (Abrek's Dream) in the same volume (31).

108. Gatuev, *Zelimkhan*, 19.

109. Guha, "Chandra's Death," *Subaltern Studies V*, ed. Ranajit Guha (Delhi: Oxford UP, 1987), 140.

110. The two writers collaborated on a translation from Ossetian to Russian of the legend of Amirani (the Georgian name for Prometheus), the giver of fire to humanity against the will of the gods. See Gatuev and Marr, *Amran: Osetinskii epos* (Moscow: Academia, 1932).

111. Marr, "Kavkazskaia poeziia i ee tekhnicheskie osnovy v osveshenii lingvisticheskoi paleontologii," *Literaturnikh razyskaniia* (Tbilisi: AN Gruzinskoi SSSR,

1947), 115. Cited in V. A. Mikhankova, *Nikolai Iakovlevich Marr* (Leningrad: AN SSSR, 1949), 259.

112. Frantz Fanon, *Black Skin, White Masks* (New York: Grove Press, 1967); Susan Buck-Morss, "Hegel and Haiti," *Critical Inquiry* 26.4 (2000): 821–865.

113. In, for example, V. Matveev, "Severnyi Kavkaz: abreki, kachagi, i drugie," *Orientir* 4 (2002): 9–11.

114. Jürgen Habermas, *The Structural Transformation of the Public Sphere* (Cambridge: MIT Press, 1991).

115. Bobrovnikov, "Bandits," 261.

116. Hegel, *Elements of the Philosophy of Right* (Cambridge: Cambridge UP, 1991), 275 (=§257).

117. For this argument, see chapter 4 and the epilogue.

118. Lauren Benton, *Law and Colonial Cultures* (Cambridge: Cambridge UP, 2002), 11. For a discussion of legal pluralism in the context of Caucasus societies, see Bobrovnikov, *Musul'mane*, 98–102.

119. Benton, *Law and Colonial Cultures*, 12.

120. For a lucid comparative account of Sufi anticolonial jihad across the colonized world, see Michael Kemper, "The Changing Images of Jihad Leaders," *Nova Religio* 11.2 (2007): 28–58.

TWO Regulating Rebellion

1. The Avar version of this text, originally composed in the ʿ*ajamī* (Arabic) script, was deemed lost until very recently, when it was discovered by D. M. Malamagomedov and published in the volume titled *Khunzakhskie predaniia o Khadzhimurade* (Makhachkala: DNTs RAN, 2009). See T. M. Aitberov, "Ot redaktora," in the aforementioned volume, for a description of the Avar manuscript.

2. Gamzat Iasulov, "Predaniia o Khadzhi Murate," *Dāghistān mejmūʿasï-Dagestanskii sbornik*, ed. A. A. Takho-Godi, B. G. Mallachikhanov, and D. M. Pavlov (1927), 3:7–49. Future references to this text are given parenthetically by page number. The two earlier *Dagestanskii sborniks* appeared in 1901 and 1903 under the rubric "issue [*vypusk*]" rather than *tom* (volume).

3. For a recent brief biography, see A. A. Isaev, "Alibek Takho-Godi," *Khunzakhskie predaniia*, 5–12. For a more detailed study, see A. M. Magomedov, *Alibek Takho-Godi* (Makhachkala: Dagestanskoe knizhnoe izd-vo, 1993).

4. Marshall, *The Caucasus under Soviet Rule* (London: Routledge, 2009), 62.

5. Alibek Takho-Godi, "Predislovie," ed. Dzakho Gatuev, *Poeziia gortsev Kavkaza: Sbornik* (Moscow: Gosliizdat, 1934), 3–26.

6. See Aitberov, "Ot redaktora," 4.

7. For Takho-Godi's activities in this capacity, see *Nauchnoe nasledie A.A. Takho-Godi*, ed. A. A. Isaev (Makhachkala: RAN, 2006), 2:9ff.

8. In both Sunni and Shīʿa traditions, *khums* is a "one-fifth share of the spoils of war and, according to the majority of Muslim jurists, of other specified forms of income, set aside for variously designated beneficiaries" (A. Zysow, "Ḳhums," *EI²*).

9. Here it is worth recalling the lineage leading from the archetypal folkloric hero of the Chechen *illi* to the Chechen abrek (discussed more fully in Gould, "The Lonely Hero"). For the latter, see Vagapov, "Odinokii geroi."

10. As for al-Qarākhī himself, he passed the remainder of his life following Shamil's surrender as a *qāḍī* in Temir Khan Shura, in the employ of the Russian administration (*Āthār*, 205).

11. *Tadhkirat Sayyidī ʿAbd al-Raḥmān ibn Ustādh Sheykh al-Ṭarīqah Jamāl al-Dīn al-Ḥusaynī fī bayān aḥwāl ahālī Dāghistān wa-Chichān allafahu wa-katabahu fī Tiflīs fī sanat 1285*, ed. M.S. Saidov, A. R. Shikhsaidov, and Kh. A. Omarov (Makhachkala: Dagestanskoe knizhnoe izd-vo, 1997).

12. Ḥasan al-Alqadārī, *Āthār-i Dāghistān* (St. Petersburg: n.p., 1302/1894–95), 208. I am deeply grateful to Vladimir Bobrovnikov for furnishing me with a scan of this edition.

13. Given that he was from the mixed Chechen-Qumuq village of Enderei, Ḥājjī Tashaw would likely have been of mixed ethnic background. For my purposes, however, his intellectual profile, which converged with the discourse of Chechen transgressive sanctity, is of greater importance than the question of whether he was himself Chechen.

14. The citation in this sentence is from Kemper, *Herrschaft*, 296. For the geography over which Ḥājjī Tashaw claimed sovereignty, see Michael Kemper, "The North Caucasian Khālidiyya and 'Muridism,'" *JHS* 5 (2006): 162–164, and Anna Zelkina, "Islam and Society in Chechnia," *JIS* 7.2 (1996): 257–259.

15. For these details of Ḥājjī Tashaw's biography, see Smirnov, *Miuridizm*, 61–62.

16. See, in addition to the sources cited here, Dettmering, *Russlands Kampf gegen die Sufis*, 217–219.

17. A. B. Zaks, "Tashev Khadzhi," *Voprosy Istorii* 4 (1993): 144. Zaks's doctoral thesis (based on Russian sources) was defended in 1944 (the year of the Chechen deportation) but was banned from publication by the conditions of Soviet censorship. An abstract of this monograph was first published in Grozny in 1972 (and republished in 1992) under the title *Tashev Khadzhi-spodvizhnik Shamilia*. For this publication history, see Kemper, "Einige Notizen zur arabischsprachigen Literatur der jihad-Bewegung in Dagestan und Tschetschenien in der ersten Hälfte des 19. Jahrhunderts," *MCRCA* 2, 78n63.

18. See the citation from this work in Kemper, *Herrschaft*, 299.

19. Ḥājjī Tashaw, *Asʾilatuhu al-ʿadīd min makān al-baʿīd* (IIAE, f. 14, op. 1, no. 1690), folios 5b–6a. Cited and translated in Kemper, *Herrschaft*, 298–299, and Kemper, "Einige Notizen," 84–85. Kemper is to my knowledge the only scholar whose account of Ḥājjī Tashaw's beliefs is based on his own Arabic writings.

20. For a detailed study of Bāyazīd, see M. ʿAbdur Rabb, *The Life, Thought and Historical Importance of Abu Yazid al-Bistami* (Dacca: Academy for Pakistan Affairs, 1971). For Bāyazīd's legacy among the Naqshbandī, see Muhammad Hisham Kabbani, *Classical Islam and the Naqshbandi Sufi Tradition* (Fenton, MI: Islamic Supreme Council of America, 2004), 129–138. The Khālidiyya sheykh al-Bākinī, an Avar from northern Azerbaijan, discusses Bāyazīd in his *Ṭabaqāt al-Khwājagān al-Naqshbandiyah* (Damascus: Dār al-Nuʿmān lil-ʿUlūm, 2003), 48–49.

21. Ḥājjī Tashaw's desire to institute *sharī ͑a* is noted in Zaks, "Tashev Khadzhi," 142, and Smirnov, *Miuridizm*, 62.

22. Zaks reports that the last recorded mention of Ḥājjī Tashaw's activities occurs in the reports of the Caucasus regiment and that there is a local (presumably Chechen) saying that he died his "own death [*svoei smertiu*]" ("Tashev Khadzhi," 145).

23. Aleksandre Qazbegi, "Mamis mkleveli," *Txzulebata sruli krebuli oṭx tomad* (Tbilisi: Sabchota sakartvelo, 1948), 1:303.

24. Kovalevskii, *Vosstanie Chechni i Dagestana*, 10. For further discussion of *taips* in Chechen society, see Magomed Mamakaev's foundational *Chechenskii taip (rod) v period ego razlozheniia* (Grozny: Checheno-Ingushskoe izd-vo, 1973); and Christian Dettmering, "Reassessing Chechen and Ingush (Vainakh) Clan Structures in the 19th Century," *CAS* 24.4 (2005): 469–489.

25. Ian Chesnov, "'Byt' Chechentsem. Lichnost' i etnicheskie identifikatsii naroda," in *Rossiia i Chechnia. Obschestva i gosudarstva*, ed. Dmitrii Furman (Moscow: Sakharov Foundation, 1999), 63–101.

26. Steve Caton, "'Salam Tahiyah': Greetings from the Highlands of Yemen," *American Ethnologist* 13.2 (1986): 296.

27. Michael Kemper, "Communal Agreements (*ittifāqāt*) and ʿādāt-Books from Daghestani Villages and Confederacies (18th–19th Centuries)," *Der Islam* 81.1 (2004): 124.

28. Caton, "Salam Tahiyah," 292.

29. Compare Vassan Giray Jabagi's statement that "the main role was played by Muslim clergy" in all Daghestani rebellions, in his "The North Caucasus in the Wake of the Russian Revolution, 1917," *CAS* 10.1–2 (1991): 132.

30. A. Runovskii, "Dnevnik polkovnika Runovskogo," *AKAK* 12 (1904): 1476.

31. See ʿAbd al-Raḥmān, "Predislovie k rukopisnomy sochineniu Dzhmaleddina traktat," *al-Ādāb al-marḍiyah fī al-ṭarīqah al-naqshbandīyah* (1905; Oxford: Society for Central Asian Studies, 1986), 25. ʿAbd al-Raḥmān's preface (originally published in *SSKG* 2 [1869]: 3–6) was composed in Arabic (according to the edition in *SSKG* 3), but the Arabic text is not included in the published version of *al-Ādāb al-marḍiyah.*

32. Recorded in *Tarjamat maqālā fā al-ustādh al-kāmil al-sheikh al faḍā'il al-Ḥājjī Kunta Sheikh* (Petrovsk [Makhachkala]: Tip. A. M. Mikhailov, 1911), cited in Akaev, *Sheikh Kunta Hajji*, 53 and 122n135. This compendium of Kunta Ḥājjī's sayings, translated into Qumuq from an unknown language, is not available to me but was recently studied in M. Albogachieva, "'I am entrusted with only prayer beads by Allāh, and I will take neither a dagger nor a rifle in my hands' (Kunta-Ḥājjī Kishiev, his preaching and followers)," *Manuscripta Orientalia* 17.2 (2011): 12–20 (first page reproduced at 14).

33. See Sh. V. Megrelidze, *Zakavkaze v Russko-Turetskoi voine 1877-1878 gg* (Tbilisi: Metsniereba, 1972), 66.

34. ʿAlī Qāḍī al-Salṭī, "Istoriia shariatskogo vosstaniia," *Vosstaniia dagestantsev i chechentsev v posleshamilevskuyu epokhu i imamat 1877 goda*, trans. T. M. Aitberov, Iu. Dadaev, and Kh. A. Omarov (Makhachkala: Fond Shamilia, 2001), 69.

35. Nadhīr ad-Durgilī, *Nuzhat al-adhhān fī tarājim ʿulamāʾ Dāghistān*, ed. Michael Kemper and Amri R. Shikhsaidov (Berlin: Schwarz Verlag 2004), 132–139. Also see Tagirova and Shikhsaidov, "ʿAbdarraḥmān Ġāzīġumūqī," 333–334.

36. Kemper, *Herrschaft*, 217–224.

37. The Arabic gloss on the manuscript, dated 1873–1874, is given in *Bāriqat*, p. 7, in Arabic pagination (see Barabanov, "Vvedenie," 16–17, for a description of the manuscript in which the gloss was found).

38. The anonymous glosser further specifies the meaning of *murīd* in terms that suggest a consciousness of newness. "In these meanings," he writes, "the word [*murīd*] is used throughout *Bāriqat*" (7 in Arabic pagination).

39. [Ḥājjī ʿAlī al-Chūkhī], "Skazanie ochevidtsa o Shamile," *SSKG* 7 (1873): 7.

40. See Michael Kemper, "Khālidiyya Networks," *WDI* 42.1 (2002): 43.

41. Kemper, "Khālidiyya Networks," 43.

42. Musaev, *Musul'manskoe dukhovenstvo*, 109–110.

43. ʿAlī Qāḍī al-Salṭī, "Istoriia shariatskogo vosstaniia," 74. For ʿAlī Qāḍī as a student of al-ʿUrādī, see al-Durgilī, *Nuzhat*, 144/102 (Here and elsewhere where al-Durgilī is cited, the first reference is to the Arabic manuscript held in *IIAE* and reproduced in the 2012 edition [*Uslada umov*], followed by a reference to the Arabic transcription in the 2004 edition [*Die Islamgelehrten Daghestans*]). ʿAlī Qāḍī al-Salṭī also transcribed a treatise by Ghāzī Muḥammad against *ʿurf*, which is translated and discussed in Michael Kemper, "Ghazi Muhammad's Treatise against Daghestani Customary Law," *Islam and Sufism in Daghestan* (Helsinki: Academia Scientiarum Fennica, 2009), 85–100.

44. Magomedov, *Vosstannie gortsev Dagestana v 1877*, list 48.

45. ʿAbd al-Raḥmān al-Thughūrī's first son Muḥammad Ḥājjī (also referred to as Ḥājjī Muḥammad) was a "*nāʾib* in Sogratl under Shamil," as Kemper notes on the basis of Gaidarbekov's unpublished *Anthology of Daghestani Arabic Poetry* (*Antologiya dagestanskoi poezii na arabskom yazyke* [1965]), held at *IIAE*, fond 3, op. 1, no. 3560, 76 (Kemper, "ʿAbd al-Raḥmān al-Thughūrī," *EI*[3]). Also see Abuzar Aidamirov, *Khronologiia istorii Checheno-Ingushetii* (Grozny: Kniga, 1991), 71.

46. ʿAlī Qāḍī al-Salṭī, *Opisanie vosstanniia 1877 goda* (trans. from Arabic by K. M. Barkuev [c. 1963]), IIAE, f. 1, op. 1, no. 430/3255, list 1–2. This account diverges significantly from the account of ʿAlībek Ḥājjī's death given in an older manuscript of ʿAlī Qāḍī's text, translated in "Istoriia shariatskogo vosstaniia," 128–129. According to Aitberov, Dadaev, and Omarov in the introduction to their translation of ʿAlī Qāḍī's text, Barkuev's translation is based on an abbreviated copy that was made of the Arabic original in the "middle of the twentieth century," and which is held at IIAE, IIAE, f. 1, op. 1, no. 365/3286, list 1-8 ("Opisanie materiala," 14). Aitberov, Dadaev, and Omarov based their translation primarily on a more recent and detailed manuscript, obtained from the private collection of Darbishmagomed Karagishnev from the village of Ingisho, and that appears to have been copied between the end of the nineteenth and the beginning of the twentieth centuries. I have consulted both translations.

47. N. Semenov, "Khronika Chechenskogo vosstaniia 1877 goda," *Terskii Sbornik* 1 (1881): 92, and N. A. Smirnov, chief ed., *Ocherki istorii checheno-ingushskoi*, 140.

48. ʿAlī Qāḍī, "Istoriia shariatskogo vosstaniia," 95–96.

49. Aitberov, Dadaev, and Omarov, notes to "Istoriia shariatskogo vosstaniia," 208n16. These scholars argue that the corruption of *ʿādāt* was a major reason for the mountaineers' turn to *sharīʿa* as a means of resisting colonial rule.

50. Michael Kemper, personal correspondence (July 2014). Also see Kemper's "'Adat against Shari'a: Russian Approaches towards Daghestani 'Customary Law' in the 19th Century," *Ab Imperio* 3 (2005): 147–174, to which my "*Ijtihād* against *Madhhab*" is a homage and response.

51. Michael Kemper, personal correspondence (July 2014).

52. Akhlakov, *Geroiko-istoricheskie pesni avartsev*, 150.

53. ʿAlī Qāḍī al-Salṭī, *Opisanie vosstanniia 1877 goda*, 60, 75.

54. R. Magomedov, *Vosstannie gortsev Dagestana v 1877*, IIAE, f. 1, op. 1, no. 318/187, list 20. The citation from the Soviet poet Suleiman Stalskii (d. 1937) quoted at the end of this typescript dates it to the mid-Soviet period.

55. Magomedov, *Vosstannie gortsev Dagestana v 1877*, list 26.

56. Magomedov, *Vosstannie gortsev Dagestana v 1877*, list 46. According to Magomedov, Ḥājjī Muḥammad, ʿAbd al-Raḥman Ḥājjī, ʿAlībek Ḥājjī, Uma Duev, Dagaza Zalmaev, Abas-Bats-Oshi, Nika Qāḍī, and Qāḍī Aḥmed all found refuge in Sogratl.

57. Giorgi Anchabadze, *Vainakhy* (Tbilisi: Kavkazskii Dom, 2001), 40.

58. My translation from the Russian version in Akhlakov, *Geroiko-istoricheskie pesni avartsev*, 154. This unpublished Avar poem is said by Akhlakov to be from his own personal collection (Akhlakov, n169).

59. For details on the deportations to Siberia, see *Repressii 1878 goda. Ssilka i pereselenie gortsev posle podavleniia reaktsionogo vosstaniia 1877 goda*, IIAE, f. 1, op. 1, no. 1365/226.

60. Austin Jersild, "Imperial Russification: Daghestani mountaineers in Russian exile," *CAS* 19.1 (2000): 8.

61. RGIA, f. 1286, op. 39, 1878–79, d. 362, 1.18, cited in Jersild, "Imperial Russification," 7 and 15n18.

62. RGIA, f. 565, op. 5, 1878–84, d. 19814, 1.25, cited in Jersild, "Imperial Russification," 8 and 15n23.

63. V. Ivanenko, "Razlad mezhdu ugolovnym zakonom i narodnym obychaem na Kavkazie i ego vliianie na prestupnost'," *Russkaia mysl'* 4.4 (1904): 205 (more fully discussed in Gould, "*Ijtihād* against *Madhhab*").

64. On these differing attitudes, see Michael Kemper, "Khalidiyya Networks in Daghestan and the Question of Jihād," *WDI* 42.1 (2002): 41–71.

65. Musaev, *Musul'manskoe dukhovenstvo*, 150.

66. Musaev, *Musul'manskoe dukhovenstvo*, 151.

67. Kemper, "Daghestani Legal Discourse," 275.

68. Khaled Abou El Fadl, *Rebellion and Violence in Islamic Law* (Cambridge: Cambridge UP, 2001), 65. This provision was invoked by, among others, the Shāfiʿī jurists Ibn al-Mundhir (d. 930) and al-Māwardī (d. 1058).

69. For Shamil's legal code (*niẓām*) in Russian translation, see "Nizam Shamilia," *SSKG* 3 (1870): 1–18. For the Ottoman origins of the text on which this Russian translation is based, see Kemper, *Herrschaft*, 287n139.

70. For the Ottoman interest in Shamil, see most recently Candan Badem, *The Ottoman Crimean War: 1853–1856* (Leiden: Brill, 2010), 149–152.

71. ʿAlī Qāḍī al-Salṭī, "Istoriia shariatskogo vosstaniia," 49–50.

72. The precise nature of the oath to which ʿAlī Qāḍī refers is unclear. He may have had in mind either a personal oath taken by Shamil or the temporary armistice with nonbelievers that is referred to as *dar al-ʿahd* in Islamic sources. See Muḥammad Abū Zahra, *Al-ʿalāqāt ad-duwaliyyah fī al-islām* (Cairo: Dār al-fikr al-ʿarabī, 1984), 57, and Sami A. Aldeeb Abu-Sahlieh, "La migration dans la conception musulmane," *Oriente Moderno* 74 (1994): 222.

73. ʿAlī Qāḍī al-Salṭī, "Istoriia shariatskogo vosstaniia," 64.

74. P. I. Kovalevskii, *Vosstanie Chechni i Dagestana*, 27. Admittedly, this work, written from a colonial point of view, does not directly reflect mountaineer perceptions.

75. "Obvinitel'nyi akt," *Protokol doprosov i obvinitel'nyi akt i prigovor suda uchastvovuiushchim vostaniia 1877 v Chechne*, fond 1, op. 1, no. 183/1314, list 226. Although certain Chechen leaders such as Kunta Ḥājjī were openly opposed by the *ʿulamāʾ*, both Shamil and ʿAlībek Ḥājjī were all formally legitimated by the *ʿulamāʾ*.

76. For example, Khojaev, *Chechentsi v Russko-Kavkazskoi Voiny*, 304–305.

77. ʿAlī Qāḍī al-Salṭī, *Opisanie vosstanniia*, list 1; "Istoriia shariatskogo vosstaniia," 51. The two different titles for the same work are the result of editorial decisions; the Arabic manuscript bears no title.

78. ʿAlī Qāḍī al-Salṭī, *Opisanie vosstanniia 1877*, list 1-2.

79. ʿAlī Qāḍī al-Salṭī, *Opisanie vosstanniia 1877*, list 2.

80. ʿAlī Qāḍī al-Salṭī, "Istoriia shariatskogo vosstaniia," 63.

81. When there are contradictions between the versions given for different historical events—and there are many such contradictions for the 1877 uprising, even within the same work (e.g., between the two extant manuscripts of ʿAlī Qāḍī's narrative)—I have endeavored to give the different versions as contained in the sources without adjudicating among them. Such an approach seems most appropriate for an anthropological approach to the study of a literary archive. Notes 233–238 (on p. 245) of the commentary helpfully document the convergences between ʿAlī Qāḍī's version of the 1877 uprising and colonial narratives; my interest lies more in their divergences.

82. Rudolf Bultmann, "Is Exegesis without Presuppositions Possible?" in *The Hermeneutics Reader*, ed. Kurt Mueller-Vollmer (New York: Continuum, 1985), 244.

83. ʿAlī Qāḍī al-Salṭī, "Istoriia shariatskogo vosstaniia," 128.

84. The title of this work is the same as al-Qarākhī's chronicle, *Bāriqat al-suyūf al-Dāghistānīyah fī baʿḍ al-ghazawāt al-Shāmilīyah* (Istanbul: al-Maṭbaʿah al-ʾUkhuwwah, 1327/1909), but it contains only the poetic portions of a late manuscript of al-Qarākhī's text.

85. ʿAlī ibn Muḥammad al-Jurjānī, *al-Taʿrīfāt*, ed. Gustav Flügel (Lipsiae: Vogel, 1845), 171.

86. L. Gardet, "Fitna," *EI*² 2:931. Gardet attributes these views to the Khwaraij.

87. Niẓām al-Mulk, *Siyāsat-nāma* (= *Siyyar al-mulūk*), ed. Charles Schefer (Paris: Ernest Leroux, 1891), 5. Niẓām al-Mulk's treatment of *fitna* is discussed in Rebecca Gould, "The Political Aesthetic of the Medieval Persian Prison Poem, 1100–1200" (PhD diss., Columbia University, 2013), 204.

88. Abū Dāwūd, *Sunan*, 35:4230. Also see the commentary of Muḥammad Shams al-Ḥaqq ʿAẓīmābādī, *ʿAwn al-maʿbūd: sharḥ Sunan Abī Dāwūd* (Madina: al-Maktabah al-Salafiyah, 1968–1969), 11:358–361. My citations are from the text as given by al-Qarākhī (p. 219).

89. Michael Kemper, personal correspondence (July 2014). I thank Kemper and Shamil Shikhaliev for sharing with me their readings of this cryptic section from *Bāriqat*.

90. Zelkina, "Islam and Society in Chechnia," 250. Also see Shikhaliev, "Sufische Bildung," 158n51.

91. Akaev, *Sheikh Kunta Hadji*, 67 (order of clauses slightly altered in translation).

92. See Bobrovnikov, "Bandits," 258.

93. Ippolitov, "Uchenie zikr," 4. Although Ippolitov says nothing about his sources, his Chechen wife (concerning whom see A. I. Ivanov, "Natsionalno-osvoboditel'noe dvizhenie," 11) may have been a source of information.

94. Aitberov, Dadaev, and Omarov, "Vvedenie," *Vosstaniia dagestantsev i chechentsev*, 4.

95. Khadzhi-Murad Khashaev, *Obshchestvennyi stroi Dagestana v XIX veke* (Moscow: AN SSSR, 1961), 72.

96. Musaev, *Musul'manskoe dukhovenstvo*, 102.

97. By contrast, another recent dissertation on the subject of the 1877, by A. I. Ismailovna, "Vosstanie gortsev Chechni i Dagestana v 1877-1878 gg." Grozny, 2007), is based mostly on colonial sources and does not move beyond Soviet orthodoxies.

98. Yirchi Qazaq, *Lyrika* (Makhachkala: Dagestanskoe knizhnoe izd-vo, 2001), 71 (trans. Jambul Akkaziev, modified). I thank Jambul Akkaziev for bringing this text to my attention and for his help with translation.

99. The view that the 1877 rebellion was primarily feudal in origin also animates contemporary Russian scholarship, as evidenced, inter alia, in M. M. Bliev and V. V. Degoev, *Kavkazskaia voina* (Moscow: Roset, 1994).

100. Natal'ya A. Tagirova and Amri R. Shikhsaidov, "ʿAbdarraḥmān Ġāzīġumūqī und seine Werke," *MCRCA* 1:317.

101. For overviews of al-Ghāzīghumūqī's writings, see, in addition to Tagirova and Shikhsaidov, "ʿAbdarraḥmān Ġāzīġumūqī," Shikhsaidov, "Vospominaniia Abdurakhmana iz Gazikumukha," in ʿAbd al-Raḥmān, *Tadhkira*, 6–9, and I. K. Krachkovskii, "Arabskaia rukopis' vospominanii o Shamile," *Izbrannye sochineniia* 6:559–584.

102. *Kavkaz* 72–76 (13–27 September 1862), trans. A. Runovskii. Republished that same year in Tbilisi under the title *Vyderzhki iz zapisok Abdurrakhmana syna Dzhemaleddinova, o prebyvanii Shamilia v Vedenie i o prochem* (Tiflis: Glavnoe upravlenie namestnika Kavkazskago, 1862). Al-Ghāzīghumūqī's success in the Russian public sphere is particularly noteworthy because he does not appear to have been fluent in Russian during his initial debut.

103. See Gadzhiev, "Abdurakhman i ego vospominannie," 129, for details concerning this as-yet-unpublished letter.

104. "Daghestnis da chechnetis datsema osmaleta tsakezebit 1294 tsels [*suqūṭ dāghistān wa chachān bīyarā' al-uthmān fī sana 1294*]," ed. Nana Qanchaveli, *Mravaltavi. P'ilologuri-istoriuli ziebani* 4 (1975): 230–253. The unique copy of this manuscript is an autograph, held in *KSXI*, no. 749, and cataloged in *KAXK* 2, 438–439.

105. The most recent and accessible (Arabic-Russian) edition of this text is edited and translated by S. M. Guseikhanov and M. A. Musaev, *Dagestanskii vostokovedcheskii sbornik*, ed. A. A. Isaev, M. A. Musaev, and G. A. Orazaev (Makhachkala: DNTs RAN, 2008), 52–65. References to this work are given parenthetically.

106. For a detailed discussion of the peculiarities of 'Abd al-Raḥmān's Arabic, and in particular of his transliterations, see Tagirova's introduction to *Khulāṣat*, 29–39. More generally on the lexical specificities of Daghestani Arabic, see Krachkovskii, "Arabskaia rukopis' vospominanii o shamil'," *Izbrannye sochineniia* 6:559–584.

107. Umalat Laudaev, "Chechenskoe plemena," 3–4.

108. Aitberov, Dadaev, and Omarov, "Opisanie materiala," 14. The authors add that, not only is it impossible for an Arabist ignorant of Avar to fully understand 'Alī Qāḍī's meaning; even an Arabist fluent in Avar will sometimes be unable to discern the correct meaning (14).

109. Akhlakov, *Geroiko-istoricheskie pesni avartsev*, 160.

110. To avoid confusion with 'Abd al-Raḥmān al-Ghāzīghumūqī, I depart from convention in referring to sheykh 'Abd al-Raḥmān al-Thughūrī as al-Thughūrī rather than as 'Abd al-Raḥmān.

111. For recent scholarship on al-Thughūrī, see Kemper, "al-Thughūrī," *EI*[3], and Z. A. Magomedova, *Shekh Nakshbandiiskogo tarikata—Abdurakhman-Khadzhi iz Sogratliia* (Makhachkala: Epokha, 2010). For an important Soviet-era account, see Ali Kaiaev, *Terâcim-i ulemâ-yı Dagıstan*, eds. Tûbâ Işınsu Durmuş and Hasan Orazayev (Ankara: Grafiker Yayınları, 2012), 71–90. Also see M. A. Abdullaev, *Deiatel'nost' i vozzreniia sheikha Abdurakhmana-Khadzhi i ego rodoslovnaia* (Makhachkala: Iupiter, 1998), which includes a Russian translation of his Arabic work, *al-Mashrab al-Naqshbandī*, 200-268.

112. See M. A. Abdullaev, *Deiatel'nost' i vozzreniia*, 36; Kemper, "Khālidiyya Networks," 50.

113. By contrast, M. M. Gasanov suggests that al-Thughūrī's punishment took place after his son's execution (*Natsional no-osvoboditel naia i klassovaia bor'ba narodov Dagestana v 60-70-e gody XIX v.* [Makhachkala: Iupiter, 1997], 93).

114. For the relation between the spiritual authority of sheykh and the political authority of the ruler in another Islamic, specifically a Chistiyya, geography, see Simon Digby, "The Sufi Shaykh and the Sultan," *Iran* 28 (1990): 71–81. For an anatomy of the relation between worldly and spiritual power from the vantage point of *uṣūl al-fiqh*, see Knut Vikør, *Between God and the Sultan: A History of Islamic Law* (London: Hurst & Co., 2005).

115. Shikhsaidov, "Vospominaniia Abdurakhmana iz Gazikumukha," 9. Barabanov makes a similar observation in his introduction to the Arabic edition of *Bāriqat* ("Vvedenie," 12).

116. Kemper, "Ghazi Muhammad's Treatise," 93.

117. See the citation from ʿAbd al-Raḥmān's preface to *al-Ādāb al-marḍiyah*, 119n219.

118. Ali Gasanov, "Ot perevodchika," *Asari-Dagestan* (Makhachkala: Izdanie Dagestanskogo Nauchno-Issledovatel'skogo Instituta, 1929), 168.

119. Ali Gasanov, "Ot perevodchika," 167.

120. Al-Alqadārī, *Dīwān al-Mamnūn* (Temir Khan Shura: Mavraev, 1913), 112.

121. For example, Aitberov, Dadaev, and Omarov note that the oldest manuscript of ʿAlī Qāḍī's historical chronicle, which they used as the basis for their edition, includes an Arabic poem by Ḥasan on this event (13).

122. Cited from an unpublished manuscript in IIILGT, doc. 186, in Akhlakov, *Geroiko-istoricheskie pesni avartsev*, 161, and attributed to the Avar bard Murti.

123. For these polemics, see Nadhīr b. al-Ḥājj Nika Muḥammad al-Durgilī, *Al-ijtihād wa al-taqlīd* (IIAE, Fond Magomed Saidov, op. 1, no. 35a, pp. 1–30).

124. For these works, see Michael Kemper's provocative essay "Daghestani Shaykhs," in *Daghestan and the World of Islam*, ed. Moshe Gammer and David J. Wasserstein (Helsinki: Annales Academiae Scientiarum Fennicae, 2006), 95–107. Kemper has kindly provided me with a scan of Ḥasan's *Dīwān*, which is cited here parenthetically.

125. By contrast, the first page of the 1905 edition of Jamāl al-Dīn's *al-Ādāb al-marḍiyah* (originally published in Petrovsk [Makhachkala] by A. M. Mikhailov; reprinted in Oxford, 1986) states that the text was "permitted by the censor [*dozvoleno tsenzuroiyu*] [in] St. Petersburg." Given that Mavraev was unable to publish al-Qarākhī's *Bāriqat* during the tsarist era because of his inability to secure the censor's approval (see Barabanov, "Vvedenie," *Bāriqat* 15), the absence of the censor's imprimatur from Ḥasan's books does not demonstrate the absence of censorship in late imperial Daghestan.

126. For Mikhail Nikolaevich's involvement with the Circassian deportations, see Walter Richmond, *The Circassian Genocide* (New Brunswick, NJ: Rutgers UP, 2013), 86–87.

127. *Jirāb al-Mamnūn* (Temir Khan Shura: Mavraev, 1912). For a study of this work, see my article with Shamil Shikhaliev, "*Taqlīd* and Modernity: Ḥasan al-Alqadārī (d. 1910) and Daghestani Islam under Russian Rule," under review).

128. See the analysis in Kemper, "Daghestani Shaykhs," 103.

129. In addition to the poems discussed here, taken from Daghestani biographical dictionaries, see Najm al-Dīn ibn Muḥammad ibn Dunūghūnah al-Dāghistānī, in *Ashwāq Dāghistān ilá al-Ḥaram al-Sharīf*, ed. Muḥammad al-Ḥabash (Damascus: Dār al-Nūr, 1995), for a selection of Najm al-Dīn's religious verse.

130. The most complete biography of Najm al-Dīn at present is by Khadzhi Murad Donogo, *Nadzhmuddin Gotsinskii* (Makhachkala: Ministerstvo obrazovaniia i nauki RF, 2005).

131. Kemper, "Khalidiyya Networks," 70 (citing *Maktūbāt al-Qaḥḥī* [Damascus, 1998], 268–270).

132. By contrast, followers of the Qādiriyya *ṭarīqa* cultivated the vernacular in writing and chants (*dhikr*). See Zelkina, "Some Aspects," 499n49.

133. Al-Durgilī, *Nuzhat*, 64/88 (on Yūsuf al-Yakhsāwī) and 81–85/116–121 (on ʿAbd al-Raḥmān al-Thughūrī).

134. Al-Durgilī (*Nuzhat*, 81/115) mentions *qaṣīdas* by the Sufi sheykh Ilyās al-Tsudaqārī (d. 1908) and Shuʿayb ibn Idrīs al-Bākinī (d. 1912) for sheykh ʿAbd al-Raḥmān.

135. The only version of this text that I have been able to locate is the Russian translation provided by Donogo Hadji Murad in *Gotsinskii*, 317. The author indicates that the Arabic original belongs to the collection of T. Karagishieva.

136. Krachkovskii, "Arabskaia literatura na Severnom Kavkaze," 619. Krachkovskii states in a footnote (618n2) that he obtained the Arabic text of Najm al-Dīn's poems from the Daghestani Arabist M. S. Saidov; these Arabic texts remain unpublished and are not mentioned in *Katalog arabskikh rukopisei: kollektsiia M. S. Saidova*, ed. A. R. Shikhsaidov (Machachkala, 2005).

137. This rehabilitation was inaugurated in 1956, when the Soviet journal *Voprosy istorii* convened a conference in Moscow that marked a return to the anticolonial rhetoric of early Soviet activists such as Aslanbek Sheripov. On this rehabilitation, see Moshe Gammer, "Shamil in Soviet Historiography," *MES* 28.4 (1992): 729–777.

138. Cited in Krachkovskii, "Arabskaia literatura na Severnom Kavkaze," 619.

139. Dzakho Gatuev, "Sheikhism v Chechne," f. 1, op. 1, no. 282/1539, IIAE.

140. Although Gatuev says nothing about his informant Djenar Ali Mulla, a handwritten emendation to his typewritten text reinforces his importance: "It is necessary to note that the storyteller speaks in our era" (list 20).

141. This story of Deni related here is a paraphrase of the text, not a direct translation. I cite directly from the original where relevant. Except when discussing figures and terms that appear elsewhere in this book, my transliterations follow Gatuev's Russian spelling. The material in parentheses is my own interpolation and is not in Gatuev's text.

142. Concerning the family of Prince Bekovich-Cherkasskii, see Paul Bushkovitch, "Princes Cherkasskii or Circassian Murzas: The Kabardians in the Russian Boyar Elite 1560–1700," *CMR* 45/1–2 (2004): 9–29 (21 for this prince).

143. Nikolai Nikolaevich held this post until the abdication of Tsar Nicolas in 1917. For a pan-Caucasus perspective on the years described here by Gatuev, see Michael A. Reynolds, *Shattering Empires* (Cambridge: Cambridge UP, 2011), 191–218.

144. "Jamal al-Din" may refer to Aslanbek Sheripov's father, Jamal al-Din Sheripov.

145. For these mimetic dynamics in a later Soviet period, see Alexei Yurchak, *Everything Was Forever Until It Was No More: The Last Soviet Generation* (Princeton, NJ: Princeton University Press, 2006).

146. For an illustration of Shamil's medal with this inscription, see V. V. Degoev, *Imam Shamil'*, 187.

147. Kemper, *Herrschaft*, 300.

148. Kemper, *Herrschaft*, 300.

149. Walter Benjamin, "Über den Begriff der Geschichte," in *Gesammelte Werke*, ed. Hermann Schweppenhäuser and Rolf Tiedemann, vol. 1, pt. 2 (Frankfurt am Main: Suhrkamp, 1991), 696.

THREE The Georgian Poetics of Insurgency

1. In a precise sense, *leki* refers to the Lezgi, but the term was rarely used in this specific way in literary Georgian. For a similarly broad inflection to Lezgi in classical Arabic sources, see Genko, "Arabskii iazyk i kavkazovedenie," 95. For *vainakh* in the Chechen-Ingush language, see Johanna Nichols, "Origin of the Chechen and Ingush," *Anthropological Linguistics* 46.2 (2004): 131.

2. For this period in Georgian history, see Tariel Mumladze, *Lekianoba Sakartveloshi* (Tbilisi: 2011); and Darejan Megreladze, *Lekianoba* (Tbilisi: SSIP Istoriuli memkvidroba, 2012). For a valuable Daghestani perspective, see M. A. Musaev, "Vzgliad na 'lekianoba' v kontekste izucheniia pravovyh zakluchenii dagestanskih uchenyh-bogoslovov XVIII v.," *Fundamental'nye issledovaniia* 10.14 (2013): 3223–3228.

3. The two best-known examples of such texts are Vazha's "Aluda ketelauri" and "Stumar-mazpinzeli," in his *Txzulebata sruli krebuli at tomad*, ed. Giorgi Leonidze (Tbilisi: Sabchota sakartvelo, 1964), 3:58–73 and 3:207–237 (respectively).

4. For an early usage of *daghestani* as an ethnic denominator, see the martial ode in Nikoloz Baratashvili, *Txzulebani* (Tbilisi: Saxelmtsipo gamomcemloba, 1945), 40–41, analyzed in Harsha Ram and Zaza Shatirishvili, "Romantic Topography and the Dilemma of Empire," *Russian Review* 63.1 (2004): 13–24.

5. For a recent study of the 1812 uprising, see Akaki Gelashvili, *Kaxeṭis 1812 tslis ajanqeba* (Tbilisi: Artanuji, 2003). For a collection of primary source documents, see Shoṭa Xanṭaje, *Dokumentebi Kaxeṭis 1812 tslis ajanqebis istoriisaṭvis* (Tbilisi: Tbilisis universitetis gamomcemloba, 1999).

6. Batonishvili is best known to Persian historiography under the name Eskandar Mīrzā. For a Georgian account of these events, see Ivane Bukurauli, *Daghestnis sami imami* (Tbilisi: Tbilisis universitetis gamomcemloba, 2005), 51.

7. For Georgian literary and folkloric treatments of Arsena, see appendix I.

8. Except where otherwise noted, all citations from Titsian are to the best (though incomplete) three-volume edition of his collected works: *Rcheuli*, ed. I. Abashidze, R. Gargiani, and D. Sturua (Tbilisi: Literatura da xelovneba, 1966).

9. For Titsian's modernism, see the excellent studies of Harsha Ram: "Towards a Crosscultural Poetics," *Comparative Literature* 59.1 (2007): 63–89; "Masks of the Poet, Myths of the People," *Slavic Review* 67.3 (2008): 567–590; and "Decadent Nationalism," *Modernism/modernity* 21.1 (2014): 343–359. For Georgian literary modernism generally, see Soso Sigua, *Kartuli modernizmi* (Tbilisi: Gamomcemloba Didostati, 2002).

10. In keeping with my effort to follow transliteration methods specific to different languages, *Ḥājjī Murād* references the historical individual, *Hadji Murat* references Tolstoy's Russian novella (a precise transliteration would be *Khadzhi Murat*), and *Haji-Muradi* (ჰაჯი მურადი) references Titsian's lost translation.

11. On this translation, see G. Tsurikova, *Titsian Tabidze* (Leningrad: Sovetskii pisatel', 1971), 279 and n373.

12. The fullest version of this essay is in Georgian: "tolstois dreebi," *Rcheuli*, 3:7–30. A truncated portion of "tolstois dreebi" appears in Russian under the title "Tolstoievskie

dni" in *Stat'i ocherki, perepiska*, ed. Bebutov (Tbilisi: Literatura da xelovneba, 1964), 115–117 (Bebutov simply states that this speech was "delivered at the [Tolstoy] jubilee gatherings in Moscow," 287, without giving further information concerning date or venue). Yet a third essay, in Russian, is Titsian's "Lev Tolstoi v Gruziia," *Stat'i, ocherki, perepiska*, 113–114 (Bebutov's editorial note reads: "Printed from manuscript. Written on two pages of the notebook bearing the title 'Chairman of the All-Georgian Writers Union.' Published in [in Russian] in the magazine *Verchernii Tbilisi* on 2 November 1960," 287).

13. Muriel Atkin, *Russia and Iran, 1780–1828* (Minneapolis: U of Minnesota P, 1980), 165.

14. Paolo Sartori and Ido Shahar, "Legal Pluralism in Muslim-Majority Colonies," *JESHO* 55 (2012): 657.

15. In addition to Titsian's Georgian version, there exists an early Armenian translation by I. Tanyelian made only two years after its Russian publication *Hach'i Murat* (Tiflis: Aghanian, 1914). For the Armenian reception, also see Nanor Kebranian, "Beyond 'the Armenian': Literature, Revolution, Ideology and Hagop Oshagan's *Haji Murat*," *Journal of the Society for Armenian Studies* 12.2 (2010): 131.

16. On Tolstoy's debt to Chechen material, see U. Dalgat, "Gorskie pesni, predanie i skazka v 'Khadzhi-Murate' L. N. Tolstogo," *Izvestiia* 2.3 Literatura (Grozny: Checheno-ingushskii nauchno-issledovatel'skii institut, 1951), 6–23. There is a rich body of literature concerning Tolstoy's sojourn in the Caucasus in general and the home where he stayed specifically. See, inter alia, A. Opul'skii, *L. N. Tolstoi na Kavkaze* (Ordzhonikidze: Severo-Osetinskoi knizhnoi izd-vo, 1960).

17. The conference proceedings were published as *L. N. Tolstoi i Sheikh Kunta-Khadzhi Kishiev*, ed. V. Kh. Akaev (Tula: Iasnaia Poliana, 2006).

18. For Tolstoy's campaigns in the Caucasus, see L. P. Semenov, "Lev Tolstoi i Kavkaz," in *Kavkaz i L. Tolstoi, 1828-1928*, ed. L. P. Semenov (Vladikavkaz: Ingushskii nauchno-issledovatel'skii institut kraevedeniia, 1928), 4.

19. Paul Friedrich, "Tolstoy and the Chechens," 115.

20. L. N. Tolstoi, *SS v 22 tomakh*, ed. Mikhail Borisovich Khrapchenko et al. (Moscow: Khudozheshtvennaia literatura, 1978–1985), 14:99. Future references to this volume are given parenthetically.

21. For the censorship and publication history of *Hadji Murad*, see A. P. Sergeenko, "*Khadzhi-Murat*" *L'va Tolstogo: istoriia sozdaniia povesti* (Moscow: Sovremennik, 1983).

22. L. N. Tolstoy, "Nabeg," in *PSS L'va Nikolaevicha*, ed. P. I. Biriukov (Moscow: I. D. Sytin, 1912–1915), 2:18.

23. L. N. Tolstoy, "Nabeg," *Sochineniia* (Moscow: Tipolitografiia Kushnerev, 1885–1895), 37.

24. Diary entry dated 8 July 1854, in Tolstoy, *SS v 22 tomakh*, 21:127.

25. Titsian states: "მე მომიხდა ამ ზაფხულს სწორედ 'ჰაჯი მურატის' თარგმნა." This implies that the translation occupied him for the entire summer. The translation was never published. A detailed search for this translation in consultation with Nino Tabidze at the Georgian Literary Museum in May 2013 yielded no leads.

26. Tabidze, "Lev Tolstoi v Gruziia," 113.

27. Tabidze, "Lev Tolstoi v Gruziia," 113.

28. Tabidze, "Tolstois dreebi," 8.

29. Titsian Tabidze, "Tolstoievskie dni," *Stat'i, ocherki, perepiska,* ed. Bebutov, 116. This passage does not appear in the Georgian version of this essay.

30. Tsurikova, *Titsian Tabidze,* 279.

31. Tsurikova, *Titsian Tabidze,* 289.

32. Tabidze, "Lev Tolstoi v Gruziia," 113.

33. Author's personal interview with Nitka Tabidze (Tbilisi, 2006); also see Gould, "Landslide," *Guernica* (2010).

34. Tsurikova, *Titsian Tabidze,* 279.

35. The translator is listed as Sh. Tagukashvili (Tbilisi: Saskolo biblioteka, 1938). The only extant copy of this edition that I have been able to locate is held by the Georgian National Library in Tbilisi, record number 891.71-3.

36. Tsurikova, *Titsian Tabidze,* 280.

37. Rayfield, for example, ranks Titsian's poetry below Pasternak's and argues that "the Titsian Tabidze which Pasternak discovered had been partly created by him. . . . Tabidze could not be called an innovator but he was far more than an imitator" ("Pasternak and the Georgians," *Irish Slavonic Studies* 3 [1982]: 40). "Gunib" is not mentioned in Rayfield's classic survey of Georgian literature, *Literature of* Georgia, 3rd ed. (Richmond, Surrey: Curzon Press, 2010).

38. Tsurikova, *Titsian Tabidze,* 304.

39. Osip Brik, *Shamil'* (Leningrad: Khudozhestvennaia literatura, 1940).

40. Tsurikova, *Titsian Tabidze,* 281-282.

41. Harsha Ram, "Notes" to Tabidze, "With Blue Drinking Horns," *Modernism/modernity* 21.1 (2014): 341n64.

42. For recent controversies surrounding Shamil's *besedka,* including an effort to destroy it by local youth, see Rebecca Gould, "The Modernity of Premodern Islam," *Contemporary Islam* 5.2 (2011): 175.

43. Titsian Tabidze, "Gunib," *Rcheuli,* 1:106.

44. A Russian translation of "Gunib" by Pavel Antokol'skii (1898–1973) appeared in *Pobratimy* (Tbilisi: Literatura i iskusstvo, 1963), 204, and is available in Tabidze, *Avtoportret'* (St. Petersburg: Vsemirnoe slovo, 1995), 158. Also see the analysis by Makhach Musaev, "Rebekka Gul'd ob Imame Shamile," *Dagestan* (2014).

45. For the revival of interest in Shamil, see Michael Kemper, "Red Orientalism," *WDI* 50.3 (2010): 435–476; and Lowell R. Tillett, *The Great Friendship* (Chapel Hill: North Carolina University Press, 1969).

46. An earlier translation of this text, also by me, is available in *Metamorphoses* 17.1 (2009): 70–71.

47. *Hadji Murad,* 14:58–62.

48. For an overview of Orbeliani's life and writings, see Giorgio Kereselidze, "Grigol Orbeliani," in *Krebuli: kʿarṭuli literaturisa, istoriisa da xelovnebis organo,* ed. Givi Kobaxidze (New York: Rausen Brothers, 1957), 90–137.

49. See Harsha Ram, *The Imperial Sublime* (Madison: U of Wisconsin P, 2003) and the engagement with Ram's concept in Gould, "Topographies of Anticolonialism," *Comparative Literature Studies* 50.2 (2013): 89–91. Georgian texts in this tradition include Baratasvili, *Txzulebani*, 40–41, and Grigol Orbeliani, *Saghamo gamosalmebisa* (Tbilisi: Merani, 1989), 179–199.

50. The verse numbers given here correspond to my translation; for the Georgian original, see appendix II.

51. Aleksandre Proneli, *Mtis artsivi shamili* [Shamil, the eagle of the mountain] (Tbilisi, 1914).

52. M. A. Musaev, *Musul'manskoe dukhovenstvo*, 217.

53. Ram's work on the imperial sublime demonstrates that both relationships to power are conceivable within Romanticism. See in particular Ram and Shatirishvili, "Romantic Topography."

54. See the entry for მაშფოთებელი in Donald Rayfield, Rusudan Amirejibi, and Reuven Enoch, *A Comprehensive Georgian-English Dictionary* (London: Garnett Press, 2006), 2:870.

55. Nikolo Mitsishvili, *Hadji Muradis mochrili tavi* (Tbilisi: Intelekti, 2010), 85. Future citations from the poem are taken from this edition.

56. L. P. Semenov, "Khadzhi-Murat v khudozhestvennoi literature," *Kavkaz i L. Tolstoi*, 32.

57. When Titsian alludes to this conflict in his 1916 essay "With Blue Drinking Horns" (332), he criticizes Chavchavadze for mimicking the Russian critic Vissarion Belinskii.

58. Paul Manning, *Strangers in a Strange Land* (Brighton, MA: Academic Studies Press, 2012), 116.

59. Grigol Orbeliani, *Saghamo gamosalmebisa*, 166. On the conflict between fathers and sons in Georgian literature, see Roza Devdariani, *Grigol Orbelianis shemokmedeba* (Kutaisi: Kutaisis saxelmtsipo universitetis gamomcemloba, 2002), 71–79.

60. For a brief biographical sketch of Orbeliani's life, see *Gruzinskie romantiki*, ed. G. L. Asatiani and T. P. Buachidze (Leningrad: Sovetskii pisatel', 1940), 116–117. For the 1832 Georgian rebellion, see Stephen Jones, "Russian Imperial Administration and the Georgian Nobility," *SEER* 65.1 (1987): 53–76.

61. Rayfield, *The Literature of Georgia*, 154.

62. Charles King, *The Ghost of Freedom* (New York: Oxford UP, 2008), 14.

63. For Chavchavadze's translations of the first three authors, see Aleksandre Chavchavadze, *Txzulebani* (Tbilisi: Merani, 1986), 230–238. For the others, see Rayfield, *The Literature of Georgia*, 148.

64. Cited in Beso Zhghenti, "Aleksandr Kazbegi," in Qazbegi, *Izbrannye proizvedeniia* (Tbilisi: Zariia Vostoka, 1955), 11; also see the discussion in Rebecca Gould, "Aleksandre Qazbegi's Mountaineer Prosaics," *Ab Imperio* 15.1 (2014): 361–390.

65. For Orbeliani's *muxambazis*, an example of which may be found in his *Lirika, eposi, targmanebi: 1826-1883* (Tbilisi: Sabchota mtserali, 1948), 9–10, see Harsha Ram, "Sonnet and the Mukhambazi," *PMLA* 122.5 (2007): 1548–1570; and Paul Manning and

Zaza Shatirishvili "Exoticism and Eroticism of the City," *Urban Spaces after Socialism*, ed. T. Darieva, W. Kaschuba, and M. Krebs (Frankfurt: Campus Verlag, 2011), 261–281.

66. Chavchavadze's words are cited in *Gruzinskie romantiki*, 117.

67. The relationship between Georgia and the Islamic northern Caucasus appears different from the vantage point of the northeastern Georgian highlands, which is the primary background against which Vazha Pshavela's works transpire. The perspective adopted here is that of Tbilisi-based Georgian literary culture.

68. See I. Kh. Sulaev, *Musul'manskoe dukhovenstvo Dagestana i svetskaia vlast'* (Makhachkala: Delovoi mir, 2004), 158 and 175, for primary sources pertaining to Akushinskii. Also see Michael Reynolds, "Native Sons," *Jahrbücher für Geschichte Osteuropas* 56 (2008): 246, for his rivalry with Najm al-Dīn.

69. For one biography of this Georgian poet, whose verse is available in *Tʿxzulebatʿa sruli krebuli*, ed. A. Baramidze and S. Iordanishvili (Tbilisi: Kartuli tsigni, 1931), see Giorgi Natroshvili, *Vitʿa davghamdi, ise gavtʿendi: tsigni Davitʿ Guramishvilis tsʿxovrebasa da shemokʿmedebaze* (Tbilisi: Nakaduli, 1960).

70. Titsian, *Rcheuli*, 3:120–121. For a close reading of this poem in relation to its Russian rendition by Pasternak, see Harsha Ram, "Towards a Crosscultural Poetics of the Contact Zone," *Comparative Literature* 59.1 (2007): 68–89.

71. Mixeil Javaxishvili, *Arsena Marabdeli: romani*, ed. Nana Suxitashvili (Tbilisi: Sakartvelos Matsne, 2005), 244. Donald Rayfield provides the best overview of the censorship to which this text was subjected in multiple editions in "Time Bombs," *Art, Intellect and Politics*, ed. G. M. A. Margagliotta and A. A. Robiglio (Leiden: Brill, 2013), 584–589.

72. Rayfield, "The Death of Paolo Iashvili," *SEER* 68.3 (1990): 663. Based on Georgian archival sources made public only recently, Rayfield's is by far the best account of the final days of Titsian and his contemporaries.

73. For Gamsaxurdia's biography, see Dimitri Benashvili, *Konstantine Gamsaxurdia* (Tbilisi: Sakartvelos SSR metsnierebata akademiis gamomcemloba, 1962).

74. This story was recalled by Nitka Tabidze, who narrated to me the circumstances leading up to her father's arrest in 2006 (see n33 above), and who passed the memory on to her daughter Nino after her death, whom I interviewed in 2013. It is confirmed through archival documents in Rayfield, "The Death of Paolo Iashvili," 655.

75. Archives of the Georgian Union of Writers, LXCA, f. 8, a. 20, o. 30.

76. Rayfield, "The Death of Paolo Iashvili," 662.

77. The source for this information is interviews with Nitka and Nino Tabidze, conducted during 2006 and 2013.

78. Rayfield, "The Death of Paolo Iashvili," 640.

79. See Grigol Robakidze, "Imam Shamil," *Kaukasische Novellen* (Leipzig: Insel-Bücherei, 1932), 69–79.

80. The account given here follows D. Tuallagov, *Prigovorennye k bessmertiiu* (Vladikavkaz: Alaniia, 1993), 149–211; Gudaev, *Abrek Zelimkhan*, 352–355; and the entry on Gatuev in *Liudi i sud'by*, ed. Ia. V. Vasil'kov and M. Iu. Sorokina (St. Petersburg: Peterburgskoe vostokovedenie, 2003), 113. Vasil'kov and Sorokina give the date of Gatuev's arrest as November 16, 1937.

81. For contemporaneous repressions among the Daghestani intelligentsia, see G. B. Musakhanova and S. Kh. Akhmedov, *Nasledie, vozvrashchennoe narodu* (Makhachkala: IIILGT, 1990).

82. Soslanbek Gatuev, "Otets," *Zelimkhan: povest' i ocherki* (Ordzhonikidze: Irfon, 1971), 207.

83. V. Shalepov, "Dzaxo (Konstantine) Gatuev. Vstupitel'naia stat'ia," *Zelimkhan: povest' i ocherki*, 14.

84. The most important research on Shamil's imamate under way during Titsian's lifetime was undertaken by N. I. Pokrovskii, whose monograph, completed in 1941, was published only during the post-Soviet period. See Pokrovskii, *Kavkazskie voiny i imamat Shamilia* (Moscow: ROSSPEN, 2009).

85. See Édouard Glissant, *Poétique de la relation* (Paris: Gallimard, 1990). Glissant's conception of relation has recently been productively theorized for comparative literature in recent years by Natalie Melas in her *All the Difference in the World* (Stanford: Stanford UP, 2007).

86. Khalid Dudaevich Oshaev, "O druge i cheloveke Dzakho Gatueve," *Zelimkhan* (Ordzhonikidze: Irfon, 1971), 201–202.

87. Terry Eagleton, *The Ideology of the Aesthetic* (New York: Wiley, 1990), 3.

88. Rasul Gamzatov, *Pesni gor. Pis'mena. Patimat: kniga stikhotvorenii* (Moscow: Sovremennik, 1983), 98–99.

FOUR Violence as Recognition, Recognition as Violence

1. Walter Burkert, *Homo necans* (Berkeley: U of California P, 1983), 3.

2. For an early account of my fieldwork in and around Chechnya, see Rebecca Gould, "Behind the Wall of the Caucasus," *Gettysburg Review* 18.2 (2005): 291–307.

3. My understanding of the sexual contract follows Carol Pateman, *The Sexual Contract* (Stanford: Stanford UP, 1988).

4. Beginning with her name (sometimes given as Aiza or Luisa in lieu of Aizan), nearly every detail in Gazueva's story admits of variations. One account records a different verbal exchange between Gazueva and Gadzhiev in which Gazueva arrived armed at the police station and asked to see the general. When the general refused, she said: "Wait a moment!" and exploded the bomb strapped on her chest (see Surkho, "Pravda o shaidke Aize Gazuievoi," *Chechen News* 10 August 2010). As with any history primarily disseminated orally, certain aspects of Gazueva's story vary according to the transmitter.

5. Anna Politkovskaia, "Smert' voennogo komendanta," *Novaia Gazeta*, 14 January 2002.

6. "Memorial" Human Rights Center, "Terror with Terror."

7. Gazueva's suicide was preceded by at least two others: that of Khava Barayeva and Luiza Magomadova, who together drove a truck loaded with explosives into a Russian barracks in the Chechen village Alkhan-Yurt.

8. My information concerning Aizan Gazueva's life and death is taken from multiple sources. In addition to my informants, I draw on the accounts in Politkovskaia, the "Memorial" report, and the news agencies cited here.

9. See the famous passage in Walter Benjamin, "Das Kunstwerk im Zeitalter seiner technischen Reproduzierbarkeit (Erste Fassung)," in *Gesammelte Schriften*, ed. Rolf Tiedemann and Hermann Schweppenhäuser (Frankfurt am Main: Suhrkamp, 1991), 1, pt. 2:469.

10. Khalili, *Heroes*, 217.

11. Lori Allen, "Getting by the Occupation," *Cultural Anthropology* 23.3 (2008): 460.

12. Allen, "Getting by the Occupation," 471, drawing on Michael Hardt and Toni Negri, *Empire* (Cambridge: Harvard UP, 2000), 113. Tishkov plots a similar psychic topography for war-torn Chechya (*Obschestvo v vooruzhennom konflikte* [Moscow: Nauka, 2001]); for an abridged English translation, see his *Chechnya: Life in a War-Torn Society*.

13. Khalili, *Heroes*, 217. Also see Rebecca Gould, "The Materiality of Resistance," *Social Text* 118 (2014): 1–22.

14. Khalili, *Heroes*, 94. For Pankisi parallels, see Gould, "Secularism and Belief."

15. For this particular juncture in Chechen history, see Anatole Lieven's *Chechnya* (Cambridge: Harvard UP, 1998) and Matthew Evangelista's *The Chechen Wars* (Washington, DC: Brookings Institution Press, 2002).

16. Derluguian, *Bourdieu's Secret Admirer*, 38.

17. The exact phrase is "prave narodov na samoopredelenie," in *Rossiia i Chechnya*, ed. I. N. Eremenko and Yu. D. Novikov (Moscow: RAU Universitet, 1997), article 4. Also see Politkovskaia, *Vtoraia Chechenskaia* (Moscow: Zakharov, 2002), 275.

18. James Hughes, *Chechnya* (Philadelphia: U of Pennsylvania P, 2007), 112.

19. A case in point is the recent and influential work of Valery Tishkov (p. 24 of this volume and n12, this chapter). While rich in ethnographic detail, Tishkov's depoliticization of the conflict stands in tension with his ethnographies, written by largely uncredited Chechen native informants. For critical engagements with Tishkov's work, see Bruce Grant, "Sense and Sense Making"; and Rebecca Gould, "Chechens through the Russian Prism," *Transitions Online* (2005).

20. Compare Allen, "Getting by the Occupation," 476.

21. Harootunian, "Postcoloniality's unconscious," 146.

22. The names used here have been changed to protect my informants. While I have refrained from divulging specific information concerning Zeynap's acquaintances or projects, evidence for Chechen support for Gazueva's actions is easily obtainable online, so no statement made here constitutes a security risk for those involved. But I have preferred to err on the side of caution.

23. Jean Comaroff and John L. Comaroff, "Law and Disorder in the Postcolony: An Introduction," in *Law and Disorder in the Postcolony*, Jean Comaroff and John L. Comaroff, eds. (Chicago: U of Chicago P, 2006), 2–3.

24. Ruslan Shamaev, "Piat' let nazad molodaia zhenshchina Aizan Gazueva vzorvala sebia i ubila Gaidara Gadzhieva," *Prague Watchdog/Radio Svoboda*, 29 November 2006.

25. Frances Hasso, "Discursive and Political Deployments by/of the 2002 Palestinian Women Suicide Bombers/Martyrs," *Feminist Review* 81.1 (2005): 27.

26. Hasso, "Discursive and Political Deployments," 24.

27. Claudia Brünner, "Occidentalism Meets the Female Suicide Bomber," *Signs* 32.4 (2007): 957–972.

28. Khalili, *Heroes*, 203. Whereas writers such as Petra Procházková have skillfully documented the lives of Chechen women during the war (see *La guerre russo-tchetchene* [Paris: Le serpent à plumes, 2006]), this sensitivity is missing from most reportage or scholarship on Chechen female suicide bombers. The only monograph-length study of *shahidki* is Yulia Yuzik, *Nevesti Allakha* (Moscow: Kultura, 2003), the author of which maintains that "democracy is completely unsuited for the North Caucasus" (Dmitri Volchek, "Avtor knigi 'Nevestyi Allakha,'" *Radio Svoboda*, 2010).

29. For sheykh Jarrar's distinction, see Lori Allen, "There Are Many Reasons Why," *Middle East Report* 223 (2002): 36. For suicide in modern Islamic societies, see "Suicide," *EWIC* 3: 450–456.

30. Sudakov, "Basaev sam sozdal otraid zhenschina-smertnits. Oni uzhe rabotaet," *Pravda* 15 May 2003.

31. M. Schwirtz, "Leading Russian Rights Lawyer Is Shot to Death in Moscow, along with Journalist," *New York Times*, 19 January 2009. As with her documentation of Gazueva's suicide, Politkovskaia's reports on this trial, first published in the *Novaia Gazeta*, and later in *Vtoraia chechskaia*, are outstanding in their analytical depth.

32. "Russian Colonel Who Killed Chechen Girl Is Shot Dead," *BBC News*, 10 June 2011.

33. For a report on this massacre, see *By All Available Means* (Moscow: Memorial Human Rights Center, 1996).

34. A detailed source on the Baraeva-Magomedova suicide act is Anne Speckhard and Khapta Akhmedova, "Black Widows," in *Female Suicide Terrorists*, ed. Yoram Schweitzer (Tel Aviv: Jaffe Center, 2006), 63–81. The fundamentals of this presentation are retained in a more recent version by the same authors: "Understanding the Motivations and Life Trajectories of Chechen Female Terrorists," in *Female Terrorism and Militancy*, ed. Cindy Ness (London: Routledge, 2008), 100–121.

35. Speckhard and Akhmedova, "Black Widows," 3.

36. Speckhard and Akhmedova, "Black Widows," 17.

37. G. W. Bowersock, *Martyrdom and Rome* (Cambridge: Cambridge UP, 1995), 5.

38. Goldziher, *Muhammedanische Studien*, 2:389.

39. *Musnad* 5.87; *Ṣaḥīḥ* 1.198, 4.315ff.

40. Franz Rosenthal, "On Suicide in Islam," *JOAS* 66.3 (1946): 245.

41. Arendt, *The Human Condition* (Chicago: U of Chicago P, 1958), 55.

42. Musaev, *Musul'manskoe dukhovenstvo*, 105.

43. Talal Asad, *On Suicide Bombing* (New York: Columbia UP, 2007), 17.

44. Ranajit Guha, *Dominance without Hegemony* (Cambridge: Harvard UP, 1998), 72.

45. Guha, *Dominance without Hegemony*, 95.

46. Vivek Chibber, *Postcolonial Theory and the Specter of Capital* (London: Verso, 2013).

47. Saba Mahmood, "Feminist Theory, Embodiment, and the Docile Agent," *Cultural Anthropology* 6.2 (2001): 210. Mahmood appears to be engaged in an indirect critique of Guha's notion of agency as well. See especially 227n14.

48. Upendra Baxi, "'The State's Emissary,'" in *Subaltern Studies VII*, ed. Partha Chatterjee and Gyanendra Pandey (Delhi: Oxford UP, 1992), 249.

49. Baxi, "'The State's Emissary,'" 252.

50. Baxi, "'The State's Emissary,'" 254n37.

51. Baxi, "'The State's Emissary,'" 254.

52. See, for example, Matthew Evangelista, *Gender, Nationalism, and War* (Cambridge: Cambridge UP, 2011), 158.

53. Asad, *On Suicide Bombing*, 42. While the shift away from motives is useful for accounting for a specific social phenomenon, the broader focus of this book on the aesthetics of violence prevents me from regarding Asad's quest for causes as adequate in itself. While anthropology rejects psychology's quest for motives, literary aesthetics problematizes the historiographic and social-scientific reliance on causal explanations.

54. Michel Foucault, *The History of Sexuality: Vol. 1.* (Harmondsworth: Penguin, 1981), 143.

55. Giorgio Agamben, *Homo sacer* (Stanford: Stanford UP, 1998), 83. For the relevance of Agamben to Muslim women, see Jenny Edkins, "Sovereign Power, Zones of Indistinction, and the Camp," *Alternatives* 25.1 (2000): 25.

56. See Agamben's assertions that "the production of a biopolitical body is the original activity of sovereign power" (6) and bare life or sacred life is the always-present and always-operative assumption of sovereignty (106). For a perceptive critique of the Foucauldian concept of sovereignty, see Raia Prokhovnik, *Sovereignty* (New York: Imprint Academic, 2008), 163–202.

57. Mia Bloom, "Female Suicide Bombers," *Daedalus* 136.1 (2007): 102. Although cited here as a major motivational factor in female suicide bombings, no concrete instance of a suicide bomber who had been raped is offered.

58. For further analysis, see Claudia Brünner, *Männerwaffe Frauenkörper?* (Vienna: Braumüller, 2005), 95–110.

59. Benjamin, "Das Kunstwerk," 476.

60. Benjamin, "Das Kunstwerk," 477.

61. Hannah Arendt, *The Human Condition*, 55.

62. Benjamin, "Das Kunstwerk," 481.

63. See Claudia Brünner, "Occidentalism Meets the Female Suicide Bomber," 963. Brünner's critique is addressed to the writings of Joyce Davis, Mia Bloom, and Rosemary Skaine.

64. Benjamin, "Das Kunstwerk," 506.

65. Frances Hasso, "Discursive and Political Deployments," 44.

66. See, for example, Mia Bloom, "Women as Victims and Victimizers," which is a simplified version of her more nuanced article, "Female Suicide Bombers," *Daedalus* 136.1 (2007): 94–102.

67. H. Hindawi, "Palestinian Father Expresses Shock over Daughter's Suicide Bombing," *Associated Press Worldstream*, 13 April 2002; Hasso, "Discursive and Political Deployments," 29.

68. Jean-Klein, *Palestinian Martyrdom Revisited* (Ithaca: Cornell Law School, 2002), 7–8.

69. Reuters, *Mein Leben ist eine Waffe* (Munich: Bertelsmann, 2002), 11.

70. Agamben, *Homo sacer*, 2, 109, 181.

71. In addition to Mahmood's critique of political theories that theorize agency solely in terms of resistance in *The Politics of Piety*, Prokhovnik's distinction between power and sovereignty in Foucault is particularly relevant here. "While the great strength of Foucault's account of sovereignty is that it highlights the importance of power in social relations," argues Prokhovnik, "one of the weaknesses of Foucault's account is that it sees resistance to social power as the only possible form of politics, thereby . . . nullifying politics as a separate sphere of action and level of attention from the social" (200–201).

72. Asad, *On Suicide Bombing*, 80.

73. Asad, *On Suicide Bombing*, 49.

74. Asad, *On Suicide Bombing*, 96.

75. Asad, *On Suicide Bombing*, 91.

76. Hannah Arendt, *On Violence* (New York: Harcourt Brace, 1969), 64 (emphasis added).

77. Asad, *On Suicide Bombing*, 90.

Epilogue

1. For the classic elaboration of the Schmittian state of exception, see Carl Schmitt, *Politische Theologie* (Munich: Duncker and Humblot, 1922).

2. Walter Benjamin, "Zur Kritik der Gewalt," *Gesammelte Schriften*, 179–202. All future references are given parenthetically to this edition. I have discussed the relation between Schmitt and Benjamin in Rebecca Gould, "Laws, Exceptions, Norms: Kierkegaard, Schmitt, and Benjamin on the Exception," *Telos* 162 (2013): 77–96.

3. For a reconstruction of the contents of this planned book, see Tiedemann and Schweppenhäuser, "Anmerkungen," in Walter Benjamin, *Gesammelte Schriften*, II Erster Teil, 943–946.

4. See Max Weber, "Politik als Beruf," in *Gesammelte Politische Schriften*, ed. Johannes Winckelmann (Tübingen: Mohr, 1988), 505–560, later elaborated on in *Wirtschaft und Gesellschaft. Grundriss der verstehenden Soziologie* (1922), §17. The reference to Sheripov is to his *Iz chechenskikh pesen* (Vladikavkaz: Terskii Narodnii Sovet, 1918).

5. Walter Benjamin, "Das Recht zur Gewaltanwendung [1920]," *Gesammelte Schriften*, ed. Rolf Tiedemann and Hermann Schweppenhäuser, vol. 6 (Frankfurt am Main: Suhrkamp, 1991), 105.

6. Jan-Werner Müller, "Myth, law and order: Schmitt and Benjamin read reflections on violence," *History of European Ideas* 29.4 (2012): 469.

7. Walter Benjamin, "Über den Begriff der Geschichte," 697. *Ausnahmenzustand*, translated here as "state of emergency," is a direct allusion to Schmitt.

8. Jacques Derrida, "Force of Law," in *Acts of Religion*, ed. Gil Anidjar (New York: Routledge, 2002), 259.

9. In a rich bibliography of scholarship on Prometheus and the Caucasus, see Georges Charachidze, *Promethée ou le Caucase* (Paris: Flammarion, 1986); Jacqueline Duchemin, *Prométhée* (Paris: Belles lettres, 1974), 142–157; and Kevin Tuite, "Achilles and the Caucasus," *Journal of Indo-European Studies* 26 (3–4): 289–343.

10. See Galaktion Tabidze's 1938 poem "Amirani."

11. For a contemporary Georgian critique, see Zaza Abzianidze, "Homo bellator," *Druzhba Narodov* 12 (2000): 170–172.

12. Judith Butler, "Critique, Coercion, and Sacred Life in Benjamin's 'Critique of Violence,'" in *Political Theologies*, ed. Hent de Vries and Lawrence E. Sullivan (New York: Fordham UP, 2006), 219.

13. Müller, "Myth, Law and Order," 469.

14. See Claude Lévi-Strauss, *La pensée sauvage* (Paris: Plon, 1962), which elaborates a literary anthropological methodology kindred to the one pursued in this book.

15. Susan Sontag, *Regarding the Pain of Others* (New York: Farrar, Straus and Giroux, 2003), 13.

16. Sontag, *Regarding the Pain of Others*, 35.

17. See Rebecca Gould, "*Ijtihād* against *Madhhab*," and the concluding remarks at the end of the introduction.

18. This event has gone almost entirely unreported in Azeri and Russian media, and I did not become aware of it until after I left Zaqatala. See the brief mention in V. A. Shnirel'man, "Identichnost' i politika postsovetskoi pamiati," *Politicheskaia kontseptologiia* 1.2 (2009): 227; and the newspaper report by Marko Shakhbanov, "Vol'nitsa dlia ubiits," *Chernovnik*, 3 February 2005.

19. "15 let diskriminatsii [15 Years of Discrimination]," dated 27 December 2007 and signed by thirty residents of Zaqatala and Belokany. This open letter notes that a library and museum had been planned near Shamil's monument for the past fifteen years but that the government had obstructed the realization of this project.

20. For an overview of Jar society in the first half of the nineteenth century, see I. P. Petrushevskii, *Dzharo-Belokanskie vol'nye obshchestva v pervoi treti XIX stoletia* (Tiflis: Nauchno-issledovatel'skogo instituta Kavkazovedeniia, 1934).

21. Bruce Grant, "An Average Azeri Village (1930)," *Slavic Review* 63.4 (2004): 706.

22. For *Hadji Murat* as ethnography, see Vladimir Goudakov, "Les oeuvres caucasiennes de Léon Tolstoï comme document ethnologique," *Autour de Tolstoï* (Paris: Institut d'études slaves, 1997), 35–43.

23. Interview with Mullah Mahir, Bash Shabalid (July 2006). For more on Sheykh Baba's background, see Grant, "Shrines and Sovereigns," *CSSH* 53.3 (2011): 660, esp. n. 5.

24. Mullah Mustafa was exiled to the Solovetsk Islands in northern Russia and executed in 1937 (Grant, "Shrines," 660).

25. Grant, "Shrines," 678. While Grant correctly denominates Mullah Mustafa's poem as a *ghazal*, I would add that the poet's declaration in his poem that "I have not the strength to complain [*şikayət halım ola ya bənim* (677)]" aligns it with the classical Islamic complaint poem (*shikāyyāt*). For other usages of the *shikāyyāt* in Caucasus literary modernity, see al-Alqadārī, *Dīwān*, 49.

Glossary

Arabic = A; Chechen = C; Georgian = G; Russian = R; Pan-Caucasian = PC

abrek—(PC) social bandit who features in most Caucasus cultures, especially folkloric and literary texts; *abrechestvo* is the Russian term for the phenomenon of social banditry

ʿādāt—(A) communal law; came into particular tension with *sharīʿa* in Shamil's imamate

ʿalīm—see *ʿulamāʾ*

ʿajamī—(A: ʿ/j/m = "to be mute, dumb") in Daghestan and other parts of the Islamic world, the term for the slightly modified Arabic script that was used for writing in vernacular languages, including Caucasus vernaculars such as Avar and Chechen; can also mean the Persian language

Amirani—(G) the Georgian counterpart to the Greek Prometheus, who stole fire from Zeus in order to give it to humanity. In Chechen folklore, the story of Pxarmat parallels that of Amirani

aul—(PC) a mountain village in the Caucasus

A.H. (after *hijra*)—(A: "separation"; "emigration"); marks the beginning of the Islamic calendar, when, in 622 of the Common Era, the Prophet Muḥammad departed from Mecca to Medina, thereby founding the first Islamic state

ayā—(A: "sign"; pl. *ayat*) verse within a sura (q.v.) of the Quran

basmala—(A) collective noun for the phrase *b-ismi-llāhi r-raḥmāni r-raḥīmi* (In the name of God, the Most Gracious, the Most Merciful); recited before each sura (q.v.) of the Quran; frequently uttered during prayer and in sacerdotal settings

besedka—(R: "place for conversation") a small outdoor structure where gatherings and meetings take place; current name for the site of Shamil's surrender near Ghunib *druzhba narodov*—(R: "friendship of peoples") Soviet term used to denote solidarity among the different peoples of the Soviet Union

duʿā—(A: "invitation") prayer, addressed to God; in poetry, a concluding prayer for the patron's well-being

dzhigit—(PC) courageous young mountaineer, given to performing feats of bravado

fiqh—(A) practical jurisprudence, *sharīʿa* (q.v.) as seen from a jurist's point of view

faqih—(A: pl. *fuquhā*) jurist, scholar of Islamic law

fatwā—(A: pl. *fatawā*) nonbinding Islamic legal opinion issued by a *muftī* or *qāḍī* (q.v.)

fitna—(A: "temptation, strife, discord"; pl. *fitan*) civil war

ghazawāt—(A: *ghazw*, "raid, attack") in Central Asia and the Caucasus, often used interchangeably with jihad to signify holy war; *gʿazot* in Chechen

GULAG—(R: acronym for *glavnoye upravleniye lagerei i kolonii*, "main administration of the camps and colonies") the Soviet system of forced labor camps that was most widespread during the Stalinist period and to which many poets and other dissidents were banished

hadith—(A: "story, saying") stories and sayings of the Prophet

ḥājjī—(A) someone who has performed the *ḥājj* (pilgrimage), one of the five pillars of Islam

ijāza—(A: "permission") a license to transmit, and to teach, texts received from a particular Sufi sheykh

illi—(C) epic song or ballad in Chechen folklore; the genre includes stories about abreks

ʿibrat—(A) moral lesson; admonition

imam—(A: *imām*, "person in front") political leader, title given to Ghāzī Muḥammad, Shamil, ʿAlībek Ḥājjī, Muḥammad Ḥājjī, and Zelimkhan

intifāḍa—(A: "shaking off") term for the Palestinian uprisings of 1987–1993 and 2000–2005

jadid—(A: "new") Muslim intellectuals across Central Asia and the Caucasus who, in the concluding decades of the nineteenth century and the early decades of the twentieth, advocated for educational reforms and for combining Islamic values with European knowledge

Kalmyk—Mongolian language widely spoken in the northern Caucasus

khalīfa—(A: kh/l/f = "to represent, to succeed, to rule on behalf of") deputy of a Sufi sheykh; in other contexts, the *khalīfa* (often Anglicized as *caliph*) was the political leader of the Islamic world until the Mongol destruction of Baghdad in 1258

muftī—Muslim jurist endowed with the authority to deliver a *fatwā* (q.v.)

murīd—(A: "seeker") a Sufi adept; in the mid-nineteenth century Caucasus, the word came to signify someone who was nominally affiliated with the Naqshbandiyya-Khālidiyya *ṭarīqa* and who was also in the service of Imam Shamil; Soviet sources coined the term *muridizm* to stereotype Islamic anticolonial militancy in the nineteenth-century Caucasus

murshid—(A) teacher of a *murīd* (q.v.)

muxambazi—(from P: *mukhammas*) Georgian strophic poem comprising five rhyming distiches *nāʾib*—(A: "deputy, agent, lieutenant") lieutenant in the Caucasus imamate; governor and commander of usually one community

nabeg—(R: "raid") used during the nineteenth century to describe incursions by the Russian army on mountain villages, as well as incursions by mountaineers on neighboring peoples

nakh—(C: "people") Chechen, Ingush, Kist, Batsbi

namaz—(A) ritual prayers recited by Muslims five times a day

namestnik—(R: "replacement") viceroy; term used for the highest office in the Russian administration in the Caucasus

Naqshbandiyya—(A/P) *ṭarīqa* (q.v.) that was founded in Bukhara by Bahāʾ al-Dīn (d. 1384) and took root in the Caucasus; the Naqshbandiyya-Khālidiyya *ṭarīqa* tended to be more oriented to jihad than other *ṭuruq* active in the Caucasus

nisba—(A) the element of a Muslim's name that indicates their place of origin

NKVD—(R) Narodnii Komissariat Vnutrennikh Del ("National Commision of Internal Affairs"), Stalin and Beria's secret police, 1934–1954

OMON—(R) Otriad Militsii Osobogo Naznacheniya ("Special Purpose Police Unit"), 1979–present

pensionerka—(R: "retiree") an elderly woman (counterpart to male *pensioner*), who survives on a small pension from the state, often in a condition of poverty

qāḍī—(A: "judge") judge who administers *sharīʿa*; under Shamil's imamate, responsible for a single mosque

qaṣīda—(A: q/ṣ/d = "to intend, aim for") a panegyric ode; the normative poetic genre from which most other poetic genres derive in the Arabic literary tradition

Qumuq—Turkic language widely spoken throughout Daghestan, and once proposed as the official lingua franca; also refers to the speakers of the Qumuq language

razboinik—(R) bandit; sometimes used in Russian sources to refer to the abrek

shāhid—(A: "witness"; pl. *shuhadāʾ*) martyr; in contemporary Russian, female suicide bombers are known as *shahidki* (sing. *shahidka*), a grammatical feminization of *shāhid* (Arabic for "witness, martyr")

sharīʿa—(A: "road, path") the body of laws and regulation formulated by Muslim scholars over the centuries for private and public affairs; it is comprised of the *ḥadīth*, mediated by the Quran, and interpreted by *ʿulamāʾ*

shikāyāt—(A: noun made from *shikwā*, "complaint") poem of complaint in Arabic and Persian

silsila—(A: "chain") chain of teachers within a Sufi network

sūra—(A) chapter in the Quran; consists of *ayat* (q.v.)

taip—(C) clan; also spelled *teip*

takhalluṣ—(A: "exit") refers to the transition between sections of a *qaṣīda* in Arabic poetics; came to signify a poet's penname in late medieval Persian

ṭarīqa—(A: "path"; pl. *ṭuruq*) Sufi method, system, or school

Turki—literary term for the Azeri language; written in the Arabic script

ʿulamāʾ—(A: ʿ/l/m = "to know"; sing. *ʿalīm*) scholars learned in Islamic traditions; experts in *ḥadīth* and *fiqh*

umma—(A) the community of Islamic believers
uṣūl al-fiqh—(A: "principles of jurisprudence") the basic rules that guide Islamic legal theory
vainakh—(C) collective term for the Chechen, Ingush, Kist, and Tsova-Tush ethnic and linguistic group; literally means "we people"
vazhkatsoba—(G) courage, masculinity
Yā Sīn—(A) the thirty-sixth *sūra* in the Quran; its recitation is associated with preparation for death
zakon—(R) law, as promulgated by an empire, a state, or a bureaucratic administration; often at odds with local forms of *ʿādāt* and *sharīʿa*

Bibliography

Manuscripts and Archives

al-Salṭī, ʿAlī Qāḍī. Untitled manuscript with Russian heading: *Opisanie vosstanniia 1877 goda v dagestane i podavleniia ego russkim tsarismom*, trans. from Arabic into Russian K. M. Barkuev, f. 1, op. 1, no. 430/3255, IIAE.

Gatuev, Dzakho. "Sheikhizm v Chechne," f. 1, op. 1, no. 282/1539, IIAE.

Magomedov, R. *Vosstannie gortsev Dagestana v 1877*, f. 1, op. 1, no. 187/1318, IIAE.

"Nadzhmuddin Gotskinskii," f. 6, op. 1, no. 47, IIAE.

"Obvinitelnii akt." *Protokol doprosov i obvinitelni akt i prigovor suda uchastvovaniim vostaniia 1877 v Chechne*, f. 1, op. 1, no. 183/1314, IIAE.

Polozov, V. *V debriakh Zakavkaz'ia*, Bakhmeteff Archive, Manuscripts and Rare Books Library, Columbia University, New York.

Repressii 1878 goda. Ssilka i pereselenie gortsev posle podavleniia reaktsionogo vosstaniia 1877 goda, f. 1 op. 1 no. 1365/226, IIAE.

Primary Sources

Abu'l Fidā. *Kitāb taqwīm al-buldān*, ed. Joseph Toussaint Reinaud, Fuat Sezgin, and William de Slane (Frankfurt am Main: Institut für Geschichte der arabisch-islamischen Wissenschaft, 1992).

Abzianidze, Zaza. "Homo bellator," *Druzhba Narodov* 12 (2000): 170–172.

Aflākī, Shams al-Dīn Aḥmad-i. *Exemplary Acts of the Mystics* [*Manāqeb al-ʿarefīn*], trans. John O'Kane (Leiden: Brill, 2002).

Aidamirov, Abuzar. *Darts: roman* (Grozny: GUP, 2006).

———. *Exa bu'sanash* (Grozny: Kniga, 1990).

al-Alqadārī, Ḥasan. *Āthār-i Dāghistān* (St. Petersburg: n.p., 1302/1894–1895).

———. *Dīwān al-Mamnūn* (M. M. Mavraev: Temir Khan Shura, 1913).

———. *Jirāb al-Mamnūn* (M. M. Mavraev: Temir Khan Shura, 1912).

al-Bākinī, Shuʿayb ibn Idrīs. *Ṭabaqāt al-Khwājagān al-Naqshbandiyah* (Damascus: Dār al-Nuʿmān lil-ʿUlūm, 2003).

al-Dāghistānī, Najm al-Dīn ibn Muḥammad ibn Dunūghūnah. *Ashwāq Dāghistān ilá al-Ḥaram al-Sharīf*, ed. Muḥammad al-Ḥabash (Damascus: Dār al-Nūr, 1995).

al-Durgilī, Nadhīr. *Nuzhat al-adhhān fī tarājim ʿulamāʾ Dāghestān* (*Die Islamgelehrten Daghestans und ihre arabischen Werke*), ed. and trans. Michael Kemper and Amri R. Shikhsaidov (Berlin: Klaus Schwarz Verlag, 2004).

———. *Nuzhat al-adhhān fī tarājim ʿulamāʾ Dāghistān* (*Uslada umov v biografiiakh dagestanskikh uchenykh: dagestanskie uchenye X-XX vv. i ikh sochineniia*), ed. and trans. A. K. Bustanov, M. Kemper, and A. R. Shikhsaidov (Moscow: al-Madzhani, 2012).

al-Ghāzīghumūqī, ʿAbd al-Raḥmān. "Daghestnisa da chechnetis datsema osmaleta tsakezaebit 1294 tsels (=suqūṭ dāghistān wa chachān bīyarāʿ al-uthmān fī sana 1294)," ed. Nana Qanchaveli, in *Mravalt'avi. P'ilologuri-istoriuli ziebani* 4 (Tbilisi, 1975): 230–253.

———. *Khulāṣat at-tafṣīl ʿan ahwāl al-imām shāmwīl*, ed. and trans. M. A. Tagirova (Moscow: Vostochnaia literatura RAN, 2002).

———. "Padenie dagestana i chechni vsledtvie podstrekatel'stvo osmanov v 1877 godu. Predoslovie, texst, perevod, kommentarii [=*suqūṭ dāghistān wa chachān bīyarāʿ al-uthmān fī sana 1294*]," ed. and trans. S. M. Guseikhanov and M. A. Musaev, in *Dagestanskii vostokovedcheskii sbornik*, ed. A. A. Isaev, M. A. Musaev, and G. A. Orazaev (Makhachkala: DNTs RAN, 2008).

———. *Tadhkirat Sayyidī ʿAbd al-Raḥmān ibn Ustādh Sheykh al-Ṭarīqah Jamāl al-Dīn al-Ḥusaynī fī bayān aḥwāl ahālī Dāghistān wa-Chichān allafahu wa-katabahu fī Tiflīs fī sanat 1285*, ed. and trans. M. S. Saidov, A. R. Shikhsaidov, and Kh. A. Omarov (Makhachkala: Dagestanskoe knizhnoe izd-vo, 1997).

al-Ghāzīghumūqī, Jamāl al-Dīn. *al-Ādāb al-marḍiyah fī al-ṭarīqah al-naqshbandīyah*, ed. Marie Broxup (Oxford: Society for Central Asian Studies, 1986).

al-Mulk, Niẓām. *Siyāsat-nāma (= Siyyar al-mulūk)*, ed. Charles Schefer (Paris: Ernest Leroux, 1891).

al-Qarākhī, Muḥammad Ṭāhir. *Bāriqat al-suyūf al-dāghistāniyah fī baʿd al-ghazawāt al-shāmiliyah*, ed. A. M. Barabanov and I. G. Krachkovskii (Moscow: AN SSSR, 1946).

al-Salṭī, ʿAlī Qāḍī. "Istoriia shariatskogo vosstaniia v Chechni i Dagestane i Imamata 1877 goda," in *Vosstaniia dagestantsev i chechentsev v posleshamilevskuiu epokhu i imamat 1877 goda: materialy*, trans. T. M. Aitberov, Iu. Dadaev, and Kh. A. Omarov (Makhachkala: Fond Shamilia, 2001), 39–130.

Antokol'skii, Pavel, trans. *Pobratimy: stikhi o Gruzii: iz gruzinskikh* (Tbilisi: Literatura i iskusstvo, 1963).

Avtorkhanov, Abdurakhman. *Memuary* (Frankfurt am Main: Possev Verlag, 1983).

ʿAẓīmābādī, Muḥammad Shams al-Ḥaqq. *ʿAwn al-maʿbūd: sharḥ Sunan Abī Dāwūd* (Madina: al-Maktabah al-Salafiyah, 1968–1969).

Bakarov, Musa. *Obarg Zelamkhekh dagaletsamash* (Grozny: Kniga, 1990).

Bakikhānūf, ʿAbbāsqulī Āqā. *Gulistān-i Iram*, ed. ʿAbd al-Karīm ʿAlīzādah (Baku: Idārah-i intishārāt-i ʿIlm, 1970).

Baratasvili, Nikoloz. *Txzulebani* (Tbilisi: Saxelmtsipo gamomcemloba, 1945).

Bobrovnikov, Vladimir, ed. *Obychai i zakon v pis' mennykh pamiatnikakh Dagestana V—nachala XX v.* (Moscow: Mardzhani, 2009).

Dykhaev, Vakha, ed. *Antologiia checheno-ingushskoi poezii* (Grozny: Checheno-ingushskoe knizhnoe izd-vo, 1981).

———. *Nokhchiin sovetski literatura: 9-10 klassashna uchebnik* (Grozny: Noxch-Ghalghain knizhni izd-vo, 1978).

Dzhambekov, Sh. A., ed. *Nokhchin folklor* (Grozny: Kniga, 1990).

Gamzatov, G. G., A. I. Osmanov, and A. M. Magomeddadaev, eds. *Mukhammad-Amin i narodno-osvoboditel'noe dvizhenie narodov Severo-Zapadnogo Kavkaza v 40-60 gg. XIX veka: sbornik dokumentov i materialov* (Makhachkala: RAN Fond Shamilia, 1998).

Gamzatov, Rasul. *Pesni gor. Pis'mena. Patimat: kniga stikhotvorenii* (Moscow: Sovremennik, 1983).

Gasanov, Ali. "Ot perevodchika, *Asari Dagestan (Istoricheskie svedeniia o Dagestan)* (Makhachkala: Izdanie Dagestanskogo Nauchno-Issledovatel'skogo Instituta, 1929).

Gatuev, Dzakho. *Zelimkhan: Iz istorii narodno-osvoboditel'nogo dvizheniia na Severnom Kavkaze* (Rostov and Krasnodar: Severnoe Kavkazskoe izd-vo, 1926).

———. *Zelimkhan: povest' i ocherki* (Ordzhonikidze: Irfon, 1971).

Gatuev, Dzakho, and Nikolai Marr. *Amran: Osetinskii epos* (Moscow: Academia, 1932).

Gatuev, Soslanbek. "Otets," in *Zelimkhan: povest' i ocherki* (Ordzhonikidze: Irfon, 1971), 204–208.

Guramishvili, David. *T'xzulebat'a sruli krebuli*, eds. A. Baramidze and S. Iordanishvili (Tbilisi: Kartuli tsigni, 1931).

Iasulov, Gamzat. *Khunzakhskie predaniia o Khadzhimurade*, ed. D. M. Malamagomedov (Makhachkala: IIAE, 2009).

———. "Predaniia o Khadzhi Murate," translated from the Avar by Koisubulinets Katsarilov, in *Dāghistān mejmūʿasï—Dagestanskii sbornik*, ed. A. A. Takho-Godi, B. G. Mallachikhanov, and D. M. Pavlov (Makhachkala, 1927), 3:7–49.

Ibn Rusta, Aḥmad Iṣfahānī. *Kitāb al-aʿlāq al-nafīsa*, ed. de Goeje (Brill: Leiden, 1892).

Ikskul', V. Ia. *Kavkazskie povesti* (Vladikavkaz: Ir, 1993).

Ismailov, M. A., T. M. Aitberov, and Akbiev A. S. *Antologiia pamiatnikov prava narodov Kavkaza* (Rostov-na-Donu: Severo-Kavkazskaia akademiia gos. sluzhby, 2010).

Jabushanuri, Gabriel. *Hoi, ghilghos daghrublulo ts'ao: lek'sebi, baladebi* (Tbilisi: Gulani, 1991).

Javaxishvili, Mixeil. *Arsena Marabdeli: romani*, ed. Nana Suxitashvili (Tbilisi: Sakartvelos matsne, 2005).

Kaiaev, Ali. *Terâcim-i ulemâ-yı Dagıstan: Dag ıstan bilginleri biyografileri*, eds. Tûbâ Işınsu Durmuş and Hasan Orazayev (Ankara: Grafiker Yayınları, 2012).

Kazak, Yirchi. *Lyrika* (Makhachkala: Dagestanskoe knizhnoe izd-vo, 2001).

Kazem Beg, Mirza. *Derbendnameh, translated from a selected Turkish version and published with notes* (St. Petersburg: Imperial Academy of Sciences, 1851).

Lavrov, L. I., ed. *Epigraficheskie pamiatniki Severnogo Kavkaza na arabskom, persidskom i turetskom iazykakh* (Moscow: Nauka, 1966–1980).

Leontievich, F. I. *Adaty kavkazskikh gortsev* (Odessa: Tip. P.A. Zelenago, 1881).

Mamakaev, Magomet Amaevich. *Chechenskii taip (rod) v period ego razlozheniia* (Grozny: Checheno-Ingushskoe izd-vo, 1973).

———. *Miurid Revolutsii* (Grozny: Checheno-Ingushskoe knizhnoe izd-vo, 1963).

———. *Zelamkha* (Grozny: Nokhch-g'aliain knizhni izd-vo, 1968).

———. *Zelimkhan*, trans. V. V. Timofeev (Grozny: Checheno-ingushskoe knizhnoe izd-vo, 1983).

Naqshabandī, Khālid ibn Aḥmad. *Kitāb bughyat al-wājid fī maktūbāt ḥaḍrat mawlānā Khālid* (Damascus: Maṭbaʿat al-Taraqqī, 1334/1916).

Orbeliani, Grigol. *Saghamo gamosalmebisa* (Tbilisi: Merani, 1989).

Oshaev, Khalid Dudaevich. "O druge i cheloveke Dzakho Gatueve," *Zelimkhan: povest' i ocherki* (Ordzhonikidze: Irfon, 1971).

O tekh kogo nazyvali abrekami: sbornik rasskazov, povestei, legend, skazok, stikhotvorenii i sotsial'no-ekonomicheskikh ocherkov o Chechne i chechentsakh (Grozny: Chechenskogo otdela narodnogo obrazovaniia, 1927).

Pshavela, Vazha. *Txzulebata sruli krebuli at tomad*, ed. Giorgi Leonidze (Tbilisi: Sabchota sakartvelo, 1964).

Qazbegi, Aleksandre. *Kha'rzhinarsh: Davtsiinarg, Tsitsia, Elisa*, translated from the Georgian by I. Margoshvili (Grozny: Nokhch-g'aliain knizhni, 1961).

———. *The Prose of the Mountains: Tales of the Caucasus*, trans. Rebecca Gould (Budapest: Central European UP, 2015).

———. *Txzulebani* (Tbilisi: Sabchota msterloba, 1948).

Robakidze, Grigol. *Kaukasische Novellen*, trans. Käthe Rosenberg (Leipzig: Insel-Bücherei, 1932; reprinted, Munich, 1979).

Runovskii, A. "Kodeks Shamilia," *Voennyi sbornik* 2 (1862): 327–386.

Shamil, Imam. Omarov, Kh. A. *100 pisem Shamilia* (Makhachkala: DNTs RAN, 1997).

Shanidze, Akaki. *Kartuli xalxuri poezia Xevsuruli* (Tbilisi: Saxelmtsipo gamomcemloba, 1931).

Sharafutdinova, R. Sh., ed. *Araboiazychnye dokumenty epokhi Shamilia* (Moscow: Vostochnaia Literatura, 2001).

Sheripov, Aslanbek. *Stat'iash a, qʿamelash a sbornik: gochiina o'rsiin sholgha arakhetsnachunna thera, nisdarsha, thetokharsh a desh* (Grozny: Nokhch-Ghalghain knizhni izd-vo, 1977).

———. *Stat'i i rechi*, 2nd ed., ed. E. P. Kireev and M. N. Muzaev (Grozny: Checheno-ingushskoe knizhnoe izd-vo, 1972).

Tabidze, Titsian. *Avtoportret': Izbrannnye stikhotvoreniia i poemy* (St. Petersburg: Vsemirnoe slovo, 1995).

———. "Gunib," *Metamorphoses: Journal of the Five-College Seminar on Literary Translation* 17.1 (2009): 70–71 (Georgian text; English trans. Rebecca Gould).

———. *Lek'sebi, poemebi, proza, tserilebi* (Tbilisi: Merani, 1985).

———. *Rcheuli natsarmoebi*, eds. I. Abashidze, R. Gargiani, and D. Sturua (Tbilisi: Literatura da xelovneba, 1966).

———. *Stat'i, ocherki, perepiska*, ed. Bebutov (Tbilisi: literatura da xelovneba, 1964).

Tolstoi, L. N. *Hach'i Murat*, translated from Russian into Armenian by L. I. Tanyelian (Tiflis: Aghanian, 1914).

———. *Haji-murati*. Trans from Russian into Georgian Sh. Tagukashvili (Tbilisi: Saskolo biblioteka, 1938).

———. *PSS L'va Nikolaevicha*, ed. P. I. Biriukov (Moscow: I. D. Sytin, 1912–1915).

———. *SS v 22 tomakh*, ed. Mikhail Borisovich Khrapchenko et al. (Moscow: Khudozheshtvennaia Literatura, 1978–1985).

Secondary Sources

Abdullaev, M. A. *Deiatel'nost' i vozzreniia sheikha Abdurakhmana Khadzhi i ego rodoslovnaia* (Makhachkala: Iupiter, 1998).

Abdullaev, Ziaudin. *Mir domu tvoemy: Izbrannaia proza narodov Severnogo Kavkaza* (Nal'chik: Elbrus, 2003).

Abou El Fadl, Khaled. *Rebellion and Violence in Islamic Law* (Cambridge: Cambridge UP, 2001).

Abu-Sahlieh, Sami A. Aldeeb. "La Migration dans la Conception Musulmane," *Oriente Moderno* 74 (1994): 219–283.

Abū Zahra, Muḥammad, *Al-ʿalāqāt ad-duwaliyyah fī al-islām* (Cairo: Dār al-fikr al-ʿarabī, 1984).

Afsaruddin, Asma. *Striving in the Path of God: Jihad and Martyrdom in Islamic Thought* (Oxford: Oxford UP, 2013).

Agamben, Giorgio. *Homo sacer: Sovereign Power and Bare Life*, trans. Daniel Heller-Roazen (Stanford: Stanford UP, 1998).

Aitberov, T. M., Iu. Dadaev, and Kh. A. Omarov. *Vosstaniia dagestantsev i chechentsev v posle Shamilevskuiu epokhu i imamat 1877 goda: materialy* (Makhachkala: Fond Shamilia, 2001).

Akaev, V. Kh. *L. N. Tolstoi i sheikh Kunta-Khadzhi Kishiev: problemy mira i gumanizma: materialy respublikanskoi nauchno-prakticheskoi konferentsii, 5 dekabria 2003 g., st. Starogladovskaia, Chechenskaia Respublika* (Tula: Iasnaia Poliana, 2006).

Akaev, V. V. *Sheikh Kunta Hadji: Zhizn' i uchenie* (Grozny: Nauchno-Issledovatel'skii Institut, 1994).

Akhlakov, A. A. *Geroiko-istoricheskie pesni avartsev* (Makhachkala: AN SSSR, IIILGT, 1968).

Alam, Muzaffar. *The Languages of Political Islam: India, 1200–1800* (London: C. Hurst & Co., 2004).

Albagachiev, R.-Kh. Sh. *Sheikh, Ustaz, Ovliia Kunta-Khadzhi Kishiev* (Nal'chik: Tetragraf, 2013).

Albogachieva, M. "'I am entrusted with only prayer beads by Allāh, and I will take neither a dagger nor a rifle in my hands' (Kunta-Ḥājjī Kishiev, his preaching and followers)," *Manuscripta Orientalia* 17.2 (2011): 12–20.

Alcalay, Ammiel. *After Jews and Arabs: Remaking Levantine Culture* (Minneapolis: U of Minnesota P, 1992).

Alibekov, Manai. *Adaty kumykov* (Makhachkala: Izdanie Dagestanskogo nauchno-issledovatel'skogo instituta, 1927).

Alibekova, P. M. *Zhizn' i tvorcheskoe nasledie Dibir-Kadi iz Khunzakha* (Makhachkala: IIALI DNTS RAN, 2009).

Alikberov, A. K. *Epokha klassicheskogo islama na Kavkaze: Abu Bakr ad-Darbandi i ego sufiskaia entsiklopediia 'Rayhan al-haqa'iq'* (Moscow: Vostochnaia literatura, 2003).

———. "Ob avtore istoricheshkoi khroniki XI v. *Tārīkh al-Bāb wa Shirwān,*" *Rukopisnaia i pechatnaia kniga v Dagestane*, ed. A. A. Isaev (Makhachkala: AN SSSR, IIILGT, 1991), 119–121.

Allen, Lori. "Getting by the Occupation: How Violence Became Normal during the Second Palestinian Intifada," *Cultural Anthropology* 23.3 (2008): 453–487.

———. "There Are Many Reasons Why: Suicide Bombers and Martyrs in Palestine," *Middle East Report* 223 (2002): 34–37.

Allen, W. E. D. *A History of the Georgian People: From the Beginning Down to the Russian Conquest in the Nineteenth Century* (London: Kegan Paul, 1932).

Anchabadze, Giorgi. *Vainakhi: chechentsy i ingushi* (Tbilisi: Caucasus House, 2001).

Anchabadze, Yu. D. "'Ostrakizm' na Kavkaze," *Sovetskaia etnografiia* 5 (1979): 137–144.

Appadurai, Arjun. "Grassroots Globalization and the Research Imagination," *Public Culture* 12.1 (2000): 1–19.

Arendt, Hannah. *The Human Condition* (Chicago: U of Chicago P, 1958).

———. *On Violence* (New York: Harcourt Brace, 1969).

Asad, Talal. *Formations of the Secular: Christianity, Islam, Modernity* (Stanford: Stanford UP, 2003).

———. *The Idea of an Anthropology of Islam* (Washington, DC: Center for Contemporary Arab Studies, Georgetown University, 1986).

———. *On Suicide Bombing* (New York: Columbia UP, 2007).

Atkin, Muriel. *Russia and Iran, 1780–1828* (U of Minnesota P, Minneapolis, 1980).

Barabanov, A. M. "Poiasnitelnye Znachki v Arabskikh Rukopisiakh i Dokumentakh Severnogo Kavkaza," *Sovetskoe Vostokovedenie* 3 (Moscow: AN SSSR, 1945), 193–214.

Barrett, Thomas M. "The Remaking of the Lion of Daghestan: Shamil in Capitivity," *Russian Review* 53.3 (1994): 353–366.

Bates, Thomas R. "Gramsci and the Theory of Hegemony," *Journal of the History of Ideas* 36.2 (1975): 351–366.

Baxi, Upendra. "'The State's Emissary': The Place of Law in Subaltern Studies," in *Subaltern Studies VII*, ed. Partha Chatterjee and Gyanendra Pandey (Delhi: Oxford UP, 1992), 247–264.

Benashvili, Dimitri. *Konstantine Gamsaxurdia: tsxovreba da shemokmedeba* (Tbilisi: Sakartvelos SSR metsnierebata akademiis gamomcemloba, 1962).

Benitez-Rojo, Antonio. *The Repeating Island: The Caribbean and the Postmodern Perspective*, trans. James E. Maraniss (Durham: Duke UP, 1997).

Benjamin, Walter. "Das Kunstwerk im Zeitalter seiner technischen Reproduzierbarkeit [1935]," in *Gesammelte Schriften*, ed. Rolf Tiedemann and Hermann Schweppenhäuser (Frankfurt am Main: Suhrkamp, 1991), 1, pt. 2: 431–508.

———. "Das Recht zur Gewaltanwendung [1920]," in *Gesammelte Schriften*, ed. Rolf Tiedemann and Hermann Schweppenhäuser (Frankfurt am Main: Suhrkamp, 1991), 6:104–108.

———. "Über den Begriff der Geschichte [1940]," in *Gesammelte Schriften*, ed. Rolf Tiedemann and Hermann Schweppenhäuser (Frankfurt am Main: Suhrkamp, 1991), 1, pt. 2: 690–708.

———. "Zur Kritik der Gewalt [1921]," in *Gesammelte Schriften*, ed. Rolf Tiedemann and Hermann Schweppenhäuser (Frankfurt am Main: Suhrkamp, 1991), 2, pt. 1: 179–202.

Benton, Lauren. *Law and Colonial Cultures: Legal Regimes in World History, 1400–1900* (Cambridge: Cambridge UP, 2002).

Berdiaev, S. K. *Razboi na Kavkaze: Iz vospominanii starogo administratora* (Paris: Pascal, 1930).

Berdiaev, Sergei. *Chechnia i razboinik Zelimkhan* (Paris: Pascal, 1932).

Bessaïh, Boualem. *De l'emir Abdelkader à l'imam Chamyl: le héros des Tchétchènes et du Caucase*, 2nd ed. (1997Alger: Casbah, 2009; first ed. Alger: Dahlab, 1997).

Bliev, M. M. and V. V. Degoev. *Kavkazskaia voina* (Moscow: Roset, 1994).

Bloch, Ernst. "Non-Synchronism and the Obligation to Its Dialectics," trans. Mark Ritter, *New German Critique* 11.2 (1977): 22–38.

Bloom, Mia. *Dying to Kill: The Allure of Suicide Terror* (New York: Columbia UP, 2005).

———. "Female Suicide Bombers: A Global Trend," *Daedalus* 136.1 (2007): 94–102.

———. "Women as Victims and Victimizers: Woman Are Both Victims and Perpetrators of Terrorist Violence." IIP Digital. http://iipdigital.usembassy.gov/st/english/publication/2008/05/20080522172353srenodo.6383936.html#axzz3pmuULPSD.

Bobrovnikov, V. O. "Abreki i gosudarstvo: Kul'tura nasiliia na Kavkaze," *Vestnik Evrazii* 1.8 (2000): 19–46.

———. "Bandits and the State: Designing a 'Traditional' Culture of Violence in the Russian Caucasus," in *Russian Empire: Space, People, Power, 1700–1930*, ed. Jane Burbank, Mark von Hagen, and Anatolyi Remnev (Bloomington: Indiana UP, 2007), 237–267.

———. *Musul'mane Severnogo Kavkaza: Obychai, pravo, nasilie. Ocherki po istorii i etnografii prava Nagornogo Dagestana* (Moscow: Vostochnaia literatura, 2002).

———. "Nasilie i vlast' v istoricheskoi pamiati musul'manskogo pogranich'ia (k novoi interpretatsii pesni o Khochbare)," in *Imperiia i natsiia v zerkale istoricheskoi pamiati*, ed. I. Gerasimov, M. Mogilner, and A. Semyonov (Moscow: Novoe izd-vo, 2011), 297–327.

———, ed. *Obychai i zakon v pis'mennykh pamiatnikakh Dagestana V—nachala XX v.* (Moscow: Mardzhani, 2009).

Bodin, Jean. *On Sovereignty: Four Chapters from* The Six Books of the Commonwealth, trans. J. H. Franklin (Cambridge: Cambridge UP, 1992).

Botiakov, Iu. M. *Abreki na Kavkaze: Sotsiokul'turnyi aspekt iavleniia* (St. Petersburg: Peterburgskoe vostokovedenie, 2004).

Bowersock, G. W. *Martyrdom and Rome* (Cambridge: Cambridge UP, 1995).

Brünner, Claudia. *Männerwaffe Frauenkörper? Zum Geschlecht der Selbst- mordattentate im israelisch-palästinensischen Konflikt* (Vienna: Braumüller, 2005).

———. "Occidentalism Meets the Female Suicide Bomber: A Critical Reflection on Recent Terrorism. Debates: A Review Essay," *Signs: Journal of Women and Culture in Society* 32.4 (2007): 957–972.

Buck-Morss, Susan. "Hegel and Haiti," *Critical Inquiry* 26.4 (2000): 821–865.

Bultmann, Rudolf. "Is Exegesis without Presuppositions Possible?" in *The Hermeneutics Reader: Texts of the German Tradition from the Enlightenment to the Present*, ed. Kurt Mueller-Vollmer (New York: Continuum, 1985), 242–248.

Burbank, Jane. "The Ties That Bind: Sovereignty and Law in the Late Russian Empire," in *One Law for All? Western Models and Local Practices in (Post-)Imperial Contexts*, ed. Stefan B. Kirmse (Frankfurt: Campus Verlag, 2012), 153–179.

Burkert, Walter. *Homo necans: The Anthropology of Ancient Greek Sacrificial Ritual and Myth* (Berkeley: U of California P, 1983).

Burt, J. "Hypotaxis and Parataxis," in *The Princeton Encyclopedia of Poetry and Poetics*, ed. Roland Greene et al. (Princeton: Princeton UP, 2012), 650.

Butler, Judith. "Critique, Coercion, and Sacred Life in Benjamin's 'Critique of Violence,'" in *Political Theologies: Public Religions in a Post-secular World*, ed. Hent de Vries and Lawrence E. Sullivan (New York: Fordham UP, 2006).

Caton, Steve. *"Peaks of Yemen I summon": Poetry as Cultural Practice in a North Yemeni Tribe* (Berkeley: U of California P, 1991).

———. "Power, Persuasion and Language: A Critique of the Segmentary Model in the Middle East," *IJMES* 19.1 (1987): 77–102.

———. "Salam Tahiyah: Greetings from the Highlands of Yemen," *American Ethnologist* 13.2 (1986): 290–308.

Chakrabarty, Dipesh. "Reconstructing Liberalism?" *Public Culture* 10.3 (1998): 457–481.

Charachidze, Georges. *Promethée ou le Caucase: Essai de mythologie contrastive* (Paris: Flammarion, 1986).

Chesnov, Ian, "'Byt' Chechentsem. Lichnost' i etnicheskie identifikatsii naroda'," in *Rossiia i Chechnia. Obschestva i gosudarstva*, ed. Dmitrii Furman (Moscow: Sakharov Foundation, 1999), 63–101.

Clastres, Pierre. *Archéologie de la violence. La guerre dans les sociétés primitives* (Paris: Éditions Payot, 1977).

Clifford, James. *The Predicament of Culture: Twentieth-Century Ethnography, Literature and Art* (Cambridge: Harvard UP, 1988).

Clifford, James, and George Marcus, eds. *Writing Culture: Poetics and Politics of Ethnography* (Berkeley: U of California P, 1986).

Comaroff, Jean, and John L. Comaroff, "Law and Disorder in the Postcolony: An Introduction," in *Law and Disorder in the Postcolony*, Jean Comaroff and John L. Comaroff, eds. (Chicago: U of Chicago Press, 2006), 1–56.

Cooper, Frederick. *Colonialism in Question: Theory, Knowledge, History* (Berkeley: U of California P, 2005).

Dal', Vladimir. *Tolkovyi slovar' zhivogo velikorusskogo iazyka* (St. Petersburg: Tipografiia Imperatorskoi Akademii nauk, 1869).

Dalgat, U. "Gorskie pesni, predanie i skazka v 'Xadji-Murate' L. N. Tolstogo i ikh khudozhestvennoe znachenie," *Izvestiia* 2.3: Literatura (Grozny: Checheno-ingushskii nauchnoissledovatel'skii institut, 1951), 6–23.

Daniel, E. "Historical Literature," in *Encyclopedia of Arabic Literature*, ed. Julie Scott Meisami and Paul Starkey (London: Routledge, 1998), 289–293.

Dale, Stephen. *The Garden of the Eight Paradises: Bābur and the Culture of Empire in Central Asia, Afghanistan, and India: 1483–1530* (Leiden: Brill, 2004).

———. "The Poetry and Autobiography of the *Bâbur-nâma*," *JAS* 55.3 (1996): 635–664.

———. "Steppe Humanism: The Autobiographical Writings of Zahir al-Din Muhammad Babur (1483–1530)," *IJMES* 22.1 (1990): 37–58.

Dean, Mitchell. *Governmentality: Power and Rule in Modern Society* (London: Sage, 1999).

Degoev, V. V. *Imam Shamil': Prorok, vlastitel', voin* (Moscow: Russkaia panorama, 2001).

Derluguian, Giorgi. *Bourdieu's Secret Admirer in the Caucasus: A World-System Biography* (Chicago: U of Chicago P, 2005).

Dettmering, Christian. *Russlands Kampf gegen die Sufis: die Integration der Tschetschenen und Inguschen ins Russische Reich 1810–1880* (Oldenburg: Dryas-Verlag, 2011).

Devdariani, Roza. *Grigol Orbelianis shemokmedeba* (Kutaisi: Kutaisis saxelmtsipo universitetis gamomcemloba, 2002).

Digby, Simon. "The Sufi Shaykh and the Sultan: A Conflict of Claims to Authority in Medieval India," *Iran* 28 (1990): 71–81.

Donogo, Khadzhi Murad. *Nadzhmuddin Gotsinskii: obshchestvenno-politicheskaia bor'ba v Dagestane v pervoi chetverti XX veka* (Makhachkala: Ministerstvo obrazovaniia i nauki RF, 2005).

Duchemin, Jacqueline. *Prométhée: histoire du mythe, de ses origines orientales à ses incarnations modernes* (Paris: Belles lettres, 1974).

Duncan, James. *In the Shadows of the Tropics: Climate, Race and Biopower in Nineteenth Century Ceylon* (Aldershot: Ashgate, 2012).

Dzidzioev, V. D. *Ot Soiuza ob'edinennykh gortsev Severnogo Kavkaza i Dagestana do Gorskoi ASSR (1917-1924 gg.): nachal'nyi etap natsional'no-gosudarstvennogo stroitel'stva narodov Severnogo Kavkaza v XX veke* (Vladikavkaz: Severo-Osetinskogo Gosudarstvennii Universitet, 2003).

Eagleton, Terry. *The Ideology of the Aesthetic* (New York: Wiley, 1990).

Edkins, Jenny. "Sovereign Power, Zones of Indistinction, and the Camp," *Alternatives: Global, Local, Political* 25.1 (2000): 3–25.

Eremenko I. N., and Yu. D. Novikov, eds. *Rossiia i Chechnya: 1990-1997 gody: dokumentyi sviditelstvuyut* (Moscow: RAU Universitet, 1997).

Evangelista, Matthew. *The Chechen Wars: Will Russia Go the Way of the Soviet Union?* (Washington, DC: Brookings Institution Press, 2002).

———. *Gender, Nationalism, and War: Conflict on the Movie Screen* (Cambridge: Cambridge UP, 2011).

Fanon, Frantz. *Black Skin, White Masks* (New York: Grove Press, 1967).

———. *Les damnés de la Terre* (1961; Paris: La Decouverte, 2002).

Fil'shtinskii, I. M. *Arabskaia literatura v srednie veka. Arabskaia literatura XIII—IX vekov.* (Moscow: Nauka, 1977).

Foucault, Michel. *The History of Sexuality, Vol. 1: An Introduction*, trans. R. Hurley (Harmondsworth: Penguin, 1981).

———. "La gouvernementalité," in *Dits et écrits III (1976–1979)* (Paris: Gallimard, 1994), 635–657.

———. *Politics, Philosophy, Culture: Interviews and Other Writings, 1977–1984*, ed. Lawrence D. Kritzman (London: Routledge, 1988).

Freud, Sigmund. *Gesammelte Werke: Bd. Werke aus den Jahren 1917-1920*, ed. Anna Freud (Frankfurt am Main: S. Fischer, 1986).

Friedrich, Paul. "Tolstoy and the Chechens: Problems in Literary Anthropology," *Russian History/Histoire russe* 30.1–2 (2003): 113–143.

Gadamer, Hans-Georg. *Hermeneutik: Wahrheit und Methode* (Tübingen: Mohr, 1993).

Gadzhiev, V. G., and Kh. Kh. Ramazanov, eds. *Dvizhenie gortsev severo-vostochnago Kavkaza v 20-50kh gg. XIX veka. Sbornik dokumentov* (Makhachkala: Dagestanskoe knizhnoe izd-vo, 1959).

Gammer, Moshe. "Collective Memory and Politics: Remarks on Some Competing Historical Narratives in the Caucasus and Russia and Their Use of a 'National Hero,'" *Caucasian Regional Studies* 4.1 (1999). http://poli.vub.ac.be/publi/crs/eng/0401-03.htm.

———. "The Imam and the Pasha: A Note on Shamil and Muhammad Ali," *MES* 32.4 (1996): 336–342.

———. *The Lone Wolf and the Bear: Three Centuries of Chechen Defiance of Russian Rule* (London: Hurst, 2006).

———. *Muslim Resistance to the Tsar: Shamil and the Conquest of Chechnia and Daghestan* (London: Frank Cass, 1994).

———. "Shamil in Soviet Historiography," *MES* 28.4 (1992): 729–777.

Geertz, Clifford. *Works and Lives. The Anthropologist as Author* (Stanford: Stanford UP, 1988).

Genko, A. N. "Arabskii iazyk i kavkazovedenie," *Trudy vtoroi sessii Assotsiatsii arabistov* (Moscow-Leningrad: AN SSSR, 1941), 81–110.

Geraci, Robert. *Window on the East: National and Imperial Identities in Late Tsarist Russia* (Ithaca: Cornell UP, 2001).

Geshaev, Musa. *Izvestnie chechentsy* (Moscow: n.p., 1999).

Glissant, Édouard. *Poétique de la relation* (Paris: Gallimard, 1990).

Goldziher, Ignáz. *Muhammedanische Studien* (Halle an der Saale: Max Niemeyer, 1889–1890).

Goudakov, Vladimir. "Les oeuvres caucasiennes de Léon Tolstoï comme document ethnologique," in *Autour de Tolstoï: le Caucase dans la culture russe* (Paris: Institut d'études slaves, 1997), 35–43.

Gould, Rebecca. "Aleksandre Qazbegi's Mountaineer Prosaics: The Anticolonial Vernacular on Georgian-Chechen Borderlands," *Ab Imperio: Studies of New Imperial History and Nationalism in the Post-Soviet Space* 1.2014 (2014): 361–390.

———. "Antiquarianism as Genealogy: Arnaldo Momigliano's Method," *History and Theory* 53.2 (2014): 212–233.

———. "Behind the Wall of the Caucasus: Crossing into Chechnya," *Gettysburg Review* 18.2 (2005): 291–307.

———. "Chechens through the Russian Prism," *Chechen Times*, 18 February 2005.

———. "The Death of Caucasus Philology: Towards a Discipline beyond Areal Divides," *Iran and the Caucasus* 17.3 (2013): 275–293.

———. "The Engaged Outsider: Politkovskaya and the Politics of Representing War," *Spaces of Identity* 7.2 (2007): 7–30.

———. "How Newness Enters the World: The Methodology of Sheldon Pollock," *CSSAAME* 28.3 (2008): 533–557.

———. "*Ijtihād* against *Madhhab*: The Meanings of Modernity in Early Modern Daghestan," *CSSH* 57.1 (2015): 35–66.

———. "Laws, Exceptions, Norms: Kierkegaard, Schmitt, and Benjamin on the Exception," *Telos: A Quarterly Journal of Politics, Philosophy, Critical Theory, Culture, and the Arts* 162 (2013): 77–96.

———. "The Lonely Hero and Chechen Modernity: Interpreting the Story of Gekha the Abrek," *Journal of Folklore Research* 51.2 (2014): 199–222.

———. "The Modernity of Premodern Islam in Contemporary Daghestan," *Contemporary Islam* 5.2 (2011): 161–183.

———. "The Political Aesthetic of the Medieval Persian Prison Poem, 1100–1200" (PhD diss., Columbia University, 2013).

———. "Secularism and Belief in Georgia's Pankisi Gorge," *JIS* 22.3 (2011): 339–373.

———. "Topographies of Anticolonialism: The Ecopoetical Sublime in the Caucasus from Tolstoy to Mamakaev," *Comparative Literature Studies* 50.1 (2013): 87–107.

———. "Transgressive Sanctity: The Abrek in Chechen Culture," *Kritika: Explorations in Russian and Eurasian History* 8.2 (2007): 271–306.

Grant, Bruce. "An Average Azeri Village (1930): Remembering Rebellion in the Caucasus Mountains," *Slavic Review* 63.4 (2004): 705–731.

———. *The Captive and the Gift: Cultural Histories of Sovereignty in Russia and the Caucasus.* Ithaca: Cornell UP, 2009.

———. "Sense and Sense Making in the Caucasus," *American Anthropologist* 108.2 (2006): 385–388.

———. "Shrines and Sovereigns: Life, Death, and Religion in Rural Azerbaijan," *CSSH* 53.3 (2011): 654–681.

Greenblatt, Stephen. *Renaissance Self-Fashioning: From More to Shakespeare* (Chicago: U of Chicago P, 1980).

Gritsenko, N. P. *Klassovaia i antikolonial'naia bor'ba krest'ian checheno-ingushetii na rubezhe XIX-XX vekov* (Grozny: Checheno-ingushskoe knizhnoe izd-vo, 1971).

Gudaev, Lema. *Abrek Zelimkhan: Argumenti i Fakti* (Grozny: Knizhnoe izd-vo, 2011).

Guha, Ranajit. "Chandra's Death," in *Subaltern Studies V*, ed. Ranajit Guha (Delhi: Oxford UP, 1987), 135–165.

———. *Dominance without Hegemony: History and Power in Colonial India* (Cambridge: Harvard UP, 1998).

———. *Elementary Aspects of Peasant Insurgency in Colonial India* (Delhi: Oxford UP, 1983).

Habermas, Jürgen. *The Structural Transformation of the Public Sphere: An Inquiry into a Category of Bourgeois Society*, trans. Thomas Burger (Cambridge: MIT Press, 1991).

Hammond, Marlé. *Beyond Elegy: Classical Arabic Women's Poetry in Context* (Oxford: Oxford UP, 2010).

Hardt, Michael, and Toni Negri. *Empire* (Cambridge: Harvard UP, 2000).

Harootunian, H. D. "Postcoloniality's Unconscious/Area Studies' Desire," *Postcolonial Studies* 2.2 (1999): 127–147.

Hart, David M. *Banditry in Islam: Case Studies from Morocco, Algeria, and the Pakistan North West Frontier* (Wisbech: Middle East & North African Studies Press, 1987).

Hart, Matthew. *Nations of Nothing but Poetry: Modernism, Transnationalism, and Synthetic Vernacular Writing* (Oxford: Oxford UP, 2010).

Hasso, Frances. "Discursive and Political Deployments by/of the 2002 Palestinian Women Suicide Bombers/Martyrs," *Feminist Review* 81.1 (2005): 23–51.

Hegel, Georg Wilhelm Friedrich. *Elements of the Philosophy of Right*, trans. H. B. Nisbet (Cambridge: Cambridge UP, 1991).

Hindawi, H. "Palestinian Father Expresses Shock over Daughter's Suicide Bombing," *Associated Press Worldstream*, 13 April 2002. Lexis-Nexis Academic Universe.

Hobsbawn, Eric. *Bandits* (1969; New York: New Press, 2000).

———. *Primitive Rebels* (Manchester: Manchester UP, 1959).

Hobsbawm, Eric, and Terence Ranger. *The Invention of Tradition* (Cambridge: Cambridge UP, 1983).

Hughes, James. *Chechnya: From Nationalism to Jihad* (Philadelphia: U of Pennsylvania P, 2007).

Imber, Colin. "What Does Ghazi Actually Mean?" in *The Balance of Truth: Essays in Honour of Professor Geoffrey Lewis*, ed. Ç. Balım-Harding and C. Imber (Istanbul: Isis Press, 2000), 165–178.

Ippolitov, A. "Uchenie zikr i ego posledovateli v Chechne i Argunskom Okruge," *SSKG* 2 (1869): 1–17.

Isaev, A. A. *Katalog pechatnykh knig i publikatsii na iazykakh narodov Dagestana: dorevoliutsionnyī period* (Makhachkala: IIILGT, 1989).

———. "K voprosy o datirovke darginskikh zapisei na poliakh arabskikh rukopisei XV v," *Istochnikovedenie istorii i kul'tury narodov Dagestana i Severnogo Kavkaza* (Makhachkala: DNTs RAN, 1991), 85–89.

———. *Magomedmirza Mavraev—Pervopechatnik i prosvetitel' Dagestana* (Makhachkala: DNTs RAN, 2003).

———, ed. *Nauchnoe nasledie A. A. Takho-Godi: knigi, staṭi, doklady, vystupleniia, pis'ma*, ed. A. A. Isaev (Makhachkala: RAN, 2006).

Iser, Wolfgang. *Prospecting: From Reader Response to Literary Anthropology* (Baltimore: Johns Hopkins UP, 1989).

Iurov, A., and N. V. Iurov. "1840, 1841 i 1842–i gody na Kavaze," *Kavkazskii Sbornik* 10 (1886): 225–404.

Ivanov, A. I. "Natsional'no-osvoboditel'noe dvizhenie v Chechne i Dagestane v 60–70kh gg. XIXv.," *Istoricheskie zapiski* 12 (1941): 165–199.

Jabagi, Vassan Giray. "The North Caucasus in the Wake of the Russian Revolution, 1917," *CAS* 10.1–2 (1991): 119–132.

Jaimoukha, Amjad M. *The Chechens: A Handbook* (London: Routledge, 2005).

Jameson, Fredric. *A Singular Modernity: Essay on the Ontology of the Present* (New York: Verso, 2002).

Jean-Klein, Iris. *Palestinian Martyrdom Revisited: Critical Reflections on Topical Cultures of Explanation* (Ithaca: Cornell Law School, 2002).

Jentsch, Ernst. "On the Psychology of the Uncanny (1906)," trans. Roy Sellars. *Angelaki* 2.1 (1997): 7–16.

Jersild, Austin, "Imperial Russification: Daghestani Mountaineers in Russian Exile, 1877–1883," *CAS* 19.1 (2000): 5–16.

———. *Orientalism and Empire: North Caucasus Mountain Peoples and the Georgian Frontier, 1845–1917* (Montreal: McGill-Queen's UP, 2002).

Kandelaki, M. B. *Iz obshchestvennogo byta gortsev Gruzii—institut amanatstva* (Tbilisi: Metsniereba, 1987).

Karny, Yo'av. *Highlanders: A Journey to the Caucasus in Quest of Memory* (New York: Macmillan, 2000).

Kaviraj, Sudipta. "On the Advantages of Being a Barbarian," in *At Home in the Diaspora: South Asia, Europe, the United States*, ed. Jackie Assayag and Véronique Bénéï (Bloomington: Indiana UP, 2003), 148–162.

———. "An Outline of a Revisionist Theory of Modernity," *European Journal of Sociology* 46.3 (2005): 497–526.

Kemper, Michael. "ʿAdat against Shariʿa: Russian Approaches towards Daghestani 'Customary Law' in the 19th Century," *Ab Imperio* 3 (2005): 147–174.

———. "The Changing Images of Jihad Leaders: Shamil and Abd al-Qadir in Daghestani and Algerian Historical Writing," *Nova Religio: The Journal of Alternative and Emergent Religions* 11.2 (2007): 28–58.

———. "Communal Agreements (*ittifāqāt*) and ʿĀdāt-Books from Daghestani Villages and Confederacies (18th–19th Centuries)," *Der Islam* 81.1 (2004): 115–151.

———. "Daghestani Legal Discourse on the Imamate," *CAS* 21.3 (2002): 265–278.

———. "Daghestani Shaykhs and Scholars in Russian Exile: Networks of Sufism, Fatwas and Poetry," in *Daghestan and the World of Islam*, ed. Moshe Gammer and David J. Wasserstein (Helsinki: Annales Academiae Scientiarum Fennicae, 2006), 95–107.

———. "Einige Notizen zur arabischsprachigen Literatur der jihād-Bewegung in Dagestan und Tschetschenien in der ersten Hälfte des 19. Jahrhunderts," *MCRCA* 2, 63–99.

———. "Ghazi Muhammad's Treatise against Daghestani Customary Law," in *Islam and Sufism in Daghestan*, ed. Moshe Gammer (Helsinki: Academia Scientiarum Fennica, 2009), 85–100.

———. *Herrschaft, Recht und Islam in Daghestan—Von den Khanaten und Gemeindebünden zum gihad-Staat* (Wiesbaden: Ludwig Reichert Verlag, 2005).

———. "An Island of Classical Arabic in the Caucasus: Dagestan," in *Exploring the Caucasus in the 21st Century*, ed. Françoise Companjen and Lia Versteegh (Amsterdam: Amsterdam UP, 2011), 63–90.

———. "Khalidiyya Networks in Daghestan and the Question of Jihād," *WDI* 42.1 (2002): 41–71.

———. "The North Caucasian Khālidiyya and 'Muridism': Historiographical Problems," *JHS* 5 (2007): 151–167.

———. "Red Orientalism: Mikhail Pavlovich and Marxist Oriental Studies in Early Soviet Russia," *WDI* 50.3 (2010): 435–476.

Kemper, Michael, Amri Shikhsaidov, and Natalya Tagirova. "Biblioteka Imama Shamilia," in *Dagestan i musul'manskii vostok. Sbornik statei*, ed. A. K. Alikberov and V. O. Bobrovnikov (Moscow: Mardzhani, 2010), 259–272.

Kereselidze, Giorgio. "Grigol Orbeliani," in *Krebuli: k'art'uli literaturisa, istoriisa da xelovnebis organo*, ed. Givi Kobaxidze (New York: Rausen Brothers, 1957), 90–137.

Khalid, Adeeb. "Russian History and the Debate over Orientalism," *Kritika* 1.4 (2000): 691–699.

Khalili, Laleh. *Heroes and Martyrs of Palestine: The Politics of National Commemoration* (Cambridge: Cambridge UP, 2007).

Khojaev, Dalkhan. *Chechentsi v Russko-Kavkazskoi Voiny* (Grozny: Seda, 1998).

Khoruev, Iu. V. *Abreki na Kavkaze* (Vladikavkaz: Severo-Osetinskii Gosudarstvenii Universitet, 2010).

King, Charles. *Extreme Politics: Nationalism, Violence, and the End of Eastern Europe* (New York: Oxford UP, 2009).

———. *The Ghost of Freedom: A History of the Caucasus* (New York: Oxford UP, 2008).

Knysh, Alexander. "Sufism as an Explanatory Paradigm: The Issue of the Motivations of Sufi Movements in Russian and Western Historiography," *WDI* 42.2 (2002): 139–173.

Kofman, Sarah. *Quatre romans analytiques* (Paris: Éditions Galilée, 1974).

Kovalevskii, P. I. *Vosstanie Chechni i Dagestana v 1877-1876 gg* (St. Petersburg: M. I. Akinfiev, 1912).

Krachkovskii, I. Yu. *Izbrannie sochineniia*, 6 vols. (Moscow: AN SSSR, 1960).

Kudriavtsev, A. A. *Puti razvitiia severokavkazskogo goroda: po materialam Derbenta domongolskoi poru* (Stavropol: Stavropol'skii Gosudarstvennoe Universitet, 2003).

Kurbanov, M. R., and Zh. M. Kurbanov. *Narody Dagestana: istoriia deportatsii i repressii: tragediia i uroki* (Makhachkala: Lotos, 2009).

Latour, Bruno. *Nous n'avons jamais été modernes* (Paris: La Découverte, 1991).

Layton, Susan. *Russian Literature and Empire: Conquest of the Caucasus from Pushkin to Tolstoy* (Cambridge: Cambridge UP, 1995).

Li, Tania Murray. *The Will to Improve: Governmentality, Development, and the Practice of Politics* (Durham: Duke UP, 2007).

Lieven, Anatole. *Chechnya: Tombstone of Russian Power* (Cambridge: Harvard UP, 1998).

Magomedov, A. M. *Alibek Takho-Godi: zhizn', mirovozzrenie, tvorcheskoe nasledie* (Makhachkala: Dagestanskoe knizhnoe izd-vo, 1993).

Magomedov, M. G., and A. R. Shikhsaidov. *Kalakoreish: krepost' kureishitov* (Makhachkala: Iupiter, 2000).

Magomedov, R. *Pamiatnik istorii i pis'mennosti dargintsev XVII veka* (Makhachkala: Dagestanskoe knizhnoe izd-vo, 1963).

Magomedova, Z. A. *Sheikh Nakshbandiiskogo tarikata—Abdurakhman-Khadzhi iz Sogratliia* (Makhachkala: Epokha, 2010).

Mahmood, Saba. "Feminist Theory, Embodiment, and the Docile Agent: Some Reflections on the Egyptian Islamic Revival," *Cultural Anthropology* 6.2 (2001): 202–236.

———. *Politics of Piety: The Islamic Revival and the Feminist Subject* (Princeton: Princeton UP, 2005).

———. "Secularism, Hermeneutics, and Empire," *Public Culture* 18.2 (2006): 324–327.

Manning, Paul. *Strangers in a Strange Land: Occidentalist Publics and Orientalist Geographies in Nineteenth-century Georgian Imaginaries* (Brighton: Academic Studies Press, 2012).

Manning, Paul, and Zaza Shatirishvili. "Exoticism and Eroticism of the City: 'Kinto' and His City," in *Urban Spaces after Socialism: Ethnographies of Public Places in Eurasian Cities*, ed. T. Darieva, W. Kaschuba, and M. Krebs (Frankfurt: Campus Verlag, 2011), 261–281.

Marshall, Alex. *The Caucasus under Soviet Rule* (London: Routledge, 2009).

Matveev, V. "Severnyi Kavkaz: abreki, kachagi, i drugie," *Orientir* 4 (2002): 9–11.

Meeker, Michael E. *Literature and Violence in North Arabia* (Cambridge: Cambridge UP, 1979).

Megreladze, Darejan. *Lekianoba* (Tbilisi: SSIP Istoriuli memkvidroba, 2012).

Megrelidze, Sh. V. *Zakavkaze v Russko-Turetskoi voine 1877-1878 gg* (Tbilisi: Metsniereba, 1972).

Meisami, Julie Scott. *Structure and Meaning in Medieval Arabic and Persian Lyric Poetry: Orient Pearls* (London: Routledge, 2003).

Melas, Natalie. *All the Difference in the World: Postcoloniality and the Ends of Comparison* (Stanford: Stanford UP, 2007).

Memorial Human Rights Center. *By All Available Means: The Russian Federation Ministry of Internal Affairs Operation in The Village of Samashki, April 7–8, 1995: Independent Research by the Observer Mission of Human Rights and Public*

Organizations in the Conflict Zone in Chechnya (Moscow: Memorial Human Rights Center, 1996).

———. "Terror with Terror." http://www.memo.ru/eng/memhrc/texts/terror.shtml.

Meskhidze, Julietta. "Shaykh Batal Hajji from Surkhokhi: Towards the History of Islam in Ingushetia," *CAS* 25.1–2 (2006): 179–191.

Messick, Brinkley. *The Calligraphic State: Textual Domination and History in a Muslim Society* (Berkeley: U of California P, 1993).

Mikhankova, V. A. *Nikolai Iakovlevich Marr: Ocherk ego zhizni i nauchnoi deiatel'nosti* (Leningrad: AN SSSR, 1949).

Miklukho-Maklai, N. D. "Opisanie tadzhikskikh i persidskikh rukopisei Instituta narodov Azii AN SSSR," *Istoricheskie sochineniia*[3] (Moscow: Nauka, 1973), 396–399.

Miller, B. *Taty, ikh rasselenie i govori (Materialy i Voprosy)* (Baku: Obshhestva Obsledovaniia i Izucheniia Azerbaidzhana, 1929).

Minorsky, Vladimir. *A History of Sharvān and Darband in the 10th–11th centuries* (Cambridge: Heffer, 1958).

———. *Istoriia Shirvana i Derbenda X-XI vekov* (Moscow: Vostochnaia Literatura, 1963) [revised edition of *A History of Sharvān and Darband*].

Mir-Hosseini, Zeba. "Muslim Women's Quest for Equality: Between Islamic Law and Feminism," *Critical Inquiry* 32.4 (2006): 630–645.

Mitchell, Timothy. "Society Economy, and the State Effect," in *State/Culture: State-Formation after the Cultural Turn*, ed. George Steinmetz (Ithaca: Cornell UP, 1999), 76–97.

Muchembled, Robert. *Une histoire de la violence: de la fin du Moyen Âge à nos jours* (Paris: Éditions du Seuil, 2008).

Müller, Jan-Werner. "Myth, Law and Order: Schmitt and Benjamin Read Reflections on Violence," *History of European Ideas* 29.4 (2012): 459–473.

Mumladze, Tariel. *Lekianoba Sak'art'veloshi: istoriul-literaturuli narkvevi natsqveti tsignidan "K'art'velt'a maoxarni"* (Tbilisi: Metsniereba, 2011).

Musaev, M. A. *Musul'manskoe dukhovenstvo 60–70–x godov XIX veka i vosstanie 1877 goda v Dagestane* (Makhachkala: IIAE DNTs RAN, 2005).

———. "Rebekka Gul'd ob Imame Shamile," *Dagestan* 10 (2014). http://journaldag.ru/52-rebekka-guld-ob-imame-shamile.html.

———. "Vzgliad na 'lekianoba' v kontekste izucheniia pravovyh zakluchenii dagestanskih uchenyh-bogoslovov XVIII v.," *Fundamental'nye issledovaniia* 10.14 (2013): 3223–3228.

Musakhanova, G. B., and S. Kh. Akhmedov. *Nasledie, vozvrashchennoe narodu: materialy o zhizni i tvorchestve repressirovannykh poetov i pisatelei Dagestana* (Makhachkala: IIILGT, 1990).

Natroshvili, Giorgi. *Vit'a davghamdi, ise gavt'endi: cigni Davit' Guramishvilis ts'xovrebasa da shemok'medebaze* (Tbilisi: Nakaduli, 1960).

Neimatova, M. Kh. "Epigraficheskie pamiatniki i ikh znachenie v izuchenii sotsial'no-ekonomicheskoi istorii Azerbaidzhana XIV-XIX vv." (PhD diss., University of Baku, 1968).

Nichols, Johanna. "Origin of the Chechen and Ingush: A Study in Alpine Linguistic and Ethnic Geography," *Anthropological Linguistics* 46.2 (2004): 129–155.

Opul'skii, A. *L. N. Tolstoi na Kavkaze: literaturno-kraevedcheskii ocherk* (Ordzhonikidze: Severo-Osetinskoii knizhnoii izd-vo, 1960).

Pateman, Carol. *The Sexual Contract* (Stanford: Stanford University Press, 1988).

Petrushevskii, I. P. *Dzharo-Belokanskie vol'nye obshchestva v pervoi treti XIX stoletia* (Tiflis: Nauchno-issledovatel'skogo instituta Kavkazovedeniia, 1934).

15 let diskriminatsii. 27 December 2007. http://www.miacum.am/gazeta/2007/12/25/15_let_diskriminacii_pismo_putinu_i_alievu.

Pohl, Michaela. "'It cannot be that our graves will be here': The Survival of Chechen and Ingush Deportees in Kazakhstan, 1944–1957," *Journal of Genocide Research* 4.3 (2002): 401–430.

Politkovskaia, Anna. *A Small Corner of Hell: Dispatches from Chechnya*, trans. Alexander Burry and Tatiana Tulchinsky (Chicago: U of Chicago P, 2003).

———. "Smert' voennogo komendanta. Pochemy Umer General Gadzhiev? Predistoria odnogo is samogo gromkikh ubistv ushedshego goda v Chechne," *Novaia Gazeta*, 14 January 2002. http://politkovskaya.novayagazeta.ru/pub/2002/2002-02.shtml.

———. *Vtoraia chechenskaia* (Moscow: Zakharov, 2002).

Pollock, Sheldon. "Cosmopolitan and Vernacular in History," *Public Culture* 12.3 (2000): 591–625.

———, ed. *Forms of Knowledge in Early Modern Asia: Explorations in the Intellectual History of India and Tibet, 1500–1800* (Durham: Duke UP, 2011).

Prakash, Gyan. *Another Reason: Science and the Imagination of Modern India* (Princeton, NJ: Princeton UP, 1999).

Procházková, Petra. *La guerre russo-tchetchene: paroles de femmes*, trans. from Czech by Barbora Faure (Paris: Le serpent à plumes, 2006).

Prokhovnik, Raia. *Sovereignty: History and Theory* (New York: Imprint Academic, 2008).

Quṭb, Sayyid. *In the Shade of the Quran [fī ẓilāl al-Qur'ān]*, trans. M. Adil Saladi and Ashur A. Shamis (London: Muslim Welfare House Publishers, 1979).

Ram, Harsha. "Decadent Nationalism, 'Peripheral' Modernism: The Georgian Literary Manifesto between Symbolism and the Avant-garde," *Modernism/Modernity* 21.1 (2014): 343–359.

———. *The Imperial Sublime: A Russian Poetics of Empire* (Madison: U of Wisconsin P, 2003).

———. "Masks of the Poet, Myths of the People: The Performance of Individuality and Nationhood in Georgian and Russian Modernism," *Slavic Review* 67.3 (2008): 567–590.

———. *Prisoners of the Caucasus: Literary Myths and Media Representations of the Chechen Conflict* (Berkeley: Berkeley Program in Soviet and Post-Soviet Studies, 1999).

———. "Sonnet and the Mukhambazi: Genre Wars on the Edges of the Russian Empire," *PMLA* 122.5 (2007): 1548–1570.

———. "Towards a Crosscultural Poetics of the Contact Zone: Romantic, Modernist and Soviet Intertextualities in Boris Pasternak's translations of T'itsian T'abidze," *Comparative Literature* 59.1 (2007): 63–89.

Ram, Harsha, and Zaza Shatirishvili. "Romantic Topography and the Dilemma of Empire: The Caucasus in the Dialogue of Georgian and Russian Poetry," *Russian Review* 63.1 (2004): 13–24.

Rayfield, Donald. "The Death of Paolo Iashvili," *SEER* 68.3 (1990): 631–664.

———. *Literature of Georgia: A History*[3] (Richmond, Surrey: Curzon Press, 2010).

———. "Pasternak and the Georgians," *Irish Slavonic Studies* 3 (1982): 39–46.

———. "Time Bombs: The Posthumous and Post-Soviet Reinterpretation of Two Georgian Novels," in *Art, Intellect and Politics: A Diachronic Perspective*, ed. G. M. A. Margagliotta and A. A. Robiglio (Leiden: Brill, 2013), 584–589.

Rayfield, Donald, Rusudan Amirejibi, and Reuven Enoch. *A Comprehensive Georgian-English Dictionary* (London: Garnett Press, 2006).

Reuters, Christoph. *Mein Leben ist eine Waffe. Selbtsmordattentäter. Programm eines Phänomens* (Munich: Bertelsmann, 2002).

Reynolds, Michael. "Native Sons: Post-Imperial Politics, Islam, and Identity in the North Caucasus, 1917–1918," *Jahrbücher für Geschichte Osteuropas* 56 (2008): 221–247.

———. *Shattering Empires: The Clash and Collapse of the Ottoman and Russian Empires 1908–1918* (Cambridge UP, 2011).

Richmond, Walter. *The Circassian Genocide* (New Brunswick: Rutgers UP, 2013).

Rosenthal, Franz. "On Suicide in Islam," *JOAS* 66.3 (1946): 239–259.

Rozen, B. F. "Opisanie ekonomicheskogo polozheniia i politicheskogo sostoianiia piemen Chechni i Dagestana," in *Materialy po istorii Dagestana i Chechni*, vol. 3.1, eds. G. E. Gruimberg and S. K. Bushuev (Makhachkala: Dagestanskoe Gosudarstvennoe izd-vo, 1940), 233–247.

Sablukov, Gordii Semyonovich. *Kalam sharif =Koran* (1907; Moscow: MP "Mif," 1991).

Saidov, M. S. "The Daghestan Arabic Literature of the Eighteenth and Nineteenth Centuries," *Papers Presented by the USSR Delegation, XXV Congress of Orientalists* (Moscow: Oriental Literature Publishing House, 1960), 1–13.

———. "Vozniknovenie pis'menosti u avartsev," *Iazyki Dagestana* 1 (1948): 136–140.

Sartori, Paolo, and Ido Shahar. "Legal Pluralism in Muslim-Majority Colonies: Mapping the Terrain," *JESHO* 55.4–5 (2012): 637–663.

Schimmelpenninck van der Oye, David. *Russian Orientalism: Asia in the Russian Mind from Peter the Great to the Emigration* (New Haven: Yale UP, 2010).

Schmitt, Carl. *Politische Theologie. Vier Kapitel zur Lehre von der Souveränität* (München: Duncker and Humblot, 1922).

Schwirtz, M. "Leading Russian Rights Lawyer Is Shot to Death in Moscow, along with Journalist," *New York Times*, 19 January 2009.

Scott, David. "Colonial Governmentality," *Social Text* 43 (1995): 191–220.

Scott, James C. *Domination and the Arts of Resistance: The Hidden Transcript of Subordinate Groups* (New Haven: Yale UP, 1992).

Sen, Ranjit. *Social Banditry in Bengal: A Study in Primary Resistance, 1757–1793* (Calcutta: Ratna Prakashan, 1988).

Sergeenko, A. P. "*Khadzhi-Murat*" *L'va Tolstogo: istoriia sozdaniia povesti* (Moscow: Sovremennik, 1983).

Shakhbanov, Marko. "Vol'nitsa dlia ubiits," *Chernovnik*, 3 February 2005, http://www.chernovik.net/print.php?new=1962.

Shakhbiev, Zaindi. *Sud'ba checheno-ingushskogo naroda* (Moscow: Rossiia Molodaia, 1996).

Shamaev, Ruslan. "Piat' let nazad molodaja zhenshchina Aizan Gazuieva vzorvala sebia i ubila Gaidara Gadzhieva," *Prague Watchdog/Radio Svoboda*, 29 November 2006, http://www.watchdog.cz/index.php?show=000000-000019-000002-000169&lang=2.

Shikhaliev, Shamil. "Sufische Bildung in Dagestan," *Repression, Anpassung, Neuorientierung: Studien zum Islam in der Sowjetunion und dem postsowjetischen Raum*, ed. Michael Kemper, Anke von Kügelgen, and Raoul Motika (Weisbaden: Reichart Verlag, 2013), 141–168.

Shikhsaidov, A. R., T. M. Aitberov, and G. M. R. Orazaev. *Dagestanskie Istoricheskie Sochineniia* (Moscow: Vostochnaia literatura, 1993).

Shikhsaidov, Amri. "Arabic Historical Studies in Twentieth-Century Dagestan," in *The Heritage of Soviet Oriental Studies*, ed. Michael Kemper and Stephan Conermann (London: Routledge, 2011), 203–216.

———. *Epigraficheskie pamiatniki Dagestana X-XVII vv, kak istoricheskii istochnik* (Moscow: Nauka, 1984).

Shnirel'man, V. A. "Identichnost' i politika postsovetskoi pamiati," *Politicheskaia kontseptologiia: Zhurnal mezhdunarodnikh issledovanii* 1.2 (2009): 209–230.

Sidorko, Clemens P. "Nineteenth Century German Travelogues as Sources on the History of Daghestan and Chechnya," *CAS* 21.3 (2002): 283–299.

Sigua, Soso. *K'art'uli modernizmi* (Tbilisi: Gamomcemloba didostati, 2002).

Smirnov, N. A. *Miuridizm na Kavkaze* (Moscow: AN SSSR, 1963).

———, chief ed. *Ocherki istorii checheno-ingushskoi assr s drevnieshikh vremen do nashikh dnei* (Grozny: Checheno-Ingushskoe knizhnoe izd-vo, 1967).

Speckhard, Anne, and Khapta Akhmedova. "Black Widows: The Chechen Female Suicide Terrorists," in *Female Suicide Terrorists*, ed. Yoram Schweitzer (Tel Aviv: Jaffe Center, 2006), 63–81.

———. "Understanding the Motivations and Life Trajectories of Chechen Female Terrorists," in *Female Terrorism and Militancy: Agency, Utility, and Organization*, ed. Cindy Ness (London: Routledge, 2008), 100–121.

Stewart, Devin J. "Rhymed Prose," in *Encyclopaedia of the Qur'an*, ed. Jane Dammen McAuliffe (Leiden: Brill, 2005), 4:476–483.

Subrahmanyam, Sanjay. "Connected Histories: Notes towards a Reconfiguration of Early Modern Eurasia," *Modern Asian Studies* 31.3 (1997): 735–762.

Sudakov. "Basaev sam sozdal otraid zhenschina-smertnits. Oni uzhe rabotaet," *Pravda*, 15 May 2003.

Sulaev, I. Kh. *Musul'manskoe dukhovenstvo Dagestana i svetskaia vlast': bor'ba i sotrudnichestvo: 1917-1921 gg.* (Makhachkala: Delovoi mir, 2004).

Sulava, Aleksandre. *Legendaruli abreki Zelimxani* (n.p.; n.d.). Xeroxed copy courtesy of Khvtiso Mamisimediashvili, Tbilisi State University, Department of Folklore, November 2005.

"'Surkho,' Pravda o shaidke Aize Gazuievoi," *Chechen News*, 10 August 2010, http://www.chechenews.com/world-news/breaking/875–1.html.

Tagirova, Natal'ya A., and Amri R. Shikhsaidov. "ʿAbdarraḥmān Ġāzīġumūqī und seine Werke," *MCRCA* 1:317–339.

Tillett, Lowell R. *The Great Friendship: Soviet Historians on the Non-Russian Nationalities* (Chapel Hill: U of North Carolina P, 1969).

Tishkov, Valery. *Chechnya: Life in a War-Torn Society* (Berkeley: U of California P, 2004).

———. *Obschestvo v vooruzhennom konflikte* (Moscow: Nauka, 2001).

Tolz, Vera. *Russia's Own Orient: The Politics of Identity and Oriental Studies in the Late Imperial and Early Soviet Periods* (Oxford: Oxford UP, 2011).

Trabulsi, Amjad. *La critique poétique des arabes* (Damascus: Institut français de Damas, 1958).

Tsagareishvili, Sh. V., ed. *Shamil'—stavlennik sultanskoi Turtsii i angliyskikh koloniztorov* (Tbilisi: Gosizdat Gruzinskoi SSR, 1953).

Tsaroieva, Mariel. *Peuples et religions du Caucase du Nord* (Paris: Éditions Karthala, 2001).

Tsurikova, G. *Titsian Tabidze: Zhizn' i poeziia* (Leningrad: Sovetskii pisatel', 1971).

Tuite, Kevin. "Achilles and the Caucasus," *Journal of Indo-European Studies* 26.3–4(1998): 289–343.

———. "Ethnographie et fiction en Géorgie," *Célébrer une vie: actes du colloque en honneur de Jean-Claude Muller*, ed. Kiven Strohm and Guy Lanoue (Montréal: Département d'anthropologie, Université de Montréal, 2007), 161–169.

Uzhakova, Rosa Kerimovna. "Chechenskii i ingushskii roman 20-70 gg. Istoriia i sovremennost" (PhD [*kandidatskaia*] diss., Moscow: Academy of Sciences, USSR, Gorky Institute of World Literature, 1984).

Vagapov, I. S. "Odinokii geroi v checheno-ingushkom illi," *Izvestiya voprosi checheno-ingushskoi literature* 5.3 (1968): 95–116.

van Ess, Josef. "From Wellhausen to Becker: The Emergence of *Kulturgeschichte* in Islamic Studies," in *Islamic Studies: A Tradition and Its Problems*, ed. Malcolm H. Kerr (Malibu: Undena Publications, 1980), 27–52.

Vasil'kov, Ia. V., and M. Iu. Sorokina, eds. *Liudi i sud'by: Biobibliograficheskii slovar' vostokovedov-zhertv politicheskogo terrora v sovetskii period (1917–1991)* (St. Petersburg: Peterburgskoe vostokovedenie, 2003).

Vikør, Knut. *Between God and the Sultan: A History of Islamic Law* (London: Hurst & Co., 2005).

Volchek, Dmitri. "Avtor knigi 'Nevestyi Allakha'—o terrorisme v Rossii," *Radio Svoboda*, http://www.svobodanews.ru/content/article/2002048.html (interview with Yulia Yuzik, 2010).

Weinstein, Jeremy. *Inside Rebellion: The Politics of Insurgent Violence* (Cambridge: Cambridge UP, 2007).

Wixman, Ronald. *The Peoples of the USSR: An Ethnographic Handbook* (Armonk: M. E. Sharpe, 1984).

Yoshimi, Takeuchi. "Asia as Method (1960)," in *What Is Modernity? Writings of Takeuchi Yoshimi*, ed. and trans. Richard F. Calichman (New York: Columbia UP, 2005), 149–166.

Yuzik, Yulia. *Nevesti Allakha: litsa i sud'byi vsekh zhenschin-shahidok, vzorvavshikhsiia Rossii* (Moscow: Kultura, 2003).

Zelkina, Anna. "The Arabic Linguistic and Cultural Tradition in Daghestan: An Historical Overview," in *Arabic as a Minority Language*, ed. Jonathan Owens (Berlin: Mouton de Gruyter, 2000), 89–111.

———. *In Quest for God and Freedom: Sufi Responses to the Russian Advance in the North Caucasus* (New York: New York UP, 2000).

———. "Islam and Society in Chechnia: From the Late Eighteenth to the Mid-Nineteenth Century," *JIS* 7.2 (1996): 240–264.

———. "*Jihād* in the Name of God: Shaykh Shamil as the Religious Leader of the Caucasus," *CAS* 21.3 (2002): 249–264.

———. "Some Aspects of the Teaching of Kunta Hâjjî: On the Basis of the Manuscript by ʿAbd al-Salâm written in 1862 AD," *JHS* 1–2: (2000): 483–508.

Acknowledgments

From the conception of this book to its publication, I have acquired many debts and friendships, both within and outside the field of Caucasus studies. Among scholars of the Caucasus, I wish to thank (in alphabetical order) Vladimir Bobrovnikov, John Colarusso, Bruce Grant, Leah Feldman, Iwona Kaliszewska, Ali Aydin Karamustafa, Michael Kemper, Hirotake Maeda, Paul Manning, Lauren Ninoshvili, Harsha Ram, Mike Reynolds, Oliver Reisner, Dana Sherry, and the late Moshe Gammer. Particular thanks go to Bruce Grant, who has been a generous reader of my work for many years and who introduced me to the Eurasia Past and Present series editor Doug Rogers. I am grateful to Doug and to the other two series editors, Catriona Kelly and Mark Steinberg, for their support of this project and for their serious engagement with my work. Working with my editor, Jaya Aninda Chatterjee, has been a pleasure from beginning to end, and I am grateful for her literary acumen.

For their assistance in and around Chechnya, many of those whom I most wish to thank cannot be named. Among Chechens in the diaspora, I have learned much from Lyoma Usmanov and Aset Chadaeva. I am proud to have been affiliated with the Chechnya Advocacy Network since its founding in 2004. In Daghestan, Shamil Shikhaliev and Makhach Musaev generously shared their wide learning of Daghestani manuscripts. In Georgia, Tamriko Bacouradze, Paata Bukhrashvili, Kevin Tuite, and Darejan Gardavadze demonstrated generosity in many ways. I am particularly grateful to Nitka Tabidze and to the deceased Nina Tabidze for generously sharing their memories of Titsian during my visits to their home.

For financial support for fieldwork and other research, I am grateful to the International Research and Exchanges Board, American Councils for International Education, Columbia University, and Yale-NUS College. Yale-NUS was particularly generous in its support of this book. I am grateful to my mentor (and now amazing friend) Petrus Liu for his generous support for my research, and especially for his friendship. Yale-NUS's excellent librarians Rebecca Maniates and Toby Teng have demonstrated considerable skill in obtaining difficult materials in a timely manner, as have the reference librarians of the University of Illinois at Urbana-Champaign. I am grateful to Janice Pilch (Rutgers) for her expertise on matters of copyright. Finally, I would like to thank the students of Yale-NUS College, in particular my research assistants Pei Yun Chia and Regina Hong, for their intellectual stimulation and engagement with my work. The timely assistance of Regina Hong has been particularly priceless for the final round of proof-checking.

Yale University Press demonstrated uncanny foresight in selecting ideal peer reviewers for this book. I am particularly grateful to Paul Manning for his untiring engagement with the nuances of the Georgian side of my argument, and for the interest he took in my work for so many years, ever since our first conversation at the home of Paata Bukhrashvili.

Beyond this specific project, I am indebted to Giorgio Ganis, Francesca Orsini, Asghar Seyed-Gohrab, Sunil Sharma, Justine Landau, Prashant Keshavmurthy, Alireza Korangy, Allison Busch, Thibaut d'Hubert, Nile Green, Alexander Key, Barney Bate, and Pranav Prakash. Each of these friends, colleagues, and mentors has enriched my life and mind in various ways. As the first teacher to support my work, and indeed the first person to suggest that I become a scholar, my undergraduate adviser Liza Knapp deserves a special mention of thanks. As the teacher who guided me through graduate school and into the world, Sheldon Pollock will always have a prominent place in every book I write.

I have been particularly blessed while working on this project in its final stages, during which I was a member of the community of scholars at the Institute for Advanced Studies in Central European University (Budapest) and at the University of Bristol. For making my ten months in Budapest all that it promised to be, I wish to thank Éva Fodor and Éva Gönczi. For enabling me to create a new life at the University of Bristol, I owe deep thanks to Robert Villain and Michael Basker, whose visions have renewed my sense of what is possible to achieve within the university. I also want to extend my thanks to my new colleagues at Bristol: Charles Burdett, Rajendra Chitnis, Ruth Coates, Connor Doak, Susan Harrow, Rebecca Kosick, Lucas Nunes-Vieira, Carol O'Sullivan, and Claire Shaw.

I cannot end without extending a heartfelt thanks to the intelligence, innately critical spirit, integrity, and generosity of the person who supported this book from an early stage. For so much that I have written, I can only think to myself: you were there first. The purity of your intellect teaches me endlessly about how scholarship works.

My mother and two sisters, Kate and Beth Gould, labored over this manuscript, in their generous efforts, which I hope were not fruitless, to make it more approachable for the general reader. My gratitude for the love they have shown me over the long course of its gestation, as well as long before this book was conceived, is a permanent source of inspiration. Having dedicated my first book to my mother and my second book to my sister Beth, I now take the opportunity to dedicate this monograph to my sister Kate, who has shared countless hours of conversation with me as I lived through its contents. I also want to express my gratitude to Anna Boyd, Moe Boyd, and Robert Byus for their lifelong support. For looking after me as child, and for his enthusiasm for my work, I thank my father, Christopher Gould.

Index

Page numbers followed by "f" or "t" indicate material in figures or tables.

trangressive sanctity — trangressive toward whom? colonial law? or is it an internal contradiction?

is it just martyrdom? or a theorization of?

other (anticolonial discourses) in which violence is legit?

the disciplinary orientation of this book is hard to grasp

trangressive sanctity puts indigenous & colonial law into closer relation (61)

stance wrt postcoloniality?

how does TS differ from moral authority?

impressive literary historiography of the Caucasus

also impressive: differentiating subregions of the Caucasus

and: understanding of the social contexts & nuanced diffs.

and: a way to mediate btwn the many strands of language, culture, law & religion present in the region

I find the defense of lit. unnecessary

could we say it's about inventing the region?